# BURNOUT

USA TODAY BESTSELLING AUTHOR

## REBECCA JENSHAK

Rebecca Jenshak

www.rebeccajenshak.com

Cover Design by Lori Jackson Designs

Illustration by Sarah Jane

Editing by Margo Lipschultz

Proofreading by Sarah at All Encompassing Books and Rebecca at Fairest Reviews Editing Services

# PROLOGUE
*Knox*

**A**drenaline thrums under my skin as I sit on my bike behind the gate. The purr of the engine idles under me and sweat trickles down the nape of my neck.

My teammate Link is beside me on a red Honda, identical to my own, talking loudly as he drums absently on his handlebars. "This one is mine. It's time for the Link era."

He repeats it like a mantra until I can't help but engage. I snort and shoot him a sideways glance.

"You have something to say, Holland?"

"Nope." I shake my head, then under my breath ask, "The fucking Link era?"

He either has super-hearing or can read my thoughts because he doesn't drop it. "You don't think so?"

"It's anybody's race," I tell him. "You're a good rider. Stay on your bike and don't get sloppy."

In response I get an eye roll before he brings his goggles down in place. "Like I'd take advice from you. I might be younger, but I've been racing longer. You've been lucky this season. Mike and the rest of the team got caught up in your underdog comeback story, but they'll see. I'm about to show everyone what *I* can do. If you're smart, you'll stay out of my way. Maybe they'll keep you around to block for me next season."

His words get to me more than I care to admit. I have worked my ass off to claw my way back, but I can't get back those years I was absent while taking care of my brothers.

I push Link and everything else out of my mind. This is it. It's the last race of the motocross season. I came in second on moto one earlier today, so I need to cross the finish line first on this moto to win the race. And I *need* to win.

It's easily a hundred degrees out here, but the crowd is fired up and they're on their feet, gathering around the perimeter of the track to cheer us on as we speed by.

I love this sport. There's nothing better than racing on dirt with the sun shining overhead.

Tension is palpable behind the starting line. Each of us in our own world while we wait for the signal. I'm visualizing myself thirty minutes from now standing on the podium with a first-place trophy in hand.

"Are you watching, Mom?" I mutter the question quietly and lift my left hand to the mouthpiece on my helmet and kiss the rose tattoo inked between my thumb and pointer finger. "This one's for you. Happy birthday."

Ten years without her and I don't know how I've survived a single second of it. It feels like another life and like yesterday all at

6

once. She would have been fifty today and I know she'd get such a kick out of watching me race.

Dad might have been the one who taught me to ride, but she was the one who always told me that no dream was too crazy and that I was capable of doing anything I put my heart and soul into.

The girl holding the thirty-second card turns it sideways and walks off the track, the official right behind her. It's time.

I rev my engine and stare straight ahead, blocking everything else out. When the gate drops, I move on instinct alone. Muscle memory mixed with a desperate determination to end this season on top has me tearing past the other riders on the straightaway.

It's always a clusterfuck until we make it through the hole shot. Dirt sprays behind us and we jockey for position while trying to avoid crashing. Ten seconds is all it takes to separate the serious contenders from the rest of the pack. My speed is my biggest asset and I use it every chance I get.

The usual guys are out front early. Three of us have been fighting it out for podium spots all season. There are always a few other riders that manage to hang on at the start of the race, but thirty minutes with me breathing down your neck is enough to make almost anyone crack under the pressure.

I don't let up. I use every straight stretch, every whoop, every jump to edge my way around anyone standing between me and the finish line.

Around the halfway point, I find myself in third place. I push back my frustration and concentrate on doing everything I can while I bide my time. All it takes is one fuck-up, one slip from the guys in front of me and I can pull ahead. Once I'm in the lead, there's no stopping me. I've never lost a lead. I just have to get there.

As I'm coming around the final corner of the track, I clock a bike on my tail. Red flashes in my peripheral and I grind my teeth as my teammate Link hits the booster at the finish line at the same time as me.

Link could be a good rider if he wasn't so aggressive. He takes too many risks. And coming from another rider, that's saying something because we're all fucking nuts. He has more DNFs than wins. The last thing I need is him crashing in front of me and costing me valuable seconds.

I'm on the inside line, gaining on him as we go around the first corner again. He manages to keep up with me, furthering my irritation. I can't shake this kid. He finally makes a mistake on the next jump, landing on soft dirt that stalls him. I breathe a sigh of relief and return my focus to the leaders.

I get through the next section of the track cleanly and close some of the distance. Second place is within reach on the next lap if I can just find a good line to get around him. He's tiring. I can see it. I can *feel* it.

My brothers used to say that when it came down to the last five minutes of a race, I could find another gear and that's what it feels like now. I push away all distractions. I only care about the next ten minutes.

Second place takes a corner too fast, and his back tire slides out, giving me an opportunity to pass him.

One more person stands between me and victory.

As I'm taking a series of small jumps, that fucking red bike returns. I let my gaze shift to him only long enough to see a cocky smirk splashed across his face. If we can both manage to finish in the top three, that'd be huge for Thorne Racing. I want that, but I want to be first more.

I keep my corners tight and grit my teeth any time Link tries to cut in front of me. Less than three minutes to go. I need to make a move soon if I'm going to take the lead.

I see my opening as we ride side by side uphill. After the next turn is a rutty spot before a double jump. Link struggled with it in our practice runs. It's hard to get enough speed going into it and at this point everyone is tired.

I'm dialed in. I hit the first jump and shift my body weight and the bike to one side, whipping to realign and get a better line. I've got him and he knows it. But instead of taking it like a good sport, Link maneuvers his bike closer. There isn't room for him to go inside on me, but he goes for it anyway. His front tire clips my back one just enough to send me off the track and down a steep embankment. I'm thrown from my seat and land flat on my back.

For the first time since the race started, the noise of the crowd comes back into focus. Their gasps are just audible over the ragged breathing slipping from my lips. Everything hurts, but none of it matters. I bring the rose tattoo on my left hand up to my mouthpiece as black crowds into my vision. "Sorry, Mom."

# CHAPTER ONE
*Avery*

**W**hen I reach the end of the beam, I raise my hands over my head and spin around on the balls of my feet. This is it. The final combination of my routine. I could do it blindfolded. When I sleep, all I dream about is this routine. It won me a silver medal at the last Olympics nearly two years ago, so there's no way I'm ever going to forget it.

I visualize this routine all day, every day. While eating or showering or daydreaming in class. There's nowhere I'd rather be than on top of the balance beam.

I inhale as I prepare for my dismount. A full twisting double pike. It's one of the most difficult dismounts. Few people perfect it because it's so hard to land cleanly without getting hurt. It requires speed and power, twisting and somersaulting off the end and landing square with the beam, chest high. No one in collegiate gymnastics even attempts it. Having a clean routine is more important than difficulty. But I love the challenge.

I'm not a risk-taker by nature, but gymnastics has always let me be someone I'm not outside of the gym.

Or it did.

I haven't done this dismount in months. Sometimes when I'm feeling exceptionally sorry for myself, I wonder if I'll ever do it again.

I push that thought away and stand taller.

"You've got this, Avery." The cheer comes from my left where my teammates are watching. Their eyes feel like pinpricks along my skin. My breathing shifts and my right knee locks.

I go into my round-off slower than I'd need to pull off the tricky dismount and instead of risking reinjuring myself, I do a simple layout onto a mat next to the beam.

I don't look up as they clap because I'm afraid of what I'll see on their faces. *Poor Avery with the bad knee. Poor Avery who still isn't back to where she was before the injury. Poor Avery, poor Avery.*

"Next up," Coach calls as I walk off the mat. My knee twinges in pain as I cross over to get my water bottle.

A few of the guys from the men's team are still practicing on the parallel bars in the corner. Tristan flips and tucks and spins into a dismount as I get nearby. Breathless, but with his ever-present smirk, he swaggers toward me. "And that's how it's done, Ollie."

He always calls me that because my last name is Oliver. It's my least favorite nickname of all time.

Tristan Williams, two Olympic gold medals to his name, and widely regarded as the number one collegiate male gymnast in the country. Widely regarded by me as the most annoying person in the world.

"How what's done? How to be an asshole or hop on the dismount?" I ask with a fake smile.

"At least I'm doing dismounts. What the hell was that beginner shit?" He waves a muscular arm toward the beam.

I avoid him, leaving a wide berth between us as I continue to the side of the gym where my stuff is stashed. I swipe my water bottle off the floor and take a long drink before I turn around. He's still standing there, hands now on his hips, as he waits for my answer.

"What?" I ask with all the sass I can muster. I drop down onto the floor and remove the wrap from my knee.

"Why aren't you practicing?" He enunciates each word carefully.

"I am practicing."

"No, you're not. You've been hobbling around for the past hour doing half-assed routines and flaking out on dismounts like you injured yourself yesterday instead of months ago. How much longer are you going to blame the knee?"

I narrow my eyes at him. His expression morphs into barely contained glee at riling me up. I swear he enjoys pissing me off.

"I'm sorry, did you get a medical degree over the summer that nobody told me about?"

After an exaggerated eye roll, he asks, "What are you doing tonight? You want to hang out?"

"Who, me? The girl doing half-assed routines?" I ask in a sugary sweet voice, then drop the act. "Pass. I'd rather watch paint dry than listen to you talk about how awesome you are all night."

I'm half kidding for the sake of this game of trading insults we like to play, but he does have a really high opinion of himself. And I definitely don't want to spend my Friday night with him.

He huffs a short laugh. "I'm always going to tell it to you straight,

Ollie. You're better than this." He waves a hand to the floor as if to indicate everything I'm doing out there. "Get out of your head."

I swallow the lump forming in my throat as he walks off to rejoin the guys. Tossing the wrap to the floor, I bend my right leg and stare at the red and slightly swollen skin around my knee. The vertical scar just below is still raised and ugly. I extend it back in front of me and stretch forward. It's still a little weaker than my left leg, so it's hard to tell if the pain I'm feeling is from that or if I've pushed it too hard.

The doctors thought I would be completely healed by now. I thought so too.

We're a month into the new school year. Full practices began this week, but all summer I was in the gym, rehabbing my knee and keeping up with my skills as best I could with one leg.

After the disaster that was last season, I need to come back stronger than ever.

A few minutes after six, Coach calls practice for the day. I grab my bag and slip my bare feet into my slides. Before I can get out the door, my name is yelled from across the gym.

I pause, but don't glance back, hoping I heard wrong.

"Avery," she repeats, still yelling. "Can I see you before you leave?"

I don't have to look over my shoulder to know it's Coach Weaver. The dread filling my stomach tells me, as does the thick German accent. When I do make eye contact, I nod and backtrack across the gym to the beam corner.

She's talking with a couple of freshman girls when I approach, so I hang back. The way these girls look at her, all awe-inspired with a heavy dose of fear, makes me smile. I remember feeling that exact way last year. To be honest, she still terrifies me, but she's a great coach. I like her style. She says little, but it makes everything she does say feel that much more impactful.

"Hi, Coach," I say when the others go.

"Avery." Her voice lowers and she takes a step closer, gaze traveling down to my knee before returning to my face. "How is the knee holding up?"

"Good," I say cheerily. Too cheerily. "It's a little swollen, but the doctor said that was to be expected."

"And how are *you* holding up?"

The question surprises me enough that I don't try to sugarcoat my answer. "I'm frustrated. I thought that I'd be back at one hundred percent by now, but my knee is still locking up on me."

"When you're tense, your body is tense."

I nod, letting her words wash over me with the shame.

"One day at a time. Next week, I want you to work exclusively on floor."

"Floor?" My brows pinch together.

"Yes. No beam, no vault. Nothing risky. You can practice your skills on the floor."

It feels like ten steps backward, which, for the record, is not the direction I want to be going.

"But, Coach—"

"That's all. Enjoy your weekend. Ice that knee tonight."

The walk back to my dorm does little to clear my head, but as soon as I push into the suite I share with my roommate, Quinn, I find myself smiling at the scene in front of me. She's in a backbend, which wouldn't be all that odd if she weren't wearing a black leather miniskirt, white tank top and platform boots, and watching an old episode of *Friends*.

"How can you watch TV that way?" I ask as I toss my bag into my room on the right side of the suite and then drop onto the couch in the shared living area.

She lifts one leg and then the other, kicking over to stand upright. "I've seen this one so many times I can recite it by heart."

Quinn drops back onto the ground in the splits, facing me. "How was practice?"

"Not great." At the reminder, I get up and pull an ice pack from the mini fridge, then sit back down and prop up my leg to ice my knee. "I froze on beam again."

"Is your knee hurting?"

"Yes. No. I don't know. It still feels off and it's swollen from the little bit of tumbling I did this week."

"I think that's normal. It'll take time, but it's only September. You have plenty of time."

I thought that too. Right after the surgery, then this summer when I was cleared to work out, but I feel years away from competing and the season is looming.

"Coach told me that next week she wants me on floor only."

My roommate's dark brows rise, but she's slow to speak, like she's considering her words carefully. "Maybe that's best."

My face heats and my expression must show my outrage because she quickly adds, "For now. A-babe," she says, using the nickname she gave me. It's way better than 'Ollie.' "You're the best gymnast on the team. She isn't worried about you perfecting routines, she just wants to make sure your knee is good to go and your head is on straight."

It's logical, or maybe I just want to believe it so I don't have to think of it as another setback. But it annoys me that it's basically what Tristan said too.

"Maybe you're right. I think I'm just cranky because I ran into Tristan." I groan as I think of his stupid smirk. "I can't believe I kissed him. Bleh."

"You were drunk and fresh off a breakup. And he is really hot, so it's forgivable."

I shudder at the memory. Tristan is cocky and entitled. He's a great gymnast, I'll give him that, but his personality sucks.

"Where did you run into him?" Quinn asks, moving out of the splits and into a handstand. She's the only person I know that could manage to still look cool and collected with her skirt bunching up like a belt around her hips.

"At the gym. Some of the guys stayed after their practice."

"Of course they did, what else do they have to do on a Friday night?"

"You mean like us? You're tumbling in party clothes and the only place I'm heading is to the shower and bed." For not going all out at practice this week, I still feel like I got run over by a bus.

"Not true. *We* are going out. And I'm just making sure I haven't lost all my skills. I might not be competing anymore, but dropping into the splits or busting out an aerial are great party tricks." She drops back to her feet and fixes her clothes. Somehow, she still looks fab, not a lock of dark brown hair out of place.

I laugh at the big smile on her face. She's one hundred percent serious and I love her for it. Quinn and I joined the Valley U gymnastics team together as freshmen, but at the end of last year she quit so she could have more of a life. It's hard to blame anyone for wanting more free time. I spend two to three hours at the gym every day, and most days even more. Add school and studying to that, and there isn't a lot of time for anything else.

I love it too much to quit, but I understand Quinn's decision.

"*We* are?" On a scale of one to ten, my desire to go out is hovering around negative five.

"Yes. Colter's performing tonight and I promised him we'd stop by."

"Oh."

"He wants you to see how much you helped him," she clarifies.

"Yeah, of course. It's just…can't you take some video for me? It'll take me at least an hour to get ready and I'm not really in the mood."

She shakes her head slowly from side to side. "You said that last weekend."

I open my mouth to protest.

"And the weekend before."

My lips clamp closed. Dammit.

She laughs and places both hands on her hips. "It'll be fun."

Quinn and her boyfriend Colter are the cutest couple ever. She's all petite and sweet-looking (even in her leather and boots) and he's this wild and crazy freestyle motorcycle guy. I adore them, but the last time I went out with the two of them I felt like a third wheel.

As if she can read my thoughts, she says, "Colter will be busy, so it'll be like a fun girls' night with great eye candy."

I laugh when she sticks her bottom lip out in a hopeful pout.

"Okay. Okay." I hold my hands out. "Help me up and find me something to wear?"

"Done," she says, gripping me and tugging with more force than her little frame looks like it'd be capable of. "I laid out two different outfit options on my bed for you."

"Are either of them sweats?" I ask hopefully.

"Go." She points toward the bathroom with a laugh.

# CHAPTER TWO
*Avery*

The sound of engines revving cuts through the night as Quinn throws her arm out the passenger window of my Bronco and points to an empty spot in the fairgrounds parking lot.

"There," she says.

"I thought you said this was a small event?" I cut the wheel and head toward the parking space.

"My man is a big deal." She shrugs and flashes me a smile.

A glint of shiny black and silver in the corner of my eye causes me to slam on the brakes. I yelp as the motorcycle stops directly in front of me. It looks brand new, sleek and gleaming under the lights.

The rider is in all black, the same color as his motorcycle, from head to toe. The only sliver of skin visible is his knee from a rip in his black jeans. I can't see his eyes through the dark visor of his helmet, but a shiver rolls down my spine as we're locked in a stare-off that feels intense and heavy.

"Asshole," I mutter and hit the top of my steering wheel.

He speeds off and disappears between the rows of vehicles.

Once I'm parked, Quinn leads me into the event. The stadium is outdoors with bleachers on two sides of the track.

There are a lot of people here. Families with small kids wearing ear protection, some couples, and along the fence that separates the crowd from the track, motorcycles are parked in groups, their owners standing next to them watching the action.

A large ramp is set up in the center of the track and around it, smaller ramps of varying sizes. The riders are taking turns racing up the main ramp and performing tricks: flipping upside down, twisting around in the air while holding on to only the seat or handles with their feet flung out to the side or above their head, and then landing seconds before they scramble back to a seated position.

"Are we late?" I ask Quinn as I follow her to the far section of bleachers.

"No. They're just warming up," she says, shouting over her shoulder to be heard over the noise.

I get some looks as we approach another big group of people along the fence. More guys with their bikes and girls crowding around them. The girls are all in short shorts or tight jeans. Black is the popular color choice on all of them. I bypassed Quinn's outfit suggestions in favor of one of my own. Maybe my light pink lacy dress and white sneakers weren't the right choice for an event like this, but I haven't gone out since the first week of school and I wanted to look cute.

One guy in particular catches my eye. I'm ninety-nine percent sure it's the guy from the parking lot, but they all look similar. He's abandoned his jacket, and the black tank top he's wearing shows off his muscular arms and back and the ink that decorates everything from his back down to his fingers.

He's sitting on his motorcycle with one hand resting on his thigh and the other holds his helmet. Something about the pose screams confidence and ease.

A crowd has formed around him, guys and girls all vying for his attention. By my best guess he's in his early to mid-twenties. His hair is a medium brown, short and wavy, with a sort of tousled look probably thanks to the helmet, or maybe he was running his fingers through it. Or more likely, judging by the woman standing closest to him eyeing him up like a prize, someone else was running their fingers through it.

It's clear they're all excited to see him, but I can't hear enough to know why he's important enough to have people focusing on him instead of the track. He must feel me staring at him because as Quinn and I get close, he glances back at me.

He doesn't quite meet my stare. Instead, his gaze sweeps over my dress and bare legs lazily, and then down to my feet where he focuses so long you'd think I was barefoot or wearing six-inch heels covered in pink glitter.

Self-consciously, I look down. My plain white shoes are already collecting dust from the track, but otherwise I'm not sure why they're getting so much attention from mister tattooed motorcycle hottie.

When I glance back up, his stare has finally made its way to my face. My breath catches as his eyes narrow and dark brows lift. A cocky challenge with a hint of intrigue like he isn't sure what to make of me. I just caught him checking me out and he looks at me like I'm the one that should be embarrassed.

I'm too stunned by his reaction to do anything but stare back.

When I pass him only a few feet separate us. The air is charged around him. He hasn't moved at all and something about it has me feeling like I'm walking a catwalk in front of him. Or a plank.

I don't like the way my heart races or my face flushes under his scrutiny.

As soon as we're past him, I hurry to walk side by side with Quinn.

"Are you sure I'm dressed okay?" I ask my friend as she finally finds a spot in the bleachers she likes and starts to ascend the stairs.

With a quick once-over, she nods. "You look hot. Nobody else I know could pull off that dress. And I don't know how you still have your summer tan."

It's because I lived in the pool this summer while rehabbing my knee.

We sit in an empty row about halfway up. We have a nice view of the riders who are still taking warm-up jumps on the track. I spot Colter, as does Quinn, judging by her smile.

"I feel like I should have worn something…"

"Something what?" She arches one brow at me quizzically.

"Less pink and lacy."

She laughs softly, only tearing her gaze from her boyfriend for a second. She takes off her leather jacket and holds it out to me. "Put this on."

"Are you sure?"

"You look amazing as is, but if it makes you feel more comfortable." Another shrug.

I slip my arms into the buttery soft sleeve and shrug into it. The leather is warm from her skin and at least on the top half now I look more like the rest of the crowd. "Wow. I automatically feel like a badass. You might not get this back."

Quinn snorts. "I know where you live, bitch."

Everyone gets to their feet when the announcer's voice crackles over the speakers. He welcomes everyone to the event as the riders sit impatiently on their bikes. I can almost see the adrenaline coming off them. My own excitement builds. I haven't seen Colter in action since last spring. He's talented and fearless. Also a smidge crazy, but in a truly loveable way.

When he first switched from racing dirt bikes to freestyle, he worked out a bunch with me and Quinn. The control and strength required to pull off some of the tricks he does is insane.

The announcer calls out each rider, introduces them and provides a list of accomplishments as they take off around the track waving at the fans, then circle back to speed up the ramp.

It really is incredible, some of the things they're able to do. When it's Colter's turn, he does a backflip, then brings his legs up behind him so he's flying horizontally above the bike.

Quinn screams next to me, bringing both hands up around her mouth. When he lands it, he circles around, riding close to the fence, standing upright. He kisses his fingertips and then points at her before speeding off.

The event continues with the riders, seven of them in total, doing synchronized tricks while loud music pumps from the speakers. Their timing, technique, even the height they soar in the air is nearly identical. They do backflips, and a bunch of other tricks that look terrifying.

The only other time I've seen Colter in action was at a small track where he practices. I went with Quinn once and that was fun, but this...this is so much more than I imagined. My own heart races with excitement as their feats get more and more jaw-dropping.

After some time, they pull out of line and stop at one end of the track, then one-by-one they each take their turn on the track, alternating between all the ramps, performing stunts and getting the crowd into it.

It smells like fumes and burnt rubber, with a touch of gasoline, and the music is so loud I can feel it vibrating in my body. It's electric.

The announcer calls out the tricks after they complete them. The names make me chuckle: Hart Attack, Kiss of Death, Rigamortis, Holy Grab, Oxecutioner, and a bunch more.

"Whoever named these has a sick sense of humor," I yell over the noise.

But also, it's a good reminder that one wrong move and these guys could get seriously hurt. These guys are bonkers.

"Most of them are named after riders," she replies without removing her gaze from the track.

When it's Colter's turn, my eyes are glued to his every move. He's good. The best of the group, maybe. And because of all the time we spent together while he was working on handstands and upper body control, I notice that he's improved a ton in that area. His lines are straight and his movements smooth.

When he flips the bike and lets go with everything except one hand gripping the seat, I hold my breath with everyone else. And when he lands it cleanly, I feel a shot of pride that I had some small part in helping him make it look so effortless.

I stand with Quinn when he's done, clapping and cheering loudly. Colter drives by us again, this time going up on one wheel and showing off for his girl. The guys in the front yell and heckle him as he goes by. My attention is drawn back to the guy from earlier.

He still hasn't moved from his bike, but he looks as comfortable on it as if it were his own personal throne. His gaze flicks to me and for several long seconds we're locked in another stare-off.

I glance away first and take a seat back on the hard bleacher.

"Wasn't he fantastic?" Quinn asks, her smile as wide as her face.

"Yeah. He really was. I can't believe how much he improved over the summer. Did you keep working with him?"

"Me?" She scoffs. "No. I'm not patient enough. That was all you."

"You were there too." For months Colter worked out with us. It was nice because I got to know my best friend's boyfriend and give him the stamp of approval. He's really great and Quinn is absolutely gone for him.

"Yeah, but I mostly sat around and gawked at him."

"You still mostly sit around and gawk at him."

She beams. "He's hot. Gawking is required."

Without thinking, I chance another look down at the guy on his bike. Speaking of hot…he has a whole bad boy, break your heart but look good while doing it vibe. He reaches forward and wraps his fingers around the handlebar. The movement makes his shirt strain against his back and side and his bicep flexes under all that ink. If danger had a look, it's this guy in his all-black ensemble and matching motorcycle.

"Damn," I mutter.

He looks back and catches me staring. A smug smile tips up the corners of his lips. I quickly glance away and back to the track, but not before heat creeps up my neck.

"Right?" Quinn asks with awe in her tone. "She's the only chick on the team, but she is representing the ladies well. Also, she's so sexy. Her red hair really does it for me."

"Huh?" My head snaps toward my friend in confusion.

She motions to the track where a woman takes off her helmet, freeing her red hair with a shake of her head, and waves to the crowd.

Quinn continues, "You think I could talk Colter into sleeping with her and letting me watch?"

"Seriously?"

"I'm mostly kidding, but I have thought about it. Colter's open to all sorts of things in theory but I think he'd kill any guy that came at me naked. And I'd probably do the same with anyone who tried to put hands on my man. What about you?"

I shake my head with a laugh. "You two are perfect for each other."

"You've never thought about hooking up with multiple people?"

"No, not really. My sex fantasies are more one-on-one," I admit. "I can barely find one person I want to hook up with, so the odds of finding more seem unlikely."

"True. You are very picky. Except Tristan."

I wrinkle my nose at the memory. He kissed like it was a competition and he was determined to win. My lips hurt just thinking about it.

The woman on the motorcycle stands on the seat of her bike and raises her arms.

"She's hot though, right? When she first joined the team, I was so jealous that Colter was spending so much time with her, but he says red hair doesn't work for him. Something about being traumatized by the Chucky movies as a kid."

"She is pretty hot." I nod.

The crowd loves her, men and women alike. Speaking of men, I feel *his* stare on me and glance back down at the hot asshole to find him watching me again. He's not ogling so much as staring like he's amused by me. I lift my chin defiantly, then turn my face toward Quinn. "That guy down there keeps looking at me."

She pries her gaze from the redhead and scans for him. "Which one?"

"Black shirt, tattoos, hot as sin?"

Her laughter is muted by the noise of an engine revving. "In this crowd, you have to be more specific."

"The one sitting on his motorcycle."

A few seconds later, I know she's found him when her voice croons, "Oooh. He is pretty."

Pretty? The man is all hard edges and tough demeanor. Handsome and striking, yes. Pretty? Not exactly.

"Is he still looking this way?"

"No. Well, maybe he was, but now he's a little occupied." Her voice takes on a playful singsong tone.

I look back at him in time to see a stunning brunette straddle the seat of his motorcycle, facing him. Her arms dangle over his shoulders. He isn't touching her at all, but he's eating up the attention, judging by the way he leans closer to her. Almost lazily he cups the back of her head and brings her mouth to his, kissing her in a way that makes my stomach bottom out.

"Do you know him?" I ask Quinn.

"No, but I recognize some of the guys with him. They're local riders. Colter will know. We can ask him later. Maybe Colter can introduce you and we can double date!"

"No thanks. He is so not my type."

"That man is everyone's type for at least a night."

She's probably not wrong about that.

The rest of the event goes by quickly and before I know it, Quinn is dragging me to a side area of the parking lot where Colter and the other riders are loading their equipment into trailers. A small crowd has formed nearby, and I spot my tattooed bad boy among them, but I'm careful not to get caught staring at him again.

Quinn takes off in a run toward her man. He's still dressed in all his gear, minus the helmet. He catches her and holds her up to kiss her, which he does, quite thoroughly. I walk slowly toward them, closing the distance while they say hello to each other like it's been months instead of hours since they've seen each other.

Colter lowers Quinn back down to stand in front of him, but keeps his arms locked around her. He's a head taller than her and uses that height advantage to smile at me over her. "Hey, Avery."

"Hey, yourself." I smile at him. Colter is really easy to like. The fact that he makes my friend so happy is just a bonus.

"What'd you think of the show?" he asks.

"It was incredible. Your lines were straight and clean. I'm so proud."

His smile widens. "Thanks."

More of the crew is working around us. Colter drops another kiss to Quinn's lips. "I gotta help the guys. Are you two sticking around for a bit? There's a cooler of drinks in the back of my truck."

My friend looks to me hopefully.

"Yeah." I lift one shoulder in a small approving shrug.

"Cool. Grab a drink. I'll be back soon." He kisses Quinn again. Seriously, these two can't get enough of each other and it's as heartwarming as it is nauseating to witness. When Colter is gone,

Quinn turns on her toes to grin at me. One look at how happy she is makes it hard to be anything but happy for her.

I'm not looking for that, but it would be nice if the universe could send me a gorgeous, sweet man that wants to make out occasionally. After the crappy year I've had, that doesn't seem like too much to ask for.

# CHAPTER THREE
## Knox

"**K**nox fucking Holland." Colter steps down from his lifted truck, a big smile splashed across his face. In all the years I've known him I don't think I've ever seen him without that same goofy, happy smile on his face.

My own much rarer smile loosens as I approach my longtime friend.

"You made it," he says, striding toward me with a huge grin on his face. We shake hands and he pulls me into a one-armed hug. "What'd you think?"

"I think I could still kick your ass in any race."

His dark eyes dance with amusement as he laughs. "No way. You're lucky I quit when I did. I'd be stealing all that prize money from you."

"You name the time and place, and we'll test that theory," I say, knowing he won't take me up on it. Neither of us let the other's ribbing get to us. I've known Colter since we were kids. We grew up in Valley together, met in elementary school, and have been racing dirt bikes just as long. About a year ago, the same time I started competing again, he switched to freestyle. Now he spends his days doing crazy stunts on his bike instead of racing.

Coincidence that he stopped racing at the same time I came back? I think not. I don't blame him. I'm fucking fast.

"I'll race you as soon as you can do the Kiss of Death double backflip." His expression dares me to attempt the crazy stunt where the rider flips the bike and holds on to the handlebars for dear life with their legs straight up in the air.

"I like all my bones *inside* my body."

His shoulders shake with his laughter. Someone calls out to him and tosses him a beer. He nods his thanks as he catches it in one hand. "Want one?" he asks, offering it to me.

"No thanks."

With another nod, he flicks the top a couple of times before opening it. He takes a long drink before asking, "Honestly, what'd you think?"

"That was some cool shit. I had no idea you were doing tricks like that. Are you planning on competing at the next X games?"

"Fuck, I dunno. Right now, this tour is all I can think about. We're booked nearly every weekend from now until Christmas."

"Seriously?" I'm not sure what I pictured when I heard he was touring and doing freestyle events, but it was a lot more casual than the event they pulled tonight.

"Yeah." He shakes his head and takes another drink. "Up and down the West Coast. Monster truck rallies and fairs, you name it."

"That's really cool, man."

"Thanks. How are things going for you? I was sorry to hear that Thorne dropped you. You had a hell of a season. That kid Link is a real piece of work."

I huff a short laugh. "Yeah, he's something all right."

"Have you already signed with someone else?"

"No, not yet."

He looks at me with a barely contained surprised expression.

"I'll figure it out." I try to wave it off, but the truth is it stung. After Link crashed into me at the final race, he went on to win. I was lucky I wasn't injured, just banged up. But I was pissed. I said some things, he said some things, and then I lost my head. I pushed him in front of the media and our team owner, Mike, and that was that. They cut me loose.

"No doubt. You had a hell of a year. You're the guy to beat next season and everyone knows it. I bet you have a new team by the end of the week. You'll be out of this desert heat and training on a fancy track next to the ocean with dieticians and specialized workouts and all that shit."

"Nah. I was planning on coming back here anyway. It's Flynn's senior year of high school, so I need to stick around as much as possible."

"Baby Holland is a senior?" Colter's brows rise in disbelief. "Damn. It doesn't seem possible that we graduated more than five years ago now."

I nod my agreement. It doesn't seem possible to me either, but that's because I didn't graduate. I understand what he means though. And it's all the more reason I need to be here to make sure Flynn finishes school and gets a scholarship to one of his top colleges.

"Seriously, you killed out there." I turn the conversation back to

Colter. "I'm impressed. The atmosphere, the energy, the whole event was cool as hell."

"You've never been to a freestyle event before?"

"Just the small ones at races. I always wanted to go to the X Games, but it's never worked out."

He beams at me, looking more like the gangly bucktoothed kid he was fifteen years ago. "Well, hey, if you're looking for something to do until you get the team thing worked out, we can always use another person."

"Freestyle?"

"Why not? I've seen you pull a few tricks."

"Yeah, just messing around."

"That's all we're doing."

He's underselling the talent it takes to flip a bike while moving around above it, and then land it clean, for sure.

"I don't think so." My only focus for the next few months is to train my ass off and convince Mike to bring me back on with his team.

"If you change your mind, say the word. Even if you don't want to run tricks, we can always use more hands setting up and tearing down. We leave on Thursday night or Friday morning and come back late Saturday or Sunday. Quick turnaround. Lots of fun. I'll add your pay directly to the Knox Holland fine fund in anticipation for all your future fights."

"Fuck off." I scratch the side of my face with my middle finger.

Laughing, he cuffs me on the shoulder. "Come on, I want to introduce you to some of my team."

Colter leads the way, stopping to grab another beer out of the cooler in the back of his truck. "Are you sure you don't want something to drink?"

"I'm sure." As much as I'd like to drown my sorrows in a bottle, I need to be clearheaded to figure out my next move. I can't have worked this hard for it all to be over after one season.

I could try to jump on another team. Though, that seems unlikely. All the top teams are set with big name riders they aren't going to let go of unless someone gets hurt or retires. I don't see where there will be an opening for me. Maybe I can jump onto a small team. But they don't have the same budget, so I'd probably be better off with a couple of sponsors. The nice part of a team is that they take care of a lot of the bullshit so I can just race.

He grabs another for himself and then walks up to a group of people chilling in front of an old, beat-up RV. I recognize the shirtless guy sitting on the steps of the vehicle not just from tonight's event but from several over the years.

"Knox, this is Sam, but we call him Oak," Colter says, pointing to the guy. Then he tips his head toward me. "Knox and I grew up racing here in Valley. I used to let him kick my ass on the track."

*Let?*

"You wish." I scoff, then offer a hand to Oak. He's tall and thin with locs that come down past his shoulders. "I've never seen anyone land a Volt that easily. That was awesome."

"Hey, thanks, man." We shake and then Colter moves to the only woman on the team.

She has long, fiery red hair and a *don't fuck with me* expression. Sexy but not my type. The energy she puts off is too much like my own. I'm not interested in fucking a version of myself. The smirk she gives me says, *right back at ya, buddy.*

"This is Brooklyn."

"You look familiar," I say as I step closer and get a better look at her face. There's something about the wide set of her eyes and the way she holds her mouth that reminds me of someone. "What's your last name?"

"It's not important." She suddenly looks bashful and that's an odd look on her. Now I'm intrigued.

"Her dad is—" Colter starts but she punches him in the stomach before he can finish. He doubles over and wheezes through a laugh, but as soon as he gets a hold of himself, he mouths the name to me.

My brows shoot up as I piece it together. "No shit?"

"Tell anyone else and I'll castrate you," she says to me before punching Colter again and then turning away with a flip of her ponytail.

Colter stands upright and lets out a breath.

"She seems sweet," I say dryly. I think my balls just crawled up inside of my body for protection.

His voice is still strained as he says, "She takes a little bit to warm up, but she's great at organizing the events and working with the venues."

"I guess she's not close with the old man."

"She just wants to make a name for herself. Can't be easy being the daughter of a legend."

I huff a short laugh. Yeah, I wouldn't know anything about that. The only thing legendary about my dad is how shitty he was at being one.

"And this is Shane. House mom of the group." Colter winks.

The big guy sitting on an overturned crate sends the man next to me a mock smile before glancing my way and giving me a chin jut. "Hey. Knox Holland, right?"

"Yeah, that's right." I cross my arms over my chest.

He nods slowly, then reaches up and strokes his beard. "I was in Salt Lake City for the championship last month. I'm sorry about how things went down."

Fresh anger and disappointment surge through me. I ball my hands and drop them to my sides. I don't know what else to say but "Thanks."

Before either of us can say anything else, a petite dark-haired girl squeezes by me and throws herself at Colter's side.

He wraps an arm around her waist and then places a quick kiss on her lips. "Babe, I want you to meet someone."

He turns them so they're facing me. I recognize her instantly. She was sitting with the smokeshow, prissy chick earlier tonight.

"Hiiii," she drawls out, scanning me with a smile like she's in on some inside joke.

"Hey, I'm Knox," I say.

"Knox and I went to school together," Colter tells her. He leans down and kisses her neck. "This is my girlfriend, Quinn."

"Nice to meet you." She lifts a hand and wiggles her fingers. Her boyfriend keeps kissing her neck as she reaches out that same hand and pulls another girl closer. *The smokeshow.*

My lips curve as I get a good look at her up close. Long blonde hair is curled around her heart-shaped face, and her eyes are a bright, almost neon, blue. She's wearing this light pink lacy dress thing that's short and tight. My mouth goes dry. She's hot, no doubt about it. I stare hard, taking in her long, tan legs all the way down to her dirty white sneakers. They're the only part of her that isn't prim and perfect. Where the hell did she think she was going tonight in that outfit, and how did she end up here?

At some point she put on a short black leather jacket over the dress, like she was trying to blend in with her surroundings. It didn't help. She sticks out in this place, all prissy and pink. Even her vehicle sticks out. Retro Bronco with a custom paint job in light pink. It's a sea of black and chrome around here, and then there's her.

"This is my friend, Avery. I think you two had a run-in earlier." Quinn giggles before nuzzling into Colter and the two of them get more serious about making out.

Avery and I stand and stare at each other for a beat, neither saying anything at first, but Quinn and Colter don't seem to be coming up for air.

"Hi," she says, then shuffles uncomfortably.

"I'm Knox."

I don't know why I don't say more. I just sort of stare at her. I'm not one for getting tongue-tied around a woman, but she's just so prissy. Undeniably hot, but high maintenance. I'd be better off letting Brooklyn claw my eyes out than messing with this one. But damn if I'm not tempted to ask her if she wants to hop on my bike and go for a ride.

"Are you a freestyle racer too?" she asks.

"Rider."

"What?"

"Rider, not racer."

"Right. Whatever. You knew what I meant." Her tone is harder than I expected, and I find myself holding in a chuckle. Smokeshow is sassy.

She looks at her friend for an out, but Quinn is still kissing Colter, so she glances back at me. "So, are you?"

"They aren't racing bikes, they're riding them. So, they're riders," I clarify. "And I ride motocross."

"What's the difference?"

"When I'm riding, I *am* racing."

Her tongue darts out to wet her pink lips. They're big and full, sort of pouty in a way that makes me want to kiss her to see what they feel like against mine.

One of the guys I was hanging out with earlier calls my name and I glance back at him. He motions toward his motorcycle, indicating he wants to take off and go for a ride.

"I could show you."

"Show me?" Her voice rises several octaves on the last word.

"Yeah. You want to go for a ride with me?" Excitement thrums under my skin at the thought of her on the back of my bike.

Those perfect lips part into an "o" but no sound comes out as she considers my question. I'm pretty sure she's trying to figure out how to politely tell me to fuck off. I laugh, knowing damn well she won't say yes even before she shakes her head.

"I'm not going anywhere with you. I don't even know you."

"Colter will vouch for me." Though as I glance over at him, he's still got his tongue down his girlfriend's throat. "Afraid you might get dirty?"

"Afraid I might die," she quips. "I'm familiar with your driving skills, remember?"

My mouth quirks up on one side. "You mean when you nearly ran me over?"

"You came flying out of nowhere." Her tone sharpens and she attempts to glare at me, but she's just so damn adorable, my smile widens.

"One ride, princess."

"Princess?" She scoffs, looking even more like a stuck-up, prissy chick.

"I'll have you back before your friend comes up for air. You might even like it."

"Doubtful since you'd be there. Why don't you go ask your girlfriend?"

"My what?"

"The girl you were making out with earlier. Does she know you're off flirting with other women?"

"Sounds like you were keeping tabs on me tonight. I'm flattered." I step forward and lower my voice. "She's not my girlfriend, and I just asked if you wanted to go for a ride on my bike, not my dick. Though…"

Her jaw goes slack, and her cheeks flush a pretty pink. "The answer to both of those would be a hard no."

"Your loss." I wink at her and take a step back then flick my gaze to Colter. I raise my voice so that maybe he'll hear me over the sound of him making out. "I gotta get going, man."

His mouth pulls away from his girl, but he keeps his arms around her. "Thanks for coming. See you next week at the track?"

"You can count on it." I nod to his girlfriend and then take one last look at Avery. "Later, princess."

# CHAPTER FOUR
## Knox

I'm driving to pick up Flynn from basketball practice the following week when my phone vibrates in the cupholder. I pull over and stare down at the name on the screen with something like hope blooming in my chest. I pick it up, thumb hovering over the screen. I hit accept on the call and bring it to my ear. "Hey, Mike."

"Knox." My old team owner's voice is upbeat and casual, giving me further hope that this call is good news. "Hey, how's Valley?"

"Good," I answer succinctly. "I've been training every day, working hard."

"Yeah, I got your messages. I'm glad everything is going well."

"It is. I'm feeling stronger than ever, and my times have never been better."

"I'm really happy to hear that. Truly."

"Does that mean you're going to give me another chance?"

I hold my breath. This is it. I need back on the team. I need another shot. I've come too far for it to all be over before it's really started.

His sigh twists my insides into knots. "Your riding was never the problem, Knox."

"I'll steer clear of Link."

"I'm sorry, but I haven't changed my mind."

"This is bullshit." My anger gets the best of me and the words fly out before I can stop them. "I can win. I'm *going* to win."

All season I raced hard for them, bringing the Thorne team a lot of top finishes. I went from a has-been rider that everyone had forgotten about in the five years I'd been gone, to a top contender over the course of the season. That championship was mine to lose. Then one mistake and they toss me out. Me, instead of the guy who cost me the race. Accidents happen on the track, but Link knew what he was doing. He knew the risk and he decided he didn't care. He was reckless and it cost me everything.

"It was never your ability to win that was the problem. You're a talented rider, no doubt about it, but I've got two other guys to think about. This isn't Team Knox. We're a tight-knit group. We want guys that can work together and help each other out."

I barely keep the words "Like Link helped me out?" from tumbling from my lips. This is bullshit.

"I like you, Knox, I do, but you've got a bad attitude, and your temper gets the best of you."

"He cost me the championship!" I yell, wrapping my fingers around the steering wheel and squeezing hard. I don't care that I'm proving his point by losing my cool. Link fucked up. Not me.

"And you caused a scene and broke your contract by fighting

with your own teammate."

I was pissed when I saw Link on the podium celebrating what should have been my victory. All I could see was red. I was so fucking close. Five years of sitting on the sidelines waiting for an opportunity and then there it was, so close I could almost feel that trophy in my hands…and then it was gone.

"It won't happen again," I say through gritted teeth.

He barks a short laugh. "It wasn't an isolated event. You and Link were bickering all season. I know he isn't perfect, but you should have been setting an example, not fanning the flames."

"I said it won't happen again." I can keep my mouth shut and my hands to myself. I can do anything if it means getting another chance.

"Even if I believed that, I couldn't convince the rest of ownership. We just can't have that kind of atmosphere. You're a liability we can't afford."

"Come on, Mike. One more shot, that's all I'm asking."

"I'm sorry," he says again, voice resolute. "I really am, but you won't be racing with us next season."

I close my eyes and let my head fall back.

At my silence, he adds, "If I were you, I'd spend the next few months reflecting on your actions. If you want to make this a career, you need to grow up and figure out how to stop letting your temper get the best of you. The racing world is small, and people talk."

Grow up? He thinks I need to grow up. It's laughable, really. He has no idea the responsibilities I had thrust on me at an early age or how much rests on my shoulders. I'm not looking for pity, I'd do it all over again. But now is my shot.

I just want to race. I want to *win*. And I'll do whatever it takes to prove myself.

I park outside of the gym at Valley High School as Flynn is pushing out of the double doors with some of his basketball teammates. When he spots my truck, he juts his chin at his friends and then takes off at a jog toward me.

Flynn opens the passenger door and tosses a wad of Valley High crimson red material into the back with his duffel.

"What's all that?" I ask.

"The new warmups came in."

"Shit. I completely forgot." I shift the truck into park. "Is your coach still in there?"

Flynn looks at me, a confused expression marring his sweaty brow. His reddish-brown hair is plastered to his forehead.

"To pay him," I clarify. Flynn mentioned needing the money for warmups, but with everything going on, it slipped my mind.

"I already paid him."

"Did you get a job when I wasn't paying attention?" I ask, knowing damn well he didn't. Keeping up with his schoolwork while playing sports is a full-time gig. I've done my best to make sure that he doesn't have to stress about money for whatever he needs so he can focus on normal teenage stuff.

I want him to have the high school experience I didn't. Our mom passed years before I was a senior and our dad was rarely around. Hendrick had already left for college, so it was on me to make sure we had a place to live and food to eat, plus clothes and school shit. I dropped out as soon as I turned eighteen and got a job at a local HVAC company so that we could all stay together, but even working full-time, extra cash to do things like go out with friends was rare.

It's why I quit racing for a while. Motocross can get expensive with the constant bike upkeep and entry fees. The time away from work and my brothers was hard too.

Archer and Brogan helped out when they could, getting jobs over the summer and after school when it wasn't football season, but I never wanted my brothers to feel like they needed to give up things or pick up my slack. One of us putting our dreams on hold was more than enough.

Flynn was only eight when Mom died. We protected him the most. It was never discussed, but looking back, I can see how we all gave up things so he could have the most normalcy.

"Hendrick gave me the money," my little brother says as I'm pulled from my own thoughts.

Annoyed, not at him, but at myself for forgetting and then making it someone else's problem, I do my best to keep my voice level as I reply, "I told you I'd give it to you."

"I know, but I forgot to remind you and I needed it today, so I asked Hendrick when he dropped me off this morning."

I nod, working my jaw back and forth. I should be thankful, but instead it makes me feel like I'm failing.

The one day I didn't take Flynn to school. It's usually me who drops off and picks up, but this morning I was on the phone making calls and worrying about my career, so when Hendrick offered to take our baby brother, I agreed. The other option—letting Flynn borrow my car—was absolutely not happening. He has his license, but drives like shit. He's wrecked one car already.

"What's for dinner? I'm starving. Coach made us run for thirty minutes today because a couple of guys were messing around." It's more words than Flynn usually says on our drive home, and I know it's because he's trying to smooth over my fuck-up. He can read me better than anyone.

We talk back and forth the entire ride, but the unease I feel doesn't abate. As soon as we get to the house, Flynn heads straight for his bedroom.

Archer and Brogan are in the living room watching TV, and Hendrick and his fiancée, Jane, are sitting at the dining room table.

"Hey," Hendrick calls as I set my keys on the kitchen counter. It's followed by a chorus of hellos from everyone else. I murmur a greeting back distractedly as my gaze snags on the half-eaten lasagna.

"You made dinner?" The question comes out more accusatory than intended. It's rare that anyone else cooks around here unless you count microwaveable meals.

"Jane did." Hendrick looks at her like she invented the meal instead of cooked it. My oldest brother has it bad.

My stomach growls. It smells good and I skipped lunch. "Thanks, Hollywood."

She shoots me a playful glare at the nickname. Jane starred in a TV show when she was younger. I never watched it, but I've heard her sing a time or two and her voice is incredible.

I fill a plate and take it to the dining room table. It'd be rude not to eat it, even if I was planning on grilling steaks tonight.

Jane's doing homework at the table. She's in her final year at Valley U, same as Brogan and Archer. Hendrick sits beside her, leaned back in a chair with a mug of coffee in front of him, studying her.

When Flynn comes out of his room to make a plate, it reminds me of the money. I drop my fork and grab my wallet, pull out some bills and plop them in front of my older brother.

"What's this?" Hendrick asks, eyeing it carefully.

"It's to pay for Flynn's warmups."

One brow rises and his head cocks to the side, then he pushes the cash back toward me. "Fuck off. I don't want your money."

"I'm not letting you pay for the warmups."

"Why not?"

I know a loaded question when I hear one. "I'd already set aside the money. It just slipped my mind and I forgot to give it to him."

I can tell Hendrick wants to argue, so I add, "If you won't take it, I'm just going to shove it in the tip jar the next time I'm at the bar."

"Can you make sure I'm working when you do?" Brogan asks without looking back at us from where he sits facing the TV.

Flynn takes a seat at the end of the table. His stare volleys between us. We're a stubborn bunch, so it's not abnormal that two or more of us would be bickering. All-out fights are less common, but also not out of the question.

Clearly annoyed, but resigned, Hendrick accepts the money. He hasn't taken it yet, but he lets it sit between us as he resumes his position, leaning back with one arm resting behind Jane's chair.

He can't be paying for things right now anyway. He just opened a bar about a year ago. It's doing well, but something always needs to be fixed, and he and Jane are planning a very elaborate and over-the-top wedding for next summer.

We all fall back into comfortable silence. I'm lost in my thoughts as I eat, turning over the day in my head. I got a good practice in at the track, but I'm still thinking about my call with Mike.

With a mouthful of food, Flynn mumbles, "Did you find a new team today?"

All eyes dart to me. I shake my head. The food I'm chewing doesn't have quite the same appeal and I push my plate away from me. "No, not yet."

After another beat of silence from everyone, Hendrick asks, "How many have you reached out to?"

All of them. "A couple."

"You'll find a team," Flynn says optimistically. "You're the best rider. They'd be dumb not to grab you while they have the chance."

"Yeah, we'll see," I say, voice raw. My skin feels tight, and my mouth goes dry. I clear my throat and stand. When my plate is cleared and put in the dishwasher, I head straight out to the garage.

My body relaxes and my mind clears as I start tinkering with my bike. It's not long after when Hendrick joins me. He holds a beer out to me.

"Thanks," I say, accepting it.

He takes a drink from his bottle as he studies my movements. "I can remember the old man out here working on our bikes or messing with his motorcycle. Remember that four-wheeler he built?"

I grunt my acknowledgement.

"He was good with motors. So are you."

Being compared to my dad, even for something positive, makes me want to burn the whole garage down and stomp on the ashes.

But fuck him, he doesn't get to take this from me. His blood might run through my veins, but everything I have is because of my hard work.

"So, what's the plan? Do you have more people to contact

tomorrow or are you going to try to get Mike to change his mind?" Hendrick asks, sitting on the weight bench situated in the corner of the garage.

"I pretty much called everyone already," I admit without looking up at him. "And Mike made it clear that they weren't going to change their mind."

"Did you tell him what Link said before the race? He was trying to take you out."

"It doesn't matter. It won't change anything."

"How do you know if you don't tell him? Mike is a decent guy. If he knew the whole story—"

"Drop it, okay?" Mike knows that the accident was Link's fault. Everyone there knew it. They chalked it up to him being a young, hungry rider.

He looks like he wants to push but he doesn't. Instead, he blows out a breath and runs a hand through his hair. "I could ask my old agent if he has any ideas."

I consider his offer. Hendrick played pro football for a while, but it's been more than a year since he parted ways with his agent, and I doubt they keep in touch.

"Nah, that's all right." I don't want anyone pulling strings for me. I want to earn this on my own. I crack open the beer and take a drink, then set it on the ground so I can go back to working on my bike.

"I could take Flynn to school again tomorrow, so you have time to figure it out."

"I got him."

"All right, well I can pick him up then."

"No, it's cool." It's not like I have a lot else to do. Work out, train, and try to figure out how I'm going to manage everything on my own next season.

Hen laughs, drawing my attention away from my bike. His eyes are lit with amusement and his lips curve into a smirk.

"What?" I ask, lifting one brow in challenge.

"You're the stubbornest person I've ever met. You don't want anyone else to help with Flynn or pay for shit or make dinner or call in favors."

I stare at him, waiting for the reason that's bad. I like to do things on my own, why does that make me stubborn?

"We want to help," Hendrick says. "You riding again has been fucking awesome for all of us. You're an inspiration. Especially to Flynn."

I want to roll my eyes or tell him their help isn't necessary, but something in my brother's expression stops me. He levels me with a deep, worried look. "Let us fucking help. You're not in this alone. I'm sorry that so much responsibility fell on you when Dad took off and I was gone, but I'm back now, Archer and Brogan are pitching in more, and Flynn would do anything to see you succeed. You're his fucking hero, so start acting like it instead of pretending your dreams are secondary. It's important for him to see you go after what you want."

His words linger between us for a few quiet moments, then one side of my mouth quirks up. "Damn, Henny. When did you turn into a motivational speaker?"

"Did it work?" he asks, grinning and taking another drink.

"If there were any other options, then yeah, maybe, but I don't think there are." I understand what he's saying, but I don't see a way to fix this.

He nods slowly.

"I saw Colter last weekend and some of the local guys. I'll ride with them and on my own, do what I can." I shrug one shoulder.

"Colter." His smile widens. "I remember you two riding like bats out of hell together. Mom was always afraid you were going to kill yourself trying to beat him."

"Trying to?" I scoff. "I'm way faster."

"Is he still racing?"

"No, he's all-in on freestyle. He's really fucking good too."

"That doesn't surprise me. You and he were always the best around."

"He asked me to tour with his team during the off-season."

"Doing freestyle?"

I wave it off. It's not like I'm seriously considering it. "He said I could travel with them and help set up and tear down until I was ready to perform."

"You should do it."

"Why?"

"You need a team and he's offering one."

Not the right kind of team, though. None of his guys or Brooklyn race.

"Hear me out." Hendrick leans forward and his eyes are bright. Every inch of him is brimming with excitement. "Thorne dropped you because you were a bad teammate."

I clamp my jaw down at the reminder. *Thanks a lot, bro.*

"Show them you can be part of a team."

"It's a distraction and hours wasted that I could be training for next season." Freestyle is fun to watch, but riding is what I want to do.

"Replace the hours that you're moping around here with practicing some tricks. How hard could it be?"

Really fucking hard probably, but his excitement is so palpable that I find myself considering it.

"I'd be gone most weekends."

"So? We survived during the season while you were at events."

"It was summertime." Brogan and Archer were chilling and enjoying the months off from college, and Flynn just had sports camps and practices to juggle.

"We will manage," Hendrick reassures me.

"I don't know," I say, but I can't shake off the idea. Could it really work?

"Promise me that you'll at least consider it, okay?"

"Why are you pushing this so hard?" It's more work for him and everyone else. It makes their lives harder, not easier.

"Because you told me once that I should fight like hell for my dreams because one of us should get a chance to chase them."

"I was talking about you," I remind him.

His dark, serious gaze locks on me. "I know you were, and I chased mine. I did what I wanted to do, and I don't regret that it's over. Now it's your time. So, fight like hell for it."

# CHAPTER FIVE
## Knox

"That wasn't bad," Colter says as I stop the bike next to him. Brooklyn snorts a laugh, the sound barely audible as she revs the engine of her green Kawasaki KX250F. It's the same kind of bike her dad rode. "I could do a better heel clicker than that when I was still in diapers."

She's probably not joking. My gaze slides to Oak.

The tall, lanky guy shrugs and his face is impassive. "At least you didn't crash."

The three of them have been watching me attempt tricks for the past hour to see where I'm at—a starting point to work from. So far, I've landed everything I've done (albeit not gracefully) but not well enough to call it good and move on to something harder. I never gave much thought to how something looked for the audience. In racing, it only matters who gets across that finish line first.

Colter hands me his phone so I can watch the jump I just did. A heel clicker is probably the simplest trick there is and even that one doesn't look very smooth as I watch it back.

On the jump, you kick your feet out and bring them around and over your arms and touch. Simple. I have thrown that trick a million times at practice or when crossing the finish line, but I never had to care what it looked like. Freestyle is all about style and finesse—something I apparently am lacking.

My timing is off. I click too early or too late when I go off the big ram, and my legs are super bent and look awkward. Have I always been so inflexible?

"Fuck," I mutter as I hand his phone back.

"Maybe you should try lifting one leg at a time," Colter says. "Get the feel of that down, switch legs, and then you can give the full trick a go again. Build on a little each time."

"I'm gonna go," Brooklyn says with a small laugh and a flick of her red hair. "It sounds like you guys are going to be here awhile and I have plans."

Oak takes off too with a salute, leaving me alone with Colter.

"Maybe this was a bad idea." I've had that thought a thousand times over since Hendrick talked me into this crazy notion.

Colter shakes his head. For some reason he's convinced I can do this. I hope he's right. "You just need more practice. Let's do it again."

With a sigh, I nod and take off toward the ramp.

I do exactly what Colter suggested, alternating bringing one leg up at a time until I feel confident, then doing the full trick again.

This time when I play back the video, it's better. Still not pretty, but I don't look like I'm about to catapult over the handlebars.

It's getting dark when we finally call it. I'm loading up my bike while Colter leans against his truck, still replaying footage from earlier.

"You made a lot of progress today," he says as he brings his gaze up from his phone. "Same time tomorrow?"

"Yeah. I'll be here." I roll my shoulders back and stretch my neck to one side. My muscles ache in a new way. I'm going to need to kick up my workout routine to add in more upper body and core.

"Cool." He pockets his phone and opens the door of his truck. "You'll get it. It takes time to get the feel of everything."

I nod, hoping like hell he is right.

At the end of day three, I've added two more tricks to my list of ones I've successfully landed, but Brooklyn has started to refer to me as Flounderella because half the time I'm struggling to get myself back in the seat after the trick. I'm slow because I want to nail the execution of the trick. All the videos, even when I manage to get the timing right, still look clumsy. I hate not being good at something. But especially something related to dirt bikes.

It's just me and Colter again, the third night in a row we've stayed until dark. The first two days he still looked optimistic, but tonight I can tell he's starting to doubt that I'll get it.

"I can do it," I say, infusing some of that confidence back into my words. I'm too stubborn to give up now. Even if I never perform with the tour, I am going to perfect the tricks I've learned.

He shoves both hands into his pants pockets. "I have an idea, but you're probably not going to like it."

One brow lifts in question. "Okay. Shoot."

"Last spring, I worked out with Avery for a few months, and it improved my strength a lot and helped with controlling my body while in the air."

"You're just mentioning this now?" My spine straightens. I'll do anything if it'll help. All last year, I had to do daily sessions with a trainer to stay in top riding shape. I'm not afraid to put in the work.

"Seriously?" The surprise on Colter's face is clear. "I thought you'd resist, or I'd have brought it up earlier."

"The team had us working out with trainers all the time. Who is she and which gym is she at?" I have my phone out, ready to put in her information.

He pauses, myriad expressions crossing his face before he says, "Avery. You met her last weekend. Quinn's friend. Her roommate too."

An image of the pretty blonde fills my head and the hope I was feeling vanishes. "She's a trainer?"

"No. She's a gymnast at Valley U."

"That prissy-looking chick is a gymnast?"

He nods his head adamantly, smirking like he's taking joy in my surprise. I run that through my mind, trying to imagine her doing cartwheels and backflips. Interesting.

"And you worked out with her? Doing what?" I'm still curious even if I don't think there's any hope of her helping me.

"Lots of stuff. Gymnastics is fucking hard. She taught me how to hold handstands, get out of them gracefully, Japanese handstands, cartwheels, somersaults, combination tumbles, and I even did a little ring work. It was tough."

A smile breaks out on my face. "What I'd give to have seen that."

"I know it sounds crazy, but it helped a lot. I made huge improvements in a shorter time than other guys."

If I know Colter, he was putting in a lot of hours riding and practicing too, which is probably what truly made the difference.

"I'm going to see her tonight. I can ask if she'd have time to help." He looks at me like he's hoping I'll take him up on it. I hate to disappoint him, but doing somersaults isn't my idea of working out.

"That's okay." I hold up a hand. "I can work out on my own and put in more time here."

"You're already here from the time you drop off Flynn in the morning until you gotta run to pick him up after practices."

"It's only the third day. Besides, my heel clicker is almost as good as yours now."

He scoffs. "Yeah-fucking-right. You wish, Holland."

I walk around to the driver's side door of my truck, open it, and pull myself up, calling out, "Just you wait, I'm going to be doing it upside down in a backflip before you know it."

# CHAPTER SIX
*Avery*

"I don't feel like doing beam today," Hope says, voice full of teen admonishment as we walk over to the right corner of the gym.

I glance back at her as I pull myself onto one of the lower beams so I can do the routine with Hope. "Why not?"

"You should see your face right now." She giggles and her expression looks every bit of her thirteen years as she smiles, showing her braces with lavender bands. "You look so offended, like you can't imagine anyone not loving beam as much as you."

"I can't," I say honestly.

The local club gym is busy tonight with young gymnasts. Boys that don't look any older than four or five to girls that are in high school and preparing for the club season competitions. I come here most evenings to get in more practice. It's nice to work out with all the energy of young competitors around me.

Hope mounts, straddling the beam, then tucking her legs before standing.

"Let's work on turns first," I suggest.

"Ugh. I was hoping we'd work on dismounts."

That's because she's good at that part. Tumbling is her strength. She is great at the floor routine and it's all she wants to work on. But with a little extra effort, she can translate some of those skills and be great at beam too.

"If your turns look good, then we'll move on to split jumps."

A little spark of excitement flashes in her eyes. Most kids would be thrilled to work on the easier skills, but not Hope. I think that's why I like working with her so much. She's fearless.

I'm not officially coaching her or anything, but since I started coming here, she's just sort of followed me around. I can't work out like I want to, so it's fun to see her improvements since I'm not making any of my own.

"Is Tristan your boyfriend?" she asks.

"What? No. Why would you think that?" I get in position beside her, then glance over my shoulder until I find Tristan across the gym. He lifts his chin slightly as we make eye contact.

"He keeps staring over here."

"He's not my boyfriend," I reiterate, turning back around.

"Why not? He's hot."

"Hot boys are usually jerks." An image of that asshole Knox at the freestyle event flashes through my mind.

"I don't think that logic works," she says. "You're pretty and not a bitch, so isn't it possible that a boy can be hot and not a jerk?"

"Aww, thanks. But I stand by my statement." I walk across the beam in time with her. We stop in the middle, and I show her one turn first, then face her so I can watch her form.

When she lifts her left leg, she wobbles.

"Stomach in. Hips under," I correct her as she gains her balance. "Let's hold the relevé for five seconds."

Hope drops down and then restarts. She brings her left leg up, foot touching the right knee and arms up in a crown position. Each time she wobbles a little less. I can tell when her focus reins in. Her jaw sets and she stops glancing around at what others are doing.

"Good. Now ten seconds."

She doesn't even talk back, just nods and then goes in again, holding the position as I count slowly to ten. On the third one, her arms come out to her sides to stop her from falling out of it.

"Dang it," she mutters.

"No, that was great. Your body lines are looking better too. Let's move on to half turns. Don't forget to drive that heel each time." I do one and then drop down to a sit on the beam with my legs dangling over one side. I still haven't been given the green light to practice on beam, and even though Coach Weaver isn't here, I don't want to push it.

She gets through a dozen or more half turns while I watch and offer small corrections before I see Hope's dad out of the corner of my eye, standing at the door to the gym. Glancing up at the clock hanging on the wall and then back at him, I hold up a hand in a wave and smile.

I let Hope get in a couple more before I say, "Your dad is here. It's later than I realized. We can work on it more tomorrow."

"Already?" Her good posture falls, and her voice goes back to the childish whine of earlier.

"Yep." I hop off the beam. "You can practice it at home after you do your homework."

She snarls at that, which pulls a laugh from me. When she comes down, I tug on one of the red braids falling down her back. "If you fail your classes, your dad will stop letting you stay late after practice to hang out with me."

"Fine," she relents, sounding entirely unhappy about it. Her voice is more upbeat when she asks, "Tomorrow can we work on floor?"

"We'll see."

I walk her to the door and say hello to her dad, who thanks me before forcing a reluctant Hope out of the gym. Then I grab my stuff and head home. She isn't the only one that needs to do some homework tonight.

But before that, I need to shower and make myself look presentable for a podcast interview. The last time I was asked to do one, I made the mistake of thinking it was audio only. It wasn't and I showed up fresh out of practice looking like a sweaty troll. Oops.

The dorm is quiet when I enter and head up to the fourth floor. Music pumps out of some of the rooms, doors are propped open, but the hallway is empty.

When I get to my room, I push into it and smile at the scene in front of me. Colter and Quinn are snuggled up on the couch watching TV. She's curled up next to him with her head resting in his lap, and Colter is absently stroking her dark hair.

"Hey," I say as I shut the door behind me.

Quinn lifts an arm lazily as Colter says, "Hey, Aves."

"What are you guys watching?" I let my bag fall from my shoulder to the floor and take a seat on the far end of the couch next to Quinn's feet.

My roommate stretches her legs out onto my lap. "*Botched*. This chick's butt implant flipped. You should have seen it. It looked so gross."

"Eww," I say.

"What are you doing tonight?" Quinn asks. "Want to hang out after you shower?" She wrinkles her nose at me like she can smell me.

I'm sweaty, but I don't stink *that* bad. "I can't. I have a podcast interview."

"This late?"

"I told them I could only do it on a weekday if it was after practice." I blow out a breath, not really wanting to get up now that I've sat down. "I should go shower and then head to the library and see if I can get one of the study rooms so there isn't a bunch of background noise during the interview."

"You can do it here. We were going to grab dinner at that Mexican place you like so much, but we were waiting on you." Quinn moves her gaze from the TV to me.

My stomach growls.

She smiles knowingly. "Want me to bring you something back?"

I press a hand to my midsection and laugh. "Yes, please."

She sits up, Colter stands, and then he pulls her to her feet and all the way to him so he can brush a kiss on her lips. My chest squeezes at how cute they are together. I was fully prepared to dislike Colter when I met him because I was certain he was going to break my friend's heart, but it's so obvious how much he adores her.

"Give me two minutes to put on shoes and grab a jacket," Quinn says as she heads toward her room on one side of the suite.

I smile at Colter as he watches her go. His gaze slowly returns to me. It's hard to say who is more obsessed with whom, him or her.

"How's the knee?" he asks.

"Okay." I tense my leg and bend it tighter to feel the joint work.

"Good. I'm glad to hear it." He shifts his weight from one leg to the other. "Do you have any extra time to train someone over the next month or so?"

"Miss me already?"

His upper body shakes with a small laugh. "Nah, not me. I've got a new guy on the team and he's struggling with some of the same things I was. I think you might be just what he needs."

"I'm flattered," I say honestly. "I won't have a ton of time once competitions start, but I work out most weeknights at the club gym. Could he come then?"

"I'm not sure what his schedule is like in the evenings. I know he's free during the day."

"I could also do before team practice every day but Fridays. I have a lab that runs late that day, but I'm free the other days."

"That might work better for him. Thanks. I mentioned you, but I thought I should ask before I gave him your contact information."

"Yeah, give him my number. I'm happy to help if I can."

He nods and turns his head as Quinn comes out of her room. "I'll tell him. Thanks, Avery."

My roommate sidles up to him. "Ready?"

He wraps an arm around her and squeezes her tight. "Ready."

"Bye." Quinn wiggles her fingers at me as she follows Colter out.

"Bye," I say, sinking into the couch and letting my head fall back into the cushion for just a second before I force myself up and to the shower.

"What did it feel like to win a silver medal as the underdog?" The interviewer, Mary, asks. She's a former gymnast herself and competed in the Olympics in the early two-thousands, but never won an individual medal.

"It was incredible," I say, a real smile curving my lips as memories flood me. I was too excited and confident to be scared or put off by people not believing I was a threat. "Being there was everything I had dreamed of, everything I had worked so hard for. I believed in myself enough that it didn't matter if no one else did."

"And now that there are certain expectations for you, how does that motivate you? Is it harder or easier to believe in yourself after something like that?" she asks. The question feels like a dart to the chest.

"Harder," I admit, but then smile wider. "But I love a challenge and I'm still one hundred percent motivated to win."

Mary loves that answer, I can tell by the way her own smile brightens. Behind her is a wall of framed photos and awards she's won. She was part of two gold medal teams and placed in who knows how many national competitions. I wonder if she looks back on her career and has regrets. I'd like to ask her, but she dives right into the next question.

"Talk me through what it was like to come off the amazing experience at the Olympics and then move to competing collegiately at Valley University. What has that been like?"

"Really good. I like the coaches and program here at Valley, and I feel like it was the right next step for me."

"But you struggled through last season even when most people would say the competition and skills required to succeed are lower than at the elite level. Why do you think you struggled so much?"

My stomach clenches and I can practically feel the sweat beading up on my forehead, but I manage to keep smiling even as I want to tell Mary to shove her annoying questions up her ass. "I think there are always going to be highs and lows. I changed a lot last year. New coaches, new routines, new city—my whole life was different, and it's taken a little adjustment period to get comfortable."

I sigh inwardly, relieved that I was able to get out an answer that sounded coherent and not bite her head off. A lot did change last year. In addition to everything I told her, there is a lot more pressure on me than ever before. The world is watching in a way they weren't when no one knew who I was. I'm nervous that I won't live up to their expectations. Or my own.

"And what about this year? Is your knee going to be healed in time to compete?" she asks.

That's the million-dollar question. "My doctors feel confident, but I'm just taking it one day at a time."

"Well, whenever you do come back, we'll all be watching to see just what Avery Oliver can do."

# CHAPTER SEVEN
## Knox

I toss my helmet to the ground, clench my jaw, and let out a low growl of frustration. The weight of Flynn's stare keeps me from completely losing my shit.

A week of practice and my improvements are minimal. At this rate I'll be ready to perform never. I so badly want to give up, but my pride won't let me.

I flop down next to my little brother, and we watch Colter and his team as they start their practice. They have another event next weekend and they're adding in a group backflip. It's a simple trick for all of them but getting the timing down so their spacing and flight are identical is harder.

Flynn had a rare day off from basketball practice, so I picked him up and brought him back to the track with me. Hendrick and Jane have been helping a lot with driving him and doing shit around the house so I can practice longer, but I've missed hanging out with him one-on-one.

"This is so rad," he says, grinning as they come around for the second time.

One side of my mouth lifts. "Yeah, they're pretty good."

The usual crew is here: Colter, Brooklyn, Oak, and another local guy, Shane, that they all refer to as "Momma Bear" but only when he isn't listening because Shane is big and burly and could beat up all of them at the same time. And then four others from all over the West Coast drove in so they could run through one last practice together before next weekend.

Last weekend's event was the smallest crowd they're expecting and more like a run-through in front of a crowd. Over the next few months, they'll go from Oregon to Texas, performing in large venues to sold-out crowds. Or I guess we'll go, since I somehow got myself roped into this.

"Do you think you can teach me how to do some tricks?" Flynn turns his head to glance at me quickly before returning his attention to the track.

My brows lift. "Fuck no."

"Why not?"

"You want to play college ball next year?"

His head bobs.

"Then let's keep you in one piece until you've signed somewhere."

He doesn't look at me or answer, but I catch an eye roll.

"Are you going to perform with them next weekend?" he asks instead.

"Doubtful. I can't land anything impressive yet. I might not ever be ready, but since I have some time on my hands it's a good way to kill time."

Flynn tears his gaze away from the riders. "Hendrick told me what you're trying to do—show your old coach that you can be part of a team without punching anyone."

I feel my brows lift. "I didn't punch anyone. I shoved him a little."

"Looked like you wanted to punch him though."

"Oh, I definitely wanted to." Might as well have for the way things ended up. "I don't know, maybe it's a stretch to think they'll take me back no matter what I do."

"Nah, I think it's a good idea."

"You do?"

"Yeah. It's like when Coach Cook benches one of us for hogging the ball. He always threatens to make us sit there until we have splinters, but he never does. He just needs time to cool down, then he gives us another chance. Your team will too."

"I hope so. I really don't want splinters in my ass."

My brother smirks and then we fall quiet as we watch the bikes take off up the ramp and spin in the air.

"We should get you home," I say, finally pulling myself off the ground. "Do you have homework tonight?"

"A little." He stands in front of me. Sometime over the last month he's shot up another inch. He's lanky still, not quite grown into his body, but he's going to be the tallest and broadest of all of us someday.

Flynn stands in front of the truck, watching the riders until my bike is loaded, then he walks backward and pulls himself up into the passenger seat, never tearing his gaze away.

"How long has it been since you rode?" I ask him.

He shrugs, lifting both shoulders up to his ears. "I don't know.

Nine years or so. I think I was eight."

Since Mom died. A lot changed after that. I silently curse myself for not taking him with me. I rode to get away from everything, but Flynn didn't have that option. That's probably why he started playing every school sport that he could.

"We should go sometime. I know some good easy spots out on the east side of town where we can take the bikes and ride."

"Yeah, sure. Whatever."

I hold back a smile at him trying not to appear too eager, but I catch the smile he's fighting.

Later that night I'm lying in bed, muscles tight and so exhausted I'm fighting sleep before it's completely dark outside. Archer and Brogan are playing video games and their voices carry through the thin walls.

Scrolling through Instagram, I heart a couple of photos of chicks I've hooked up with in the past. I can't remember the last time I went out and cut loose. Since the end of the season, I've been wound too tightly.

Messages start to pop up in response to my liking pictures, but before I click on them, I come to Flynn's most recent post. My breath catches as I read the caption. *My brother is a badass. Wait until you see the other tricks up his sleeve.* And above it is a video of me performing a heel clicker. It actually doesn't look too bad. He caught me at just the right angle.

I watch it a dozen times, rereading his words and letting them fill me with hope and determination.

I sit up, groaning as I do, and close out of the app. I text Colter before I think better of it.

ME

I'm in. Send me Avery's
information.

If Flynn thinks I can do this, then I want to do everything I can to prove him right.

# CHAPTER EIGHT
## *Avery*

"That one was better," I say as Hope completes another turn almost perfectly. After only one day, she's made huge improvements.

"Now can I work on dismounts?" Her excitement at the prospect is contagious.

"Yes, now we can work on dismounts."

She squeals and gets into position at one of the beams and prepares for a back tuck dismount into the foam pit. She's flawless and her smile widens each time she launches herself into the air.

I continue practicing some of my own skills on the mat: leaps and turns, mostly. My knee has been holding up, but I've already put a lot of strain on it today with practice earlier, so I don't want to push it too much.

"Wow!" Hope climbs onto the beam and stops. At first, I think she is amazed by my split leap with full turn, but she isn't looking at me at all.

I follow her stare into the viewing area just outside of the gym where parents and visitors can watch. I don't see anything out of the ordinary, so I glance back at her. "What?"

"Not what. *Who*." Her gaze continues to be glued to the same spot, so I turn and look again. Moms, dads, grandparents, siblings... and *him*.

Knox, the cocky motorcycle guy from last weekend, stands at the back of the room in jeans and a black leather jacket. Hope isn't the only one watching him. More than a few moms are thoroughly enjoying the eye candy.

"What is he doing here?" I ask under my breath.

His stare is heavy and aimed right at me. He lifts a hand as I dumbly stare back at him. He's as good-looking as I remember. Tall, medium brown hair that's thicker on top and shaved closer around his ears. He has sharp features and the way he holds himself, it's like he's never completely relaxed.

"I'll be right back," I say to Hope before I force my legs to move toward him.

Her eyes bug out of her head when she realizes I'm going to talk to him. I try not to let that make me nervous as I weave around the gym and enter the lobby through a side door. Knox moves toward me.

It's noisy, so I don't speak until I'm right in front of him.

"Hi," I say, letting my confusion bleed through in my tone. "Are you here to see me?"

His gaze roams down over my leotard to my bare feet and then back up to the messy bun on top of my head. "I didn't picture you as a gymnast."

I cross my arms over my chest. "Can I help you?"

"I'm not interrupting practice, am I?"

"No, not really. I'm just helping a friend. What are you doing here?"

"Colter gave me your number, but he said I might be able to catch you here, so I just swung by."

"All right," I say slowly, waiting for more. Why in the world would Colter give him my number or tell him where I was?

"He also said he talked to you about training me, but by the look on your face I'm wondering if that's true."

"Training you? For what?" It's then that I remember Colter asking about my availability. My hands drop to my hips. "You're the new guy on his team?"

"No." He shakes his head as he says the word, tone defensive, then backtracks. "I mean, yeah, but it's not permanent or anything. I have a few months until the season starts back up."

"Right. You're a rider who races." I make sure to use the right terminology, which makes one side of his mouth quirk up. "But you need help riding?"

"Colter said you had some strength and control exercises that you showed him." He crooks a hand behind his head and rubs the back of his neck. It's clear how uncomfortable he is asking for my help. So why is he?

"I mean, kind of." He's simplifying it down to a couple of exercises like I told Colter to do pushups and crunches, when the reality is we did a lot of different things. "Mostly we just worked out together."

"So, you can't help me?"

"I didn't say that." I'd been fully prepared to help Colter's new team member before I knew it was Knox, but everything about this guy has me on edge. I can't tell if he really wants my help or not. His words don't match his behavior.

"Look, you're obviously busy so let me just cut to the chase. If you could write out the exercises for me, I can swing by another day and get it from you, or if you'd prefer to show me, I can be available for an hour during the day. Are you free tomorrow?"

"I'm sorry. I don't think—"

"I'd pay you for your time, of course, and for the program."

"It's not about the money." Colter never paid a dime, though he tried a few times. I never would have taken anything from him. The truth is it was fun working out with him. "It's not really something I can write down or show you in an hour. I don't have an official plan or anything."

He's still staring at me like he can't understand why I'm not scribbling out a workout routine for him ASAP. "But Colter said…"

"Gymnastics is all about building on skills. You master one thing and then add something else," I say, but he still looks at me like I'm selling snake oil. "I'm sorry. I don't really know any other way."

He has these beautiful hazel eyes that I might describe as stunning if he wasn't shooting daggers out of them. "All right. How much time will you need to show me everything?"

"A couple hours, minimum."

"That's fine." He pulls out his phone and scrolls what I'm assuming is his calendar. "How's tomorrow from two to four in the afternoon?"

"Two hours *every* session. Colter came four or five times a week.

If you can't do that, I'd say three times each week minimum. I'd just be prepared for your progress to be slower."

"You're fucking with me." His dark brow, the one with the scar cut through it, lifts.

My face grows warm under his scrutiny.

He rephrases. "You want me to come here every day for two hours? To do what? Some handstands and shit?"

"I don't *want* you to do anything. You asked how much time it would take. That's what it took Colter." My spine stiffens and that heat that seeped into my face climbs down my neck. Handstands and shit, really? If he thinks it's such a waste of time, then why is he here?

"That seems…excessive. I'm already putting in a lot of hours on the track and working out on my own." His jaw tightens and he looks anywhere but at me. "Are you sure you can't write a few things down and I can add it into my regular routine?" He waves a hand toward where Hope is still staring at us from the beam area. "Your other students are children, and you look like you would die if you broke a nail. How hard could it be?"

The nerve of this guy coming in here to ask for help and then insulting me and my sport.

"Really hard, actually," I grind out the words.

"Fine. Whatever. Can we start tomorrow?"

"No." I drop my hands and take a step back.

"No?"

"I forgot, I'm busy tomorrow."

His handsome features twist with annoyance, but he says, "Okay. The next day?"

"Mmmm…" I tip my head up like I'm thinking. "Yeah, busy then too."

His gaze narrows. "You were free earlier."

"That was before I realized I might break a nail." I gasp dramatically, bringing my unpolished, short nails up to my chest, and glower at him. "I'd rather douse myself in lighter fluid and set myself on fire than help you."

I put another foot of distance between us. "It's so easy, right? Figure it out yourself, asshole."

# CHAPTER NINE
*Knox*

"Well, hello, sunshine." Brogan places a coaster in front of me. "Water? Beer?"

"Give me a shot of Jack."

His brows rise.

"And make it a double."

"Wanna talk about it?" he asks, before turning to get the bottle of liquor off the back shelf.

I glare at him as he fills a shot glass.

"Some people find talking to their bartenders, me specifically, therapeutic. I have a kind face and soulful eyes." He smirks and waggles his brows as he pours.

As soon as he's done, I toss the drink back and motion for another.

"Uh-uh." He holds the bottle hostage, making me glare harder. "Not until you tell me what the hell has you looking grumpier than

Hendrick before he met Jane and drinking like Archer during spring break."

"God, you're annoying," I say but my tone has no bite and I feel the tension in my chest loosening. I don't want to get drunk any more than he wants to peel me off this barstool later.

Brogan keeps himself busy behind the bar. He sets the Jack back on the shelf, pours a Dr. Pepper and puts it in front of me.

"I was a jerk," I say.

"I'm sorry, what?" He turns his head to the side and puts a hand up to his ear.

"Fuck off. You heard me."

His quiet chuckle is barely audible over the noise of the bar. "Who'd you piss off?"

I take a drink of the soda before answering. "This…girl."

That makes him laugh harder. "Tell me everything. Leave out nothing. I love it when you Holland brothers put your foot in your mouth."

Brogan is the only one of my brothers that isn't related by blood. He and Archer have been best friends forever. He was always hanging out at the house, staying over, and avoiding his place. Mom used to love to dote on him. I think she must have realized how much he needed it. I don't know all the details, but his family situation was tough and at some point, he just stopped going home. Now he's as much a Holland brother as the rest of us.

I'm considering telling him the entire story, but then a group of women at the other end of the bar waves to get his attention.

"I'll be right back. Don't leave." He points at me as he walks away.

Alone with my own thoughts, I replay the conversation with

Avery. Am I crazy or was she asking for a lot? Surely Colter didn't really spend that much time working with her.

A gymnast. I never would have guessed the prissy-looking chick in her clean white sneakers and pink lace was a gymnast. A ballerina, maybe, or a cheerleader. She has that rich, spoiled, daddy's girl air about her.

She looked good though. Her spandex leotard left nothing to the imagination. God bless it. And all that blonde hair piled on top of her head, no makeup, covered in chalk. Something about her looking a little less put together was sexy.

Not that it matters since she's undoubtedly plotting my demise after I insulted her. She caught me off guard. I mean seriously, two hours every day? I don't know when she thinks I'm going to squeeze that into my schedule.

I drop my head and mutter a curse at myself. What the hell am I going to do?

Brogan comes to stand back in front of me, but his gaze goes over my shoulder. "What's up, Colter?"

I swivel in the barstool.

"Hey." My buddy looks around at the place with wonder. "I can't believe how busy this place is. Hendrick must be thrilled."

"He's in the back counting his piles of cash right now," Brogan says with a grin. It's a funny image because it's so unlike our oldest brother, but the bar really is doing great, and I'm happy for him. It was our mom's place growing up, then it closed for a bunch of years after she passed, and Dad sold it. Just another example of him destroying something good.

"Can I get you something to drink?" Brogan asks as he tosses out another coaster in front of the empty seat next to me.

Colter slides onto the barstool. "Do you have Bud on tap?"

Brogan nods and leaves us to pour the beer into a tall, frosty glass.

Colter waits until he has his drink, takes a sip, and then turns to face me with a knowing smirk. "Heard you had a nice chat with Avery."

"How do you already know?" I ask, then remember. "She's roommates with your girl."

He nods and takes another drink. "What in the hell did you say to her? She was wound up tight, stomping around the dorm room and muttering about jerks with egos twice the size of their dicks. I had to leave so Quinn could sage their suite and calm her friend down."

Some of my earlier frustration resurfaces. "My ego? What about hers? Do you know she told me she'd rather light herself on fire than help me?"

Colter throws his head back with a laugh. I'm glad he's fucking amused.

"Seriously? What the hell?" I ask him.

"All right, so you two didn't exactly start off on the best foot."

"That's an understatement," I mutter, then look at him seriously. "Tell me something."

"Anything."

"Did you really work out with her for two hours, *every* day?"

"Yeah. Probably. I was there a lot."

"Doing what?" Disbelief makes my voice rise.

"Whatever they did. Quinn and I had just started dating, so at first it was just another way that I could hang out with her. She was on the team and they practiced every afternoon, then after, she and Avery would go to the club gym to get in extra skills practice." He shrugs, then takes another drink of his beer. "I had to get a workout in too, and it was a hell of a lot better while staring at Quinn in tight shorts and a sports bra. For such a small chick, she's got a big ass."

I close my eyes and shake my head. Quinn's a cute girl but I'm not trying to have images of my buddy's girl in my head.

"You did everything they did?"

"Well, no. I stayed off the bars and beam, and never attempted any of those crazy tumbling runs, but anything that was in the realm of doable, I did. I can almost do the splits. Wanna see?"

"Definitely not."

He grins wide. "I know it seems wild, but I swear I've never worked out harder than with those two."

"Doing handstands and splits? That's the hardest workout you've ever done? I need to introduce you to the team trainers at Thorne."

He laughs quietly. "I really thought you and Avery would hit it off."

"Why?" We're so different. She and I are from two completely different worlds.

"You're both competitive and hard-working, not to mention incredibly stubborn." He eyes me in that knowing friend way, seeing past all my bullshit. "She's this decorated Olympic gymnast, and you're on your way to being the best motocross rider the sport has seen in years…" His words trail off. "I don't know. I guess I just thought you two would get each other."

My brain is stuck on one particular phrase. "Did you say Olympic? Like *the* Olympics?"

"Yeah." He nods. "She's legit."

Fuck me. I really know how to put my foot in my fucking mouth.

"I didn't know," I say absently.

And why is Avery with a couple gold medals around her neck such a sexy image? I add a mental note to look her up later since there's no way she's ever going to help me now. Damn.

"Why would you? She doesn't walk around flaunting it. Avery's cool, and I'm not just saying that because Quinn would hurt me if I didn't. My girl is feisty. Don't make her angry unless you want to find out how hard she can punch."

"I appreciate you trying to help, but I can do this on my own. I'll call around to some trainers tomorrow." Surely someone other than Miss Priss (I mean, Miss Olympic Priss) can give me some exercises to help with the strength and coordination of the tricks on the bike. I don't need her.

Colter waves me off. "Forget about it for the weekend. I'm having a party tomorrow since a lot of the team is in town. It'll be a good chance for you to get to know everyone. Bring your swim trunks and come hang by the pool, kick back, relax, and have some fun. You do remember what that's like?"

"Fuck you, I have fun."

"He really doesn't," Brogan interrupts.

With a laugh, Colter stands and pulls out his wallet.

"I got it," I say, waving off his money.

"Thanks." He slides his wallet back into his pocket. "Two o'clock tomorrow. You better be there."

As soon as he's gone, Brogan clears the empty glass. "I like the sound of this Avery chick."

"Yeah, I bet you do."

He enjoys another laugh at my expense and then he says, "She's one hundred percent right, too. Your ego really is twice as big as your dick."

# CHAPTER TEN
## Knox

"You made it." Colter shakes out his wet hair as he gets out of the pool to greet me.

"Barely." I scan the backyard. It's huge and filled with people. Way more people than the guys and girls on the team. "I almost turned around when I saw the outside of this place because I was sure I was lost."

"It's nice, right?" He turns and looks at it like he's seeing it for the first time.

Nice? That's an understatement. It's a freaking mansion in one of the nicest neighborhoods in Valley. "Yeah, man. It's incredible."

"Brooklyn and I are renting it together. Mostly her. She's staying in the main house, and I'm in the casita over there." He motions with his head toward a small house over on the right side of the property. "Let's get you something to drink."

A few minutes later, I've got a beer in hand and Colter is

introducing me to Patrick, a young guy just out of high school, who will be coming on the tour to help set up and tear down. He's excited to talk about last season's motocross races. He's a big fan—not necessarily of me, just racing in general. It'd usually be my favorite topic, but when I spot her...everything else becomes a distant buzz.

Avery meets my gaze from across the yard, looking just as surprised to see me as I am her. My shock at her being here is quickly replaced by white hot attraction. She's wearing the smallest bikini I've ever seen, hair in braids that hang over each shoulder. Her body is insane.

"Earth to Holland." Colter elbows me.

I tear my eyes away from her. "Sorry. What?"

My buddy smiles at me all smug-like. I glare back.

"A little heads-up would have been nice," I grit out.

"Would you have come?"

He knows damn well I wouldn't have.

It doesn't take long for me to come face-to-face with Avery. She and Quinn appear while Colter is telling a story about Oak dislocating his shoulder and then going right back out for another trick not five minutes later.

Quinn nuzzles into Colter's side, and I open the circle to let Avery join. She smells like coconuts, sunscreen most likely, and warm summer days. Her skin is golden except for a small strip where the strap of her light pink bikini top has shifted, showing her tan line. I didn't realize how short she was before, but barefoot, the top of her head barely comes up to my shoulder.

She offers a stiff smile and holds herself as far away from me as she can get. It's enough to distract me from how sexy she is, and I bite back a laugh. She's all prissy and haughty, and apparently an Olympian. No wonder she was so huffy when I questioned her training methods.

I finish my beer and glance at her empty cup. "Need something to drink?"

She startles like I yelled the words at her instead of politely offering to be her personal bartender. "No thanks."

"Afraid I'll poison it?"

"It did cross my mind."

"Not really my style."

"Right. You're more of the in-your-face asshole type." Her head cocks to one side as she speaks.

Ouch. It stings and brings with it another jolt of surprising attraction to her. I don't usually like it when people treat me like shit, but she's just this sexy little thing with this tough exterior. "I guess I deserve that."

When she doesn't reply, I ask, "How about a truce?"

She eyes me skeptically with one arched brow. Damn, she's gorgeous, even when she's all pissed off. No, especially when she's pissed off. Her tone is one hundred percent disbelief when she asks, "You want to play nice?"

No, baby. I want to play dirty. Naked and really dirty. "For today anyway."

She still doesn't look like she trusts me, which, all things considered, is fair. "Come on. I'll make you a drink, and you can even watch me pour it."

She does. And doesn't even dump it over my head.

# CHAPTER ELEVEN
*Avery*

"**Y**ou're staring again."

"I am not." I tear my gaze away from Knox. Oh, I was absolutely staring. But that's just because I want to know where he is at all times so I can avoid him.

I can't believe he thought he could show up here today and play nice like he wasn't a complete asshole to me yesterday.

"Liar." Quinn glances over the top of her heart-shaped sunglasses and smiles all too knowingly. "I get it. He's hot. Stare away. In fact, I think you should go over there and make out with him."

I scoff. "Absolutely not. I'd rather die having never had sex again than let him touch me."

"Bite your tongue!" My friend gasps and flails her arm out to punch me in the shoulder. We're lying side by side in lounge chairs, soaking up the last rays of the day. I should probably put more sunscreen on. I can feel my skin burning, but this is likely the last weekend pool hang for a while. Now that practices have started, each week will just get more intense before competitions start early next year.

And since I'm still not back one hundred percent from my injury, I have a long road ahead of me. Lots of extra sessions equals less time for things like this.

Quinn sits up and turns so her legs hang over one edge of the chair. "I'm going to take a dip in the pool."

"Have fun," I singsong, and then watch as she steps into the shallow end where Colter is hanging with some friends, Knox included. Her boyfriend pulls her in front of him, wrapping both arms around her waist, all while continuing to talk. They're cute.

I close my eyes behind my sunglasses and relax. Something about lying out in the sun, music playing, people talking and having fun all around me, is just what I needed today. That jerk Knox is the exclusion from that dream scenario, obviously.

I'm about to turn over onto my stomach when a shadow falls over me. I open my eyes from their half-closed state and find the exclusion staring down at me.

"What do you want?" I ask, closing my eyes again. If I don't look at him, I can't be annoyed at how hot he is. Jerks shouldn't be allowed to be hot.

I feel him, more than see him, take the lounge chair that Quinn abandoned not long ago. "Just working on my tan."

"Can't you do that from across the yard?" I ask, then add quieter, "Or from the other side of town?"

"I'm sorry about last night."

That makes my eyes open a crack. My head falls to the side, and I take in his expression. "You sound sincere, and you look sincere, but I still don't believe you."

"I don't say things I don't mean."

"So, you meant that I'm too girly to be serious about working out?"

"That isn't what I said."

"Close enough," I mumble, focusing my attention forward again. He said I looked like I'd die if I broke a nail. Seriously? Like girls can't be feminine and also badass. What a prick.

"You weren't that nice either, if you recall," he says.

"I'm not the one who was asking a favor."

"Fair." That's all he says for a couple of minutes, and I think that's the end of it and we're going to sit here in silence until he gets bored with me, but then his voice returns, quieter this time. "I'm not good at asking for help. I hate it, actually. I'd do just about anything to avoid asking anyone for anything. So yeah, I was a jerk, and I said some shitty things. Most of which weren't about you at all, but I said them, and I'll own up to that. I am sorry though, whether you believe me or not."

He doesn't wait for a reply, not that I could form one while I'm playing his words over and over again, trying to make sense of them. Knox gets up and jumps into the pool a few feet in front of me, into the deep end. Water splashes onto my toes.

My anger has dissipated, and I'm left only with a weird sense of sadness that I can't quite put my finger on. Then I'm annoyed that one apology, where he admitted he was a jerk, has me softening toward him. This is why jerks shouldn't be allowed to be hot. It's an unfair advantage.

I flip onto my stomach and bury my face into the side of my shoulder so there's no chance of my stare going to him unintentionally.

*"I'd do just about anything to avoid asking anyone for anything."*

Why? No, scratch that. I don't care.

Seconds tick by like they're wading through quicksand. With a groan I stand and scan the yard until I find him. He's in the middle of the pool, back to me, talking to the redheaded rider, Brooklyn. I can't see his expression, but she's smiling at him like he isn't the biggest jerk on the planet.

Before I can talk some sense into myself, I climb into the pool and wade toward him. I'm not a great swimmer, despite having always loved being near water. While my friends were taking swim lessons in the summer, my parents doubled up on gymnastics practice.

The water is only five feet where he's standing, but I'm not much taller than that so I have to bob and tread, not so gracefully, to wait next to him long enough for him to notice.

Brooklyn sees me first, and when her gaze shifts, so does his.

I don't say anything. Mostly because I didn't think this through at all.

"I'm going to get another beer," the pretty redhead says when the silence turns awkward. She backs away and then swims toward the ladder.

My arms and legs are working hard to keep me afloat while Knox stands in front of me and waits for me to say something. His dark eyes are glued to me and his brown hair is darker from the water. He's muscular, tattoos all over his chest and arms, and he has a small barbell through one nipple.

Remembering why I came over, I open my lips to speak and take in a mouthful of water. Perfect. I'm going to drown yelling at this guy.

"Why are you sorry?" I ask once I can manage, moving my legs faster underneath me.

An arm comes out and wraps around my waist, and I'm hoisted to Knox's side before I know what's happening.

"What the hell?" I push off him, but his grip doesn't budge. "Let me go."

I push against him again to no avail. He's strong and his body is hard under my touch. If he weren't such an asshole, I might notice how his muscles wrap around his side and give him that nice V-cut where his red trunks hang off his hips. Or how in the sunlight his eyes have little flecks of gold.

I keep fighting him, but it's like pushing against a brick wall.

"I'm sorry because I was a jerk," he says.

"That isn't what I meant."

"Then, what did you mean?"

"Are we really going to have this conversation while you hold me hostage?" I kick my feet and wriggle, but he just slowly blinks at me like he isn't bothered at all. He's so close and the butterflies in my stomach don't care that he's a brute, they're just excited he's touching me.

Silently, he walks with me still clutched to his side as he moves into shallower water. My feet touch the bottom, and his hold loosens.

I put two feet of distance between us and adjust my top where it's shifted, showing off some serious underboob. I'm not that busty, but this suit is so small that it barely holds my full B cups.

Knox doesn't even pretend not to check me out.

"Do you just go around manhandling chicks?" I strive for annoyed, but my voice is breathy.

"As opposed to letting them drown, yeah."

"I was fine."

"Didn't look fine, shortcake." One corner of his mouth lifts in a smirk. A short joke, how original. Ugh. Why? Why couldn't I have just left well enough alone? I don't need to know why he said he was sorry. It can be one of those weird anomalies like a yeti sighting.

But I open my stupid mouth anyway. "Why are you apologizing now? Is it so I'll forgive you and agree to help?"

"No." He laughs. "There's no way I'd take your help now."

Wait, what? "Why not?"

"I'm confused."

"A normal state for you?"

He chuckles, chest shaking with real amusement. "Cute. A dumb comment from a blonde."

My jaw drops. "I'm not dumb."

"Neither am I, princess."

"And I am not a princess."

He reaches out and tugs on one of my braids. "You look like Elsa."

"Ooooh. The best Disney princess, good burn." I cross my arms over my chest.

"You would know."

Ugh. I drop my arms to my sides and take a step forward. "I'm good at what I do and I helped Colter. Why the sudden change of heart?"

Last night he was set on it, then he insulted me and I said no, and now *he's* changed his mind?

"Aside from self-preservation?" His gaze drops from my face again, taking in my closed-off body language.

"I'm flattered you think I could harm you."

"More like I don't want to waste my time. I've got a limited amount of it, and I can't afford to squander it fighting with you and not making any progress. Pity though. You're sexy when you're pissed off." He winks. He actually freaking winks at me.

And is that supposed to be a compliment? Am I not sexy the rest of the time? Ugh, this man. I think he's the most infuriating person I've ever met.

"Then why bother apologizing?"

"Seemed like the nice thing to do."

"You aren't nice."

"Fine. I take it back. Happy?" He smirks like arguing with me is a perfectly pleasant way to pass an afternoon.

"No," I grit out.

"Take the apology or don't, princess, but you should put on some more sunscreen. You're starting to burn." He ducks down into the water until his shoulders disappear underneath the surface. He looks far less intimidating and almost playful, but I'm too keyed up to enjoy it.

After I get out of the pool and apply sunscreen—not because Knox told me to but because I was already thinking I needed to—I find Colter and Quinn sitting around an unlit firepit with a group of guys that are introduced as out-of-town riders. My friend gives up her seat for me and sits on Colter's lap.

Knox stays away. He and Brooklyn seem to be hitting it off. Although she has some competition with a pretty brunette in a thong bikini with an impressive boob job. She sits at the edge of the pool showing off her body and smiling at him. He smiles right back.

None of that earlier tension in his body is visible. He looks totally relaxed. Ugh. I hope she smothers him in her perfect, perky tits.

As the day ends, the mood of the party shifts. More people arrive, bringing new energy and making me feel zapped from the sun. Most of the people in the pool get out and sit around one of several fire features in the yard. There are three, plus another large seating area at the back of the yard.

Quinn and I pull on shorts over our suit bottoms, and Colter lets us raid the fridge in his house.

"Your nose is pink." Quinn tosses two pretzels in her mouth as she stares at my face.

I bring a hand up and then grimace when my skin is warm to the touch. "Is it bad?"

She and Colter both shake their heads.

"Oh well, no one here to impress anyway," I say.

"Hey. Some of my guys are cool as hell." Colter looks between me and Quinn to back him up.

"Most of them are in relationships though," Quinn says. "And that one kid is like seventeen."

"He's nineteen," Colter insists.

"We're not into anyone younger than us," she says. "Right, Ave?"

"I guess." I take a pretzel from the bag she's holding.

"I saw you and Knox talking a couple of times." She beams. "Spill."

"There's nothing to tell really."

"I don't care," she says. "I want to know every word he said."

I think back. "Umm...well, first he apologized, and then we argued over if he meant it or not. Then I think we insulted each other some more. He said I was sexy when I was pissed off, that he didn't care if I accepted his apology or not, and that he no longer wanted my help because he couldn't afford to waste time fighting with me. I'm sure I'm forgetting a few insults."

"He said you were sexy?" The smile on Quinn's face is way too excited. And her boyfriend's matches.

"When I'm pissed off." Which is really only around him.

"Still. That's nice."

"You're sexy, baby," Colter says to her.

She turns to face him. "Aww. You too."

Colter drops a hand to one side of her neck and kisses her sweetly.

I take the bag of pretzels from Quinn without her noticing, hop up to sit on the counter, and chow down while I watch them be all cute.

My friend is flushed when they come up for air. I'm used to them being like this, so I pick up the conversation like nothing happened.

"No. He wasn't trying to be nice. He also implied I was dumb because I'm blonde." Only after I suggested he was, but I leave that part out. "He's annoying. I swear he was getting off on it. I wonder if his mom knows he's a chauvinistic asshole who insults women for fun."

Colter shakes his head. "His mom died when he was pretty young, so doubtful. Although he's always had a certain charm with the ladies."

My heart stops beating, and I get the sick feeling in my stomach like when I'm midair on a dismount and know it's not right or when I've put my foot in my giant mouth. I swallow the suddenly very dry pretzel crumbs. "I'm such a jerk. I had no idea."

"Why would you?" Colter shrugs. "I know Knox isn't sunshine

and rainbows, but he's a good guy. He's been through a lot and his first instinct when his back is against the wall is to fight."

"Makes sense," Quinn says quietly. "I'd be a trainwreck if I'd lost a parent as a kid."

"Agreed, but it's not just that. He…"

Quinn and I are hanging on Colter's every word, but he must think better of saying more because he shakes his head again. "Just cut him some slack, all right? For me? You don't have to help him, but know that he has his reasons for not being the most easygoing guy."

I manage to nod.

"Thanks," Colter says, then stands straight. "I should get back outside. Some of the guys are going to head home tonight and I want to say goodbye."

He and Quinn start for the door.

"You coming?" she asks, looking over her shoulder.

"Yeah, I'll be right out. I'm just going to splash some water on my face."

When I return to the party the music is louder, some girls have started dancing, and people are back in the pool splashing around.

I find Knox by himself, standing near the back door of the main house. He's pulled on a white T-shirt and is staring down at his phone as I approach. Slowly, his chin lifts.

"Princess," he says by way of addressing me.

I take a cleansing breath and remind myself that I promised Colter I'd cut his friend some slack.

"I can't promise that training with me won't be a waste of time or that it will do for you what it did for Colter. Partly because I didn't really set out to help him or anything, it just sort of happened, and because every time I talk to you, I end up wanting to strangle you. But I'm at the gym every evening until eight or so. If you can come by for an hour a few times a week, I'll do my best to help."

He says nothing, but his brows lift slightly.

I hold my breath. "Are you in?"

# CHAPTER TWELVE
## Knox

When I show up to the gym on Monday evening, Avery silently leads me to a back area where no one else is working out. The floor is purple, and every step feels like I'm walking on a springboard.

"I've already warmed up, but I'll walk you through some exercises that you can do on your own when you get to the gym." She takes a seat and then waits for me to do the same.

While we do some stretching, she talks continually. And she is all business. I don't understand half the exercises she outlines for our warm-up, but I follow along, all the while admiring her toned legs and the ease with which she can move her body.

I'm not out of shape by any means, but my movements aren't nearly as graceful as hers. Caterpillars, duck walk, bouncing with our hands raised—I got some looks from people around the gym while doing that last exercise so I'm sure I looked awesome. For twenty minutes, that's all we do. Then she shows me a handstand. I'm trying to keep an open mind, but my session is winding down and this is all shit I could have done (but definitely wouldn't have) at home.

"You wanna try?" she asks, tucking a loose strand of hair behind one ear.

I drop my hands to the floor and kick my feet up in the air above me. I hold it for a few seconds, then let my feet fall back and stand upright. "Next."

"You're strong enough to hold yourself in the position, but let's work on controlling it as you enter and exit."

"Enter and exit? You mean kicking my feet up into the air and down?"

"Watch when I do it." Her movements are slower, more fluid, but it looks exactly like what I think I did. "Try again."

I do the same thing, holding it longer. My T-shirt falls up around my armpits so I can't see shit. I'm wobbly, but strong enough to stay in the position for a while. I'm about to drop back when her fingers wrap around my calves. Her tiny fingers are cold. Like her icy heart.

"Use your hands to balance," she says.

"Yeah, no shit," I mutter.

I can't see it, but I'm pretty sure she rolls her eyes.

"I'm serious. Focus on pressing your fingers into the floor and gently shift your weight until you find it."

She continues to hold on to me while I play around with my hand position. "How does that feel?"

"Uhh…fine I guess."

When her touch is gone, I drop my legs and stand tall.

"Take off your shirt," she says, staring across the gym and waving to someone.

"Excuse me?"

Her gaze lazily comes back to me. "Take off your shirt. It's getting in the way."

Amused, I pull it off and ball it in my hands. "If you want to see me naked, all you gotta do is ask, princess."

"Skinny guys don't really do it for me." She turns on her heel.

The fuck? I toss my shirt to the side. "I'm not skinny. I'm lean."

Her eyes peruse my chest with an almost bored expression. "Have you ever done a handstand press?"

"Let's say no." I hold in a sigh. How is doing a handstand on the floor going to help me get better at flipping a motorcycle in the air? I was hesitant agreeing to this and I should have listened to my gut. I really am trying to keep an open mind, and I admit I was curious about training with her after I found out she was an Olympian, but this just doesn't seem like a good use of my time. I had to ask Hendrick to pick up Flynn after practice today so I could be here.

"It looks like this." Her stance widens and she leans over, feet still on the ground, and places her hands on the ground in front of her. Slowly, her legs come up and together as she gets into the traditional handstand position. She comes out of it the same way. "Got it?"

I mirror her position and attempt it. It's harder, but I manage to do it. Or at least I think I do. When I drop back and look at her, she doesn't look at all impressed.

"The best way to practice is against a mat." She takes off toward the back wall. A large blue mat is pushed up against the wall. She faces it and then goes into the handstand the same way but using the wall as a guide. "Work on that. I'm going to say hi to a friend."

With a flip of her ponytail, she leaves me in the dark corner of the gym. The place is busy tonight. Lots of kids about middle school age, some younger, a few that look around Flynn's age, and then others that I'd guess are older like Avery.

She stops at the beams where a group of girls are practicing cartwheels on the skinny bar. They can't be more than six or seven years old, but they whip their little bodies through the air and somehow land without falling off like they've been doing this since they could walk. Their skill levels vary, but they're all damn impressive.

Except one little girl. She's practicing on the lowest beam. It can't be more than a foot off the ground and there's a mat below it. The child is in tears as she tries over and over, foot slipping off every time she tries to land the cartwheel. The other girls are staring, and the coach is trying to console her.

Avery approaches slowly, talks to the coach for a moment, then walks over to the crying girl and squats down in front of her. I can't read her lips like Archer would be able to, but the soft smile she offers tells me she's encouraging, maybe soothing her. When the little girl nods her head, Avery stands. The little girl tries again, and this time Avery spots her, realigning her legs as she comes down. They do that a couple times. The coach starts instructing the other girls and soon they all get back to work on their own cartwheels.

I keep working on my handstand, but in between each one, I stop and watch how Avery helps her. She's up on the beam with her now. The little girl watches as Avery does the simple cartwheel.

Her movements are so fluid and graceful, so controlled, I realize as I wobble through another handstand.

I drop down to the floor and give up all pretense of practicing. Avery looks over from the beam and arches a brow. I smile back.

She really is sexy. Today she's in a royal blue leotard. It cuts up high on her hips and makes her legs look about ten times longer than they are. Every inch of her is made of steel.

After Avery assists the little girl with a few more cartwheels, the class breaks up and heads toward the door. The girl hugs Avery around the stomach before darting off behind her peers.

I glance up at the giant clock on the wall, noting the time, as she walks back to me.

"Sorry, that took longer than I thought," she says.

"It's fine."

She glances at the clock. "It's been an hour."

"Yep." Sixty minutes and all I've learned is that Avery likes super muscular dudes and is surprisingly good with little kids. Neither of which is going to do a damn thing to help me improve my freestyle skills.

"Do you have a few more minutes?"

"I've already wasted an hour, what's another few minutes?"

# CHAPTER THIRTEEN
*Avery*

I'm trying really hard not to lose my shit with Knox.

Since the minute he showed up, he has seemed completely disinterested. He's done everything I've asked, but he looks like he'd rather be anywhere else.

I take a seat on the floor and he does the same, somehow making the action seem twice as hard.

"Spread your legs out like you did standing." I show him. "Then place your hands on the ground and shift your weight so you're in a straddle like this."

Knox watches closely as I hold myself up by my hands, then he tries it. He's not quite flexible enough to straighten his legs completely, but he manages to get into the straddle somehow.

He's strong and his body is agile. I was messing with him when I said he was skinny. He isn't as ripped as Tristan, but I prefer Knox's body type. He's muscular and cut without being too bulky.

Between his muscles and all his tattoos, he's had all the girls in the gym admiring him since the second I made him take off his shirt. Hey, if he's going to be a jerk, I might as well get something out of this.

I like his tattoos a lot. He has a floral design down the left side of his arm and covering part of his chest. It's stunning. Roses and vines, and other objects that I can't quite make out without staring harder than I should.

He has more tattoos on his hands, chest, right arm, back, and one on his upper thigh that I catch a glimpse of each time he does a handstand and his shorts bunch up. But the roses are my favorite. I wouldn't have expected it, but they look good wrapping around his muscular bicep.

I can tell he has potential beyond what he's capable of now. He might have thought it was dumb, but a few minor adjustments with his hands and some repetition against the mat, and his handstands already look better.

"Good," I say. "Point your toes a little."

He wobbles as he shifts his gaze to his socked feet. Seeing him attempt to point his big toe is the bright spot on my day.

After another practice earlier where Coach Weaver kept me off beam and forced me to practice skills on the floor instead, my irritation bubbles just under the surface. The worst part is I'm a little relieved every day that she keeps me from pushing too hard. It's another day I don't have to worry about trying and failing.

And to make matters worse, an article came out today with the top five collegiate-level gymnasts to watch this year. I'm not on it except for a footnote in the last paragraph that if I could get back to performing like I did two years ago, I might be a threat. *If. **If.** IF!*

"Now press up into the handstand from this position," I say, refocusing my attention.

His brows lift in surprise, but he doesn't say a word as he attempts it. He doesn't know where to put his legs or how to move and there's a few seconds where he gives up and just holds the straddle, looking like I asked him to do the impossible. He drops back on his butt. It's the first time in the past hour that he's looked defeated, and I take a little pride in that.

"You might need to start with raised bars on the floor until your flexibility improves. It should look like this." I go into the straddle and then press into a handstand.

When I sit back in front of him, he cracks a smile. His tone is teasing when he asks, "Did that win you a gold medal?"

"I didn't win an individual gold and no."

"Gold, silver, basically the same."

"Yeah? You'd be happy coming in second?"

"Fuck no," he answers quickly, then adds, "But it's still cool that you went and placed."

"Careful, you're treading awfully close to a compliment."

"Your workout sucks. Better?"

"You can't talk shit about a workout when you can't even do the exercises right."

"Sure, I can," he says, but he has the smallest grin as he does so. He checks the clock on the wall. It's at least the third time I've caught him checking the time. I'm sure he has things to do, women's hearts to break and all that. Wouldn't want to keep him from it.

"I guess that's it for today. Tomorrow I'll set up some bars and we'll see if you can get up that way."

"Can't wait," he says dryly.

"You don't have to come if you don't want to," I remind him. I'm doing this for free, giving up the same amount of time that he is.

"Thanks for the permission, princess." He's quick to get to his feet, grab his shirt, and head out.

The next night I half-expect him not to show up. I'm working on beam skills while Hope does dismounts onto a mat. Even when she doesn't quite nail it, her smile never falters.

When Knox comes into the gym, he scans it, looking for me. In those seconds before he spots me, I drink him in. Black athletic pants, black shirt, black shoes. Black heart, probably. But damn is he good-looking.

"Who's that?" Tristan's voice startles me. He stops next to the beam and stares toward Knox.

"A friend of Quinn's boyfriend." I hop down. "We're training together."

He scoffs, walking with me toward the door where Knox is taking off his shoes and shirt. "He's not really your type, Ollie."

"Good thing I'm not dating him then. Besides, how would you know what my type is anyway?"

"Easy. Me."

He's so cocky and so wrong. I mean, sure, he's attractive, but he isn't the kind of guy I'd typically go out with. Nolan, my last boyfriend, was an athlete—he was on the basketball team, but he was also sweet and romantic. So not like Tristan, who probably thinks letting a girl sleep over is romantic. Then again, Nolan ended up cheating on me, so I guess he wasn't that sweet after all.

Knox looks up and his gaze sweeps over my bare legs and today's pink leotard before sliding to Tristan.

Tristan crosses his beefy arms and puffs out his chest. Ugh, boys. I don't bother introducing them.

"Ready?" I ask Knox.

He glances at Tristan one last time and then nods.

I take him back to the corner where we worked out yesterday and lead him through the same stretches to warm up.

It goes faster tonight and Knox doesn't speak until I'm placing the parallel bars on the floor for him to work on press handstands. "Your boyfriend is staring."

I don't have to look to know he's talking about Tristan. I've felt his eyes on me. "He's not my boyfriend."

"Does he know that?"

"Point your toes."

With a grunt, he does while I continue stretching. My knee aches tonight. The doctor warned me that it would continue to be sorer than the rest of me as I keep pushing myself in the gym.

"What about you?" I ask, standing and doing arm circles to get some blood flowing.

"He's not my boyfriend either."

"Yeah, no kidding," I reply dryly. Then perk up. "Though not a terrible visual."

I'm trying to decide who'd be the more dominant one. Tristan is bigger, but no, it'd definitely be Knox.

He smirks and pauses between sets. "Sorry to burst your bubble, but I don't do the relationship thing."

"No, really? I'm shocked. Another guy who is afraid of feelings," I say with all the annoyance I feel.

Hope waves to me from the beam, grinning so big at Knox.

I wave back and cross my fingers she doesn't come over here. She might drool on him if he gets too close.

"What about you?" he asks.

"What about me?" I play dumb purposely to delay answering.

"Do you date or just chew up boys and spit them out for fun?"

An unladylike snort erupts from me. For some reason I like the idea that he thinks I have that kind of prowess. "I'm also not doing the relationship thing right now."

"I'm surprised, princess."

"Why? Because I'm a girl and we're supposed to wear our heart on our sleeve at all times, so big, bad playboys like you can stomp all over it?"

"Single. Got it."

"Yep. By choice." It feels very important right now that he knows that part.

"Yeah, I got that too. The Ken doll over there would love to change your mind." With another smirk, Knox goes back to working on the press. He's improved a ton in just a day.

I don't comment and Knox says, "Maybe you should let him. You look like you could use some tension relief."

I roll my neck. "He wouldn't know how to relieve my tension if I gave him a manual."

Knox's deep laughter catches me by surprise. "I knew it. You already hooked up with him."

Dammit. I did not mean to share that.

"We made out once," I clarify, feeling my cheeks warm. "And it's never happening again."

"Not if he has anything to say about it."

"I think you're ready for something else." My irritation level is high and all I want is to get up on the beam for a little while to recenter.

I put the bars away and then lead Knox over toward the beams. I guess I'm going to have to chance Hope drooling on him because she's still working on dismounts when we get there. I run my hand along an empty beam. "Is it okay if we join you?"

"Oh my god, of course!" Her smile is locked on Knox.

"You want me to get up there?" Both dark brows lift, and he shakes his head.

"While it would be fun to see you attempt it, no. Beam is way too advanced for you." I point to the rings dangling from the ceiling behind us. "I thought you could work there while I get in some extra practice."

"Too advanced?" He doesn't look convinced.

"She's right," Hope says. "It's harder than it looks."

"Is that right?" He smiles at her, a real smile and not one that's laced in indifference or flirty innuendos.

"This is my friend Hope," I say, tipping my head toward her.

"Hey, Hope. I'm Knox. You're pretty awesome. I saw you flipping off, spinning...I don't know. Looked complicated."

"Thanks. Avery has been helping me." She is lit up with excitement at his words.

Knox keeps smiling at her. He's so...polite and complimentary with her. My face must show my surprise because when he glances back at me, his expression shifts. "What?"

"Nothing." I look away.

Hope watches Knox wrap his fingers around the rings. "You're kind of old to start training to be a gymnast."

I laugh, then bite down on my bottom lip to stop. "He's not a gymnast."

"Are you trying to get with Avery then?" she asks.

"Hope," I admonish.

"What? It's just a question." She keeps on despite my face turning red. "This guy in my musical theater class joined just so he could get Anna Laurie to date him, and it worked."

"He's not here to date me, he's training like Colter did with me and Quinn."

She thinks about that for a second. "Colter's dating Quinn, right? I thought him training with you guys was just an excuse to spend time with her."

Well, crap. That's at least partly true. "Yes, but that's not what's happening here."

She addresses Knox. "Too bad. You're hot, and Avery needs a new boyfriend. Her last one wasn't as hot as you and he was a lying, cheating—"

"Okay. That's enough sharing." I very deliberately avoid looking at Knox. I love that girl but she has got to learn how not to say every thought that pops into her head. Or I need to stop telling her stuff.

"Oh, there's my dad. I gotta go." She jumps down off the beam and waves at me, then Knox. "Hope to see you next time."

She's gone in a flash, leaving me to deal with her outburst. I glance over at Knox and find him smiling at me all smug-like.

"You're not that hot, she's just thirteen and you're walking around without your shirt on," I tell him.

He nods absently. "Is she talking about Tristan? The lying, cheating ex?"

"No. I told you Tristan and I didn't go out."

"Just an unsatisfying hookup." That playful smirk gets bigger.

"A drunken mistake that's never happening again," I say more to myself than him.

"He was that bad?"

I sneak a peek at Tristan. Calling him bad seems unfair considering how drunk we both were. "I don't think so. We were bad together."

Knox's stare slowly sweeps down and then back, giving me a very thorough once-over. "Princess, if it sucked, it was all on him."

"So, same time tomorrow?" I ask on Thursday when our time is up. Four days we've trained together, and he's seemed more frustrated each day. The only time he's been pleasant is with Hope.

Today he barely said two words. He's improved in every skill I've given him, and Hope has shared more tidbits that made me turn a hideous shade of red, but none of it has seemed to improve his mood.

"No." He shakes his head. "I'm going out of town with Colter and the team."

"Oh, right." I pull on sweats and slip into my shoes. "Are you doing tricks yet?"

I know it sounds bad but working together I sort of forgot the point of all of it. Most of our sessions I'm just trying to get through it without wanting to strangle him.

"Unlikely." With another small shake of his head, he says, "Just setting up and tearing down until I get better."

"Are the sessions helping?"

"You mean the handstands and shit you have me doing?" He arches a brow like the answer is obvious. "Not as far as I can tell."

Ouch.

"O-kay. Any suggestions?"

"If I had any idea how to do this myself, I wouldn't have come to you for tumbling lessons." He pulls on his T-shirt. The movement makes his hair messy, and I find myself wanting to run my fingers through it.

"If you think this whole thing is dumb, why do you keep coming back?"

He shrugs. "Last resort, I guess."

# CHAPTER FOURTEEN
*Avery*

Tristan lives in an off-campus apartment complex that is filled with college students. It's especially popular with the hockey team, who live two buildings over.

We're hanging out at his place on the balcony and noise from several other parties combines to make it feel like all of Valley U is here. Most of the gymnastics team is here, guys and girls. Tristan's neighbors across the hall, Nico and Whitley, are on the university golf team and brought a lot of their teammates, too.

It's still early and the atmosphere is chill and friendly. It was a long week and Quinn didn't even have to convince me to come. I needed to do something other than obsess over training—mine and Knox's.

I keep replaying his words from yesterday. *Last resort, I guess.*

I don't like thinking of the time I've devoted to him as a last-ditch effort, but I knew he was hesitant when he agreed to it. The real issue, the thing making me want to chew on my fingernails and mess up my manicure, is wondering if I'm making any difference at all. He said he didn't think so and that stung.

"Need a refill?" Tristan asks as I stare out at the party around me, not really seeing it.

I shake my head to clear my thoughts. "No, I'm good."

He takes the empty camping chair next to me. His blond hair falls into his eyes and he pushes it back with a flick of his head. "How's your knee?"

"Fine," I say quickly.

His gaze narrows and drops to my bare legs. "You're still holding back in practice."

"Yeah, no kidding. Coach has me on mats still. She wants me to ease back into things, so I don't reinjure myself."

"Bullshit."

If I had any beer left in my cup, I'd be tempted to toss it at him.

"She's coddling you. You could already be back at one hundred percent if you wanted to be. What I don't get, is why aren't you pushing yourself? We're two months out and everyone is looking to see if you're going to let this setback end your career or if you're going to be hungry enough to let it fuel you to dominate."

Tristan has been competing in the spotlight since he was sixteen. He's been to the Olympics twice and medaled both times. He doesn't get it. No one has ever doubted his talent or chalked it up to luck.

"Admit it." He leans closer and lets his fingertips brush my thigh. "At least to me. I know you, Ollie."

"Just because I let you feel me up once when I was drunk doesn't mean you know me." Moving my leg away from his touch, I stand.

"I think I do want a refill."

Inside the apartment, I step into the kitchen and mix another drink. A splash of vodka with strawberry soda. Quinn is in the living room playing video games. She hands off the controller after she wins another round of Mario Kart and bounces toward me.

She takes my cup without asking and drinks while eyeing me closely.

"You're welcome," I mutter dryly, but I'm not really upset. I start to make another drink for myself.

"Why do you have a murderous look in your eye, and who do I need to yell at?" Her eyes widen over the cup.

Tristan walks in and I glower as we make eye contact. He keeps going, walking through the living area and disappearing down a hallway toward the bedrooms.

He has a two-bedroom apartment even though he doesn't have a roommate. He turned the spare bedroom into a workout room. I know because that's where we made out. One minute I was poking fun at him for having a home gym and the next he was kissing me. Ugh. Never again.

"Oh. I see. I should have known." My best friend raises her voice and yells after him. "You're an asshole, Williams."

It makes me laugh, how loyal she is even without knowing what happened.

"I'm sorry," she says more sincerely. "What'd he do?"

"Just being his usual charming self." I take a sip then cough. I got a little too heavy-handed with the splash of vodka on my redo drink.

She gives me a sympathetic smile. "Do you want to go? I heard the hockey guys have people over."

"No. It's fine." I don't want him to know how much his words are messing with my head.

"I can Saran wrap his toilets or call in a noise complaint."

Smiling, I shake my head. "Just don't leave me alone."

She links her arm through mine. "Never."

"Quinn, you're up," someone yells from the living room.

Her eyes light up with excitement, then she catches herself. "I'm done for the night."

"Go," I tell her. "I'll watch."

"You hate video games."

"No, I don't. I'm just not any good at them. I can be your personal cheerleader." She just might have to tell me when to cheer because I have a hard time following most of them.

I settle into a spot between Quinn and a freshman golfer. Everyone else is playing, so I keep myself occupied by scrolling through my phone and drinking faster than normal. Occasionally I glance up to check what's happening in the game. Quinn's excitement level is my best indicator. When she wins, she's loud and jumps around, and when she loses, she sits quietly and pouts.

Her phone pings three times in a row, vibrating on the couch between us.

"It's Colter," I tell her after a quick glance at the screen.

"Tell him I'm dominating Mario Kart. He'll be so proud," she says over her shoulder.

I snap a picture of her in deep concentration mode, then text it to him with her exact words. He replies with, Atta girl 🖤

I snort a laugh. "He's very proud."

She beams at the second-hand compliment.

I reply back asking how the tour is going.

COLTER

**Awesome. At a fair in Chandler tonight.
Packed crowd.**

I hesitate, wanting to ask him if Knox rode in the event, but for some reason it feels weird to ask. Then I say screw it, we're working together. It'd be weird not to ask, right?

COLTER

**Nah, not yet. He's getting there though. I
really appreciate you training with him.**

"Not that I'm any help," I grumble to myself.

Quinn screams out in victory, dropping the controller and reaching for the phone. So fast I'm not sure how it happens, she has Colter on FaceTime. She's telling him how incredible she is and he's backing her up and smiling big.

It's loud in the room. A big group of guys from the golf team just arrived.

"I can't hear you," Quinn says.

"Go have fun, babe," he tells her. "Text me when you get home."

"Wait," I say before she can hang up. I motion for her to hand me the phone.

"Avery wants to talk to you." She hands the phone over and I move out of the living room and down the hall where it's a little quieter.

"What's up?" Colter looks concerned as he waits for me to talk.

"About Knox…" I start and blow out a breath. "I'm not sure I'm helping him at all."

He cracks a smile. "I'm sure that's not true."

"I think it might be."

"Okay. So, what do you need from me?"

"I don't know. Ideas? What is he struggling with?"

"Landing tricks."

"Specifically," I push.

He runs a hand through his hair. "Knox is a beast on the bike. He can make it do anything he wants. But he questions himself in the air when he's not in full control. Freestyle is all about losing control without really ever losing control, you know?"

I nod. I do actually. Beam is sort of the same way. It's about trust.

"You could always ask him," Colter starts.

I make a face that has Colter chuckling. "Get to know the guy. He's not so bad."

Quinn bounces back to my side.

"I'm handing you back to your girlfriend now," I say.

While Quinn says goodbye, I chew on my thumbnail and think about Colter's words.

"Okay." Quinn interrupts my thoughts as she slides her phone into the front pocket of her shorts. "I need another drink and then let's walk over to the hockey party."

While she's filling her cup, my phone pings. When I pull it out, it's a text from Colter. A short video of a rider racing up the ramp and sailing through the air doing some sort of trick where his body lifts from the bike. I can tell by the way the rider moves that it's Knox.

I watch it five times, slowing it down, zooming in, examining every piece of it. I'm not even sure what I'm looking for exactly.

Something that will help, I guess. On my sixth rewatch another text comes in from Colter. No words, just a number.

And I know just whose number it is.

# CHAPTER FIFTEEN
*Knox*

LOVING BROTHERS

HENDRICK

**Valley High won. Flynn was MVP. Twenty-one points.** 🔥

BROGAN

**He killed. The other team tried three different defenses to shut him down. #unstoppable**

ARCHER

**Who the hell changed the group name again?**

HENDRICK

**Do you even have to ask?** ** **Brogan**

BROGAN

ARCHER

Knox, how's the event? Are you riding tonight?

ME

Nah. Probably be awhile still. Congrats, little brother. How many assists?

HENDRICK

He's probably not checking his phone. He went over to Pete's house after the game.

BROGAN

Speaking of partying...I'm out. Later, losers.

HENDRICK

So much for loving brothers, huh?

Shaking my head, I fire off a text to Flynn outside of our group chat to tell him congrats and let him know I'll be home late tonight if he needs a ride home.

We're about thirty minutes from the start of the event. Everything is set up and Colter and his team of riders are warming up and making any final tweaks as the crowd settles in.

My part is mostly done. I'm on standby if anyone needs anything, but everyone is pretty hands-on here. If they need something, they don't wait around for someone to do it. I guess that's a luxury I forgot about, having an entire team around me dedicated to making sure I had whatever I needed.

Colter drives off the track and stops in front of me. "Pretty cool, right?"

"Yeah."

He grins knowingly. "Not long before you'll be warming up with us."

"I don't know about that."

"How are things going with Avery?"

"Honestly?" I ask. When he nods, I say, "I'm not sure it's helping."

"Stick with it. Maybe it's not the answer for you, but I swear it made a huge difference for me. She's tough as nails."

"Yeah," I agree, chuckling. "That she is."

"I can't tell if you two are going to kill each other or tear each other's clothes off."

"Definitely the first." Not that I haven't thought about the latter.

Laughing, he drops one foot to the ground and stares at me through the visor opening of his helmet. "Why don't you go sit in the crowd?"

Confusion mars my brow. "Kicking me off the crew already?"

His eyes dance with amusement. "Get some distance from it. Watch the tricks. Really watch. You're so close to nailing it."

I've been watching for two weeks, but I'd hop around on one foot blindfolded if he thought it would make a difference.

"What about Patrick?"

"He can handle himself." With a rev of his engine, Colter takes off.

I check with Pat, make sure he has my number, and let him know where I'll be in case he needs anything. Then I head out the side gate.

Colter hadn't been kidding about the Valley event being small by comparison to the others planned. This stadium is packed, and the energy is high. It thrums under my skin, reminding me of when I used to enter small local races as a kid. The motocross events are bigger and flashier, but there's no matching the energy here. It's simple in a way I forgot it could be. Maybe that's just me romanticizing it from the sidelines.

I miss being out there. I even miss Mike and his frequent pep talks on doing better, working harder. Like I haven't put in the effort to be the best. I've worked my tail off for that. No pep talk needed. It's a primal desire deep inside of me. I don't want to do anything unless I'm trying to be the best.

I find a spot at the top of the first section and settle in. A little kid is bouncing on the bleacher next to me. He's holding a toy motorcycle in his hand, eyes glued to the track. His mother shoots me an apologetic look that isn't necessary. I still feel like that about racing. I've just learned to keep my body still while my insides jump with uncontainable excitement.

I'd written Colter's advice off when he asked me to go sit in the crowd. I've watched them do these tricks a million times back at the practice track. But there's something about the stadium lights and the extra adrenaline in their movements that has me seeing it with fresh eyes.

My phone vibrating in my pocket pulls me back down from the clouds. I'm getting to my feet, expecting Pat. Definitely not Avery.

I sit back down as I read her message twice.

UNKNOWN

So I've been thinking. Maybe you're
right and my workouts suck. Also, this
is Avery.

Smiling, I tap out a reply.

ME

No, it isn't. Avery would never
admit her workouts suck.

In response she sends me a selfie of her scowling directly at the
camera.

ME

Did hell freeze over? Feels pretty
warm here in Chandler, but maybe
it hasn't reached me yet.

AVERY

To be fair, you haven't exactly been a
picnic to work with. If we're going to do
this, then I need to know you're in it.

ME

I showed up all week and did
handstands. What more proof
do you need? Blood oath?

AVERY

Tempting.

Dots dance along the bottom of the screen indicating she's

typing more. I glance back up at the track. We're at a short break in the jumps and Brooklyn is riding around while standing on top of her bike. When she hops down and stops in front of the fence, she revs the engine and burns out. The crowd loves it.

I drop my gaze back to my phone.

AVERY

I will do everything I can to help you, but I need you to be open to whatever I throw at you.

ME

I draw the line at cartwheels.

She sends another scowling selfie. I look past her to the background of this one. She's somewhere in a crowd. An apartment or house maybe. There are guys behind her and one of them is definitely checking her out.

ME

Where are you?

AVERY

Don't change the subject, buddy.

Buddy? Seriously?

Colter and the team line up for one of their synchronized tricks. The timing is damn beautiful. A shot of pride rushes through me. Which is the only explanation for what I type next.

ME

Fine. I'm in. I'll do anything you want.

A few minutes pass without a response.

AVERY

**Wow. That was easier than I expected.
This is Knox, right?**

I snap a selfie and hit send.

AVERY

**The alien did a very good job with your
face. It looks almost identical.**

ME

**Is that your way of saying you
like my face?**

AVERY

😊 **See you Monday.**

ME

**I'll be there.**

I'm about to pocket my phone again when she sends one more.

AVERY

**Oh and Knox...there'll definitely be
cartwheels involved.**

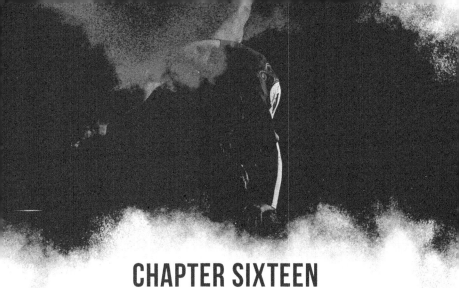

# CHAPTER SIXTEEN

*Avery*

"I'm not getting up there."

All the optimism I clung to this weekend dissipates as Knox aims a stubborn scowl at me.

"You said anything," I remind him.

With a sigh, he walks closer to the beam. He pauses for a second like he's not sure how to get on. Oops. I forgot for some people it's not as easy as breathing. Before I can hop down and show him how, Knox hoists himself up with a lot of impressive upper body strength.

I fight a grin as he stands tall, wobbling a bit as he finds his balance. I can tell by the look on his face that laughing right now would be ill-advised.

After warming up and a little trampoline work into the pit, I have my fingers crossed that this works. And if it doesn't, well, at least I got a few minutes up on beam. What Coach Weaver doesn't know won't hurt her.

"Okay." I find a smidge of composure. "I want you to do a back tuck dismount into the pit."

One dark brow arches.

"It's perfectly safe. So easy a five-year-old could do it," I mock.

"Oooh. Can I show him?" Hope asks with a pleading expression from her spot on a neighboring beam.

Before I've nodded, she's already getting into position. She adds a cartwheel before the back tuck, landing it on a mat instead of in the pit.

Knox's jaw works back and forth.

"Want to see it again?" I ask.

"No," he says gruffly. When Hope gets back up, he silently, still grimacing at me, offers her his fist.

She taps her knuckles against his with glee and her face goes pink.

"One time and we'll get back down on the floor," I say to him.

"Then, what's the point? Are you messing with me?"

"You said anything, and I want to see if you meant it."

With a huff, he finally moves to the end of the beam. He hesitates.

"Don't overthink it. Just like we did before."

"Yeah, except now I'm balancing on a tightrope." His cheeks puff out with a breath and then he goes for it.

My relief is immediate. He did it. I walk over to see his face as he surfaces from the pit.

"Is that a smile?" I ask, hands on my hips.

He tries to wipe it from his face, but his lips betray him.

"Fun, right?" I ask.

"I don't know. I think I blacked out. Are you done hazing me now?"

"Yes." I hop down from the beam. "And you passed the test."

Maybe there's hope for him yet. I need him to trust me. And sure, watching him get on the beam was fun, but the real point was that he's not going to fight me at every turn.

"Okay. Let's keep doing back tucks into the pit but focus on your form."

He's following me one second and the next I look back and he's stopped to check his phone.

I walk back toward him. "Setting up a hookup later?"

"No." He's scowling at his phone as his fingers fly over the screen.

I wonder if he scowls during sex.

"We've only got thirty more minutes," I remind him. Usually, I'd be game to stay at the gym until they kicked me out, but tonight I'm meeting up with some classmates to study for a psychology quiz.

"Something came up. I gotta go."

"Now?"

"Yeah." He shoves his phone in his pocket and jogs off without so much as an apology.

I start to follow him, but he's quick and I'm too stunned to catch him.

What the fuck?

I'm still fuming the next day. I waited all night for a text that explained his hasty departure. I almost caved and texted him to make sure everything was fine.

As I perch on a chair facing the door, my gaze is glued to it, waiting to see if he'll show. I don't get it. One minute he is all in, and the next he's bailing early with no explanation.

No more. I can't handle it. I can't help him if he doesn't want to take this seriously. I'm done.

Knox walks in three minutes early. He's staring out into the gym as he walks, but then something pulls him to look at me.

His steps slow as he approaches. "Hey."

"Hey," I parrot. I had planned to play this cool and professional. Simply let him know this wasn't going to work and walk off. But with him standing in front of me, all my frustration resurfaces. "You're alive."

"Uhh...yeah."

"I didn't think you were going to show." That's a lie. I don't know how, but I knew he'd be back, if only to tell me my workouts are shit and he's quitting.

"Why wouldn't I show?"

"I don't know, maybe because you ducked out early yesterday or you've made every workout seem like torture."

"Something came up." His brows furrow. "You were standing right next to me. I told you I had to leave early."

"Let's just call this training together idea a big giant fiasco and move on." I'm exhausted. I can't fail myself and him too. "I'll text you some exercises you can add into your workout routine."

It's what I should have done in the first place. One and done and out of mind. I stand and brush past him out to the parking lot.

Knox jogs after me, catching me as I reach my Bronco. "Wait, Avery. I'm sorry."

Funny, he couldn't find that word yesterday. "No, I'm sorry. This was never going to work. You're—"

"My little brother is failing math," he blurts out.

All right. Not what I expected. "O-kay."

"His GPA is almost below the requirement to play sports, so yesterday his coach texted me and wanted to meet immediately."

I have so many questions but the first one out of my mouth is, "Why did he text you?"

"Because I'm Flynn's guardian." He rakes a hand through his hair. His obvious discomfort makes me feel like shit.

"Why didn't you just tell me that instead of storming out of here with no explanation?"

"I don't like talking about my fucked-up family stuff, all right? I can be all in and not want to share every detail of my life." His jaw hardens as his mouth pulls into a straight line.

I chew on my bottom lip. Crap. Crap. Crap. I'm a flaming pile of dog shit. I thought he was blowing me off and I might have overreacted a teeny tiny bit.

"So, are we good?" he asks, looking more composed, but his dark eyes are hard.

I feel like I should be asking him that. "Yeah, we're good, Knox, but I'm still not sure this is a good idea. I don't know how to help you. I thought getting you out of your comfort zone this week would help, but maybe I'm out of my depth."

"You already have helped."

Words I never dreamed of hearing from Knox Holland. "What do you mean?"

"Look." He shoves his phone in front of me. The movement brings him closer. His arm presses against mine and I get a whiff of his cologne.

It's a struggle to focus on the screen. The video is shaky, but I can tell it's him. When he's at the highest point of the jump, his legs fly out to the side and he lets go with one hand. It happens so fast that I don't have time to be scared it'll go wrong. It takes my breath away.

I keep watching the video of him landing and then riding toward the camera, body language clear that he's thrilled with the jump, until he stops it.

"That looked great," I tell him honestly.

"I know." He wears a proud grin. Totally transformed from the frustrated, rough edges just moments ago.

"I don't think I helped with that."

"No, you did. Look, you're right. I've given you a hard time. And I still maintain that cartwheels are bullshit, but I don't know, something about all of it has me more aware of my body. Even when I'm up in the air."

"Really?" A flame of hope blooms in my chest.

"Really." Knox pulls back and stands in front of me. "Don't quit on me."

"All right. I'm in if you are."

"We're still doing this?" he asks again, voice filled with cautious optimism.

"Yes." I unlock my Bronco. "But not tonight."

His gaze drops over my bare legs and then flicks up like he's finally realizing I'm not in gym clothes. I swear there's disappointment in his expression when his eyes drift back to mine. "Why not? Hot date?"

"I have a study session tonight."

His cocky and playful grin is back in an instant. "Oh, okay."

"Rest up," I tell him as I open the door of my vehicle. "You're going to need it tomorrow."

# CHAPTER SEVENTEEN
*Knox*

"**D**o you actually practice on that thing or do you just like using it as a seat?" I ask as I walk into the gym and find Avery sitting on the beam. More often than not that seems to be where she's waiting for me.

Without replying, she pushes herself up to a standing position, does some sort of fancy turn, and then does a cartwheel and backflip off the end closest to where I'm standing.

Her head is held high as she stands upright on her toes, then glances at me.

"Better?" she asks, dropping down onto flat feet.

"I don't know. I might need to see it again." Or a dozen more times. She's hot as fuck showing off. Especially when it's for my benefit.

"I've already practiced today. It's your turn." She bumps her small body against mine before walking off toward the trampoline run.

All week she's had me doing flips and twists into the pit. It's kind of fun. Not that I'd admit that to her. It's also exhausting. I can't remember ever being this sore. Again, not that I'd admit that to her.

We fall into stretches without her saying anything. I have the whole routine memorized at this point. She leans forward, basically folding her body in half with her legs wide. I'm doing a less flexible version where my fingers don't even reach my toes.

Laughing, she scoots closer and lines her feet up with mine.

"Give me your hands." She leans forward, stretching out her arms toward me.

It's embarrassing how far she has to lean until I can reach her fingertips. We join hands and she sits back an inch.

"Ouch," I say as my muscles protest the extra stretch.

She just grins and pulls a little harder.

"You're tiny, but terrifying," I tell her.

"Thank you." She smiles sweetly.

"So really, do you practice at night or do you just like to hang out here?"

She takes a moment to answer. "I hurt my knee earlier this year at a competition. I hyperextended it and messed up my ACL. Over the summer, I had surgery and completed rehab, but I haven't been able to practice much. Coming here is routine, I guess. I do what I can on the mats. That was the most skills I've done on beam in a month."

If that was her rusty, then I'd kill to see her on top of her game. "Looked pretty good to me for not having done it in a while."

"Pretty good?" She scoffs and smiles.

"Sorry about your knee."

"Thanks."

We switch up the stretch and I pull her toward me. Her flexibility is impressive and sends a dozen dirty thoughts racing through my mind.

"Knox?" she asks.

I clear my throat. "Sorry, what?"

"I asked about your shoulder."

"It's fine." I landed a little rough on a trick two days ago and my right shoulder has been bugging me. Nothing I can't handle. I wouldn't have even mentioned it to her, but yesterday it was all I could do to hold a handstand for a few seconds.

She studies me for a moment like she's trying to determine if I'm bluffing.

"Really." I break away from our stretch and go up into a handstand, then push off the floor to pop myself back to my feet.

When I come down, she's watching me still from the floor with an amused expression. "Okay. I was going to take you at your word, but if you want to show off for me, then by all means. I love a good show."

She leans back, arms propping her up, and stares at me with those bright blue eyes. I like having her eyes on me.

"If you want a show, then you should watch me race."

She cocks her head to one side. "Is that an invitation?"

I find myself nodding. "Yeah. Any time."

She holds out her hands and I reach down and help her to her feet. I pull a little too hard. She's so small. And she trips forward into my chest. She's laughing and so am I.

"Smooth," she says, sarcasm mixed in with her laughter. We linger there a beat, her cheek resting against my bare chest and me holding on to her.

Avery steps back and drops her gaze, breaking the moment. "Why don't we work on your backflip a little more. It was looking good yesterday."

I follow her lead, silently doing each thing she does, but a fuck of a lot less gracefully. She has me flipping and twisting. From the floor, from a large block mat, to the trampoline.

"Okay. You're good on that. Let's try a double," she says.

I eye her skeptically. She rolls her eyes as she gets into position on the trampoline and then demonstrates. I'm so distracted staring at her toned legs and the way her leotard hugs her curves that I miss whatever she was trying to show me. She's undeniably gorgeous. That much was obvious the first time I saw her, but there's something else about her that has started to make our workout sessions blue ball hell.

She pulls herself out of the pit and waits for me. I give it my best go, but I overshoot it and almost do a triple. Her smile is wide when I come up.

With a sheepish grin, I try again. Usually while I work out, she'll eventually leave me to do something else. Beam or stretching, floor work. She never goes far, but she doesn't hover. But tonight, she stays with me. Sometimes she joins in to show me something, but mostly she's just watching.

"How long have you been doing gymnastics?" I ask.

"I started when I was three," she says. "And I've been competing since I was six. Could have been earlier, but my parents thought I was too young to be devoting all my time to one thing. Plus, it's expensive, so I guess I can't really blame them."

"Motocross too." I rest my hands on my hips as I catch my breath between flips. "Archer and I used to mow grass and do whatever odd jobs we could for people to buy parts and pay for entry fees."

"Archer?"

"My brother."

"I thought you said his name was Flynn."

"Different brother."

She cocks one brow. "How many do you have?"

"Four."

"Four?" Her eyes widen.

I nod. People always have that reaction.

"And you're the oldest?"

"Second oldest. I'm twenty-three, Hendrick is twenty-six, Archer and Brogan are almost twenty-two, and Flynn is seventeen."

I can see her working it out, trying to make sense of the dynamics. I don't expand. I doubt she wants to hear about how our mom died and then Dad took off after Hendrick was in college.

"What about you?" I ask, bridging the silence. "Any siblings?"

"Yep. I have a little brother. Tommy. He's thirteen."

"Does he do gymnastics too?"

"No. He never did. He's into music though. He plays like four different instruments. He's pretty cool as far as little brothers go." The way she talks about him, I can tell they're close.

"What about your parents?" she asks in a softer tone. "I'm assuming they aren't around if you're Flynn's guardian."

"No, they're not around." I don't say more even though I can see her face is still full of questions. I try another double backflip, once again not getting the speed quite right, and I land halfway through the third turn, eating foam.

She must be feeling sorry for me because she asks, "Should we take a break and come back to it?"

"No way."

She cracks a smile like she knew I wasn't going to give up that easily.

Twenty-five minutes later, I'm starting to get the feel of it. Avery offers me her water bottle as I rest.

"Thanks." I take a long swig and hand it back.

"Okay. Final attempt for today. You've got this. Core tight, chest high, control the rotations. Don't overthink it."

"Don't overthink?" I snort a laugh. "You gave me a dozen things to remember and then you want me to not overthink."

"Yeah, it's just that easy." She bats her lashes at me. I want to lean in and kiss her. Doubt that's on her workout plan.

I get into position and mentally run through everything she's said. My core is engaged, I'm standing tall, and when I push off, I focus on my body and the turns instead of tucking and rotating as fast as possible like I did on the others. I'm sure it's going to end badly. But by some miracle, I finally manage to get around twice and land feetfirst in the pit.

She's standing on the side, smiling at me as I make my way back to the edge to get out.

"Congrats. See? You just needed me to tell you not to overthink it." She holds out a hand to help me out. I take it but instead of pulling myself up, I pull her down.

Avery squeals in surprise as she comes down next to me in the pit. Her shrieks turn to laughter as she surfaces.

"You big bully." She shoves at my shoulder. Not hard, but I still retaliate by tossing a foam square at her. We're in an all-out war soon, laughing and tossing foam at each other.

"Okay. Okay." She holds one in front of her face. "Truce."

She peeks out to see if I'm going to agree.

"Fine." I hold up my hands in surrender, but as soon as she drops hers, I fire.

I can see her winding up to attack again, so I move toward her and wrap my arms around her to keep her from hurling more foam squares at my head.

"Let me go," she says, half-heartedly, squirming to get her arms free.

"Put the foam square down first."

"No!" She wriggles harder. The silky thin material of her leotard slides against my body. Between her outfit and me in only shorts, it's hard not to notice how perfectly she fits against me.

I've been spending so much time training at the track and then here that I haven't been doing much else. Notably missing from the calendar is sex. And I'm all too aware of it as her ass burrows into my crotch. It only takes a second for her to realize what she's grinding against. With a sharp inhale, she freezes.

"Truce." The word comes out breathy. She tosses the square to prove she's serious.

I let go of her and she practically leaps away. Embarrassment tinges her features, but then she reaches over for another foam square and tosses it directly at my face before climbing out.

I grin and follow behind her, then head to the door to get my stuff.

"Do you have study group tonight?" I ask as she slips on shorts over her leotard. I don't know much about what she does outside of gymnastics, but I'm suddenly curious. Does she go out a lot? Party?

"No, but I do need to catch up on some homework," she says

casually. "What about you?"

"No studying for me." I wink at her. "Well, what about tomorrow?"

She considers me. "Why are you suddenly so curious about my schedule? Are you planning to sneak up on me and fire foam at my head when I least expect it?"

"Tempting." I laugh. "No, I was wondering if you wanted to hang out sometime."

"We hang out every night."

"You know what I mean."

"Like a date?" she asks carefully.

"No. Not a date. A hang."

"What's the difference?"

God, she's frustrating. "If you don't want to, it's no big deal."

"I didn't say that."

But we both know she might as well have implied it.

"Tomorrow night I'm busy," she says.

I'm not sure if she is expecting me to go down the days of the week, praying she has one empty for me, but I don't. I nod and let it drop.

"I have to go to this sponsor event. It's going to be awful. Quinn was supposed to be my plus one, but now her parents are coming into town to take her out to dinner."

"Sponsor event, huh?" I think back to some of the ones I've had to attend. Dinners, drinks, mingling with rich people who don't know shit but want to pretend that they do. "Sounds like a crappy way to spend an evening."

"It's going to suck, for sure, but I can't get out of it."

I bob my head in agreement.

"Unless…you want to come?" She laughs it off like she's joking.

And maybe I'm crazy, but I don't hesitate to take her up on it. "What time?"

"I was kidding. You don't want to come. Trust me."

"Sure I do. I'm great at schmoozing."

She pauses pulling her hair out of its ponytail. "You're serious?"

"No, actually I'm terrible at it, but I'm free."

"I meant about coming." Her gaze narrows on me. "What's the catch?"

"There's no catch."

"What's in it for you?"

That shakes a laugh free from my chest. "Nothing. I promise."

I can tell she's thinking really hard about my motive so I level with her. "I owe you."

She opens her mouth to protest, but I beat her to it, quickly adding, "It's the least I can do, and I already planned to be hanging out with you anyway."

"I didn't say yes to your non-date hang out."

"I meant here, working out together."

"Oh." Her cheeks flush a pretty pink.

"Now you just won't get to boss me around and toss foam blocks at my head."

"Don't be so sure about that," she says.

# CHAPTER EIGHTEEN
*Avery*

K nox is meeting me at the event, so I'm standing in the parking lot waiting for him. I should go in and let him find me, but the truth is I need to work up the courage to face the people inside.

Everyone at Bella Hunter has always treated me well. I owe a lot to them. They were one of the first companies to reach out and want to provide funding. I hadn't even won an Olympic medal when they invited me to be part of their team. Plenty more sponsors came then, and I can't blame them for not believing in me sooner, but I always liked that the Bella team saw something in me before.

Unfortunately, with that comes the pressure to live up to their hopes.

The rumble of a motorcycle stops the tapping of my foot on the pavement. My heart lurches as he pulls into the parking lot in all black. Black motorcycle, black pants, black jacket, black helmet.

It's the same motorcycle he was driving the first night I met him. Even with my very limited knowledge of motocross, I know it's different from the dirt bike he uses to race and freestyle. It's larger, but still sleek and very Knox.

He finds a spot and cuts the engine. He's facing me, but I can't see his eyes through the visor of the helmet.

Slowly, I start toward him. He gets off the bike and lifts his helmet in one fluid movement that makes my stomach flip. He looks like an advertisement for bad boys, and everything inside me screams, *sign me the hell up.*

I really need to get it together around him. Yesterday when he pulled me into the pit and tackled me to keep me from throwing foam at him, I was rubbing myself up against him before I realized what I was doing. But intentional or not, I enjoyed it a lot. It's probably pathetic that that's the most action I've seen in months.

"Hey," I say as he sets his helmet on the seat of his bike and takes off the jacket. I'm glad I spoke first because as I get a good look at him, my tongue goes dry. He looks divine. The black dress shirt he's wearing pulls against his chest and biceps. It's tucked into black pants with a simple black belt. His hair is messy, but somehow just makes his put-together outfit that much hotter. He cleans up nice.

I'm ogling him and trying to play it cool, but I'm not the only one enjoying the view. Knox's eyeline is parked somewhere south of my chin. My skin prickles with awareness as his gaze roams over my tight dress. The way he looks at me turns my insides to lava and gives me a boost of confidence I desperately need for tonight.

"Hey," he finally returns my greeting and meets my stare. "What's wrong?"

"Nothing. Why?"

He gives his head a small shake. "You look nervous."

"No, I'm fine." A generous stretch of the truth. "Just anxious to get inside."

More like I'm anxious to hop on the back of his motorcycle and speed away from here, but for some reason I don't want Knox to know that I'm scared.

He doesn't look like he totally buys it, but he starts walking as he says, "Okay. Let's do this."

Once we're inside the restaurant, I give him the basic rundown. "Bella Hunter, the activewear brand, has been sponsoring me for almost three years now. Kelly and Michael are here. Michael is my main contact, but Kelly is the head of the company. They're just passing through on their way to visit a new store in California, so this should be pretty quick. Drinks. Maybe dinner. It depends on how many glasses of wine Kelly has. If she drinks a lot, she gets very chatty and will want to stay longer. If she doesn't, she'll want to get out of here quickly. She doesn't strike me as someone who stays in one place very long. That's probably why she travels so much. Oh, and whatever you do, don't ask about her dog. She will talk for an hour straight about her pug if you do. Drunk or not. And—"

"Hey." Knox takes my hand and pulls me back. All the flutters in my stomach screech to a halt and my pulse picks up speed as his rough fingers clasp mine. "Relax. I'm not a social pariah. I can manage small talk and not embarrass you."

"I wasn't worried about that." I wasn't. I'm more worried that I'll say the wrong thing. Like if they ask about practices and my knee. And what if they ask me about the article claiming I won't manage to get back to the level I was at before my injury?

I'm not sure he believes me, but his grip loosens on my hand until my fingers fall free. My skin tingles in the spots where he was touching me.

"There they are," I say when I spot our party.

I lead us through the busy restaurant. Kelly and Michael are both smiling at Tristan as he speaks, no doubt regaling them with stories of how awesome he is. None of them brought someone, which now makes this a little more awkward that I did. It's too late though. Tristan spots me first and his gaze goes straight from me to Knox at my side.

He stands and that draws Kelly and Michael's attention to me, and they follow suit.

"Hi." My smile isn't fake, but I do make an extra effort to show them I'm happy to see them.

"Avery. It's so nice to see you," Kelly says, holding a wine glass in one hand and stepping forward to hug me with one arm.

Knox hangs back as we all say hello, then I open my stance to introduce him. Michael and Kelly both offer a hand. Tristan doesn't but he tips his chin to him and says, "Hey, man. Are you lost?"

"Nope. I'm here for Avery." Knox doesn't give him the satisfaction of letting Tristan's words have any impact on his demeanor, but I shoot daggers at Tristan for trying to make it uncomfortable.

"It's so nice out tonight. What do you say we grab drinks and head out to the patio?" Kelly asks, looking between all of us for an answer.

None of us would be brave enough to go against her, but I'm thinking it might be good to make room for both Tristan and Knox's egos.

As we follow them out, Knox whispers, "You didn't tell me the

Ken doll would be here."

"You didn't ask."

He steps in front of me, blocking my path. His hazel eyes spark in warning. "Don't toy with me, princess. Am I here in some fucked-up game to make him jealous?"

"No." I'm slightly appalled he thinks I'd stoop that low. "I told you, I'm not interested in him."

A muscle in his cheek flexes, but he nods and turns back to catch up with our party.

The five of us sit at a table on the patio near an outdoor bar. Kelly is the only one drinking alcohol, but the rest of us order something and settle in.

"So, how are practices going?" Michael lobs the first question at me and Tristan.

Tristan waits a beat to see if I'm going to answer first. My stomach is in knots.

"Good," he finally answers. "Really good. I'm excited to start competing again."

Michael and Kelly are both pleased with his response, smiling and subconsciously leaning toward him like they're eager for more information. Tristan is good at small talk. He always knows just what to say and who to be. Not just now, but in interviews and public appearances.

"What about you, Avery?" Kelly asks, turning her attention to me. "How is the knee doing?"

"Pretty good. The doctor thinks I'll be able to keep all the skills in my beam and bar routine."

"That's great news," Michael says, giving me the same smile he had Tristan.

Kelly's expression is harder to crack. "Is it still limiting you in practice?"

"Some." My voice wavers.

"Her knee seems solid to me. She looks great in practice," Tristan speaks up for me unexpectedly. He's never this nice to me and alarm bells go off in my head. "She just needs to stop holding back and practice like her career is on the line."

And there it is. I grit my teeth but try to make my voice sweet as I say, "I'm not holding back. I'm being cautious. It's early and I don't want to risk getting hurt again by pushing too hard too fast."

"Makes sense." Michael's eyes twinkle as his smile softens reassuringly.

"That's bullshit, Ollie." Tristan shakes his head, gaze turned away from me. "You were cleared to practice. I'd be going crazy if I'd been out as long as you were. Every week you hold back is another week wasted, in my opinion."

My cheeks heat with embarrassment. I'm annoyed at him for calling me out in front of Michael and Kelly, but worst of all I'm afraid he's right. Because while part of me is going crazy, there is this constant fear that hangs over me, wondering if I'm already past the best part of my career.

"It takes a lot of time and repetition to get the feel back after an injury, but Avery is smart and talented. She'll get there and she's going to be better than ever. She's the most talented gymnast to come along in a decade. It would be stupid to set back her recovery so close to the season." Knox's voice works like a salve, soothing my wounded pride.

"A few weeks of working together and you're an expert on gymnasts," Tristan says in a sarcastic tone that has just enough playfulness in it that neither of our hosts seem to catch on to the fact that he's baiting Knox.

"No, definitely not, but I've had my share of injuries." As Knox speaks everyone listens intently. He has that kind of presence. Quiet but never fading into the background. "I broke my wrist once and it was weeks after I was cleared before I could practice normally. It isn't all brute strength and powering through. Sometimes you have to be patient and let yourself heal even when you don't want to. You can be reckless, or you can be patient, but we all know there aren't any shortcuts to stand on the podium."

"Reckless or patient?" Tristan seems amused by Knox's words. "And who gave you that advice?"

"Ricky Carmichael."

"Who?" Tristan asks, his smile twists into a mocking smirk.

"He's a motocross racer," Knox fills in. "I wouldn't expect you to know him."

I can tell Tristan isn't impressed by a remark by some motocross racer, but I could care less about what Tristan thinks right now.

"A motocross *legend*." Kelly smiles. "You know Ricky?"

"No." Knox shakes his head. "Not really. I met him once."

"I thought you looked familiar." Kelly tips her head to the side. "You rode for Thorne last season."

"Yes, ma'am." One side of his mouth lifts and his eyes widen in surprise. "You know motocross?"

"I know top athletes across all sports. It's the job." She lifts one finger from her wine glass and points between us. "How did you two meet?"

"A mutual friend introduced us," he says.

"So is Valley your home base then?" she asks.

"Yep. Born and raised right here." Knox slips his arm around the back of my chair, resting along my bare shoulders. I glance over at him. He flicks his gaze up quickly, almost disinterested, but then his knee knocks against mine under the table.

*Thank you.* I mouth the words, then take a deep breath for the first time since we sat down. I'm thankful to have the conversation out of the way and the attention on someone else. It soon turns back to gymnastics and I happily let Tristan dominate Kelly and Michael's questions.

An hour passes relatively quickly. Kelly sips on the same glass of wine the entire time and, as I predicted, announces she and Michael need to get going.

"I need to answer some emails before I turn in, but the three of you stay if you want. Dinner and drinks are on me," she insists.

We all stand to say our goodbyes. I hug Michael and then Kelly. Tristan does the same.

"We'll see you both at the Valley U showcase," Kelly says before pulling her phone out of her purse. "Knox, good luck next season."

"Thank you, ma'am."

"See you soon." Michael nods to us.

"Bye." I lift my hand in a wave.

As soon as they're gone, Tristan looks to do the same. "Are you heading out, Ollie? I can give you a ride."

"Uhh, no." I glance at Knox. "Not yet."

Tristan pauses like he's waiting for me to change my mind. Eventually he clenches his jaw and nods. "Call me if you need anything."

My shoulders sag in relief when he leaves. I survived. In no small part thanks to Knox.

"That was fun," he says dryly.

I tilt my head to the side and give him a look of disbelief.

"What?" He laughs. "It was. I nearly made the Ken doll's head explode when we walked in together. That alone was worth it."

"You take a weird pleasure in pissing people off."

"Not untrue." He smiles, then motions with his head to the indoor part of the restaurant. "Do you want to grab something to eat?"

"I'm not very hungry." My stomach is still working out the knots I tied it into earlier. A flash of what I think is disappointment crosses Knox's face. Is he upset that I don't want dinner or does he just want to spend more time together? I don't believe for a second that he wants to "hang out." Unless hang out means sex. And I can't sleep with a guy I'm training every day. If it was bad, it'd be awkward after, and if it was good, then I'd be finding more reasons to rub up against him while we work out. Neither option is smart. I'm still dealing with the daily repercussions of facing the last guy I made out with. Two of them at the gym every day would be too much.

Our walk out to the parking lot is slow. Knox's hands are in his pants pockets and he matches his pace to mine.

"Did you really break your wrist?" I ask him as we reach my Bronco. I hit the fob to unlock it and Knox opens the door for me.

"Yeah. I landed wrong during a practice and it just snapped."

I wince.

"And the Ricky Carmichael advice?"

"I was paraphrasing. I think he told me not to do anything reckless for a while. But I listened and there weren't many people I would have listened to then."

"Or now?" I joke.

He huffs a laugh and nods in agreement. "I listen to you."

"And I know how much it pains you."

"What can I say, I like to be the one giving orders." Knox's eyes darken with a playful glint. His tone promising his words are somewhere between a taunt and the truth.

My stomach flutters and my thighs clench.

"Thank you for tonight. For coming with me, for telling that story, for all of it. I was dreading answering questions about my knee and practice. Everyone wants me to already be back to where I was. No one more than me."

"You'll get there."

I nod like I agree. I hope, but I'm not sure. I feel a little surer with Knox believing it though.

"You will. I've seen the videos of you at the Olympics. You were phenomenal. You had a determination about you that I still see on your face any time you get up on the beam. Besides, I know how damn stubborn you are. You're not done."

"You looked me up?" Surprise makes my insides feel warm and fuzzy.

"Of course," he says casually.

I should have known with that line about being the most talented gymnast to come along in a generation. That was before I got injured. I bet they're reconsidering their words now.

"Lots of people think I won't get back to where I was before."

"You'll prove them wrong, princess."

My chest inflates like a balloon and my throat is thick with emotion. I couldn't talk even if I knew what to say.

Knox waits for me to climb up into the driver's seat and then closes the door. I wave from the inside and he smiles, turns and heads for his bike.

I start the Bronco, but don't move. His words swirl around in my head. *You'll prove them wrong, princess.* So certain. So confident in *me*.

*Don't do it, Ave.* No sooner than I've thought the words, I kill the engine and go after him.

He's already put on his jacket and started his bike, but he pauses when he sees me.

"Okay," I say when I reach him.

"Okay?" He sits on his motorcycle, holding the helmet in his hands. My heart races with the promise of excitement and fun. Two things I'm certain are guaranteed when Knox is in charge.

"You've done everything I asked, so tonight, you can order me around."

Knox hands me his helmet with a wicked smile I feel all the way to my toes. "Get on."

# CHAPTER NINETEEN
*Avery*

**M**y hands shake as I pull on the heavy helmet. I flip up the visor so he can see my eyes. He grins back, an approving glint in his hazel eyes. Then he scoots forward to make room for me behind him.

"Where are we going?" I ask as I climb onto the motorcycle. It is not easy in a dress.

"For a ride." He revs the engine. "Hold on tight, princess."

That's the only warning I get before he takes off. I yelp and grab hold of his jacket on either side of his waist. I lean in closer as the wind whips around us, burrowing my front into his warm back. My pulse accelerates along with the bike as he pulls out of the parking lot. I smile into the night, loving the feel of wrapping myself around him while he navigates through town and then onto a quieter, two-lane highway.

My fear lessens, but the butterflies in my stomach and the ache between my legs grow under the rumble of the seat. It's like doing a somersault on beam, but with a hot, shirtless guy staring at you while you do. Or maybe that's just the fantasy that's worked its way into my head since Knox started coming to the gym.

I'm not sure how long or how far we ride. There's an ease in being with Knox like this, where nothing is expected of me. Get on, wear the helmet, hold on tight. Easy. And exhilarating.

The motorcycle slows as we turn off onto a dirt road. There's nothing as far as I can see until suddenly there is. A track of some kind. Abandoned or in rough shape, I'm not sure which. As we get closer, I can see the track itself is in good shape. It's just everything around it that's in shambles. Rickety-looking bleachers, a shed that was once maybe used to store supplies but now is leaning so far right that I'm certain one shove and it'd fall over.

A crowd of people are parked just off the track. Motorcycles in an array of colors with their riders perched on them. And other guys and girls standing around them. There are more people sitting in the center of the track on blankets, coolers littered around them. It takes me a second to realize I'm seeing Knox's party spot. This is where he comes to hang out. I'd bet on it. Especially judging by the unimpressed glares aimed at me from several of the girls watching as Knox pulls onto the track. He stops when we reach the front of the crowd.

One of the guys standing nearby walks over to him. "Knox Holland. I didn't think you were going to make it tonight."

"Change of plans."

The guy gives me a cursory glance, but his attention quickly darts to the bike and he whistles. "Well, all right. I'll let everyone know."

"Thanks."

The guy walks backward slowly, smiling at Knox. "I'll give you twenty bucks if you let me drive her around."

"I wouldn't let you lay a finger on her for twenty bucks."

"The bike or the girl?" He smirks and lets his gaze slide over to me.

Knox gets off the bike and holds out a hand to me. "Either, but especially not the girl."

I'm struggling to figure out how to get off without flashing anyone. Knox notices and silently steps in front of me, blocking me out of view from everyone but him.

Quickly and without thinking about how I'm probably still flashing him, I throw my leg over and stand in front of him. He places both hands on either side of the helmet and gently lifts it up.

"Helmet hair," I say with a laugh as I run my fingers through my tangled hair.

"You look stunning." He brushes a blonde strand out of my face and tucks it behind my ear, then sets the helmet on his bike and then takes my hand. He guides me down to the center of the track. "Come on. It's about to start."

"Wait." I glance back. Next to his motorcycle, three others have parked. Their riders are watching us, and it could be my imagination, but they look nervous. "Are we going to watch a race?"

My heart speeds up.

"You are," he says.

I don't quite catch his meaning before he pulls me toward two girls sitting on an orange and blue flannel blanket. I recognize the redhead as the rider on Colter's team. "You remember Brooklyn?"

"Uh, yeah. Hi." I raise a hand in a wave. She doesn't reciprocate except to lift both dark brows at me.

"Stay with her, okay?" Knox asks, then without waiting for an answer, he turns to leave.

I catch him a few steps away. "Wait. *You're* racing?"

He's so casual and calm, stopping and facing me like he has all the time in the world. When I know that isn't true. It's so obvious now. The other guys are waiting for him, revving their engines impatiently.

"Don't worry. It won't take long. I'll be back before you can miss me." He tosses me a wink and then turns, finally breaking into a jog as he heads back to his motorcycle. I stand watching him until he pulls on his helmet and starts the bike, then I walk back over to Brooklyn. She tips her head toward an empty space on the blanket with a look that I wouldn't exactly call inviting.

"This is Tate," she says, motioning toward the blonde girl on the other side of her.

"Hi. I'm Avery."

Tate waves, but then our attention all goes to the guys preparing to take off.

"Are the other riders any good?" I ask without peeling my eyes from Knox. What I mean is, are they as good as he is, but I don't know how to ask that without sounding like a fangirl.

"Fletcher used to race Moto GP," Brooklyn says, and when it's clear I don't know what that is, she snorts. "He's good."

"So is Bobby," Tate adds. "But Knox has only been beaten once and I heard that he had the flu that day or something."

"Knox probably started that rumor himself." Brooklyn flashes me an amused smile. "Your boy is good, and he wouldn't have brought you here if he thought he'd lose."

My stomach dips and my face warms. "He's not mine. We're just hanging out. I'm training him."

"Oh, I know." Her smirk stays put. "The guys on the team gossip more than I do. Until tonight, I thought 'training him' was code for sex."

"Like I was sleeping with him to help him ride better?" I ask, voice too high-pitched as I ignore the throbbing between my legs at the thought.

"It's not totally ludicrous. Sex is good for confidence, which is key when you're free-falling with your bike," she says with a shrug, then looks me over closely. "But you look too wound up to be fucking him."

My mind reels and I am utterly lost for words. I manage to mutter, "Oh. Yeah, no. I'm not sleeping with him."

"Not yet, anyway." She refocuses on the track.

I wonder what they've said that's led her to believe Knox and I are sleeping together. What has Knox said? I also wonder just how well she knows Knox. Is she speaking from experience? Not that I doubt sleeping with Knox would loosen up a girl. If he's half as good at sex as he is at acting like an annoying asshole, then I understand why he's so cocky.

"He's made some improvements though. Whatever you're doing with him, it seems to be helping." Something tells me that's as close to a compliment as I'll ever get from her. I guess if she wants to think it's my magical vagina that's helping him and not the training, so be it. Not the worst thing someone's thought of me.

A woman in short black shorts and a red halter top walks onto the track holding a black and white checkered flag. Knox flips his visor down and leans forward, grasping the handles. His back tire spins and smoke plumes out behind him.

The girl lifts the flag above her head. Her body is insane. She's curvy and not afraid to flaunt it, but something tells me none of the guys are noticing right now. Even without seeing Knox's eyes, I know they're laser-focused in front of him.

The moon is hidden behind the clouds. Tall sky lights shine down on each turn. None of them have all the bulbs, but it's enough to make the black track visible in the night.

My heart races in anticipation. In one swift motion, the woman lowers the flag, and the three motorcycles take off. They speed by so fast it's hard to keep track of them. Not that I really try to follow anyone except Knox. My entire body is coiled tight as I watch him lead the pack around once and then twice.

I can barely watch, but I can't take my eyes off him either. He's going so fast. One wrong move, one slip of his attention could be disastrous. My stomach is in knots and my pulse races along beside him.

On the last lap, Knox pulls slightly ahead, but the other two are right on his tail. They're so close to him I'm not sure how they don't crash.

On the final turn, my heart is in my throat. I stand. Brooklyn and Tate do too.

"You got this," I hear Brooklyn say quietly to herself. "Punch it."

Almost like he's heard her, Knox's bike seems to find another gear than the other two and he puts distance between them as he speeds past the finish line.

I let out a whoosh of air. Oh my god, he won. I jump and clutch Brooklyn's arm. "He won!"

She eyes my hand.

"Sorry." I let go quickly and she wears an amused smile.

Brooklyn cups her hands around her mouth and yells, "Nice job, Holland."

Then she looks back at me. "Better go get your boy before someone else gives him his victory kiss."

"Victory kiss?" Tate asks, then she says, "Oh, *right*. The victory kiss. Yeah, it's not an official win until he's made out with at least one girl after crossing the finish line."

I don't bother commenting on my thoughts about that. I do not want to think about Knox kissing other girls right now. I start for him as fast as my legs can carry me. He's going around the track another time, slower now. I reach the edge of the finish line as he's crossing it again. He turns his bike sharply to the side and as Brooklyn warned, he's flocked with girls congratulating him as soon as he stops. Some guys too, but the girls are more insistent and standing closer than I'd like.

He takes it all in as he climbs off his bike and removes his helmet. Guys pat him on the back and girls press their tits into his arm. I stand back and let him soak it all up, even as I glower at the girls. Did they not see me ride in with him? I guess that's not fair since we're not a thing, but still. Basic decency. Keep your mitts off my…whatever Knox is to me.

He cuts through the group, acknowledging people but not stopping as he makes his way to me. His hair is wilder. So is his smile.

"Congratulations," I say when he reaches me.

"Thanks, princess."

I step forward and hug him. God, he smells good. Like leather and metal and sex. The really dirty, amazing kind of sex.

Brooklyn steps up beside me. "Nice ride. I wasn't sure you were going to punch it in time."

"You should never doubt me," he tells her playfully.

"Right. Of course. The great Knox Holland." She rolls her eyes and stalks off.

"She's a bundle of sunshine," I say wryly.

"She's pretty cool once you get to know her."

"So, uh, Brooklyn said something about it not being official until you've claimed your victory kiss."

"Victory kiss?" His brows lift. "And you want to be the one I claim it from? Is that what you're saying?"

"You did win." I shrug. "And you're in charge tonight, remember? So whatever you want."

"That's a dangerous thing to say to me, princess." He lowers his voice. "I'd have you bent over my bike so fast you wouldn't know which way was up."

His words make heat pool low in my stomach and my breath catches in my throat. "I'm not sure I'd mind that so much. In fact, I think I'd like it very much."

His eyes darken and he studies my face, maybe reading my seriousness. I'm so serious. He stays close. I can feel the heat radiating off him. One hand moves to my cheek. He's wearing gloves and the warm leather feels decadent. His thumb strokes my skin and then his hand drops to my neck as he eliminates the rest of the space between us.

His eyes never leave me. I've stopped breathing. "You want me to kiss you?"

I'm not capable of speaking, so I nod.

"That's not an answer."

"Yes." I manage to get out the word. Or I think I do. I can't hear it over the blood rushing and thrumming in my ears. I know it's not a great idea to make out with Knox while I'm training him, but there's already this tension between us. How much worse could it get if we kiss a little?

The seconds tick by and he still doesn't move until I add, "Kiss me, Knox."

He makes a tsking sound and his head lowers. "You just can't help but boss me around, can you?"

Oops.

"Luckily, what we want right now is the same." His lips take mine. Hard and controlling from the moment they touch me. I open immediately and his tongue sweeps in, stroking mine. A person could get lost in Knox's kisses. I do. I never want to stop.

I grab a fistful of his jacket, trying to tug him closer. He's in charge and rough, but still somehow gentle in the way he caresses my face. I'm not sure how long he kisses me like that, but when he finally eases up, the world around us comes back into focus. People talking, laughing, the sound of engines and tires on the track.

"Let's get the fuck out of here," he says, voice gruff, as I'm still reeling from the loss of his mouth on mine.

My legs are like jelly as he takes my hand and pulls me with him toward his motorcycle. I have to jog to keep up with him. There's a small crowd of guys standing around and drinking near his bike. When we get there, Knox lets go of my hand to grab his helmet. Slowly and carefully, he lowers it onto my head. As if I'm not dying to get out of here. His kisses promised so much more and I am eager for it all. I push back all other worries. They'll still be there tomorrow while this moment feels fleeting.

"On the bike, princess. And don't flash anyone in the process."

Not an easy feat, but I climb on while holding my dress tight in front of me.

Knox is about to get on himself when one of the guys stumbles over. "Legendary Knox Holland does it again." His tone is playful, bordering on mocking. "Guess it's easy to win when you've got sponsors throwing money at you and paying for all the best equipment."

"You don't know what you're talking about." Knox tries to ignore him, but the guy claps him on the shoulder and stops Knox from getting on the bike.

"Oh, that's right. They dumped your ass." The guy waggles a finger around like he's reprimanding a child. "You really need to get that temper of yours in check."

Knox's jaw flexes, but otherwise he looks unaffected and calm. "Get lost, Justin. You're drunk and making an ass of yourself."

The guy waves it off, staggering a little as if proving Knox's point. "I saw your old man hanging around here the other day."

I see the way Knox tenses. It's only for a fraction of a second and then the mask of indifference quickly slams down, but it was there.

"Good for you," Knox says, shrugging out of his hold and throwing one leg over the bike.

"You wanna talk about making an ass of yourself, he was trying to get people to race him like he isn't an over-the-hill burnout." The guy's gaze snaps to me as Knox lets one hand drop to my leg. I can feel the edge in his touch. It's soft, but solid. He needs something to anchor him and I'm happy to be that. I doubt he even realizes he's done it.

Unfortunately, the guy decides to try one last attempt at pissing off Knox. Why? I'm not sure. Knox is taller, broader, and this guy doesn't look like he could fight my brother.

"Expensive bike, expensive pussy. What'd he pay for you, honey? And can I get on a payment plan? I'm no Knox Holland, but he'll be washed up in a year or two anyway." He smiles and laughs at his own joke.

Knox is off the bike before I know it, stalking toward him and pushing him. "Stop fucking talking."

The guy is caught off guard, though he shouldn't be. He poked the bear. He stumbles back and falls on his ass. For reasons I can't comprehend, the guy is still smiling.

"Knox," I say, voice barely above a whisper, when he balls his hands into fists at his side. Everyone is watching now. Knox could kill this guy in a fight. It wouldn't even be close.

Brooklyn emerges from the crowd and rests a hand on his arm. He flinches and then focuses his attention like he wasn't aware of anyone else around. She flicks her head toward me, and Knox turns on his heel. He gets on the motorcycle and starts it, pulling away before the guy gets to his feet.

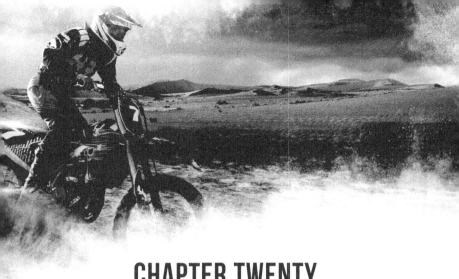

# CHAPTER TWENTY
## Knox

**A**very's hands dig into my sides as I take a turn too fast. Fuck. I let off the gas and drop my speed as I return to town. My anger has turned to frustration by the time I pull into the empty restaurant parking lot and park next to her Bronco.

I kill the engine, but neither of us moves.

"I'm sorry," I say without looking at her.

I miss the heat of her body behind me when she climbs off and stands next to the bike.

She flips the visor up and the fear or trepidation I expected to see in her eyes isn't there. "Why are you apologizing? That guy was an asshole."

"I shouldn't have taken you there." I don't know what I was thinking. She doesn't belong at some rundown track. We're from two different worlds. If she didn't see that before, she definitely does now.

"I'm fine." She removes the helmet and sets it on the back of my motorcycle. Her blonde hair is messy, and her pink dress has ridden up high on her thighs. How many tight, pink dresses does this chick own? I hope a lot. She looks fucking perfect.

My gaze drops to her lips as she says, "Seriously, Knox. I'm fine. But how are you?"

"You're worried about me, princess?" I smile at the concern in her eyes. That was just a slice of everyday life for me. It's cute that she thinks I was ever in danger. I've known Justin since we were kids. He's harmless. An asshole, no doubt, but I've never seen him throw a punch. He's taken quite a few though.

"That guy was saying some pretty shitty things to you."

"He's just pissed because his racing career never went anywhere." Failure makes people bitter. I've seen it in others, and I've felt it in myself at times. I shouldn't have let Justin's words get to me. I knew he was provoking me for a reaction, but I don't understand what he was trying to prove. That I'm hotheaded? That I can't control myself? I don't know for sure, but I fed right into it.

"I didn't know that you lost your team." Avery moves closer so that her leg brushes against mine, and her hand comes up and rests on the front of my jacket. "I'm sorry."

Amusement makes one side of my mouth pull up. "And what do you have to apologize for?"

"Nothing. I'm just sorry. What happened?"

"I got into it with a teammate after he crashed into me at the championships. I shoved him in front of the media. The league doesn't take too kindly to violence between riders and the team owners made a choice between him or me."

I expect her to look at me differently, but she doesn't.

"What did he do?"

My brows knit in confusion.

"He had to have done something to make you shove him."

"What makes you say that?"

"I just watched a guy goad you, basically begging you to hit him, and you didn't."

I think it's the first time someone has assumed it wasn't my temper that caused the whole thing and I'm taken aback that she's so quick to trust me.

"Link didn't do anything. I mean, yeah, he said some shit and crashed into me, but I shouldn't have put my hands on him. It's what he wanted."

"Then why did you?"

I work my jaw back and forth. "It was my mom's birthday. She died ten years ago. She would have been fifty. I wanted to win for her. Instead, I fucked everything up."

"You made a mistake on a really bad day. That's all."

A mistake that cost me everything.

"This isn't how I saw the night ending," I say, trying to steer us back to light conversation.

"Yeah, me neither." She smiles. "But I'm here if you want to talk about it."

When I say nothing, she takes the hint.

"Okay. Well, do you want to come back to my dorm? Quinn is probably at Colter's, but even if she's there, I have my own room."

"Another time. It's late."

Her surprise is apparent. "You're turning me down?"

My dick throbs in protest. She's standing here in that little dress looking like a goddess and I can still taste her. "I'm trying to be noble here. Don't push me, princess."

"Why?"

I get back on the bike because I don't trust myself not to touch her. "I'm not a relationship kind of guy. If we have sex, it doesn't change anything."

"Who said I was a relationship kind of girl?"

She doesn't have to say it. Maybe she's testing the waters by sleeping around for a bit, but eventually, she's going to want to settle down. I'm not made that way.

The next thing I know, she's climbing on in front of me and draping her arms over my shoulders. "I know it doesn't change anything. I'm not going to turn into a clingy stalker. You're hot, but you're not that hot."

My brows lift and a small chuckle loosens the tension in my chest. I reach out, guiding her closer with a rough grip on her hip. "Is that right?"

She's full of fiery determination until my other hand slips under the hem of her dress. Her expression goes soft and her lips part as I glide a gloved hand up her leg. I should stop. Go home. Jerk off. Call someone else. But I've never been good at doing the noble thing anyway.

I reach the top of her leg and my thumb brushes her panty-covered clit. "If I slipped off these gloves, would I feel how soaked you are for me?"

"Yes." Her eyes flutter closed.

She's beautiful. Needy and desperate for me. She wants to see what it's like to be with a guy like me, and I want her, so I stop fighting it. She knows what this is.

I increase the pressure and make quick circles over her clit until her breaths come in little pants. When she's practically grinding against my hand, I slip it under her panties and let them snap back against her sensitive core. Her body tenses and she gasps, but I'm already back to soothing the ache with my fingers gliding back over her swollen flesh.

"Knox." The way she says my name has me wishing it were more than my fingers buried inside of her.

"Come for me, princess."

She does, biting down on her bottom lip like she's trying to hold in all those sexy pants and moans. I want all of them, so I bring my mouth to hers, swallowing them as she rides my hand through the waves of pleasure.

I don't stop until she goes limp against me. Her head falls against mine and she sucks in air. I fix her panties and remove my hand. She eyes my glove as it emerges and blushes at the wetness now coating the leather.

I bring that same hand up to her lips and brush my thumb over her plump bottom lip, then kiss her again.

When we break apart, her eyes are a bright blue, and her skin is flushed. "I think I like motorcycles."

# CHAPTER TWENTY-ONE
## Knox

I stand up and clap as the buzzer sounds, ending the first half. "Atta boy, Flynn."

My brother doesn't look up, but as he heads off the court his mouth curves up in a small smile.

"I swear he gets better every game," Hendrick says.

I nod my agreement as I take my seat. It's incredible. Our baby brother is on another level when it comes to sports. Basketball isn't even his best sport.

"We're gonna grab some food." Brogan stands and Archer follows. "You guys want anything?"

Hendrick and I both shake our heads. The crowd thins out around us, everyone piling into the cafeteria to stand in the concession line.

I'm checking my phone. I had to miss today's practice session with Avery for Flynn's game, but we've been texting back and forth.

Silly stuff. She just sent me a video of a three-year-old doing the press handstand and said, "Watch this kid for tips."

I'm not even sure if she's joking. Probably not. I give it a thumbs-up and then reply, "Watch these girls for tips." And put in the link for Pornhub.

I'm laughing to myself as Hendrick leans back and props his feet up on the bleacher in front of us. "This place never changes."

"Nope," I say without looking up.

"It's weird to think about coming back here someday with our own kids and it all being exactly the same."

I lift my gaze. It takes me a second to process his words. "Kids? Is Jane pregnant?"

"What?" He waves me off. "No. I was just thinking."

"About kids?"

"Well, yeah. Eventually. Jane wants to finish school and get married first, and I want to have a house and make sure the bar is doing well."

He's serious. Damn. I knew things in his life were changing. He and Jane got engaged a year ago and she practically lives at our house, but kids? A house? Fuck.

"A little Hollywood." I smile as I think about Hendrick as a parent. He's going to be an overbearing prick to anyone who hurts his kid, and they'll most definitely have him wrapped around their finger. "I hope they get Jane's looks."

"Yeah, me too." His chest rises and falls with a short laugh.

Avery texts back a selfie of her giving me the finger. I chuckle as I send an angel emoji back.

"Who are you texting?" Hendrick asks.

"Avery. That girl that's training me."

"The gymnast," Hendrick says, more statement than question.

"Yep."

"Are you two dating?"

"No," I say quickly and slide my phone into my pocket.

"Oh, come on. Don't act like Flynn when I ask if he likes a girl. You're texting her and laughing. I'm not an idiot."

"We're just talking."

"Naked?"

"Is that how you talk to people?" I mock him. "No wonder you don't have any friends."

"You know what I mean. Are you fucking her or not?" he asks as a group of parents walk by. Their disapproving glares are priceless.

Hendrick shoots them an apologetic smile and I hide my laughter behind a fist.

Before we can compose ourselves, Archer and Brogan reappear with snacks. Brogan tosses me a bag of M&Ms. I always tell him I don't want anything, and he always gets me something. I think it's to make up for how annoying he is all the time.

Brogan sits in front of us, but Archer stands with a contemplative look on his face.

"*You make a better door than window*," I tell him and also sign. Flynn's team is stepping back onto the floor behind him. Not that I can see.

"I think I saw Dad outside," he says finally.

"What?" Hendrick sits up.

I'm frozen at first, then I shake it off. I sign instead of speaking. *No. No way he'd show up here.*

Archer had an accident when he was younger that caused him to lose his hearing. He's legally Deaf and wears hearing aids. He can read lips really well, too, but signing is the easiest way to make sure he doesn't miss anything in a big conversation.

*"It did look kind of like him, but then again it's been a while since I've seen your old man."* Brogan shrugs.

Our dad barely showed up to a single sporting event or class event in all the years Hendrick, Arch, and me were in school. I doubt he even knows Flynn hasn't graduated yet. He stopped keeping tabs on us a long time ago, and I've made sure it stays that way.

*"Where was he?"* Hendrick signs, then glances toward the cafeteria.

"In the breezeway outside. I didn't get a good look…" Arch trails off. "It probably wasn't him."

"I'll go check." Hendrick gets to his feet and takes off before I can tell him not to bother. It's not him. No freaking way.

I tap my foot and stare out onto the court as Flynn takes shots from around the perimeter. I clap and try to shake off all thoughts of dear old dad, but Archer and Brogan are still talking about it.

"When's the last time you saw him?" Brogan asks.

Archer tosses Raisinets into his mouth and thinks before replying, "I can't even remember. On my birthday last year, he sent a card."

"He did?" I ask. I didn't know about that. It's not the only time he's reached out. He texted me a few times until I blocked him, and he dropped by once a few years ago on the date of Mom's passing, but I'm the only one that saw him, and I got rid of him real fast. I didn't need him fucking with anyone else by showing up on a day we all hate.

"Yeah. But I haven't seen him since my graduation maybe. What about you?" Archer asks and waits for my answer.

"It's been a long time."

Hendrick comes back, shaking his head. "I didn't see him."

"I told you. It wasn't him," I say, but the pit in my stomach doesn't go away.

Back at home, I'm in the garage punching the bag when Hendrick comes outside.

"What are you doing up, old man?" I ask him, stopping the bag with one hand. We didn't get home until after nine and it was another hour before I made sure Flynn had done all his homework, eaten, and showered. Hendrick was in his room with Jane when I came out here. I assumed everyone had gone to bed.

He paces in front of me. "I can't stop thinking about tonight. Do you think Dad was there?"

"I don't know," I admit.

His dark brows pull together. "He stopped by the house once this summer saying he wanted to check in, asked about Flynn."

"What?" My voice rises. "Why didn't you say anything?"

"Because I knew you'd get worked up over it. You were gone at some race and when you got back you were training for the championship. I didn't want to distract you with it. I handled it and nobody else knows."

I let out a sigh of relief. Hendrick, Archer, and I are all in agreement about Dad. None of us want him around, but I'm not sure how Flynn would react. He was too young to remember what a shitty father he was. I don't want him to go through what all of us did. Dad popping in and out randomly. Each time we'd get excited when he showed up, only to be let down when he left again.

And it isn't like he was some great father when he was around anyway. It was a real mind fuck. We wanted him to be present, but then he showed up and it was like we forgot how much of an asshole he was. He and Mom fought constantly, he got irritated if we were too loud or too rowdy, which was always. My bike became my salvation.

I don't know why the fuck we wasted so many years wishing he'd finally decide he wanted to be a dad. He sucked at it. We were better off without him. We still are.

"Justin Pushner. You remember him?" I ask Hendrick.

"Yeah. He was your grade, right?"

I nod. "The other night I saw him. He said Dad was hanging around the track. I didn't believe him at the time. I thought he was just trying to get a rise out of me, but maybe he was telling the truth."

"Fuck." Hendrick runs a hand over his jaw. "Do you think he's back living in Valley?"

"I hope not." But it can't be a coincidence that two days in a row someone's mentioned him hanging around town.

# CHAPTER TWENTY-TWO
*Avery*

Colter's birthday falls on Saturday night. The guys got back sometime this afternoon, according to Quinn.

When I walk into The Tipsy Rose, I already know Knox is here. Aside from seeing his truck outside, Quinn texted ten minutes ago to inform me my "hang out buddy" was here. She meant it as an excited warning, also probably trying to hurry me up.

Coach Weaver cleared me to work on vault yesterday, and I'm desperate to make up for lost time. I needed a long soak in the ice bath before I could function enough to get ready for a night out.

Nerves I don't want to acknowledge swirl in my stomach. I'm excited to see him, but it's more than that. I'm giddy. That make-out session the other night was…there are no words. We've been texting on and off since then, but mostly just gymnastics stuff or flirty, silly things.

I spot the birthday boy first. He's sitting on a stool in front of the bar. Quinn is perched on his lap. I keep my eyes down to push through the crowd. This bar and one down the street are favorites with Valley U students, but tonight it's a mixture of us and a slightly older crowd. I see people I recognize from school, but none I know well enough to approach.

A group of guys in riding jackets eye me as I angle my body to step past them.

Quinn slides off her boyfriend's lap to greet me when she sees me approaching.

"You made it." She throws her arms around my neck and squeezes me while leaning side to side.

"Hi," I say, laughing a little. "Miss me?"

"Always," she returns without missing a beat, then pulls back and guides me with a firm grip on my hand to the bar.

"Happy birthday," I say to Colter.

"Thanks, Avery."

Then I see him. He's a few seats down, lifting a glass to his lips while talking to the bartender. Knox has already seen me, and it feels like I've given him the upper hand somehow. His gaze burns hot, and I feel a flush as he swallows and sets his drink down without ever taking his eyes off me.

"What do you want to drink?" Quinn asks me, dragging my attention away from Knox.

"Sprite, I guess."

Colter orders it for me and before it's arrived, Knox has made his way over.

"Princess," he says by way of greeting.

I roll my eyes at the nickname that is apparently not going to die. Then say his name in the same mocking tone, "Knox."

We smile at each other. I'd like to think his mind is back in that parking lot with his hand up my dress because that's where mine is as I stare at the way his fingers wrap around the glass.

Someone jostles me from behind and I'm shoved toward him. Knox reaches forward and steadies me with his free hand. Those strong fingers I was just staring at wrap around my upper arm, and I narrowly avoid face-planting into his chest.

He smells good. He looks good too. Dark gray T-shirt, jeans, black boots.

Quinn squeals, breaking the spell I'm under. "A-babe, it's our song!"

It takes a moment for the music to register, but by that time she's already grabbed my hand and is pulling me to the other side of the bar where the band is playing a remixed version of "Good 4 U."

It's really her song. Don't get me wrong, I like singing and dancing to it, but it's Quinn who considers it her personal anthem. She loves Olivia Rodrigo.

"Don't worry. He's still staring," she shouts.

"Who?"

"Knox. I knew pulling you away would drive him crazy."

I shake my head at her. "I can't decide if you're a genius or evil."

"A little bit of both." She grins.

People have gathered in front of the stage. Most are standing around watching and drinking, not really dancing. One of the great things about Quinn is she doesn't worry a lot about what other people think. She doesn't need other people to dance for her to throw her hands over her head and wiggle her hips to the beat.

And I easily fall into step with her. We cut loose for the remainder of the song, singing the lyrics along with the band.

I don't forget about Knox, but I can't see him.

The next song is slower. We turn and stare toward the stage, swaying to the beat.

"Knox looks good," Quinn says, still a little out of breath.

I hum my agreement.

"What's going on with you two? Are you planning on hooking up on the regular or was it a one-time thing?"

"I don't know. I forgot to ask him when he was making me orgasm in the empty parking lot."

She fights to hold in a laugh. I smile right back at her. Did I immediately tell her every detail when I got home the other night? Of course, I did. I *needed* to tell someone so I could relive it.

Colter comes up behind Quinn and wraps his arms around her waist. He drops a kiss on her cheek. "Hey, babe. I need my darts partner."

She looks at me for permission.

"Go. Have fun. I'm going to dance some more," I tell her with a wave of my hand.

"Come watch." She leans back into her boyfriend without moving.

"Yeah, Quinn does better with an audience." Colter drops another kiss onto her cheek.

She nods her agreement. "I do love when people are watching me beat up on unsuspecting men who assume it's my first time playing."

Yeah, that sounds like her. I follow them into a back area where there are billiards, pool, and some arcade games. This room is a little more closed off from the rest of the bar, which drowns out some of the noise from the band.

I park myself on an empty stool against the wall next to the dart boards. Quinn and Colter are playing with two of his riding buddies, Oak and Shane. I glance around for Knox but he must still be at the bar.

While I'm cheering on Quinn and giving her the audience she craves, another one of Colter's friends comes over to me.

"Hey." He drops his head to catch my gaze. "Can I buy you a drink?"

"No thanks." I never did grab my Sprite from the bar, but I don't want to give this guy the wrong idea by letting him buy me another drink.

"I'm Mitch," he says.

"Avery."

He tips his head toward Colter. "How do you know the birthday boy?"

I point toward my best friend as she raises her hands overhead in victory. I don't follow darts that closely, but I guess that was a good shot. "Quinn is my roommate."

"Ah." He moves closer and rests one side up against the wall. He's a tall guy, broad, mid-twenties, I think. He has a short beard that makes it hard to accurately guess his age. At youngest, twenty-four. At oldest maybe early thirties. He's good-looking. Striking eyes and chin-length hair that's tucked behind his ears. Objectively, I should be attracted to him, but right now I have a singularly focused addiction in the form of Knox Holland.

Mitch is about to say something else when my addiction walks into the back area. One side of his mouth pulls into a tiny smile as he approaches. I hate the way I want to squirm in my seat from the butterflies swooping low in my stomach.

Mitch stands tall and offers him a hand. "Holland. Good to see you."

"You too," Knox says.

Mitch is oblivious to Knox's intent in coming over. He thinks he's there for him, but I know better. Even if he isn't looking at me, I can feel the pull between us.

"How've you been?" Mitch asks. "I was sorry to hear about Thorne."

A flash of emotion crosses Knox's face, but he smooths it out so fast I doubt Mitch notices. "Thanks. I'm good."

"You always did land on your feet." Mitch looks back to me, angling his body to include me in their conversation. "I was just chatting with…"

Am I surprised he's already forgotten my name? Yes, yes, I am. My face flushes hot as Mitch's eyes grow wide.

Knox's smile grows bigger and mocking as he watches his friend flounder to remember my name.

"Amanda, right?" Knox takes a step closer. "I think we've met."

"Right. Amanda!" Mitch grins sheepishly.

I wasn't exactly feeling him, but *ouch*.

"My friends call me Mandy," I say to Knox, making my voice sugary sweet. "Have we met? I don't seem to remember."

"Oh, no?" His voice is low and skims over my skin like gravel. "I could have sworn we had run into each other once or twice. I can't put my fingers on it at the moment."

My face has to be red, but I smirk right back at him. I'm not backing down. "Must not have been very memorable."

Mitch's gaze is ping-ponging between us. I stand, legs a little shaky from bantering with Knox.

"Excuse me. I need to talk with my roommate." I make a beeline for an excited Quinn. She and Colter have won their game. She throws her arms around me and I congratulate her. Then she convinces me to play with her. I happily oblige so I can avoid Mitch and him calling me Amanda.

Colter grabs Knox, who is still standing nearby, and the four of us start the game. I'm not very good at getting the dart to go where I aim, but I'm confident Quinn will carry us, or at least keep us from being creamed.

"Mandy, huh?" Knox drawls.

"Only to my friends."

He leans in closer and drops his voice. "What about guys you let feel you up occasionally?"

My pulse ticks faster. "You can call me Amanda."

"Sure thing, princess." He laughs.

We don't talk a lot during the game, which we win (thank you, Quinn), but as soon as it's over, my best friend and her boyfriend head out to the dance floor.

"You look bored," Knox observes when we're alone. "I have a few ideas how to help with that."

"I'm not bored. I just don't really know anyone here except Quinn and Colter."

"And me."

"And you."

That cocky smirk stays on his face. Someone calls out to him, and he briefly glances away, nods to whoever spoke, and then refocuses.

"You don't need to hang around to keep me company. Quinn and Colter will be back soon."

"Is that your prissy way of telling me to fuck off?"

"What? No. I—"

His laughter cuts off my reply. "Come on, princess. You can slum it with me until your friend returns."

On the farthest wall, several arcade games are set up. There's a football-throwing game, an old school Donkey Kong game, and two driving games. One is a car and the other is a motorcycle.

I'm not surprised in the least when he walks straight to the motorcycle game.

"How lucky that they have a game especially for you."

He taps the seat. "Hop on."

I arch a brow.

He takes my hand and pulls me toward it. I don't object any further. At least tonight I'm in jeans instead of a dress. I sit on the red motorcycle. It's attached to a base, but still moves side to side. There's a large screen in front of it.

I run a hand along the top of the motorcycle then wrap my fingers around the handle. "I've never driven a motorcycle before."

He inserts money into the game and then presses a few buttons on the screen. I watch him more than what he selects.

"You want to watch me pretend to ride a motorcycle?" I ask.

He leans toward me and whispers, "I'd rather have you on the back of mine again, but this will do for now."

His lips are so close I could tip my head up and our mouths would meet. I consider it, but then he moves back and presses the big green button and the game comes alive.

My competitiveness sparks and I try out the gas and brake to get a feel for it. The other riders in the game are flying past me as I get my bearings.

"The idea is to be the first person to cross the finish line," he says, voice laced with humor.

"Shut up. I've got this," I tell him, even though I definitely don't have this. I spend more time trying to keep myself on the track than anything else.

I lose focus of Knox and concentrate solely on the game. I do not want to come in dead last and I'm frustrated that I keep running off the damn road.

I startle when I feel his body behind me. His chest is flush against my back and his arms come up on either side of me, hands draping over mine. He controls the bike and I'm able to speed up a little more. I come in twelfth place.

We both lean back in the seat when the race is over. I glance over my shoulder. "I had it. I didn't need your help."

"Sorry. I couldn't help it. Watching you swerve across the track was too much for me." He brushes my hair back over my shoulder. "Wanna get out of here for a bit?"

"I can't." Goosebumps rise where his fingers graze my skin.

"Why not?"

"It's Colter's birthday."

"So?"

I laugh and shake my head. "Tonight is about him."

"I already bought his drinks and told him happy birthday," he says, but he's grinning like he knows as well as I do that he needs to stick around.

"When is your birthday?"

"September fifth. Yours?"

"August second." I turn around to face him, placing both legs on one side of the bike. A beat of silence hangs between us. It isn't uncomfortable but I still hurry to disrupt it. "How was your week?"

He bites his bottom lip as he leans closer. "Had promise midweek, but the past couple of days have been underwhelming."

The blatant flirting is a surprise. I came tonight hoping to kiss him again, but he seems so certain that he's already won me over that I can't help but enjoy playing hard to get.

"Miss me?" I ask, but I don't wait for him to reply. "Or miss my awesome workouts?"

His eyes light up with amusement as he laughs.

"I hope you enjoyed your days off. I have some ideas for next week."

"Can't wait." Sarcasm coats his words, but his eyes defy his disinterest. Maybe he's not looking forward to working out, but he's excited about something.

"Do you want something to drink?" He scoots backward off the bike, and it leans to the right without his weight.

I stand too. "Water."

We go to the bar where Knox gets the attention of the bartender right away even though there are other people waiting. Her expression is familiar and friendly. I stare daggers at her as she takes his order and calls him by name. He hands me my water and then accepts a bottled beer with a thanks. Leaning one hip on the bar, he angles his body toward me. "Your friend is looking for you."

"Quinn?" I ask as I turn. Sure enough, I find her standing at the edge of the dance area, scanning the bar. As soon as she sees me, her gaze slides to Knox and then she smiles.

"I was afraid you left," she says as soon as she makes her way over. She fans her face and eyes my water.

I hand it over without her asking.

"Excuse me for a minute," Knox says, gripping me by the waist before he steps away.

When I glance over, he's sliding behind the bar to help the bartender with something. He looks so comfortable there, like maybe it isn't the first time he's helped her out. The two of them are talking back and forth but I can't make out either of their words.

"I would never leave without telling you," I say to Quinn. "But I am thinking it's going to be a short night. I barely know anyone here."

"You know Colter and he knows everyone."

"That's not the same thing."

"What about you and…" She tips her head in the direction Knox disappeared.

I glance back at the bar. He's no longer standing there, and neither is the bartender. My stomach twists with jealousy and embarrassment. Knox and I are not a thing. He asked me to leave with him and I said no. What did I really expect but for him to find someone else?

"I don't know."

She makes a short sound of disapproval, then perks up. "I saw one of Tristan's neighbors at a table with some other golf guys."

"You don't need to play matchmaker to con me into staying," I tell my best friend with a laugh. "I'm not leaving yet, but soon."

"Good. I have longer to convince you to stay out all night. After the bar, people are going over to Colter and Brooklyn's house."

Colter and some of his friends have pulled together three tables. Quinn takes a seat next to her boyfriend and I sit beside her. The guys are telling stories and talking about bikes. I don't understand a lot of it and find my mind wandering.

Knox appears at some point. I don't see him take a seat, but the next time I search for him, he's seated at the far end. And when I let myself glance at him again, a pretty girl with jet black hair and stunning colorful tattoos is sitting in his lap. He's leaned back, but she has her arms around his neck, and I don't need to hear the conversation to know she's hitting on him. Or vice versa. I'd be impressed that he's already found two girls to replace me in less than an hour if it didn't also make me so jealous. I force myself to look away when she threads her fingers through his hair.

I stay longer than I intend, but when Colter says they're going to head over to his place, I'm ready to go home.

"Are you sure?" Quinn asks, giving me wide, hopeful eyes. I know she can tell I'm upset, but I can't bring myself to say it. Knox doesn't owe me anything. So, we hooked up once. So what?

"Positive. Go have fun with your man. I'll see you in the morning."

"Okay." She hugs me, squeezing tightly.

The group disperses quickly. A lot of the guys have already left by the time I also hug Colter and wish him one last happy birthday.

At some point Knox disentangled himself from the girl that was in his lap and he hangs back clearly waiting for me. I walk over to say goodbye to him too. I don't want to leave tonight with there being any awkward feelings between us.

"See you at Colter's place?" he asks.

"No, I don't think so."

Part of me thinks he'll try to change my mind, but then his name is called from behind the bar. It's the guy bartender this time with his hands cupped around his mouth. When Knox glances back, the guy motions for him to come over. Then I see him squeeze the girl bartender's shoulder like he's reassuring her. She smiles at Knox then looks at me like she hopes I burst into flames.

I had pretty much already put it together that Knox had hooked up with her before, but the whole encounter feels icky somehow. I don't get into catfights with girls over guys. That's so not me. And Knox seems to have a flock of women ready to throw down for his attention.

"Looks like another one of your friends wants to *hang out*." I purposely use his phrasing so he knows I'm not an idiot. With a wave, I step back. "See you on Monday."

# CHAPTER TWENTY-THREE
*Knox*

The bar has cleared out by the time I finish helping Erika. Avery is long gone. I even check the parking lot in case she's waiting out there, but her Bronco isn't anywhere in sight.

Well, fuck.

I sit on my motorcycle and text Colter to see if she showed up at his place, but he replies back quickly.

**COLTER**

**No. She bailed after the bar. You coming over?**

ME

I'm not sure yet. I might head home.

COLTER

Yeah, I'll bet. Quinn says to tell you that
you're an idiot and that she hopes your
dick shrivels up and falls off.

"Damn," I mutter to myself.

ME

What the hell did I do to her?

COLTER

I'm paraphrasing here but I think the
problem might be that you hooked up
with Avery earlier this week and then
followed some other girl into the back
room at the bar right in front of her.

I read his words twice slowly until I finally piece it all together. Then I laugh. Miss Priss is jealous, and the rush of adrenaline pumping through me is like none other.

ME

Is Avery at her dorm?

COLTER

Yes.

COLTER

Oops. I mean no.

COLTER

You blew your chance, buddy. Avery is
out of your league anyway. Dumbass.

I feel my brows rise and a smile pull at my lips.

COLTER

**That was Quinn.**

ME

No kidding.

COLTER

**She's protective and hits hard. I suggest
staying on her good side.**

Too late for that.

COLTER

**I gotta go before she takes my phone
again, but just so you know Quinn is
staying at my place all night. Have fun.**

I don't text Avery first, which is likely a mistake. Who just shows up at a girl's place uninvited? I guess the answer to that is me. I do.

I was able to get the dorm name and room number from Quinn after I promised I'd let her punch me in the nuts if Avery wasn't glad to see me. That's how confident I am. She was jealous, not because she cares if I hook up with other people—I already told her I'm not a relationship guy. No, she wasn't feeling territorial. She was feeling hurt. Despite her playing it cool when I asked if she wanted to leave with me earlier, she was hoping we'd hook up again tonight. Me fucking too.

I knock on the door and then tap my thumb against my thigh. The hall is mostly quiet. I passed a few open doors with people hanging out inside, but mostly it looks like people are gone. Or asleep. I check the time. Fuck. Maybe she's already in bed. I knock louder. With every second that passes I'm more certain she's not going to answer.

I'm reaching in to get my phone so I can text her, while continuing to knock, when I hear her on the other side of the door. "Geez. I'm coming. One second."

My hand is still raised, poised to knock, as the door opens.

"Knox?" She stands there, staring at me, clearly surprised to see me. But my throat goes dry as the desert as I take her in.

Tiny pink shorts, white tank top, and about four inches of skin in between. Her hair is pulled back into a ponytail and her feet are bare. Damn. Every time I see her in different situations, I think she can't get any hotter. And somehow, I'm always wrong.

"What are you doing here?" she asks.

"Can I come in?"

"Did your other plans for the night fall through?" she asks as she steps back and opens the door wider. "How did you know where I live?"

I ignore the first question.

"Quinn," I say, walking in and glancing around at the space. It's my first time setting foot in a dorm room. It's bigger than I imagined, but otherwise basically how I've seen them portrayed in movies and shows. "I piggybacked in behind some guys coming back from a party."

There's a couch, chair, and TV in this room and then two doors off either side that I assume lead to their bedrooms. One is closed and the other is open with the light on.

"Okay, but why?"

I pick up a three-ring binder with her name on it from a small table. "What's your major?"

"I'm still undecided," she says, growing more irritated. She takes it from me and sets it on top of a backpack resting on the floor. "Knox, why are you here?"

"I wanted to see you." I pause at a picture frame sitting on top of the entertainment center and glance at a photo of Avery and Quinn. They're both in their Valley U team leotards and smiling at the camera.

"I was just about to get in bed." She crosses her arms over her chest. "Shouldn't you be at Colter's party or maybe hooking up with the bartender or some other girl?"

There it is. That little jab of jealousy I was waiting for.

"I didn't hook up with Erika."

"Who?" she asks, but she knows who I mean. Her face flushes.

"The bartender."

"Oh," she says flippantly.

"It's her first week working there. Or bartending anywhere for that matter. First weekend nights can be tough."

"Well, I'm glad she had you to help her out," she says, not sounding at all glad.

God, she's stubborn.

"Yeah. My brother wouldn't normally throw someone to the wolves like that, but he came down with the flu and no one could fill in."

"Your brother…" she trails off, the lilt of a question in her tone.

"Owns the place, yeah. I'm not much of a bartender but I know where shit is and I can change a keg, so occasionally I jump in and help if things get hectic while I'm there."

I watch the pieces come together for her and the way her body language softens as she realizes I'm telling the truth. But then her spine stiffens again. "You had so many girls hitting on you tonight, it was an easy mistake to make."

"Why weren't you one of them?" I ask. I'm genuinely curious. If she wanted to hook up with me, why didn't she just tell me?

"You don't need me to feed your ego."

"This isn't about my ego. Were you or were you not hoping tonight would end with me here?"

"Part of me was," she admits.

"Then why not just say that?" It would have saved a lot of time. We could already be naked.

Exasperation makes her blue eyes spark to life and she shrugs her shoulders high up to her ears. "Because...I don't know, okay? I haven't done casual hookups before and I don't know how to do this."

No shit. I called that the other night.

"I told you I don't do relationships."

"I know," she says. "I'm not asking for that. I'm just bad at doing this." She motions between us. "Who was the other girl? Long, black hair, tattoos."

"Just a friend I've known a long time."

"A friend you've hooked up with?"

"You really want me to answer that?"

She shakes her head. "I was jealous."

"You didn't need to be. The only person I was interested in leaving with was you."

Her gaze narrows like she's weighing the truth of my words.

"Why'd you run away instead of telling me all this at the bar?

Hoping I'd chase you?"

"No. I promise I did not expect you to show up here."

"Good. I don't chase."

"But here you are anyway."

We're in a standoff, neither of us wanting to budge. But every second I stand here is another second I'm not kissing her.

I step forward and grab her hand, then tug her toward me. Her lips finally pull into a smile.

"Here I am anyway." I brush my fingers along the curve of her neck. Her skin is warm and soft, and she leans into my touch.

We lunge at the same time, our mouths colliding in a frantic need to get closer. She tastes like mint toothpaste. My hand slides to the back of her head and I wrap my fingers around her ponytail.

I guide her toward the open bedroom. She pushes my jacket off my shoulders, and I shrug out of it and toss it toward a desk chair.

My hands slip under her shirt and she wrenches her mouth away from mine.

"Wait. I, uh…" She shifts and bites one corner of her mouth. "Can we…"

Every time she trails off or stumbles over her words it makes me pause as if she yelled stop. She's always so certain of everything.

"You want to stop?" I ask, pulling back to get a better look at her face.

"No. I mean, yes." She places her hands on my chest. "I want to hook up, but can we hold off on having sex?"

"Oh." That isn't what I expected.

"It's just that after my last relationship I promised myself I'd take things slower. I know it sounds silly considering we're only hooking up and not dating, but sex is a hard limit for me right now."

I'm silent, not because it's a dealbreaker, but because I'm trying to understand.

She continues, "Nolan—my ex—cheated on me."

I don't know what to say so I run my hand down her back in what I hope is a soothing gesture. After my dad left for good, I've been careful about who I've let into my circle. It's one of the reasons I don't do relationships. People can't disappoint you if you don't expect anything from them.

So even though I've never let anyone close enough to cheat on me, the concept is similar. She doesn't trust people. I so get that.

"I don't understand why he couldn't just be honest and tell me that he wanted to break up or sleep with other people. Instead, I had to find out through the rumor mill that he was hooking up with his ex-girlfriend at a party while I was gone at a competition."

She stops talking and looks at me like she expects me to bail now that I know sex is off the table. What a fucking prick her ex is.

"People are selfish," I say. "It didn't have anything to do with you."

"I know, but now here I am with a hot guy in my dorm room, and I'm turning down what I imagine would be very good sex."

I pull her into my body. I'm so hard the contact makes me groan. "Do you want me to go? We can do this another time."

"No. Definitely not." She bites her lip again, but this time it's as she stares at my chest and heat flushes her face. "I want to keep going. All I've thought about since the other night is having your hands on me again."

Relief floods through me. I want this girl so bad the thought of walking away is painful. It's not a feeling I'm familiar with.

"Is that right?" I sit on the bed and pull her onto my lap. Her lashes flutter and her breath hitches. My hands drop to her hips and I splay my fingers out, letting my thumb slide beneath her shorts.

"Yes." The word is breathy. She wraps her arms around my neck and rolls her hips against me.

My thumb continues to glide over her clit as she grinds on top of me. Our kisses are sloppy.

Her body quivers as she gets close.

"Can I?" she asks, letting her hands drop to the button of my jeans.

I nod and then suck her bottom lip into my mouth as she fumbles to get my jeans undone. When she succeeds, she pushes on my chest to get me to lie down.

Smiling, I lie back on the bed and crook one hand behind my head as she shimmies down my body and rids me of my pants. She removes her shorts too. My dick twitches at the scrap of pink lacy material covering her pussy. She's making a real good case for pink being my new favorite color.

Avery climbs back on top of me, straddling me with only my boxers and her panties between us. She settles on top of me, the weight of her sitting on my dick enough to pull another groan from me. I don't need to be buried inside of her tonight, but I'm not gonna say it wouldn't feel fucking fantastic.

I lift my hips and her eyes flutter closed with a moan. My hands rest on her waist. She only needs a little encouraging to start grinding into me again, taking what she needs from me and bringing me dangerously close to exploding without either of us so much as touching my dick.

She stops and stares down at me.

"What?" I ask.

She bites her full bottom lip again.

I reach up and free it from her teeth. "What do you need?"

"You. Your hands. Please? Nothing has ever felt better than the other night."

I sit up and then turn us so she's underneath me. Splayed out underneath me like a wet dream. Damn. Pleasure jolts up my spine.

I run my thumb over her bottom lip again. "This mouth of yours is sexy as fuck, princess."

Her lips curve. "Wondering what it'd look like wrapped around your dick?"

"If I hadn't been, I am now." I definitely had been.

"Me too," she says.

Fuck me, that's hot.

"Later. I'm busy." My hand dips down her body until my fingers brush against the top of her panties. I shift so I can kiss her stomach and hook my fingers on either side of the lacy material to pull them down.

"Is it all right if these come off?" I ask.

"Yes."

I can't get her out of them fast enough and then she's naked underneath me and I'm wondering if I might die from seeing her like this and not being able to fuck her.

"You're gorgeous." I slide a finger down her slit and then bring it up to my mouth. She flushes and her eyes dilate as I suck the taste of her off my finger.

"Okay if I lick you, princess?"

She nods rapidly.

I'm damn near sweating as I settle between her legs. I alternate using my fingers and my tongue. She thrashes under me, moaning my name, grinding down against me occasionally and then pulling away like she's trying to hold off the impending orgasm.

She's more patient than I am. I can't wait any longer to watch her come undone again. I hold tight to her hips and suck hard on her clit as I fuck her with two fingers. That's all it takes.

She cries out, hands fisting in my hair and body arching off the bed. Her grip loosens and then her body goes limp as the last of her orgasm shudders through her. I place soft kisses on her thighs and lower stomach and then fall onto the mattress beside her.

Our ragged breathing is the only sound until Avery starts to giggle.

"Something funny, princess?" I ask.

"No," she says, still giggling.

I let my head fall to the side to look at her. She's grinning back at me.

"You just fucked me stupid and we didn't even fuck." She starts laughing harder.

I only get her to stop when I roll back on top of her.

Her smile is contagious. Messing around with her is fun in a way I don't think I've ever experienced before.

"My turn." She pushes me back and scrambles onto the mattress between my legs.

"Always so bossy." I barely grit out the words before she pushes my boxers down, wraps her puffy lips around my cock, and takes me to the back of her throat.

I can't take my eyes off her. She glides up and down slowly. Too fucking slowly. I wrap one hand around her ponytail again and guide her over me.

"Goddamn, Avery. Your mouth was meant for sucking my

dick."

Her eyes light up and she takes me farther, gagging before she pulls back. I can't remember the last time I wanted a blow job to take longer, but the sight of her blonde hair and big blue eyes as she sucks me off is as good as the way her lips feel wrapped around me. If I had to give up sex for this blow job, then it was well worth the trade.

I hold off as long as I can, but when I'm seconds from coming down her throat, I pull her off me and finish on my stomach and chest.

My head falls back onto the bed as I catch my breath. Avery gets me a towel and I clean myself up. I'm about to get dressed to go when she flops down beside me.

"Are you staying?" she asks.

"I don't cuddle, princess."

"As in you don't like to cuddle or it's against your rules for casual hookups?"

I rub the back of my neck. "Both, I guess."

"Okay, no cuddling." She thinks for a moment. "What if we lie next to each other and watch TV until we have the energy to make out again?"

I have no idea how that's different than cuddling, but the thought of going again with her is enough to stop me in my tracks. "Deal."

"What time is it?" Avery asks, voice groggy with sleep.

"Early. Go back to sleep." I pull on my jeans and then look for my T-shirt, only to realize Avery is sleeping in it.

She curls up onto her side and yawns. "See you tomorrow?"

"Yeah." I grab my jacket off the back of her desk chair. I hesitate. I don't think I've ever been so slow to leave a chick before. I don't chase. I don't stay over or cuddle. And I don't linger like some lovesick fool. "See you tomorrow night."

The ride home wakes me up some. I'm going on barely any sleep, but I promised Flynn I'd take him riding this morning.

The house is still and quiet as I come in through the garage. I come up short when I spot Hendrick standing in the kitchen in sweats and a T-shirt.

"Where have you been?" he asks, one brow raised.

"Waiting up for me? How sweet." I toss my keys on the counter and rub a hand over my hair. "I was out."

"With a girl?" His voice dips low in a teasing tone and he grins wide.

The smell of fresh coffee draws me over to the pot. I pour some into a mug, then wince. I hate the taste, but my eyelids burn from lack of sleep. "What are you doing up?"

"I couldn't sleep anymore and my body hurts from lying in bed all day yesterday."

"You look like shit, but less so," I say as I look him over. His hair is sticking up and he's got the start of a beard going, but he no longer smells like sickness.

"I feel less like it." He rubs a hand over his face. "I gotta go into the bar today. What are you up to?"

"I promised Flynn I'd take him riding."

Hendrick's mouth pulls into a straight line and concern etches his brow. "Be careful. He hasn't ridden in a long while."

"I know." I shoot him a scathing look. I'd rather walk over hot coals than see Flynn get hurt. "I've been taking care of him a lot longer than you."

His parental mask falls and is replaced with a look of guilt. Fuck. I don't know why I said that. Hendrick feels bad enough about the time he was gone playing football and it isn't like I resent being the one that stayed back. I just want him to realize I'm not some fuck-up when it comes to Flynn.

"We're doing an easy trail down by the falls. It's just the two of us and I'll let him set the pace," I reassure him in a less accusatory tone.

Hendrick's easy smile returns. "I remember riding there. We used to drive out in the early morning, ride for a few hours, drink, swim all day, then load up and come home after dark."

I nod. I have the same memories. Hendrick and I didn't hang out much as we got older. He had his popular football friends, and I wasn't into that scene. Wouldn't have been wanted even if I had been. But every once in a while, we'd all decide to do the same thing for a day. Archer and Brogan went a few times after Hendrick graduated, but they were more interested in drinking and swimming than riding. Flynn was too young and when he was finally old enough, I didn't want anyone to come with me. Riding was my escape. I haven't done it for fun with any of them in a long time.

"I should shower and wake up Flynn." By the time we load everything up and drive out there it'll be the perfect time when the sun is low, and the air is still crisp. I unzip my jacket and then laugh.

Hendrick eyes my bare chest with amusement. "Lose a shirt somewhere?"

"Nah," I say. I didn't lose it. I know exactly where it is.

# CHAPTER TWENTY-FOUR
*Knox*

The next night when I get to the gym, Avery smiles and waves from the balance beam.

I shuck off my shoes and walk over to her. "Hey."

She hops down close to me, putting her hands on my shoulders for balance. "Hi."

Her gaze darts to my lips like maybe she's thinking about kissing me right here. Same. It's all I've thought about since I left her dorm.

"I thought we could work on adding a twist to your backflip," she says, eyes lit up with excitement.

"I can't stay." I give her an apologetic grin. "I forgot Flynn has a basketball game tonight. I have just enough time to go home and shower before it starts."

My eyes rake over her. Today's leotard is black and all I can think about is her tight body underneath.

"You could have texted."

"I could have, but then I couldn't have done this." I drop my mouth to hers in a soft, quick kiss. It's not the kiss I've been imagining all day, but the gym is full of people.

Avery smiles as I pull back, then she looks around, takes my hand and says, "Come with me."

Her little legs move so fast, I don't have time to think about where she's taking me. At the back of the gym there's another room, more like a closet. The light is on and I have just enough time to look around at all the equipment to determine it's a storage closet before her arms drape over my shoulders and she's up on her tiptoes pressing her lips to mine.

Neither of us wastes any time. I drag her flush against me and kiss her like I've been thinking about since yesterday morning. Only I'm not fucking her while I'm doing it. This will have to do for now.

"I think I'm addicted to this mouth," I say, sucking on her bottom lip. My hands roam up and down her sides from her hips to the curve of her breasts.

The sliver of restraint I'm holding on to is the only way I'm capable of pulling back before I've stripped her out of her little spandex outfit and made her come.

She smiles happily, then giggles as her gaze drops to my chest. "Oops."

I glance down at my shirt, which is now covered in chalk. "I'm heading home to shower anyway."

I adjust my hard dick. "That's going to be harder to deal with."

"Did you just pun?" Her smile grows wider.

"I gotta go. See you tomorrow."

"All right, but I'm going to be twice as bossy to make up for you flaking tonight."

I step away with a wink. "I look forward to it."

The next day I go to The Tipsy Rose to grab lunch. Brogan is standing behind the bar, leaning against it, with a textbook in front of him. He glances up when I take a seat.

"I just put your turkey burger down on the grill."

I arch a brow in question. "Tracking my location again?"

"Don't flatter yourself. I have notifications turned on for all of you. If you get within five miles of this place, I know it."

I chuckle. "How is that different from tracking my location?"

"Do you want me to spit in your food?" he asks as he pours a water and places it in front of me.

"No lunch rush today?" I glance around. There's a couple of guys sitting at a table watching bowling on TV and one other at the bar picking around a plate of fries.

"Slow day." His phone pings and he pulls it out and stares at it so long I get bored waiting and start watching the TV behind the bar. Sports highlights. Football updates, hockey predictions, and a new coach for a college basketball team. My stomach drops when they switch to discussing motocross—specifically the Thorne team changes.

"Hey," Brogan says. "That gymnast that's helping you. What's her name again?"

I glance away from the TV and blink a few times before his question registers. "Avery."

"Avery Oliver?" He turns his phone around to show me a video of some sort. I see that Ken doll Tristan before it finally pans to a clear shot of Avery.

"What the hell is this?"

"Media day."

"Why do you have a video of it?"

"They're livestreaming it."

I continue to stare at him.

"The girls are hot. A buddy follows the team social media page and sent it to me."

"And you're just creepily gawking at it?"

He rolls his eyes. "They're doing interviews, asking questions, showing some behind-the-scenes shit."

"That's like saying you get porn magazines for the articles."

"Nobody gets porno mags anymore."

I grit my teeth. Not the point, but before I can argue with him, another customer comes into the bar.

Brogan hands me his phone like he's throwing down a silent gauntlet, daring me to peek and not enjoy myself. What an idiot. I pick it up and watch as the camera girl with a bubbly voice goes down the line and asks each person their meet day breakfast. I'm already bored, but I hold out to hear Avery's answer.

When it gets to the girl in front of her, Avery is half in frame, enough I can get a good look at her. Her hair is down instead of pulled back into a ponytail or bun like she does at practice. Her leotard is a blue shiny material. Long sleeves, but cut up high on her thighs, showing off her toned legs. She has her phone in one hand and holds it up like she's scrolling it to kill time.

The camera moves over to her and she smiles, but it doesn't make her face light up like normal and she looks nervous.

"Meet day breakfast?" The girl repeats the question.

"Oh, umm…an omelet with toast and a banana."

I'm not surprised by her answer, but it's her expression that I can't stop thinking about even as the camera moves away.

I set Brogan's phone on the bar and pull out my own.

ME

**You look nervous.**

AVERY

**Uhh…Hi. Stalk much?**

ME

**I'm at the bar grabbing lunch and my brother was watching. Apparently the gymnastics team is "hot."**

AVERY

**You disagree?**

ME

**Blue just became my new favorite color. Media day?**

AVERY

**Yep. Photos, interviews, more cheesy questions. I'll be sure to let our team manager know the views we're getting are creepy dudes checking us out.**

> **ME**
>
> I doubt she'll be surprised by that. I take it you're not a fan of photos?

I glance back up at Brogan's phone still streaming. It's panned now to show someone being photographed. She's standing in front of a white backdrop with lights all around. She does jumps and poses as flashes go off quickly.

> **AVERY**
>
> No, that part isn't so bad.

> **ME**
>
> Knowing creepy dudes (aka me and Brogan) are watching ruin it for you?

> **AVERY**
>
> lol, no. I'll be sure to stick my boobs and butt out next time I'm on camera just for you.

I chuckle to myself, but despite her joking tone I can't shake the sense that there's something about today that she's dreading.

> **ME**
>
> I appreciate that. Maybe just text me that though instead of doing it on a public video. You really will have creepy dudes hitting you up.

AVERY

**You mean others like you?**

ME

**Exactly.**

She sends a photo a second later. One shoulder pushed forward, head angled to the side and her chest pushed out dramatically. She is gorgeous even when she's mocking me.

ME

**Ah perfect. Send more. I'll see if I can sell them to my brother. #gymnasticschicksarehot**

I'm smiling at my phone, but still wondering why she doesn't like media day. I thought girls loved getting dressed up and having photos taken.

Such a sweetheart.

ME

**That's me.**

ME

**So, what's the issue with media day? Why do you look like you want to be anywhere else?**

AVERY

**I don't look like that.**

ME

**You do. It's the same look you get on your face when Ken doll speaks.**

I expect her to deny it.

AVERY

**I hate doing interviews.**

Interesting.

ME

Why?

She doesn't strike me as someone who would get nervous talking to people, especially about gymnastics.

AVERY

It's always the same questions. "How's your knee?" "Are you going to be ready to compete at the start of the season?" "Will this season be better than last?" And it's not just what they ask, but what they don't ask. Everyone wants to know if the Olympics was a fluke or if I can compete at that level all the time.

The paragraph of text surprises me. I read over it a couple of times. I didn't expect her to answer so honestly, but I read the genuine fear in her words. She wants to prove herself. I get that.

ME

Those interview questions are bullshit, so give them a bullshit answer. "My knee has never been better." "I'm ready now. I can't wait to compete." "I'm in the best shape of my life."

AVERY

Lie?

ME

Eh. A stretch of confidence.
You're manifesting that shit.

AVERY

Is that what you do in interviews?

ME

No. I usually say
dumb shit I regret.

AVERY

Like that your teammate should go back
to the amateurs?

I laugh then wince at the thought of her watching that clip. I said that seconds before I shoved Link.

ME

Now who is stalking who? I'm
flattered.

AVERY

Don't be. It was the first hit when I
searched your name.

ME

Was the second my sex tape?

She types, then the bubbles go away.

ME

Kidding.

ME

You're going to show them
what a badass you are when
you start competing again, but
for now hold your head up high
and tell them whatever you
want. Don't let them make you
doubt yourself.

AVERY

ME

Is that your way of blowing off
my advice?

AVERY

No. I'm repeating your words over and
over in my head. I am a badass.

ME

Damn straight.

She goes quiet and I keep watching the live footage. People are commenting and an idea hits me. It's Brogan's account so what do I care. I smile as I type the words and hit send.

A second later the girl behind the camera reads it out loud, stepping closer to Avery. "Brogan Six says Avery Oliver is his favorite gymnast of all time and says he can't wait to watch you dominate this season. Oh, and several people are agreeing. You're a fan favorite."

Avery flushes and looks at the camera with a confused expression. The camera girl moves on and then a text pops up on my phone.

AVERY

**Thank you for that. Or thank your brother.**

ME

**You're welcome, princess.**

When they interview her twenty minutes later and the first question is, "Is your knee ready for the season?" she looks straight at the camera, smiles so big no one else could tell it's contrived, and says, "It's never been better."

# CHAPTER TWENTY-FIVE

*Avery*

"**A**re you listening?" I ask Knox.

His gaze travels up my legs. "Huh?"

I tilt my head to the side and give him my best sassy, authoritative look. His lips pull apart into a smile. "Kidding. Yeah, I heard you. Slowly up and slowly down."

The way he says the last part, I'm certain he's talking about something completely different than me. My face heats and my stomach dips. I have spent every minute since he walked into the gym tonight imagining his hands on me again. If this is part of some elaborate game to have me desperate and needy so I'm too distracted to torture him with exercise, it's working. Today's training session has been more stolen kisses and little touches than workout.

"I am going to help Hope. You stay here and work on that." Distance. That's what we need. Otherwise, I might try to jump him in the middle of the gym.

Smiling like he knows exactly what I'm doing, he nods.

Coach Weaver has lifted all bans on my practicing. I'm now doing my full routines on beam and vault. The only catch is she downgraded the skill level on my beam dismount. I'm trying to focus on the positives, but I want to be back–fully back–in time for our first competition.

"Your boyfriend is hot," Hope says when I mount the beam next to her.

"He's not my boyfriend." The words fly out quickly without thought. "We're just…I'm not…He's…" I stop myself, but her smug teenage smile appears.

"Hot boy got your tongue?"

I stick said tongue out at her. I can act her age too. "Let's see your full turn and then we'll work on back handspring layouts."

Her smile falls into a pursed look of determination as she gets into position. At least she's easy to distract.

And I am too, as it turns out, because I focus on nothing but Hope and helping her on beam skills until Knox wanders over almost an hour later.

He sits on the floor in front of us. He's sweaty and too handsome for his own good. He smiles at me as I talk Hope through a handspring layout.

There's something about the way he smiles at me. It burns into my skin and makes me light-headed. I turn back to Hope with a flick of my ponytail. "Get your arms and chest up quickly and focus on raising your hips."

"I'm doing all that," she mutters, frustrated and whiny. She glances over at Knox like she's embarrassed he's seeing her at less than perfect.

"You're doing great. Keep practicing on the mat. It'll make it easier to land it up here. It took me forever to get it."

"Show me all of it together once more?" Her dad has just arrived, and she waves at him before adding, "Please?"

"All right." I hop down onto the mat.

"No. On the beam."

I waver. It's been forever since I've done the combination pass on the beam, but her pleading eyes get the better of me.

"Fine. One time."

I pull myself back up onto the beam next to her. A quick glance at Knox shows him eyeing me with a mix of admiration and excitement. It gives me a little boost of confidence. I've done this a million times, and my knee has been feeling stronger every day.

Without giving myself too much time to worry about getting it right in front of them, I go into the back handspring, layout step out, layout step out. I stand tall, hands over head when I end. A smile tugs at the corner of my lips and a jolt of excitement tingles through my fingertips. Damn that felt good.

When I glance at Hope, her mouth gapes wide. "Damn, Avery. I hope someday I'm half as good as you."

My face heats from the compliment. "Don't be silly. You're going to be so much better than me."

She smiles wide and jumps down with a wave to me and Knox.

When I hop to the floor, Knox stands and steps forward slowly.

"That was impressive," he says.

"You've seen me do skills before."

"Yeah, but not like that."

Another shot of confidence pushes some of those lingering doubts away. Maybe I will be ready for competition season.

"What are you doing tonight?" he asks, pulling his T-shirt over his head. My least favorite part of the workout is when he puts on clothes and leaves.

"I'm not sure, why?"

"Thought we could hang out. I need to stop by the house, but after that I'm free."

"That sounds fun. I'd love to meet your brothers."

"Oh, I, uh…" He rubs at the back of his neck and one of his brows, the one with the scar cut through it, lifts. "You would?"

"Yeah, of course. Why wouldn't I?"

"I don't know. Lots of reasons. We're kind of a lot."

"If I can handle you, I think they'll be a cakewalk."

He chuckles, that cocky smirk back on his lips. "I don't think you know what you're getting yourself into, princess."

Knox pulls into the driveway of a small white house not far from the Valley U campus. I park along the curb and hop out. There are several other vehicles. His brothers', I'm assuming.

I tug on the hem of my shorts as I walk up the drive, shove my hands into my pockets, then pull them out again. I'm nervous. Four brothers and if they're anything like Knox, this could be interesting.

Knox waits for me a step outside of the open garage. There's gym equipment taking up the entire space, except a workbench with tools on it along the back wall.

"We don't have to stay," he says. "I just need to check in with Flynn and shower. We could go to your dorm."

"Trying to keep me away?"

"You should be taking me up on it."

I laugh. "Quinn and some friends from her Spanish class are there studying, so unless you want to listen to their bad pronunciation of Spanish words, I think this is the safer option."

"Don't say I didn't warn you," he says under his breath and leads me farther into the garage.

I showered after practice and then mostly sat around while I bossed Knox and Hope around the gym, but I would have brought something nicer to change into if I'd known we were going to hang out tonight. Naked hanging out, judging by the looks he gave me during his workout. All I had were the jean shorts and shirt I wore to classes today.

As soon as he pushes through the entry door from the garage into the house, noise explodes around us. Male voices talk loudly over the sound of the TV.

I barely have time to process the layout or any other details before we step into chaos. The kitchen looks out onto the living area and the dining room off to the side. Three guys are sitting on leather couches in front of the TV, another is in the kitchen with a pretty blonde girl.

"Hey," one of the guys in the living room calls when he spots Knox, then quickly turns back to the TV. He does a double take though and glances back again. His gaze goes past Knox to me. He stares really hard and for too long. I'm certain I turn crimson at his full attention. Especially when everyone else notices, and then all eyes are on me.

"This is Avery," Knox says, hitching a thumb over his shoulder. Then he signs my name. Or I think that's what he does. I learned the alphabet in elementary school, but I'm rusty with some of the letters.

He's the only one that's managing to act cool and collected. He glances back at me. "These are my brothers. And Hollywood. I mean, Jane. She's Hendrick's fiancée."

Jane is the first one to approach me. The closer she gets, the prettier she is. She looks familiar, but I can't figure out why. And she's smiling at me with this big, disbelieving look on her face. I hope she doesn't think Knox and I are dating or something. Maybe we should have chanced the Spanish study session at my dorm.

"Hi. Avery?" she asks like maybe she's afraid she didn't hear my name right.

"Yeah. Hello." I lift one hand in a wave.

"Finally, another girl around here," she says. "Thank god."

"Do you want something to drink?" the brother in the kitchen asks. His smile matches hers.

"Umm…sure."

I panic and glance at Knox for help.

Once again, he seems totally at ease, even though they're all looking at me like this is a much bigger deal. With a roll of his eyes, he says, "Don't be weird, Hollywood. She's the girl that's been helping me at the gym."

Jane nods, eyes still wide and pinned on me. Something tells me she's not really hearing him.

"O-kay." Knox comes over and puts himself between us, then turns me by the shoulders.

His innocent touch sends a rush of heat to my skin. I remember exactly what those hands can do.

In the living room, I can immediately pick out the youngest brother. He has a baby face and messy, reddish-brown hair. His cheeks are ruddy, and he's quiet but sneaking glances at me. The other two stand.

The taller of them wears a playful smirk as he steps forward and loud whispers, "Did he force you here? Blink twice if you're under duress."

I hear Knox groan behind me, and his hands fall away from my shoulders. He edges in front of me and pushes his brother away with a playful shove. He's signing again. This time as he talks. "Thank you all for making this super uncomfortable. Now you know why I don't bring people here."

His brother snickers. "I'm Brogan, and don't worry, we won't hold it against you that you're hanging out with this asshole."

Knox shakes his head and sighs like he's annoyed, but there's an ease in his stance being here. "That's Archer, you met Hendrick in the kitchen, and this is Flynn."

"Hi," I say again, waving and moving my gaze around the room.

When Knox nudges Flynn's foot and asks about school and practice, the rest of the room goes back to ignoring us.

"Sorry about that." Jane appears next to me with two glasses of wine. "It's just, there's a lot of testosterone in this house. I got excited about another girl in the house. A peace offering, or whatever you call it when you want to apologize for coming on too strong."

I can't help but smile back at her. I take the wine just so she doesn't feel bad, but after I take a sip, I feel a little more at ease.

"Are you two staying for dinner?" she asks me.

Knox isn't listening, so I shake my head. "I'm not sure."

"We're making plenty if you do."

"Can I help with anything?" I ask.

"Oh no, we've got it. Knox used to cook for us every night but since he's started working out with you, Hendrick and I have made it our thing. It's kind of fun."

I try to picture Knox cooking, but can't.

Jane walks over to the couch where Brogan is sitting and pushes his leg. "Move over and make room for Avery to sit down."

I start to protest, but Jane doesn't look like someone who is used to being told no. Brogan moves over without a second thought, eyes glued to the TV. He and Archer are playing some sort of video game.

I sit with my wine.

Brogan leans back into the couch. His shoulder brushing against mine. He's a big guy, broader than the others. "I'm surprised we haven't run into you on campus."

"You go to Valley?" I wrap my hands around the top of the glass.

"Yep," Brogan says. "Me and Archer, and Jane."

"Really?"

He nods. "Seniors. What about you?"

"Sophomore."

Something about Jane finally snaps into place. "Wait. Jane is…"

"Ivy Greene," Brogan finishes for me with a proud smile. "Yep."

"Knox never said." Ivy Greene, or Jane Greenfield, is a Valley U icon. She was a child TV star and now she goes here. I've never seen her on campus, so I was almost convinced she wasn't real.

"Something tells me there's a lot Knox doesn't say. Unless he's a lot chattier with you than he is with us."

Brogan nudges Archer next to him and signs something. Archer nods. Knox also never mentioned one of his brothers is Deaf. He didn't mention a lot of things, I guess. Not that I expected him to spill his guts to some girl he's only known for a month, but being here I already feel like I understand him better.

Since everyone else is preoccupied, I listen in on Knox talking to his youngest brother. They're talking about colleges, I think. Knox is asking him if he's heard back from a coach in Illinois. Flynn is all shoulder shrugs and head shakes. He says very little, but Knox just keeps engaging him until finally he glances away. His gaze starts to scan the room like he doesn't know where I am, then he smiles when he sees me sitting next to Brogan with wine in my hand.

"Sorry. Didn't mean to leave you to the wolves," he says, walking over to the edge of the couch in front of me.

"We don't bite," Brogan protests. "We're like really playful wolves who just want to have a good time."

"Have a good time with someone else." Knox inclines his head and takes a step back. I feel five sets of eyes on me as I follow him out of the living room and down a hallway. He stops at the last door and pushes it open, then holds out a hand for me to enter.

"I'm gonna shower quick, but I figured you might want to hang in here instead of being subjected to my brothers fawning all over you." He rolls his eyes.

"They're nice."

"They're a pain in my ass." He grabs the frame of the door that leads into what I suspect is the bathroom and stares at me for a beat. "Be right back."

Once the shower turns on, I walk around the room, greedy to explore every detail of his room. It's a pretty good size. Big enough for the king-size bed that sits in the center of one wall. The frame is simple, dark wood. And there's a matching nightstand on one side. The top is bare except for a charging dock.

I glance toward the bathroom door and then open the top drawer. A bottle of lube rolls and hits the front of the drawer next to a box of condoms. I wince at the noise and close it quickly.

The walls are painted a light gray and the curtains are black and pulled closed. I glance back at the bed, noting his black comforter and laugh. At least he's consistent.

His dresser is the same dark wood as the bed and nightstand. It sits in front of the bed. Two drawers aren't shut all the way – sock drawer and boxers. I don't snoop in the others. On top of the dresser is a stack of folded clean clothes. I drop my nose, Knox's familiar smell of leather and lemons filling my nostrils.

A TV is mounted over the dresser and the only other item of interest is his closet. It's ajar, so I walk into it. It's mostly empty. One side has clothes hanging on it. The other is bare and on the floor is what I assume is riding gear.

I hear the shower cut off and start to leave, but two pictures taped on the inside of the door catch my eye. Neither are framed, but they're taped up where Knox must look at them sometimes. One is of what I presume to be him and a woman, his mother maybe. Knox can't be more than five or six. He has the same smile. A little cautious and reserved even when I can tell he's happy. The woman is beautiful. Light brown hair and big brown eyes. Her smile is everything Knox's isn't. Big and filled with so much happiness it practically jumps out of the photo.

The other one is of him and his brothers. They're older here. Maybe even taken recently. They're standing in front of the bar at The Tipsy Rose. Knox is standing next to Hendrick, who has one arm thrown over him and the other around Archer's shoulders. Brogan is lying on top of the bar and Flynn is sitting on a stool.

I hurry out of the closet only a few seconds before Knox reappears. Dressed but hair still damp.

"That was quick," I say and then take a sip of my forgotten wine.

"Sorry. Did I leave you enough time to snoop?"

I laugh and don't even try to pretend like I wasn't doing just that. "Yes, but sadly I didn't find anything interesting. No whips or chains, ball gags."

"You must not have looked very hard." His demeanor shifts and the way he's looking at me is a lot like he did before he took his victory kiss.

"Really? Show me."

He shakes his head slowly. "Uh-uh. Not yet. I've been dying to taste you again."

My breath hitches and the next second his mouth is covering mine. Without breaking the kiss, he takes my wine. I hear him set it on the nightstand as he walks me backward until my thighs hit the edge of the bed.

Everything happens so fast. I'm on my back and he's trailing kisses down my body. Lifting my shirt so he can reach more skin and then unbuttoning my jean shorts. I help him push them down. He swats at my hands when I try to do the same to my panties. "I want to unwrap you all myself."

My stomach flutters as he inches the pink material down slowly. He pulls off my panties and spreads my legs apart. His stare burns my skin. The kisses he places along my inner thighs and low on my stomach are gentle. His eyes flick to mine as he brings his mouth down close and licks up my folds.

"Oh God," I groan loudly.

I swear I can see him smirking as he does it again. My legs quiver and I push my hips lower, desperate for more. He swats my pussy. Not hard but I'm so keyed up that it stings and then pulses with new pleasure.

"I'm in charge in here, princess. Be a good girl and hold still."

The only reason I comply is because he doesn't make me wait. His mouth covers me again. This time he adds more pressure and alternates sucking on my clit.

"Knox. Please. More." My words are broken up with cries of ecstasy. Guys have gone down on me before, but it was never like this.

One of his fingers slides into my pussy. Then he adds a second.

He nips at my thigh and pushes my legs farther apart. I'm splayed out for him, naked from the waist down and he's fully dressed. I sit up, intending to undo his pants, but Knox doesn't let up and the new angle has all his focus on my clit.

"Look at this pretty pussy. So tight. So greedy for more." He shifts slightly and pulls me farther off the bed so he can keep thrusting his fingers in and out of me while continuing to lick and suck on my clit.

I'm putty in his hands. I come hard, my entire body locking up and then shaking as the orgasm refuses to end. My arms can't hold me up any longer and I fall back onto the bed. It's almost painful how long it goes on, but that pain melts into pleasure and I chase it, grinding down onto his face. He gives me another gentle smack and then follows it with sweet licks until my body stops writhing under him.

As soon as the tremors leave my body, I'm filled with a rush of adrenaline. I sit up quickly, and we remove his shirt, then push his jeans and boxers down. They're also black.

My eyes flick to his when his dick springs free. He's long and thick, smooth and hard. Perfect. I understand why he's such a cocky asshole.

I scoot closer and wrap my fingers around his shaft, then bring my lips to the head and kiss him gently.

"Still addicted to my mouth?"

"You have no fucking idea." He drags the pad of his thumb over my bottom lip and then pushes me down onto his long, thick cock.

His throat works as he stares down at me. He pulls my shirt up but I don't want to let go of him to take it off.

Surprisingly, he doesn't take over. He lets me work my mouth down his length, taking a little more each time.

Only when I take him to the back of my throat does he wrap a hand in my hair and urge me to increase the pace. I've always loved giving blow jobs. It makes me feel powerful and sexy, but seeing Knox with pleasure painted across his face—pleasure I put there—is euphoric. He holds on to every shred of control until the last possible second. He pulls out of my mouth and jerks himself to release, coming all over my chest and onto the bottom of my shirt.

I'm too enthralled to care and he's staring at my chest like it's the best thing he's ever seen. I've always been self-conscious about my boobs. They're a little bigger than most gymnasts' but probably small on average. But right now, I'm not insecure at all.

He pulls up his pants and tucks himself away, then disappears into the bathroom. When he returns, he has a washcloth.

"This is why I wanted to take your shirt off." He smirks as he drops the cloth on the bed and pulls my shirt over my head.

"Oops."

He cleans me up and then takes my shirt and the washcloth

back with him to the bathroom.

"I think this was your plan to keep me naked," I say.

"Stay that way if you want, princess. I'll never stop you, but it might be awkward for you to sit around the dinner table with your pussy out."

He tosses me a T-shirt from the stack of clothes on top of his dresser. It takes me a second to register his words.

"I can't go out there now." I can still hear the TV and his brothers' muffled voices. "They're going to know we were in here… you know."

"I hate to break it to you, princess, but they knew why you were here the second you walked through the door."

I try to cover my face with the shirt instead of putting it on, but Knox takes it from me and pulls it down over my head. I slip my arms through and then get up and put on my panties and shorts. I love wearing his shirts. They're big and soft.

When I stand, the hem falls past my shorts. It's one hundred percent obvious I'm wearing his shirt.

"I think I'll just stay in here."

He laughs and takes my hand. "Come on. You gotta eat."

# CHAPTER TWENTY-SIX
## *Knox*

**A**very is flushed and trying to hide behind me as we walk out for dinner. Everyone is already seated at the dining room table.

I arch a brow at Jane and the smile she gives me is all the answer I need to know this family dinner is her doing. We rarely all sit and eat at the same time. Our schedules are all different and someone is always in a rush to eat and go somewhere or do something.

In the kitchen, I grab two plates and hand Avery one. I watch her take a small portion of the ravaged chicken casserole.

I consider our seating options carefully. There are empty spots across from Brogan or next to Jane. Brogan smirks like he's dying to say something that's going to make me want to beat his ass, but Jane looks more likely to interrogate the fuck out of Avery.

Pulling out a chair, I tip my head for Avery to take it and then I sit directly in front of Brogan just in case I need to kick him under the table.

"Thank you for dinner. It smells so good." She leans closer to her plate and inhales. "I miss homemade meals. I mostly live on Jimmy John's delivery and the salad bar at the cafeteria."

"It's Knox's recipe," Jane offers. She's sitting with her elbows on the table and her fork dangling absently from her fingers. She's clearly more interested in our guest than eating.

Avery steals a glimpse at me.

"I got it off the internet," I say with a shrug.

Her lips curve like she's amused by me cooking or looking up recipes. A man can only eat so many frozen pizzas and ordering takeout every night is expensive. I'm not a chef by any stretch of the imagination, but I figured out how to make a few things with the help of Google and a lot of trial and error.

"So, Avery," Jane prompts. "How long have you been doing gymnastics?"

I hold in a sigh and shoot my future sister-in-law a glare that would intimidate most people. Unfortunately, she isn't scared of me because she knows Hendrick would castrate me if I so much as touched a hair on her head.

"Since I was three."

"Competing since she was six," I add, then pause. How the hell did I remember that?

"That's right." Avery smiles at me. "It's the only thing I've ever been any good at."

"I can think of at least one other thing," I mumble just loud enough that only she can hear me.

No one else is paying attention to me because Jane launches back into the conversation.

"I love gymnastics," she says. "I watched you during the last

Olympics. Your beam routine was so good I had chills. And you had the best hair too."

"The best hair?" I mouth at Hendrick. He shrugs, but I see him fighting to hold in a laugh.

"Thank you." Avery seems genuinely thankful for the compliment as she beams at Jane. "I love your hair color. Is it naturally that blonde?"

I lean back in my chair and watch as the two girls chatter on about hair shit. Here I thought Jane was fangirling over Avery, but it looks like it's a mutual adoration.

My brothers and I all exchange a look of amusement.

As soon as there's a break in the conversation, Brogan clears his throat. He's been quiet too long. I should have known it was about time for him to pipe up. "Ave, do you have any video of Knox doing gymnastics shit?"

"Her name is Avery," I say it slowly for him and point my fork at him. "And no. She's not giving you footage of me making an ass out of myself so you can blackmail me."

One corner of his mouth lifts. "I like Ave. I'm gonna call you that. So do you?"

"Well, that depends. What's it worth to you?" Avery asks.

My jaw falls open and I turn to her as everyone else at the table bursts into laughter.

"Oh, it's worth a lot," Brogan tells her.

When I look around, my family is staring at Avery like her willingness to go along with a blackmail scheme against me makes her more endearing. Fuckers. Even Flynn is grinning.

It's hard to keep the smile off my face. These people are everything to me and she fits in so seamlessly. It's a relief and also a surprise. I couldn't be with a girl, even if it's just hooking up, knowing my brothers didn't like her.

"Speaking of Knox," Archer says, looking at Avery. "Do you go out much? Parties? Bars?"

Avery glances between us, but she makes a point of facing Archer directly before she answers. "Not that often. Practice and school keep me pretty busy."

*"How is that related to me?"* I ask and sign to Archer.

His lips twitch and then pull into a smile. "I just wondered if she knew there was a whole bunch of way cooler guys on campus. You don't need to slum it with him." He looks back at her. "I could introduce you to some teammates."

I was prepared for Brogan to talk shit, but Archer? I make the sign for asshole where Avery can't see.

She doesn't miss a beat, clearly enjoying messing with me as much as they do. "Oh, phew. I thought this was the best Valley had to offer. What a relief."

My brothers are laughing, and Jane is admonishing them while trying to keep a straight face.

I sit forward and drop a hand to her thigh. My fingers splay out over her smooth skin and squeeze. She jolts at the contact and bites down on her lip.

Leaning my body toward hers, I brush her hair back from her neck and whisper, "Careful, princess. I might be inclined to show them just how much you like my hands on you."

My heart thuds in my chest as she pins me with her big, blue eyes.

"Promise?" she whispers back, taunting me and batting her lashes.

Damn she makes me crazy. I can't get enough.

Maybe I'm not the best guy for her long-term, but it feels too good to walk away yet.

I don't know when I decided that I wasn't interested in girlfriends or relationships. It wasn't one moment that I can pinpoint. In theory, I know people can make it work, but I guess avoiding it felt like the best way to ensure there was one less area where I might turn out like Dad. Besides, I have all the responsibility I can handle here, taking care of my brothers.

Because it's not something I've ever wanted, I haven't spent a lot of time wondering what it would be like to have someone in my life like Hendrick has Jane. But I don't have to think hard about it to know Avery is the kind of person I would want by my side if things were different.

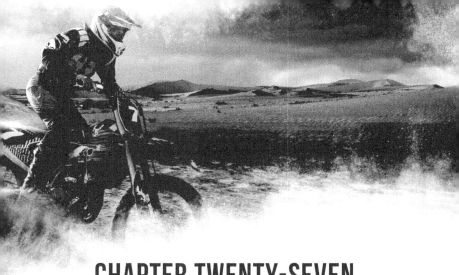

# CHAPTER TWENTY-SEVEN
## Knox

Avery is smiling as I ride over to her. She had a day off practice and came to the track after classes to watch. This old dirt track isn't much to look at. It's tucked back away from the main road where there's nothing but desert land to be seen each way you look. It's peaceful out here. All the travel during the summer, racing on tracks around the country, this one is still my favorite. It's where I learned to ride, and that makes it feel like home.

I pull my helmet off and plop down next to her on the tailgate of my truck.

"What'd you think?" I ask.

"The videos I watched made it look so easy, but in person, it's a lot scarier."

I laugh and bump my shoulder against hers. "Says the girl who flips around on a balance beam and launches herself off a vault."

"It's not that high." Her smile falls into a smirk. "You're all dirty."

I wipe my forehead with the back of my hand. "Dirt track will do that."

"It looks good on you."

I recognize the look in her eye. If I weren't covered in sweat and dirt, I'd be tempted to get her naked right here. Instead, I lean in and brush my mouth against hers, nipping at her full bottom lip and wishing I'd blown off riding today and spent the day in bed with Avery.

When I pull back, Colter is parking next to me and Brooklyn drives up next to him. It'll only be a few minutes before the rest of the group is here to start practicing.

"Hey," Colter greets us both, smiling a little bigger when he spots Avery. "I was just at your dorm."

"I know. I heard you before I left." She wrinkles up her nose.

Colter just laughs it off. "How was riding today?"

"Good." I start to get down to help him unload but Brooklyn waves me off and steps in instead.

They get both their bikes unloaded and then Brooklyn takes off to warm up.

"So, you two." Colter waggles a finger between us. "Are you like together now or what?"

Fuck. Leave it to Colter to need to define my relationships for me.

"We're just hanging out," Avery answers quickly and rolls her eyes like maybe she was having the same thought as me.

He holds his hands up defensively. "My bad."

"It usually is," I mutter just loud enough he can hear me.

"The first time Knox brings a girl around in the daylight and I'm the weird one for thinking it's more than fucking." He makes a face and then climbs onto his bike and takes off.

Joke's on him since we aren't fucking. I laugh it off, but when I glance over at Avery, she's pulled her bottom lip behind her teeth.

"Ignore him," I say. Why does everyone in my life gotta make such a big deal out of us hanging out?

"Is that true?" she asks. "You've never brought a girl around in the daylight?"

I shrug. "I don't know."

Maybe?

"Have you ever dated someone?"

Fuck. Is it hot out here?

"I guess that depends on your definition of date."

"I'll take that as a no." She's smiling and laughing though. "It's cool. I like how things are between us. I was just curious. Your brothers made it sound like you've never brought a girl home either."

"I haven't." I don't even have to think on that one. "They're nosy as fuck, and it's always been just as easy to keep girls away from all that."

She nods thoughtfully. "Makes sense. I always preferred going to my ex's place instead of him coming to mine. Quinn didn't really like him. Plus, his place was so much nicer. My bed is not big, as you know."

She laughs again and looks at me like she expects me to join in. I can't. I'm stuck on the thought of her fucking around with other guys.

Does she have a string of guys she hooks up with? She should. She's beautiful and fun. It just never occurred to me before. And it shouldn't. We're just hanging out.

"Do you two still *hang out*?" I purposely use our phrase and then hate it.

"No way."

There's a bite in her tone. I guess that'll happen when you find out your boyfriend is cheating on you. She should count herself lucky. Any guy that would cheat on Avery should have his head examined. "And the Ken doll?"

The hint of a smile twists her lips. "Don't tell me you're jealous."

"I'm not." I'm not, right?

"I told you that wasn't happening again. Tristan and I were bad together." She shudders at the thought. Me too.

She turns and hooks one leg over the top of mine after she recovers. "What about you and Brooklyn?"

The flicker of jealousy in her eyes is sexy as hell. But I don't lie to her. "We've never hooked up. She has a boyfriend."

"Really?"

I nod. "Some corporate guy. Older, I think. She doesn't bring him around."

"Huh. I thought for sure there was something between you two. At the pool party and then that night at the track you seemed close."

"Only girl I remember from either of those days is you, princess."

"Liar." But her face softens, and she wraps her arms around my neck and kisses me. "So, we're *hanging out*?"

"Mhmmm." I hold her chin and take her mouth.

"Good. I'm not ready to date anyone." Avery hops down from

the truck and stares back at me, all sass and tease. "Let alone a guy who can't even do a double nac four sixty or whatever."

I lunge for her, jumping down fast and wrapping my arms around her waist before she has time to flee. She squeals and giggles in reply.

"It's a Nac-Nac Double Backflip."

"Just like I said."

I burrow my head in the crook of her neck and bite her playfully. She wriggles around to face me and then bites me back on the chest. Her eyes are still lit up with humor.

As our laughter dies down, we don't move apart.

"I'm not hanging out with anyone else right now," she says, and the impact of those words takes a second to register. She's not hooking up with other people. Thank fuck. "And I won't as long as we're…whatever we are."

"No, me either." I brush off the weird feeling as I realize I haven't even thought about calling up another girl since Avery and I have started hanging out. Despite never having a girlfriend, I have had girls I've hooked up with exclusively before. Nothing that lasted very long, a month or two until one of us got bored. I can't imagine ever getting bored of Avery, but that doesn't mean anything. We're just good together, that's all. Besides, she's said she doesn't want anything serious either.

Her lips curve into a pleased smile. "I need to go. I promised Hope I'd stop by the gym tonight and help her."

I drop a kiss to her lips. "All right. I should get out there and perfect my double nac four sixty."

She laughs playfully. "Text me when you get back or I'll see you

Monday afternoon?"

"Yeah." Reluctantly, I loosen my grip.

Avery walks over to her Bronco, then glances back and waves before she gets in. I watch her until the dust from her tires makes it hard to see her vehicle as it turns out of the track onto the road.

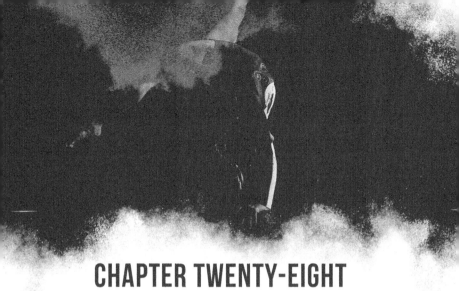

# CHAPTER TWENTY-EIGHT
*Avery*

"**I** need to go out tonight."

Quinn looks up from her laptop with a wide-eyed, confused expression on her face. "Who are you and what have you done with my best friend?"

I sit down on her bed and toss her pillow at her. "Do you have any plans or not?"

"No, but I heard the soccer team is having a pajama party."

"Really? That's perfect!" Some of the soccer team's upperclassmen live in this big off-campus house. They only throw a couple parties each year, but they're always amazing. Last semester they hosted a graffiti party where they covered the entire house in white cloth. Everyone wore clothes they could get messy and brought pens and paint to decorate everything from the ceiling to each other. People still talk about that night.

"Oh my gosh. I have so many outfit ideas." I take off toward my room to rifle through my clothing options. Technically, the sweats I have on would work but the fun in these parties is really getting into the theme.

I'm in my closet tossing out outfit options when I hear Quinn shuffle in. "Does this sudden desire to go out have something to do with Knox being out of town?"

"No," I say quickly, but the silence behind me forces me to turn and look at her. "It's not. Well, not just about that."

Her mouth pulls into a half-smile and she takes a seat on the bed, giving me her attention.

"I like him," I admit through gritted teeth.

"And?" she asks, lips pulling higher.

"Shut up. It's a problem. We're hanging out and not hooking up with other people, but we've both said we don't want a relationship so what the hell am I doing?"

"I don't know, A-babe."

Me neither. I thought about him all night and all day today. I'm totally obsessed with him. I wasn't lying to him when I said I wasn't ready to date again, but I can't help liking him. I don't know what to do, but I think I need to mix things up before I get way too attached. Keep it casual and on my terms.

"So now you know why I need to go out." It might not be the greatest plan, but it's better than sitting around waiting for him to text. "Are you in?"

"Yeah, of course," she says softly. "When have I ever turned down a party?"

Thirty minutes later Quinn and I have piled everything we're considering into a heap on my bed. Flannel pants, tank tops, slippers, sleep masks, bralettes, items that are more lingerie than pajamas, and even some face masks we vetoed immediately.

Quinn opts for a tank top and cotton shorts, and then pulls a fluffy robe on over it in case she's cold. I decide to wear a pair of black silk pants and a light pink, lacy bralette. I've definitely never slept in this outfit, but it's cute. Quinn accessorizes with the slippers, and I pull the eye mask on and wear it like a headband.

We take a dozen photos before we leave, posing and smiling at the camera to show off our outfits. I post one of me and Quinn to my Instagram before we leave and as we're walking out to my Bronco, I get a notification that Knox has liked it.

He's coming back late tonight and part of me is dying to see him, and the other part (the one trying to keep my heart from being sliced in two) thinks I shouldn't jump at every opportunity to hang out with him.

"Repeat after me. C-a-s-u-a-l," I mutter slowly to myself.

"What's that?" Quinn asks getting settled in the passenger seat.

"Nothing." I set my phone in the middle console. "Have you talked to Colter?"

"Yeah. We texted earlier. They were rain delayed the last I heard."

"Oh. So I guess it'll be later when they get back."

"I wouldn't be surprised if they stay overnight and drive back in the morning instead. Especially if it's still raining. The freeway is always a mess when it rains here."

A feeling a lot like disappointment makes my stomach twist, but that's silly because I have plans tonight anyway.

When we arrive at the party, the off-campus two-story house is already packed.

"I have died and gone to heaven," Quinn mutters as we walk through the upstairs. Some people are playing card games and others are standing around in the kitchen area taking shots.

Guys are in boxers and socks. A few have on sweatpants hung super low on their hips. Most are shirtless. And the girls are all wearing similar outfits to us, except one brave girl who is wearing a nude color, barely-there bikini. I overhear her telling someone she sleeps naked so this is as close as she could get. Clever.

Music from downstairs filters up here, but it isn't until we both have a drink in hand and start down the narrow stairway that it gets loud. I welcome it and find myself feeling like dancing and drinking more than I thought I would.

I'm with my best friend, her boyfriend and my—whatever he is—are both away for the weekend, and I just want to have fun. We sit on a couple of folding chairs set up on the opposite side of the DJ booth and dance floor where we can sort of hear each other when we talk.

I drink my first one fast, then a freshman offers me a White Claw, and I take that and drink it quick too.

"Whoa there," Quinn says.

My body feels light and I'm buzzing with happiness.

"Let's dance." I pull her in front of the DJ booth where the speakers make my insides vibrate. Nothing matters right now. Not having my routine skill level downgraded, not being left off some stupid best-of list, and not the fact Knox might be off hooking up with someone else tonight.

The thought hits me unexpectedly. Is that really what I think? He said he wasn't hooking up with other people, but this is Knox

Holland we're talking about. I don't have any reason not to trust him, but…well, I don't trust as easily as I did before Nolan.

We don't leave the dance floor until Quinn complains her scalp is getting sweaty and she doesn't want to ruin her hair.

We go back upstairs where it's cooler and quieter. Tristan is standing in the kitchen with Corey, another guy on the team. Tristan sees us before I can figure out how to avoid him.

"Hey, Ollie, Quinn." He nods to each of us as he takes a drink from his cup. He's wearing American flag briefs and I can't help but smile. It's so him. So ridiculous.

"Did you bring your gold medals too?" I ask him, avoiding giving him the satisfaction of checking him out. His body is muscular and cut, and I'm sure other girls find him attractive. I'm just not one of them anymore. His personality ruins it for me.

"No. You'll have to come back to my place for that." His gaze dips down my body.

Quinn snorts. "Smooth, Tristan."

She pulls me away and I waggle my fingers at him in a wave.

"Guess what?" she says after a fit of giggles.

"What?"

"The guys got rained out. They're almost back to Valley."

My heart rate speeds up.

"Do you want to go over to Colter's place? He said they're going to hang out there."

I pull my phone out of my bra where I stashed it while we were dancing. This outfit doesn't leave a lot of options for storage. My heart flutters seeing his name on the screen. Knox sent a text fifteen minutes ago asking what I was up to tonight. Nope, nope. No fluttering stupid heart. *Casual.*

"But we've only been here for an hour."

Her expression is clouded with confusion. "Right, but Colter and Knox...I thought you'd want to hang out with them instead."

"Did you tell Colter where we were?"

"Yeah." Her brows pull together in a cute little furrow.

I reply to Knox, reading it out loud to Quinn as I type, "At a pajama party. Heard you got rained out. You should come by if you're not busy."

I drop the location and hit send. "There. They know where to find us."

I plead to her with my eyes. I can't run to him the second he gets back into town. That is definitely the opposite of casual.

I can see the second she gives in. Her lips curve up and she puts her phone away. "Okay. Yeah. You're right. I'm hanging with my best friend. Colter can wait."

"Thank you." I take her hand and squeeze.

"Of course." She pushes her shoulders back and surveys the party. "Now, how should we celebrate our independence?"

A second later she starts singing the lyrics to Destiny's Child's "Independent Women." Smiling, I pull her back downstairs.

We get in on a game of beer pong with Tristan and Corey. Quinn is a boss at darts, but I'm the reigning beer pong champ.

"How is your aim so bad situationally?" I ask her as she misses the table entirely, hitting Tristan's red, white, and blue-covered junk instead.

"What are you talking about?" she asks innocently. "I was dead nuts."

I'm tipsy enough that I think she's hilarious.

"His cup runneth over." Corey tries to join in, but Quinn and

I are in a world of our own. Happy and giggling, and probably obnoxious to everyone around us.

Quinn and I manage to win the first game, but Tristan is too competitive to quit so we start a second game.

He and I go back and forth, neither missing and not giving our partners a chance. It's me versus him. I toss the ball straight into the cup closest to Tristan and then smile huge at him. I can't hear his groan, but I can tell he does so as he lets his head fall back and stares at the ceiling. One more cup and I am the champion. Turning to Quinn with arms stretched over my head, I find my best friend looking around the party and not even watching my awesome skills.

"Hey, you're leaving me hanging," I tell her. But then I follow her gaze.

The alcohol makes me warm and has completely removed any filter on my mouth. Luckily the music is so loud it swallows the "Holy shit!" that erupts from my lips.

Knox smirks like he heard it anyway as he saunters behind Colter across the room.

Colter is wearing a pair of sweatpants and a T-shirt. He fits in, but Knox...Knox is wearing his usual attire of black jeans and shirt. If I hadn't slept beside him, I might be tempted to believe he never removes his black uniform. With everyone else showing so much skin, he stands out as the only one not following the dress code.

Quinn hurries toward her boyfriend and jumps into his arms. He spins her around, kissing her, then sets her down and steps back to admire her outfit. "Damn, babe. You look sensational."

"Sensational," I repeat the word slowly.

Knox smirks as he closes the distance between us. "What's wrong with sensational?"

"Nothing, if you're a fifty-year-old woman." I stare at him, still in shock he's really here. "You came."

He doesn't reply, just smiles back at me.

"You aren't in pajamas," I say in case he didn't realize his mistake. Of course, he realizes. I'm definitely drunk.

"Some guy tried to stop him at the door until Knox glared at him," Colter says, aiming a smirk at his friend.

"I was hoping I wasn't going to be here long." He glances around.

"You don't have to stay." I spin back around too quickly and catch my balance by gripping the table. Tristan is watching the whole interaction, gaze pinging between me and Knox. He's holding the ball, waiting for me.

"Ready?" I ask him.

"Waiting on you, Ollie." His jaw tightens as he lets his gaze slide over to where I assume Knox is still standing.

It's hard to say why I'm disappointed Knox didn't strip down like Colter did. Or maybe it hurts that he thinks the whole idea of the party is dumb. I mean, he came when I know he didn't want to. He came to see me. Or because he wanted to hook up. But that's what we do. We hook up and work out together. We don't do themed parties and couple-y shit.

Tristan eventually tosses the ball. It hits the edge of a cup and bounces. I react too slowly, but a hand reaches in front of mine and catches it.

Knox steps up to the table, shirt removed and pants unbuttoned. He holds the ball in one hand and takes off his jeans and shoes with the other.

I bite my lip to keep my smile small as he removes everything except his black boxers. He glances over and cocks one brow like he's daring me to comment. I say nothing, but my chest tightens.

Knox takes Quinn's place, but my awesome beer pong skills are seriously hindered by the half-naked guy next to me and my aim goes to crap.

With a clenched jaw, Tristan fires another and sinks into a cup. I drink it then toss it back and miss again.

Knox catches me staring at him when I should be paying attention. He steps closer to me, his arm pressing against mine and his fingers brushing my thigh. "See something you like, princess?"

"I see lots of things I like." I move my attention away from him like I'm checking out all the guys at the party. "If you've seen one half-naked guy, you've seen them all."

"Liar." He pulls me in front of him so my back is to his chest, and wraps his arms around me.

Tristan sinks the ball in our last cup and Knox doesn't let me go as he removes the ball and downs the drink. He places it back on the table and then lets his nose drag down the side of my face. "Another game?"

"No thanks." Tristan's gaze flicks to me. His mouth is pulled tight. I don't even think he likes me that much. He just hates losing.

When he's gone, I turn in Knox's arms to look at him. My stomach flips and my pulse kicks up. What was I thinking? There's really nothing I want more than to jump Knox right now. He came here just for me. Maybe that means something. Maybe *we* could be something. "Pajama parties are really more fun with a bed, don't you think?"

His lips twist into a smirk. "Couldn't agree more."

Knox slips his shoes back on and carries the rest of his clothes as he leads me out of the party. Colter and Quinn decide to stay a bit longer, although the way they're making out on the dance floor before we've even made it up the stairs, I don't think they'll be too far behind us.

"Uber can be here in five," he says, glancing down at his phone. "I knew I should have driven instead of riding with Colter."

"My Bronco is here." I point in the direction of it parked in sight along the street.

He takes a step with me toward it and then pauses. "I don't think I can drive that thing."

"Why not?"

"It's pink."

"So?" I laugh.

He cocks his head to the side.

"Do you really want to wait five more minutes when my vehicle is right there?" I ask, hands on my hips.

He considers it, which makes me laugh.

"Come on." I take his hand and pull him quickly to it. I unlock it and climb into the passenger seat.

He gets in, looking adorably conflicted about driving my pretty vehicle. The inside is pink too—pink seats, pink dash, pink gear shift. I'm fully aware it looks like Barbie threw up inside of my Bronco. I love it.

"Only for you, princess," he says before starting it up.

I fall asleep on the ride back to my dorm and am woken when Knox opens the passenger door and tries to carry me.

"I got it," I say and stumble a few steps before he hurries to my side and helps me stay upright. Maybe I don't have it.

His laughter is the only sound in the quiet parking lot. "You are such a lightweight. You got this drunk off a few beers?"

"I'm not that drunk!" I insist, but we both know that's a lie.

In my dorm room, I fall onto my bed and stare up at the ceiling. The room is spinning.

The mattress dips with his weight and Knox holds a glass of water in front of me. "Drink this."

I sit up and take it, but I spill more of it down the front of me than I get in my mouth.

Chuckling, he takes the glass back and sets it on the nightstand then disappears. I hope he isn't leaving.

"I just need a minute and then I'll be ready to make out," I yell.

I'm met with silence. It feels like too much effort to sit up. The next thing I know, I'm being pulled back up to a sitting position. Knox smiles down at me with an expression that seems almost tender.

"Hands up."

I do as I'm told even before I realize what he wants. Knox pulls my bralette up. My skin tingles at the contact. Even in my drunken haze my body comes alive under his touch.

"Is everything you own pink?" He holds up the offending bra.

"You're one to talk, mister all black and sexy."

One side of his mouth lifts. He brings a T-shirt down over my head, covering my breasts.

"Why are you dressing me?" I ask. "Aren't we gonna…" I waggle my brows.

"Not tonight." He hits the light and then climbs into bed next to me.

Instinctively, I turn on my side and curl into him. "Thank you for coming to the party tonight. I'm sorry I drank too much."

"Happens to the best of us." He runs a hand down my hair and pulls me farther onto him so my head is resting over his heart. The steady thump is soothing.

I like him so much it actually hurts a little. "I missed you."

A beat passes, and then he says, "I missed you too."

I bury my smile into his chest and wrap my arm around his middle. "Hey, Knox?"

"Yeah?"

"You're cuddling."

# CHAPTER TWENTY-NINE
*Knox*

"That was the best one I've seen you land yet." Colter holds his fist out for a bump as I come to a stop on my bike next to him. He's grinning like Colter often does. "You're doing it, man. Another month and you'll be ready to do the entire show with us. We just need to get your timing down on the group runs."

It feels good. I like these guys, and while I was worried about switching gears to do freestyle and how it might impact my racing, it's only improved it. I'm in more control of myself and the bike. It makes the fact that I haven't heard from Mike sting a little less.

I thought someone would have called by now. If not Mike, another team. I'm eager to show everyone how I've improved, and how ready I am for the season.

"Are you heading out to train with Avery?" he asks as he stands from his seat, still holding on to the handles.

"No. She has a team dinner tonight."

He grins at me. "Seeing her after?"

"Don't be a nosy asshole. I've got enough of those at home."

He chuckles. "I like you two together."

I shoot him an amused glance. "Who are you and what have you done with my friend Colter? Once upon a time, you were the guy who was hooking up with multiple girls a night. You made me look like an altar boy."

He smiles through a grimace. "I know. I was a total player before Quinn. I've changed though."

"She seems cool, if not slightly unhinged, and I'm happy for you. But changed? Come on, really? You're saying the next time you're single you won't plow through girls to make up for lost time?"

"I'm dead serious." His tone is genuine through his light laughter. "I'm pretty sure she's the real deal. The one. All that."

I bark out a laugh, but his expression doesn't change.

"You're serious?"

"Yeah. I'm trying to save up enough for my own place so I can ask her to move in with me."

"Shit. I had no idea."

He shrugs it off. "I thought maybe…"

"What?"

"Maybe you and Avery were heading down a similar path. I've seen how you look at her and you didn't so much as glance at another chick this weekend. You like her."

I start to shake my head and tell him that while I do like Avery, it isn't serious, but something catches my attention. Or rather someone. I don't know if it's his stance, hands shoved in his pockets and one foot angled out, or the familiar beat-up, black ball cap that he's been wearing for ten years, but I know it's him in an instant.

"What the fuck?"

Colter follows my gaze. "Is that your old man?"

"He's not my anything."

I ride my bike over to my truck where he's standing. I don't look at him as I ask, "What are you doing here?"

"I heard you were doing freestyle, but I didn't believe it." There's contempt in his voice.

One sentence out of his mouth and I'm already clenching my hands into fists.

"You're not really thinking of giving up racing for this, are you?" He waves a dismissive hand toward the track where Colter is flying off a ramp. "You're better than this. I know you got dropped by Thorne, but you don't need them. You can win on your own."

"Save me the loving parent act and tell me why you're here, *Dad*?" I say the last word with all the disdain I feel. I don't call him that because he's acted like one, but to remind him he hasn't.

"I wanted to see you and your brothers. Knew I'd have to go through you first."

I look up at him, gauging his seriousness. The hair at his temples has more gray in it than the last time I saw him, and the lines around his mouth are deeper. Otherwise, he hasn't changed one bit. Out of all my brothers, I look the most like him. "Absolutely not."

His face goes red, but he manages to keep his temper in check, so his words only come out slightly strained. "Hendrick is home and engaged from what I hear, Flynn's about to graduate, Arch is doing amazing things with football. I know I've made mistakes and wasn't there when you all needed me."

"We never needed you. Mom was the real parent." God, the

number of times I wished he'd show up for me. Missed races, birthdays, and holidays. I learned how not to need him at an early age, but it took a lot longer to stop wanting him to be there. I can still remember the first time I took first place at a race. I was so excited to tell him, but by the time he came around, two months later, it seemed so stupid.

"You're right." His mouth pulls into a sad smile. "But I'm here now. Doesn't that count for something?"

"Not to me."

"But maybe to your brothers. Does Flynn even know that I've tried to see him over the years?"

Anger vibrates and prickles my skin. This isn't the first time he's shown up claiming he's different and wants to see everyone. Luckily, I've been able to intercept.

"No, because I'm not going to let you fuck with his head. You can't pop in whenever you want and pretend like you give a shit, then disappear on him. I'm not going to let you do that. Not now. Not ever."

Flynn doesn't remember him being around. It wasn't something he had to grieve and I'm thankful for that. Losing one parent was hard enough on him.

"I'm only asking to see him. He should get a say in whether or not he wants to talk to me." He tucks a piece of paper under the windshield wiper. "My number. At least think about sharing it with your brothers."

I load up my bike so fast, eager to get away from him. I throw open the door of my truck. "Stay away from all of us."

My anger has turned to a simmering boil that won't let me sit still. I pace the living room as I tell Hendrick and Archer about Dad showing up at the track. Brogan's here too. Flynn's still at practice. I came straight home so I could talk to them without him around.

*"I was afraid this was going to happen,"* Hendrick says and signs. We don't always sign entire conversations, but any time it's this important, we all do.

*"It's been more than a year since the last time he reached out to me. I was hoping he finally got the hint that we don't want him around."* I work my jaw back and forth.

*"What'd he say?"* Hendrick asks.

*"Same shit. He apologized and said he wanted to see everyone."*

*"Has he tried to contact you directly?"* Hendrick asks Archer.

Arch follows along, nodding. *"Just the one time, and Flynn's never said anything about Dad reaching out to him."*

It's quiet except for the low volume of the TV in the background. They're talking motocross, but I don't even care right now.

*"We can't continue keeping him in the dark,"* Hendrick says.

The words feel like a slap. *"Why the hell not?"*

*"He's old enough to decide for himself if he wants a relationship with Dad."*

I'm so stunned I can't even speak. Hendrick hates Dad as much as I do, I'm sure of that.

*"I hate to say it, but I agree with him."* Brogan is the next to speak. "I'm not sure if I get a say, but I can tell you if it were my dad trying to contact me, I'd at least want to know."

I look to Arch for backup. He's always reasonable.

*"Maybe they have a point."* He doesn't look happy about it, but it's clear whose side he's on.

*"Are you all serious right now?"* I glance between them. *"You've all lost your minds. There's no fucking way I'm letting him back into our lives."*

*"Flynn doesn't remember all the shit we do,"* Hendrick says.

*"Exactly. He's the only one Dad didn't fuck up, and I'm not about to let him get his chance now."*

# CHAPTER THIRTY
*Avery*

I'm about to climb into bed and watch some TV when Quinn yells my name from the living area of our dorm room.

"Yeah?" I call back.

She doesn't answer, but then there are more voices. Did she invite people over? I walk over to the door and open it. Knox smiles and waves from where he stands in the entryway of our suite.

I had to cancel our practice tonight for a team dinner and I'm so excited to see him that it takes me another few seconds to realize something is off about him. He doesn't look upset exactly, just not quite himself.

He takes a step forward, lethal like a panther. Quinn shoots me a smile as I step back to let him into my room and close the door.

"Sorry to show up unannounced," he says, glancing around my room. It's a mess.

"No, it's fine." I clear the laptop and notebook from my bed and place them on my desk, then turn around to face him.

He's smiling, but his eyes are so dark, and he's tense in a way that I don't understand but it has me almost nervous with anticipation.

"Good." He stalks forward and lifts me into his arms. His mouth covers mine, hard and demanding.

I melt into him and wrap my arms and legs around him.

"Miss me?" I smile into the kiss.

His answer is to suck on my bottom lip. He backs me up against the wall. I can feel him already hard underneath me. My pulse skitters as his mouth leaves mine and trails down my neck. One of his hands slips beneath the hem of my shirt.

He groans when he realizes I don't have on a bra. His large, calloused palm cups my breast and then squeezes. He ducks down to drop wet, open-mouthed kisses onto my neck. His teeth graze my nipple, then he flicks his tongue over it.

My head falls back. "I missed your mouth."

"Yeah?" He pulls away and looks up at me, all cocky and smug.

I nod, heart racing with the throb between my legs.

"I missed yours too." With his thumb he drags my bottom lip down and lets it go. "This fucking mouth will be the death of me."

He takes me over to the bed and drops me on top. My shorts and panties are gone in a flash and then his mouth is covering my pussy.

He's learned my body well in the short time we've been hooking up. I'm so close to getting off and he's still fully dressed.

I sit up and manage to get his shirt off.

"You're still wearing too many clothes," I protest. He grins and helps me shove his jeans and boxers down. He stands long enough to take them off, then climbs back on top of me. His body is insane.

Tattoos and muscles and the nipple piercing. None of it turns me on as much as the look in his eyes though.

I reach for him, pulling him high enough so I can kiss him. I could kiss him for hours and never get tired of it. My hips rise instinctively, desperate to be closer. The head of his dick nudges at my entrance and slips in just the smallest amount. I let out a gasp. It feels so good and it's literally just the tip.

"Fuck, sorry." Knox shifts immediately.

I almost want to tell him that it's fine and we should just have sex already, but I lose my nerve. I trust him, but I know it will make it that much harder when things between us end.

"Wait." I push him over onto his back and climb on top of him. I want him and I love the way his jaw flexes as my pussy glides over his length.

I grind over him slowly a few more times. He swallows hard and a vein in his neck pulses. I can tell how hard he's working to hold back and it pushes me to continue.

"Gonna come if you keep that up," he says, voice gravelly.

"Me too." I grind over him harder.

"Ah, fuck."

My body trembles and my arms feel like Jell-O as I hold myself up. Right before I'm about to collapse onto his chest, he takes over. With his hands on my hips, he moves me over him. I come apart, moaning his name loudly as I bury my head into him.

His release is quieter, but the grip on me is relentless as he shudders and spurts onto my stomach. Neither of us speaks as we catch our breath.

I grab my shorts and clean myself up, then find him a towel. He pulls on his boxers and jeans and I get into my favorite pair of sweats. Then we fall back onto the bed.

Knox leans against the headboard. He still has a strange expression on his face, and I know there's more to why he showed up here tonight than just a hookup. The mask he wears, closely guarding his emotions, makes him look less like the cocky guy I'm falling for and more like the jerk I thought he was when I first met him.

"How was your day?" I ask, snuggling up to his side. It hadn't occurred to me until right this second that maybe this was goodbye. My heart races and panic slowly creeps in.

"Long. How was yours?"

I swallow down the lump in my throat. "Good. Sorry I had to cancel on our training."

"It's fine. I ended up needing to deal with something anyway."

"Is everything okay?" I can't go another minute without knowing. I don't think he's cold enough to come over, hook up, and then say peace out forever, but it does cross my mind.

At first, I think he's going to wave off the question or dodge it, but he quietly mulls over his answer and then says, "My dad showed up at the track today."

"Oh." My relief is second to my surprise and I struggle to figure out what to say next.

"Yeah." He laughs bitterly.

"Does he come around a lot?"

"No." A muscle in his cheek flexes. "He was never really in the picture. My parents separated when we were little, and he came and went as he pleased. Then my mom died when I was in junior high. Cancer."

"You've been taking care of Flynn since you were in junior

high?"

He shakes his head then says, "Well, kind of. Right after she died, there was a long stretch where he stuck around. A year or so. He drove a truck so even then there were times we had to fend for ourselves while he was on the road. As time went on, he showed up less."

"And no one else knew you guys were on your own?"

"He popped in every couple of weeks. Often enough that no one really asked any questions, and we weren't about to say anything. None of us wanted to be split up or end up in the system."

My stomach clenches. My parents wouldn't even let me stay home alone until I was almost thirteen. I had thought it was dumb and I griped about not needing a babysitter. So no, I can't imagine.

He couldn't have been more than seventeen years old with only his older brother to look out for him, and three younger ones to worry about too. A fierce protectiveness surges through me, which is ridiculous because Knox doesn't need me. He's constructed his life so he doesn't need anyone.

"We managed," Knox says as if he can read my thoughts. "Then Hendrick got a full-ride scholarship for football. I don't think he wanted to leave us, but he wanted to get away from it too, you know?"

I don't know. I can't even wrap my head around it, but I nod.

"That's when our dad's absences got longer and longer until he just stopped coming around at all."

"How did you survive?"

"I dropped out of school and got a job. Arch pitched in, Brogan too. He's not even related by blood, but he did whatever he could to help us."

"Brogan isn't your real brother?" I ask.

"He's a brother, for sure, but no, not by blood." He brings his hand up to cover mine resting on his chest and runs his thumb over the top of my knuckles. "He and Archer have been best friends for as long as I can remember. Brogan didn't have the best home life. I mean, not that our house wasn't dysfunctional, but we had each other and we had Mom. He was an only child with two parents who didn't give a shit. Our mom took him in, always let him stay over, got him presents at Christmas and on his birthday just like he was one of us."

I wrap an arm around him and squeeze as hard as I can. "She sounds like an amazing woman."

"Yeah, she was cool." He lets his head fall over to rest on mine. "I can remember her watching the Olympics when they were on. She loved women's gymnastics. She'd be super impressed by you."

"What did she do?" I ask, wanting to know more about the mom that he obviously loved very much.

"She owned The Tipsy Rose. Well, it was called Rosie's Place then."

"Really?" I smile. "I wondered about the name."

"It's a nod to Mom." He confirms my suspicion as I let my gaze fall over his left arm. It explains his tattoos too. Roses—so many of them.

I sit up and look him in the eye.

"I'm really impressed by you too," he says and my heart flutters. He's complimented me before, but this feels more important. I want to hear him explain all the ways he finds me impressive someday, but not right now.

"I'm impressed by you too. It's a really noble thing you did, taking care of your brothers. Still taking care of them."

He shrugs it off. So very Knox.

"Was racing always what you wanted to do?" I ask him.

"Yeah. I stopped for a few years with everything going on. I didn't have the money or the time to be traveling to races. I thought I was done for good. I'd made my peace with it, but then Hendrick moved back home, and he encouraged me to get into it again. Told me I'd always regret it if I didn't give it a shot." He smiles in a way that makes me realize how everything they've gone through has created this tight-knit bond between them.

And it's forged him into this amazing man who would give up everything for the people he loves. It's seriously sexy.

I want to ask him more. Specifically, about his dad and what showing up at the track means, but Knox brushes his lips over mine and smiles, and I don't want to drag him back to a place that I know is touchy.

"What are you doing Sunday?" he asks.

"I have no idea. Why?"

His smile turns into a smirk. "I want to take you somewhere."

"Okay." I don't even need to know where. I want to be pretty much any place he is. I'm absolutely addicted to kissing him, but I'm also falling for him a little more with every new tidbit I learn.

# CHAPTER THIRTY-ONE
## Knox

**W**hen Avery pulls up to the house on Sunday, I'm loading the bikes into the back of my truck.

She gets out looking a little bleary-eyed and tired, but gorgeous as always. White tank top, jeans, and she's got a black beanie pulled down over her ears.

"I know you don't really like coffee, but I didn't want to show up empty-handed," she says as she steps forward and holds one out to me.

"Thanks." I take it and drop a kiss on her lips.

She looks over the bikes in the back. "What time did you get back last night?"

"Not too late." It was just after midnight when I got home from the freestyle event in California, so I am technically tired but I'm too excited about today to need caffeine to function.

"Do you want help unloading? I don't know what I'm doing, but

I can lift heavy things."

I shake my head and smile at her assumption. "You can help unload when we get where we're going."

"Wait." Her lips pull into a wide smile. "We're riding?"

"Yep." I finish strapping down the second bike.

Her smile falls into hesitation. "I don't know how to ride."

"Good thing I do."

She tells me about her weekend while I drive and then we fall into a comfortable silence. It's a nice feeling being with Avery. She's as happy staring out the window and taking in the scenery as I am. And I think it's because she doesn't need or expect things from me in the way so many other people do in my life that I find myself wanting to know things about her.

"What part of Texas are you from?"

The window is down, letting in the cool morning air, and it whips her hair around her face. She tucks a strand back as she answers, "A small town just outside of Houston."

"Do you miss it?"

"I miss my family, but other than that, not really. I feel bad, though. My brother sat through so many practices and meets for me and I don't get to do the same for him."

"Music, right?"

She beams at me. "That's right. He started out playing piano, then guitar, and the last time I talked to him he was begging our parents for a drum set. My dad will make him ask for at least two months to make sure he really wants it, but they'll give in eventually. They've always been really supportive of our hobbies."

An ache fills my chest. What would it have been like to have that kind of family growing up? It's not a line of thought I allow myself to go down very often. I had Mom and she did everything she could. Wishing things had been different feels like saying she wasn't enough. And she was. She was everything.

When we get to the trail and I start unloading the bikes, Avery's excitement morphs into a timid, almost fearful nervousness.

"This one is yours," I say as I pat the black and pink dirt bike. "In case that wasn't obvious."

Some of that fear abates as she looks it over. "This is one of your bikes? I can't believe Knox Holland owns something with pink on it."

"I don't. *You* do."

She turns to face me, brows furrowing.

"I bought it for you," I say, then shift uncomfortably because she looks stunned.

"You bought me a bike?"

"It's not new or anything. I got it off Brooklyn and switched out some of the—"

She cuts me off with a kiss and I don't finish what I was going to say, or even remember it. Avery's mouth is heaven.

"This is the nicest gift anyone has ever given me," she says when she pulls back. "I absolutely love it, but I can't accept this."

"You have to. It's a gift. And it wasn't that much. I had most of the tools and parts on hand."

She still looks hesitant to accept it.

"Wait until you see the rest of your gear." I wink.

From the back seat I get all the clothes and gear. Pink and black, of course.

"Knox. Seriously, this is too much."

"Nah, it's just enough."

I help her into the jacket. It's black with just a touch of pink on the zipper. The pants match. The helmet is one of mine, but the goggles are all pink and so are the gloves.

"Do you like it? You probably won't need the jacket once the sun comes up, but it's cold riding in the morning."

"I am never going to wear anything else," she says as she pulls the pants up. They're too big so she just wears her jeans, but everything else is perfect.

While she finishes getting ready, I grab my own gear.

That look of trepidation is back on her face when it's time to go. But she looks so sexy in her black boots, jeans, riding jacket, helmet and goggles that it's hard to concentrate on anything else.

"Good thing you have so many layers on right now." I lean down and kiss the tip of her nose through her helmet before I put mine on.

"I look okay?"

"No. You look fucking hot."

I sit on her bike to show her everything. She watches so keenly that I get a little thrill.

"Okay." I scoot back and pat the seat. "Sit down and let's go through it again."

She does, placing her ass in my crotch, her blonde hair is tickling my face as the wind blows it around. I hold it back with one hand and lean over one shoulder. I can't resist kissing her neck. I've never ridden double on a dirt bike. They're really not meant for it, but I have the sudden urge to leave my bike here and let her ride me around.

I quiz her and do my best to pay attention to make sure she gets it right, but I am distracted.

"I think you got it. We'll ride around here until you feel

comfortable to hit the trail."

She stands to get off the bike. The movement puts her ass right in my face and my hands move to it without thought.

She laughs and sticks it out farther. I swat one perky cheek. I'm going to be hard all day with her looking like she does in her riding gear.

And I'm not mad about it one bit.

# CHAPTER THIRTY-TWO
*Avery*

K nox gives me a basic rundown of the bike, all the controls and how to sit, which wasn't as obvious as I assumed. It takes a little bit for me to get it all memorized. He rides next to me as I walk the bike, focusing only on letting the clutch out, then moving my feet to the pegs as I accelerate a short distance and practicing with the foot brake.

After that, we ride side by side on a flat, open area. He lets me set the pace, but I find myself wanting to impress him more than ever, so I focus hard.

I'm not sure how long passes with him riding beside me while I get comfortable with the bike, but when I finally dare to glance over at him while riding, he's got a pleased smile on his face. "You're doing good. Follow me?"

I nod rapidly and my heartbeat picks up as he speeds up and takes the lead. He checks back frequently, only staying a little bit in front of me, but it's hard to appreciate the view while I try not to fall off the bike. Too bad. Knox is in his element on two wheels. Every movement is practiced and skilled, and I love that he brought me here to experience it with him.

He stops at the end of a trail. Beyond it is a gravel road in one direction and desert brush in the other. "We'll head back the same way. About halfway there's a turnoff. The trail is narrower and pretty bumpy in spots, but we'll take it slow. If you have any problems at all, stop or pull over and wait for me to come back. I won't lose you."

He waits for my approval.

"Okay," I say and smile, not that he can see it behind my helmet.

I can feel him smiling back though as he stands on the pedals and takes off.

"Show-off," I mutter.

Just as Knox had warned me, the trail is narrower and bumpier than the road I practiced on, but it isn't too bad until we start to get into turns that require me to continually brake and accelerate. Knox is patient and attentive, constantly checking back on me. We're going downhill and the air gets cooler the farther we go.

I breathe a sigh of relief when the path opens up and we can ride side by side again. I glance over at Knox and he motions with his head for me to look in front of us.

My next breath gets caught in my throat. The road looks out over a bluff of the mountain and there's a waterfall. Knox rides a little closer to the cliff and then stops. I pull up beside him and lift my goggles.

"Pretty cool, right?"

"It's stunning. I had no idea it was here."

"Most people don't. It's far enough away from the university that it's mostly serious hikers or riders and locals that venture out here. It's even prettier in the summer after monsoon season."

I stare at the beautiful view in front of me a few seconds longer and then look at him. "Thank you for bringing me out here."

"You're welcome." He dips his head toward my ride. "How's the bike?"

"Still in one piece," I joke.

"You're a natural."

"Not really, but it's fun to ride even if I can't go fast or do any fun tricks like you."

He revs his bike as if making my point. If I tried that, I'd probably accidentally let off the brake and drive myself off the cliff. "Fun tricks that I can only do because of you."

That is a bald-faced lie. He would have found another way. There's nothing Knox can't do. He's too stubborn.

"I'm serious," he says. "I owe a lot to you."

"You can repay me in shirtless handstands."

"Done." He winks and then leans in like he's going to kiss me but has to settle for tapping his helmet against mine.

He turns off his bike and parks it, and then motions for me to do the same. We take off our helmets and goggles and leave everything. Knox holds my hand tightly as he goes first down the steep incline of a well-trodden path toward the bottom of the mountain. The waterfall ends in a pool that's surrounded by large rocks that are hard to navigate.

Stepping up onto one of the larger boulders, he turns and takes both of my hands to pull me up next to him. Then he sits and kicks his feet out in front of him.

"This is breathtaking." I drop down beside him, mirroring his body language.

"One of my favorite places in Valley." He stares out toward the waterfall.

"Knox Holland likes waterfalls. Who would have guessed?"

"Waterfalls are awesome." His face is dirty and his hair is messy, and he's this sexy mix of playful and sweet and badass biker.

"What are the others?" I ask as I run a hand over my hair. I just realized I probably look as windblown and dirty as he does.

"Other what?"

"Favorite places."

"Oh." He leans back and lets his head drop to the side to look at me. "The practice track, The Tipsy Rose...I guess my other favorite spots around Valley aren't that exciting."

"What about outside of Valley? I know you traveled a lot for racing."

"All the tracks start to look the same. I don't really care where I am as long as I have my bike."

I place one hand behind me and lean back. The very tips of our fingers touch. "I have a favorite beam."

He lifts one dark brow in question.

"At my old club gym back home. It was perfect. The position in the gym, the feel of it. I used to lie on it just to think or visualize my routines."

"I kind of figured they were all the same."

I gasp, feigning outrage. "Are all bikes the same?"

"Point made." He scoots forward and then jumps down from the big rock we're sitting on and out of view.

"Are you crazy?" I yelp, carefully inching to the edge to make sure he didn't die. He's standing below in water that comes to his ankles, grinning up.

"Probably," is his answer. He cups his hands and drops them into the water. The freezing water. I know it's cold because after running some over his face and hair, he starts splashing me.

I squeal and move farther back.

He looks entirely too pleased with himself when I dare to peek over the side again. Knox offers me a hand.

"Are you going to splash me?" I ask before accepting it.

"Yes. But you can retaliate down here."

His fingers are ice cold as I slip my palm into his. When my feet are dangling over the edge, he brings his other hand up to my waist and pulls me down the four-foot drop into the water.

I immediately kick my foot and splash him. We do that back and forth a few times, laughing and squealing as we douse each other in the frigid water until Knox wraps an arm around my waist and tugs me against his hard chest. His mouth is warm when it covers mine. I forget all about the cold and everything else but him. We could be standing in lava and I'd probably still happily burn if it meant I could kiss Knox a second longer. There's something about him. I can't get enough of him.

"Ready to head back?" he asks when we finally break apart.

"I guess so." I like being out here, away from everything with just him. I don't want it to end.

He smiles like maybe he knows exactly how I'm feeling.

We trek back up to the bikes. This time when I sit on mine, it feels more natural. And when we ascend up the hill, I'm able to keep up with Knox without him slowing down too much.

It felt like we went so much farther than we did and we're back at the truck before I'm ready to go.

He puts my bike up first and straps it down.

"Today was really fun," I tell him as I take off the jacket. It's much warmer away from the water and out of the shade.

"Then why do you look so bummed?" he asks as he turns to get his bike.

"Because it's over."

His head tips back with a laugh.

"Will you bring me back sometime?"

"Any time you want." Instead of putting his bike in the back of his truck, he gets on it and starts it up.

"Jump on the back," he says while pulling on his helmet and then handing me mine.

My hesitation is short-lived, and I get on without questioning him. He looks me over in my jeans, tank top, and helmet and smiles. "Hold on tight, princess."

Knox takes off, accelerating quickly while I hug him around the middle. He sticks to the flatter, wider trail but it's exhilarating holding on to him while he maneuvers the bike expertly.

My face hurts from smiling so hard. Then he stops and places his feet on the ground. With one muscular arm, he circles my waist and pulls me around in front of him so I'm facing him but still straddling the bike (and now him).

If our helmets weren't on, I'd kiss the crap out of him. The way his eyes bore into mine I think he's on the same page. He revs the engine and I instinctively wrap myself around him so I don't fall off. Knox drives that way, with me staring behind us, chest pressed to his. My heart soars and I feel so light and free, but somehow safe too.

He picks up speed and then goes up into a wheelie that makes me squeal. I'm certain I can feel the rumble of his chest against mine as he laughs at me.

When Knox and I get back to his house the various vehicles that are usually parked outside are gone. Everything is quiet, at least from the driveway. The silence is a stark contrast to how loud and boisterous it was the last time I was here.

"Where is everyone?" I ask, holding my new riding jacket against my stomach.

"Flynn had practice, Hendrick's probably at the bar, and I'm not sure where Arch and Brogan are." He runs a hand through his hair. "A rare moment of peace and quiet around here."

He comes around the truck and wipes his thumb across my cheek. I follow the movement and blush.

"I'm a mess." I'm covered in dirt. My jeans got the worst of it, but I got a look at myself in the mirror in his truck and know my face and hair didn't go unscathed. "I should go back to my dorm and shower."

"You can shower here."

"I didn't bring any other clothes with me."

"Take whatever you want of mine. T-shirts are in the top drawer. Shorts and sweats are in the bottom right. Though you probably remember that from your snooping."

"Hmm…" I bring a hand up to my chin and peer up like I'm deep in thought. "What will I pick? The black T-shirt or the other black T-shirt."

He smiles, amused but not the least bit riled by my teasing. He kisses me and then steps back. "You can have the shower first. I'm going to unload the bikes."

I start for the door. "I don't think your undies are going to fit."

He doesn't miss a beat. "Guess you'll have to go without."

The house is almost eerily quiet. The evidence of the five brothers that live here is everywhere though. Empty protein shakers on the kitchen counter and miscellaneous sporting goods. And shoes—so many different pairs of sneakers.

In Knox's room, I find a clean T-shirt and a pair of sweats, then take them to the attached bathroom.

When I glance in the mirror over the vanity, my reflection makes me laugh. The ends of my ponytail are no longer blonde, but brown. And there are streaks on my face around my eyes and on my neck.

Peeling my jeans off is a challenge. The dirt has made them stiff and they stick like glue against my skin.

I fold and set them on the top of the vanity and then just stand there staring at myself, my thoughts pinging around like a pinball machine.

Today was the best day I can remember in…forever. Riding dirt bikes was fun, but that wasn't even the best part.

Knox.

Unexpectedly sweet, loyal, beyond stubborn, and the most selfless person I've ever met. He bought me a bike. A *pink* bike. Even if it wasn't expensive and he had the parts…he did it because he wanted to make me happy. I don't think anyone has ever bought me a more meaningful gift.

Nerves flutter in my stomach as I quickly wash my face and neck. I grab what I need from the nightstand and then head back out to the garage.

Knox has taken off his T-shirt. My bike is already in the garage and he's standing in the back of the truck to remove the tie-downs on his. His riding pants hang off his hips and the muscles in his back ripple as he works.

He glances over his shoulder as my steps draw closer. Those hazel eyes spark as he looks me over in my white tank top and black panties.

"Remember that time we went to the track and I watched you race?"

"Yeah." He abandons his bike and hops down from the truck.

I walk over to where his motorcycle is parked along one side of the garage and run a hand over the seat. "I said, 'you can have whatever you want.'"

I don't look at him, but I can feel his heated stare on me. "And you said something like, 'That's a dangerous thing to say. I'd—'"

"Have you bent over my bike so fast you wouldn't know which way was up," he finishes.

Turning, I lean back against the cool leather and hold up the condom I stole from his nightstand. "Is that still what you want?"

My heart beats so fast as he moves toward me at a much slower, controlled pace. Only the hungry look in his eyes gives him away.

When he finally reaches me, Knox plucks the condom from my fingers and slides it into his pocket. "I think we've already established that I don't need a condom to fuck you stupid."

One of his hands grips my hip, and his mouth takes mine swiftly, nipping at my bottom lip in a way that makes butterflies swarm in my stomach. Everything I'm feeling is so big, so hard to quantify, but I put it into my kisses and into the way I clutch at him, trying to get impossibly closer. I want more. More, more, more.

He turns me so I'm facing away from him and then he pushes me down until my stomach rests against the seat and my ass is up in the air.

All my reasons for not sleeping with him have become sort of beside the point. After Nolan cheated on me, I didn't want to trust anyone. I was scared and wanted to safeguard my heart. I thought it was my fault. Not that he cheated, but that I didn't really get to know him or his character.

Maybe I didn't or maybe I only saw what I wanted to, but Knox has never tried to hide who he is. He's always been honest with me, even when I haven't liked the answer.

I trust him. He won me over one day at a time, showing me the good and the bad.

His fingers graze softly down my spine and then his mouth drops to my shoulder. The groan that escapes him rumbles over my sensitive skin. His lips move to my neck. Kissing, sucking, and then nipping until I'm panting and pushing my ass against him.

I can feel how hard he is through his riding pants.

"I want you." The words are breathy and quiet.

He hooks a finger under the band of my panties and slides them down my legs, crouching behind me to slip them off. I have a sudden rush of nerves. His truck is blocking us from view of the road, but if his brothers came home or anyone walked up, they'd see me naked from the waist down and ass up in the air.

I stop caring the second Knox pushes my legs apart and groans.

"You are fucking perfect." His lips graze the side of my ass and then he hitches one of my legs up over his shoulder. The new position has anticipation building in my core. Long, calloused fingers glide over my clit and pussy, then back, slow and teasing.

"I'm gonna make you come, princess. Don't worry. Been thinking about this pussy all day."

My body flushes and I moan as he dips a finger inside of me.

"Knox…" I start and then gasp as he shoves two more fingers in, stretching me. Pleasure rocks through me. It's hard to think or form words.

When his mouth covers me, I stop trying to speak and let the sensations roll over me. He keeps up the rhythm with his fingers and alternates sucking and nipping. I grind into his face, unabashedly chasing the orgasm. But today it isn't enough.

"I want you," I rasp. "All of you. Fuck me stupid."

He pauses, and I arch up and glance back at him.

"Are you sure?"

"I'm positive."

He doesn't move and I wonder if maybe I made him wait so long that he doesn't want to anymore, so I add, "If that's still what you want."

His brows lift almost comically. "Princess, I've been dreaming of fucking you since the first time I saw you in that frilly pink dress and white shoes."

"Really?"

He looks me straight in the eye and there's no hint of teasing or bluffing when he says, "Really, Avery. That day and every day since."

My stomach swoops at his admission. One second I'm half-bent over the motorcycle and the next he's got me in his arms, kissing me harder than he ever has. I feel it everywhere. My hands roam over his chest and stomach and then lower to undo his pants and push them down.

He lets out a low growl when I wrap my fingers around the base of his dick, then he spins me back around and pushes me down on the bike like he can't wait a second longer.

My heart races as I wait for him. I can hear the rip of the foil and our ragged breathing. The anticipation is almost more than I can take.

My breath catches when the head of his cock nudges my entrance.

"Hold on tight, princess." He pushes in and my eyes roll back as my body stretches to accommodate him. I've barely taken him a couple of inches, but it feels so good. So full, so complete.

"So damn tight." His words are clipped as he guides me farther onto him. When I'm finally taking all of him, we both go still.

"So damn big," I say back.

He pulls out and pushes back in a few times until I can take him easily. Our movements are still slow and controlled, but it has my orgasm building fast anyway. Knox leans down, and with one hand, guides my face around enough that he can kiss me deeply while buried inside of me. It's so sensual and comforting that tears prick the back of my eyes.

Knox tears his mouth away from my lips and bites the spot where my neck and the top of my shoulder connect. His movements become faster, pounding into me harder.

I can't believe I held out so long. We could have been doing this for weeks. It feels even more incredible than I imagined.

When I start to whimper and cry out his name, Knox squeezes my ass from either side, clenching me around him tighter. "Are you going to come all over my dick, princess?"

"I'm close, but you feel so good I don't want it to end."

"Don't worry. I don't plan to stop until you've come so many times you've lost track." With that, he thrusts faster until I'm crying out and squeezing him so tight that it's hard for him to push in and out.

I barely have time to catch my breath before I feel the next wave of pleasure crashing.

"Avery," Knox says my name throaty and low. Bursts of light flash in my vision and he goes still as we both come. My legs are shaking underneath him, and I'm thankful to have something holding me up.

We're still a beat, catching our breath. His hands come up around my waist and his forehead drops to my back. It feels like he places a soft kiss on my spine.

When he finally pulls out and gets rid of the condom, I work on getting feeling back in my legs.

"Ready, princess?" he asks, walking back toward me. His riding pants are still on but undone.

"For?"

He smirks and sweeps me up and into his arms. "I'm not even close to done with you."

# CHAPTER THIRTY-THREE
*Knox*

"**A**re you listening?" Avery asks, and I bring my gaze up from her legs to her face.

"Of course."

Her hands go to her hips.

"Core tight, slow and controlled, yadda yadda." I have no idea if that's what she said, but it's a safe bet.

Avery laughs and Hope joins in.

"You've got it bad," the teenager comments in a tone that's part annoyance and part inspired.

Avery ignores both of us. "I need to work on my beam routine, so I'm trusting you two to stay out of trouble on your own."

I stare at her ass as she walks off, then get back to working on rings. Hope is doing vault, but between each run, she sits on a big mat next to the rings and chats with me. She talks nonstop, requiring me to say very little. I'm so used to Flynn and his silence that it's a nice change of pace.

She tells me about gymnastics, about the boy she likes, how her parents are concerned she's spending too much time on gymnastics and not giving other activities a chance. And then somehow blocks everything else out while she sprints and hits the springboard, flipping her little body over the vault and landing on two feet. It's impressive.

I'm taking a break and watching Avery do her thing on beam the next time Hope comes to slump on the mat next to me.

"She's worried," Hope says.

"Who? Avery?"

"Yeah. Her first competition is next weekend."

"She looks pretty ready to me," I say, and shoot Hope a questioning look. I don't want to pry, but I'm not sure I understand why Avery is worried. She's dynamite. I've seen her do this routine a few dozen times and she always nails it.

"She is," Hope says, but her tone tells me there's more that she isn't saying.

Near the end of my hour workout, I walk over to where Avery is still practicing on beam.

"Time already?" she asks when she spots me.

"Pretty much. Thought I'd see an expert in action before I take off."

She drops to sit on the beam. Her smile isn't that different than many she's given me before, but Hope's words have me questioning if it's a defense mechanism so no one realizes she's not really happy.

"Hope said your first competition is coming up?"

"Saturday," she says, letting out a breath.

I walk over and rest my hands on the beam next to where she

sits. "That first race of the season excitement and nerves?"

"Mostly nerves," she admits.

"Why?"

"I haven't competed in nine months. Not since I hurt my knee."

"It's holding up well though, right?"

She bobs her head absently. "Yeah. It feels good."

"You're ready. I've watched you."

"You mean you've stared at my ass and boobs while I worked out?"

I laugh. "Not gonna lie, done a lot of that too."

Her legs dangle off one side and she kicks her feet out in front of her. "It doesn't feel like it used to yet. I'm hesitating before my dismount and I'm wobbling sometimes on my turns."

I move to stand between her legs, resting my hands on her bare thighs. "Sometimes you need that adrenaline of competition to perfect those tiny things."

She nods like she's considering my words. "Maybe you're right. I never used to stress this much before."

"Of course I'm right. I'm always right."

She rolls her eyes. "It's just…"

"What are you really worried about?" I ask when she seems to be stuck working out how to phrase her concerns.

"What if I never get that feeling back? What if the Olympics was a fluke and I'll never be able to perform at that level again? I don't know if I could keep doing it. I love it, but I'd rather walk away than get out there and be some watered-down version of the gymnast I used to be." She blows out a breath and her blue eyes are wide with worry.

I take her hand and thread my fingers through hers. "It wasn't a fluke. Your success wasn't dumb luck, it was hard work and a fuck-ton of talent. I've seen you put in the time, day after day. You *will* get there."

She nods, but still doesn't seem fully convinced.

"Let's go," I suggest.

"Where?"

"I need to go by my place for a bit, then wherever you want."

She looks like she might want to stay in this gym forever or until she gets her routine exactly how she wants it, but I lift her off the beam before she can protest.

"If you really want to practice more after I feed you, then I'll bring you back and I'll do more handstands or something while you work out."

Her lips turn up in a weak-ass smile.

"I'll even take my shirt off for extra motivation."

A real smile finally spreads across her face. I'd do just about anything to keep it there.

At home, I get to work making dinner while Flynn sits at the table doing homework. Hendrick is at the bar, and Archer and Brogan are still at football practice but should be home any minute.

Avery washes her hands and then asks, "How can I help?"

"I got it. Take a load off, princess."

"Shut up. I'm not going to sit around while you make me food."

"Uhhh, all right. You wanna chop that onion?"

She finds the cutting board and picks a knife, then sets to work while Flynn and I chat about his day. He's got college recruitment tours coming up and I need to chat with Colter to make sure none of them conflict with the tour event dates.

"Which school is your favorite?" Avery asks my brother, glancing up from her cutting.

"Houston," Flynn says immediately.

"Really?" I ask. I didn't know he had a preference. Every time we've talked about college it's just been wherever he can play.

He nods, then blushes.

"I grew up nearby. A lot of my high school classmates went there. I have a friend that goes there, too. Well, friend might be overselling it. I trained with her before the Olympics."

Flynn and I share an amused look.

"What?" Avery says, her voice climbing with uncertainty as she glances between my brother and me. "Am I inserting myself into a family conversation?"

"What? No." That makes me laugh, which makes her confusion grow.

"Why are you laughing?" she asks, propping one hand on her hip.

"It's nothing. It's just the way you said 'I trained with her before the Olympics' like that's a totally normal thing."

"Oh." She looks more embarrassed at that than if I'd told her yes, you did in fact insert yourself into our very private family discussion. Not that I could have joked about that even with a straight face.

Still laughing, I step forward to brush my lips over hers. "You're a badass. Own it, princess."

She softens under me immediately, and it takes all I have to pull back before I forget about dinner and burn the house down. Which reminds me Flynn is watching.

I chance a glance at him as I straighten and as I suspected, he's got a curious expression on his face. I clear my throat and tip my chin at Avery. "I've got it from here."

"Are you sure?"

"Yeah," I assure her.

She goes around to the other side of the kitchen counter and sits next to Flynn. "So, why Houston?"

I expect him to shrug or say, "I don't know." Instead, he says, "They just got this new pitching coach, Luka Champe. He was a relief pitcher for the Diamondbacks in the early two-thousands, but hurt his shoulder and only played a few seasons. He retired and disappeared for a while, but then about five years ago he took a job coaching at a junior college, took a struggling program to the national championship in two years. I'd kill to play for him."

"Luka Champe." I say the name slowly. "I think I remember him. You had his card framed on your desk."

Flynn looks embarrassed that I remember, but nods.

"Are you going there to tour the school?" Avery asks him.

"Nah. It's too far." Flynn shakes his head and fiddles with a pen on the counter in front of him.

"We could probably make it work some weekend," I say as I think through my schedule. There aren't a lot of free weekends between now and the start of the motocross season.

Flynn must have already realized the same thing because he doesn't press.

"Where else are you thinking?" Avery asks him. "I loved college touring. I went to so many different schools, my parents were begging me to choose already."

She and Flynn talk colleges while I make dinner. He's enamored with her, or just really likes talking colleges, but he speaks more than I've heard him say at once…ever.

Brogan and Archer get home just as I'm pulling the enchiladas out of the oven. Avery comes back in and asks where to find plates and silverware. She sets the dining room table and although we all glance at her uneasily, no one breaks it to her that we rarely eat at the table and instead the five of us have dinner together while she carries most of the conversation.

I've turned into Flynn, barely finding my voice and instead watching how she interacts with my brothers. We're a lot to take on a good day, and yet she seems perfectly at ease while Flynn shovels food into his mouth and Archer gets up to get a second bag of tortilla chips when we finish the first. He tosses it like a football to Brogan across the room. She isn't fazed at all, or at least she has a good poker face if she's inwardly cringing at the chaos around her.

Everyone else disappears when they're done eating and Avery and I walk back into the kitchen last to put our plates in the dishwasher.

Without saying anything, she wipes down the counter while I put the leftovers in Tupperware for Hendrick.

It's only when we're done that I can see a little of that earlier worry working on her. She smiles but when she thinks I'm not looking, she chews on her thumbnail and gets this contemplative faraway look.

"Thanks for helping." I wrap my arms around her waist. I didn't hate having her help and I always hate when people help.

"Thanks for feeding me. You're a good cook."

My chest shakes with a short laugh. "I manage."

"Don't tell me cocky Knox Holland is humble about his cooking skills?" she mocks with a hand held to her throat dramatically.

I take her mouth like I've wanted to all night. Her arms go around my neck and she presses flush against me. I want nothing more than to take her into my room and stay there the rest of the night.

"Hey," I say, pulling back and looking down at her flushed face and puffy lips. "Want to go back to the gym?"

Her eyes light up, but she masks it quickly. "Why?"

"I was thinking I could get in another workout. I was a little preoccupied earlier."

"You mean you were too busy staring at my ass to focus?"

"That's absolutely what I mean."

She laughs. "You don't need to do this. I'll figure it out just like you said. I'm sure I'm worrying for no reason."

But she is worrying.

"I've been there many times. If I had a race this weekend, I'd want to be out in the garage tinkering with my bike or at the track."

Her teeth graze her bottom lip. "You don't have to come, but thank you for understanding. Text you later?"

"Yeah. Sounds good. I should probably spend some time with Flynn. See if I can figure out when to take him to Houston."

"You're a good brother." She presses a kiss to my lips that makes me want to beg her to stay, but it's her words that linger with me all night long.

# CHAPTER THIRTY-FOUR
*Avery*

**W**e travel to Lakeshore College for our exhibition meet on Saturday. It's less than two hours away so we take a chartered bus, arriving early to warm up and prepare.

Nearly all college meets are held on the host team's university basketball court. Mats and all the special flooring needed for the events are placed on top of the hardwood floor and the equipment is placed in the four corners of the gym.

The size and setup are always so similar that it should make it feel more like home, but everything is different. The spring floor is green instead of blue and feels harder than the one I'm used to, and the beam is cold and unfamiliar as I run a hand along it before I warm up.

I'm an all-around gymnast, usually competing in all four events for Valley U, but today Coach Weaver has me only on beam. I try not to let that mess with my head. I know she's giving me an opportunity to get back into things without overwhelming me at a meet that doesn't matter in our overall season standings, but that constant worry nags at me that I'll never climb my way back to where I was before my injury.

As my teammates and I stretch, I block everything else out and visualize the routine, imagining myself flawlessly executing every movement.

Beam is our last rotation today, so I cheer on my teammates on vault, floor, and bars. Upbeat music plays over the speakers and there's an energy that hums in the air. Even when it's hard and my future is uncertain, I can't imagine giving this up.

A fresh wave of nerves rolls over me when we finally make it to beam. I peel off my warmup pants and jacket and stand on the sidelines. I'm in the anchor position so I have a little time before it's my turn. *More time.* I feel like I've been waiting an eternity.

In my bag, I dig out my phone and reopen the text Knox sent earlier.

KNOX

Good luck today even though you don't need it. You've got this. Text me after. x

That little x makes my heart flutter. Knox isn't really a hugs and kisses kind of guy. He's been clear about what he wants, hanging out and hooking up. But we've been spending so much time together the lines have blurred. I know he likes me beyond hooking up, but that could just be friendship on top of sex. Is it possible he's falling for me like I am him?

The guys' team isn't competing today, but a few of them drove up to watch. Tristan walks over in his Valley blue warmup pants with a gray T-shirt.

"You ready for this, Ollie?"

"If I'm not, are you going to give me a rousing pep talk?" I ask dryly.

"Would you listen if I did?" One side of his mouth lifts and I feel some of the tension in my shoulders relax.

He's been distant since the night of the pajama party and I'm not sure if it's because he finally realized I'm not going to make out with him again or if I'm finally practicing hard enough that he decided to stop holding it against me.

"No, probably not."

He holds out a fist and I tap my knuckles against his.

"Kill it, Ollie."

When it's finally my turn, I walk to the beam like I've done a million times. I lift my hands over my head and smile at the judges, then turn and mount the beam. Sitting on it with my legs dangling on either side, I arch back and let my head graze the beam before sitting up and getting to my feet. My hands scoop down and then with my feet pointed, I walk to the middle of the beam and do my first full turn.

Because we switched the difficulty level of my dismount, the starting value of my beam routine is only a 9.9. That means I really do need to kill it.

My hands move gracefully as I move to the other end now, standing sideways and facing the judges while smiling like this is no big deal. And that's how I feel. In this moment I am invincible. It's a fleeting feeling. It happens so quickly I almost don't recognize it.

A half turn on my toes places me back into position for my

first combination. Side aerial layout step out. My heart soars with excitement and pride, but I don't acknowledge it yet. I shove it down with my other feelings and focus on the next forty seconds of my routine.

My only thoughts are about execution. Not just in the technical skills but in my dance movements as well. Practiced grace on top of precision is the goal. I land my final cartwheel and then Gainer dismount with my chest high.

Relief like I've never felt washes over me as the world around me comes back into focus. I raise my hands for the judges and then jog off to a smiling Coach Weaver. She's a force in practice, but on competition days she's our biggest cheerleader.

"Fantastic job, Avery. Your final combination was perfection."

"I wobbled a little on the half turn."

She shakes her head like it doesn't matter, but it will in my final score. "Today, you proved that you're back and ready to dominate beam like you were meant to do."

She releases me as my teammates come over to congratulate me. High fives and hugs. Tristan doesn't approach, but he tips his head to me.

My final score is 9.825. I try not to be disappointed. I know it was a good first routine of the season, but I'm already wanting to get back up there and work on my turns and switch out my dismount.

I'm also dying to text Knox and my family, but I know I need to celebrate with my team so I wait until we're on the bus headed back to Valley.

ME

**Your girl is heading home with
some bling.** 🏅

I second-guess the phrase "your girl" and hope he reads it in the
playful tone I meant it. His reply is almost instant.

KNOX

Congrats! Knew you could do it.

ME

**Thanks. How's Flagstaff?**

KNOX

Not bad. Looks like we're staying tonight
though so I won't get to congratulate
you in person until tomorrow.

ME

**Bummer, I guess I'll have to
entertain myself.**

KNOX

Only til tomorrow. Gotta make some
adjustments to my bike before tonight.
Go celebrate with Quinn. I'm sure she's
dying to take you to some party.

That does sound like Quinn.

> **ME**
>
> Okay. Good luck with your double nac four sixty 😔

And to Quinn…

> **ME**
>
> We're on our way back. I got third place on beam!

**QUINN**

My bestie is a badass! Congrats. What time will you be here? Colter and Knox aren't getting back until tomorrow.

> **ME**
>
> I'll be there in about two hours.

**QUINN**

Putting my party pants on!

> **ME**
>
> About that…how do you feel about celebrating in Flagstaff?

It takes basically no convincing on my part to get Quinn to agree to surprise the guys by driving up to Flagstaff.

We turn up the music in my Bronco and sing nonstop for the three hours it takes to get there. We arrive a little after the event has started. Quinn gets us seats and I weave through the crowd, trying to get as close to the back as I can to see if I can spot Knox.

I know from watching him practice, and him and Colter talking about the show that Knox doesn't ride in the first half. The other riders have a series of jumps that are more technical and he helps in the back until it's time for him to go out.

I can see where the riders are disappearing out a side gate when their turns are over, so I walk that way. Lucky for me, there isn't anyone to stop me. I guess they aren't worried about superfans getting back here, although the way some of the girls are dressed up for this event, I think they maybe should be. I feel a spark of jealousy at the thought of one of them hitting on Knox.

My smile widens when the man I'm looking for comes into view. He's sitting on his bike watching the event just out of sight from the crowd. He glances in my direction as I get to the last fence that separates us. He does an actual double take and then a wide grin splits his face.

My heart leaps out of my chest as he gets off his bike and walks toward me.

"What are you doing here?" he asks, linking his fingers through the fence around mine.

"I didn't want to wait until tomorrow to celebrate with you."

His smile is crooked and sexy. He removes his gaze from mine and searches down the fence. He walks to a shorter section and hops over to me. He's decked out in his riding gear, black jacket, black pants, black boots. Nobody should be able to make a single color look this good.

Knox's arms immediately wrap around my hips and he picks me up. I drape myself around him and kiss him. Or really, I should say I do my best to kiss him back. He's got full control of it and I'm just along for the ride.

His hands slide up the back of my shirt and then his fingers tangle in my hair.

"Missed this mouth," he rasps.

His words feel almost as reaffirming as nailing my beam routine did.

My mouth is tender when he finally pulls back. He gives my bottom lip one final nip. "I better get back before I miss my signal."

"Okay. Good luck."

He shakes his head as he walks off. "Don't need it now that you're here."

# CHAPTER THIRTY-FIVE
*Knox*

watch Avery walk back to the stadium seats and climb up into the middle section about halfway up. Colter rides back and grins at me. "Ready to put on a show?"

My nerves kick up. I'm doing the Superman seat grab for the first time in front of an audience tonight. It's a fun trick with a lot of variations to make it harder or give it more style. I've landed it dozens of times in practice, but it's always different in front of a crowd.

"You've got this. Piece of cake."

I nod in acknowledgment, then jut my chin toward the audience. "Your girl is here."

"Quinn's here?" His brows pull together like he's trying to understand my words.

"Yeah, she and Avery drove up."

His grin widens. "Then don't embarrass me in front of my girl,

Holland."

With a laugh, I start up my bike. "I'll do my best."

I drive around the track a few times, pulling wheelies and burning out in front of the audience. They love it and I feed off their energy, giving them more when they cheer louder.

My gaze finds Avery every time I dare look at the crowd. I swear I can see she's smiling even though it's impossible to make out her facial features from this far away.

I speed up the ramp and whip to cheers from the crowd, then go right back around, hitting the ramp faster than before. There's no other feeling quite like hitting the end of the ramp. Everything goes quiet like a collective intake of breath. It's just me and my bike hanging midair.

I let my legs come up behind me, grab the seat with one hand while keeping the other on the handle, then cross my legs for a little extra flair. All the work I've done in the gym hasn't been for nothing. My core squeezes to keep my lines straight and my upper body strength helps me hold on for dear life. One wrong move and this could end badly.

For a few seconds I'm suspended in the air above my bike. I'm flying, weightless and free. I can hear the music and the cheers, but it's white noise just like when I'm racing.

It happens so fast and then I'm scrambling back to my seat before I land. Like all the best moments in life, it's over before I can grab hold of the feeling.

The crowd is louder than before as I come around and stop in front of them. I stand on the pegs as I wave. It isn't my imagination this time when I glance up at Avery. I know she's smiling.

She's waiting for me when the show is over. Quinn runs to Colter as we come out together. Avery hangs back, a little more reserved than her friend. I wonder what it might be like to have her run and jump into my arms, so excited she can't wait to see me a second longer. I don't know when it happened, but at some point, I started picturing her in all kinds of scenarios I never gave much thought to before.

She doesn't catapult herself toward me, but I settle for the huge grin on her face as I approach.

"I bow down to the king of the nac four sixty."

"Oh, you'll bow down later all right, princess."

Her blue eyes flash with heat as I take her chin between my thumb and pointer finger and drop a kiss to her perfect mouth. All I can think about is getting her alone to show her just how happy I am she drove up to see me.

"Congrats. Seriously, you were inspiring. The crowd loved you. I thought I was going to have to fight off a couple of women talking about what they'd like to do to you."

My lips twitch with amusement at the thought of Avery being jealous of some chicks I don't know and could care less about.

"Better get me out of here before they try to steal me away," I say jokingly and wink at her.

"They'll have to go through me." There's something so adorable about her being ready to throw down to stake her claim on me.

"No chance. I've been thinking about getting you naked since you showed up." With her meet and the freestyle event, we haven't had any time alone in days.

A flush creeps up her face. "Quinn wants us all to go out together first, and then I'm all yours."

I'd rather spend all night showing her exactly how happy I am she drove up to see me, but I guess I can share her for a couple of hours.

"All right. I gotta help finish loading the truck first." Colter still has his mouth fused to Quinn's. Looks like we might be doing it without him.

"I'll come with you," Avery offers.

I like that she wants to tag along. I've noticed she's never afraid to jump in and help. It's not even a trait I realized was important to me. I've so actively avoided letting anyone in or accepting their assistance, but I like that she does it without making it a big thing.

I'm also glad she's sticking with me because it gives me an excuse to keep kissing her as we make our way through the crowd that's still gathered from the event.

I take her hand so we don't get split up. She hovers close to my back and I feel a shot of pride walking with her. Guys notice her everywhere, but right now they're checking her out and she's with me.

We come to the edge of the crowd and I drop her hand to drape an arm around her shoulders. Avery attaches herself to my side.

A man steps into my line of view but it takes me a few steps to place him. I slow and Avery moves ahead before pausing to wait for me.

"Mike," I say when we're in front of him. "What are you doing here?"

He smiles and his brows lift slightly. "You invited me."

I did. I've invited him to every event, but he's never shown up.

"I was visiting some family nearby and thought I'd check it out. That was impressive."

"Thanks." My pulse speeds up at the sight of my old team owner.

Mike's gaze shifts to Avery.

"Hello," he says.

"Hi." Avery waves and smiles politely.

"This is Avery," I tell him, then look to her. "Mike is the owner of my old racing team, Thorne."

"Oh." Her tone implies she's made the connection. "Nice to meet you."

"Same to you." He gives me his attention again. A serious expression that has me anxious and excited. "Can we talk?"

"I see Quinn and Colter not far behind us." She smiles at Mike again. "Nice to meet you."

We both watch her go. As the seconds tick by, I grow more curious. It isn't like him to show up unannounced. The ideas I had about him popping by to lure me back after seeing I                 can be a part of a team seem like the dreams of a silly kid. What does he care if I can do freestyle? His business is racing.

"When you first told me you were doing freestyle, I thought you were kidding."

"Colter and I are old friends," I say by way of explanation. "He needed help and I had some time to kill."

He nods thoughtfully. "Thinking of making the switch full-time?"

He wants to know if I'm planning on racing next season. It's on the tip of my tongue to tell him it's no longer any of his business. I've always liked Mike, but I'm still salty he dropped me. Ultimately, I decide being an asshole won't do me any favors.

"No. This was just something to focus on while I'm figuring out my next steps. Racing is still my dream."

"That was a hell of a performance to be a side gig."

"The team is great. They let me train with them, and I just tag along and do a few tricks."

He nods thoughtfully. "Being humble looks good on you. I hope it doesn't sound too condescending when I say I'm proud of you."

His words swirl around in my head. If I've changed, it's because I've seen what it's like to have a team around me that wants me to succeed. Colter, Brooklyn, all the rest of the guys. Most of all Avery.

"Thanks, Mike." I clear my throat. "How's the team looking?"

"Good. Things are good. The full team is heading back to headquarters next week."

"That's great."

His soft chuckle tells me he knows I'm bullshitting. Some of my anger has dissipated, but I'm still not quite ready to pretend I'm ecstatic that they're all doing fantastic when I'm without a team.

He doesn't say anything else and somehow, I know now he's never going to invite me back.

I clench my jaw as I watch my dreams of rejoining the team go up in smoke. There is no other plan. "Well, I should get going. Thanks for stopping by, Mike."

I start to push past him, eager to get away from him and sit in my disappointment. I wanted him to see me succeeding on a freestyle team and he did. It just didn't have the results I wanted.

Mike throws a hand out to stop me. "Actually, there's one other thing."

# CHAPTER THIRTY-SIX
*Avery*

"Congratulations!" Colter raises a glass toward the middle of the table and smiles at Knox. "I knew you'd land on your feet."

"Don't forget Avery." Quinn holds out her water to me. "Third place at the first meet of the season is no joke. You would have been first if you'd done your original dismount."

Knox and I accept our congratulations and the four of us cheers. Knox's old team owner didn't offer him a spot back on the team, but he did the next best thing. He found someone else that's looking to make a switch. Colter says Neon Punch is the newer, shinier Thorne. He's ecstatic.

Knox is…well, he's harder to read.

"Are you okay?" I ask him after Quinn and Colter leave us to go to the bar.

"I think I'm just still surprised." He shakes his head. "I really thought it was over."

"No way. You're too crazy talented to not get picked up by someone."

One side of his mouth twitches and then lifts slightly.

"So what does this mean? I assume you have to go meet them or interview or something?"

"I gotta call tomorrow, but Mike thought they'd want me in New Mexico at the end of next week."

"Next week?" I don't have time to hide the surprise in my tone.

New Mexico is where their headquarters is located. I suppose it could be worse. He'll be within driving distance.

"Most teams are already training or starting next week. Short off-season and then right back to it."

"Yeah," I say. "I get that."

I take a few days off here and there, sometimes a week right after the season, but I'd train year-round with my team if NCAA rules would allow it.

"I guess that means we won't be able to train together anymore."

"Don't pretend you're sad to have me out of your gym, princess. You've been counting the days since I showed up."

"Maybe before, but not now. It's the best part of every day."

He smiles and places a hand on my thigh. I bring that leg over his and inch closer.

"Congrats. Really. You set out to do something and you did it. I'm in awe of you."

"Right back at ya, princess."

The rest of the group shows up and we push tables together to make room. There are lots of shots and since I'm not old enough to partake, I enjoy watching as his friends push a few too many shots in Knox's direction.

With each one he gets a little freer with the PDA. I'm sitting fully on his lap now while he talks to Brooklyn around me. One of his hands rests in my lap and his fingers make absent circles.

He tries to pull me into conversations, but my mind wanders. He's going to leave next week and then what? Will we still talk or see each other?

An old song comes on the jukebox of the bar and Knox squeezes me around the middle. "Dance with me?"

"Here?"

"No, outside in the parking lot." His sarcasm is punctuated with a smirk.

It seems just as likely that's what he meant, but I slide off his lap and stand with him right behind me.

He holds my hand as he leads me out to a little area in the bar that can hardly be called a dance floor. An old guy with a graying beard tips his beer at us as we pass.

Knox wraps himself around me like he needs me to keep him upright. Which honestly could be the case at this point.

"Feeling good?" I ask him.

"Now that I got you all alone I am." He sways us slowly to the beat.

"I thought you would want to celebrate with your friends." I only promised Quinn I'd stay for one hour, but Knox hasn't mentioned leaving and I don't want to pull him away.

"I do, but if there's the option to be alone with you, you can rest assured that's always the one I'm going to choose." His words make my chest tighten.

"You're a real smooth talker, Knox Holland."

"Joel," he says.

"What?"

"My middle name is Joel."

His lids are heavy and his mouth soft. I bring a hand up to his cheek. "Knox Joel Holland. I like it."

"My dad's name is Joel. I always hated that she named me after him. I don't want to be anything like him."

"I think you've already proven how different you are. What you did, dropping out of school and taking care of your brothers, is not a small thing."

I can tell he wants to shrug it off. "You have a good heart, and it's just a name. Mine is Sarah. No reason. My mom just liked the name."

His smile returns. "Avery Sarah Oliver."

His grip around me tightens and we're quiet as we dance and stare at each other.

"Are you happy?" I ask, then add, "About Neon Punch. I can't tell. You're very hard to read tonight."

"Yeah, it's just…" His brow creases. "I guess it hasn't really sunk in yet."

"Will you move there or drive back and forth so you can be in Valley on weekends and stuff?" I ask. It's all I've been able to think about since he told me he was leaving.

"You're pretty."

Surprised laughter spills out of me. "Was that an answer?"

"I might have missed the question because I was staring at your mouth. I'm obsessed with your mouth." He leans in and kisses me while I continue to giggle at him.

We stumble back to the hotel. Well, Knox stumbles and I hold him up.

"I think you should probably take off all your clothes," he says when we get into the room. He kicks off his boots and flops onto the bed on his back.

"What a great idea," I say in my best surprised voice as I pull my shirt over my head.

His smile is lazy and carefree. "I'm full of great ideas."

"Oh yeah?" I cross the room halfway to him while unbuttoning my jeans. "Like what?"

He holds his hands out and waves me forward with his fingers.

I crawl over him, jeans still on but shirt tossed aside. His arms wrap around me and he crushes me to his chest.

I squeal and yelp like I'm protesting, but there's nowhere I'd rather be. I lick his face and then he bites my boob. We're attacking each other back and forth, but smiling and rolling around the big bed.

My next retaliation is licking his nipple piercing, and then he takes my face in both of his hands and holds me while he kisses me breathless.

From there it's a lot of scrambling hands to get each other undressed, him ripping open the condom foil at super speed and covering himself while I cling to him like I can keep him here with me no matter what. When he pushes inside of me, we both still.

"I can't get enough of you," he says, eyes so dark and serious that I wonder if he's thought the words before but is only saying them now because he's drunk.

My throat burns with the need to say *well actually, I can't get enough of you either. In fact, I'm in love with you and wondering if you could possibly reconsider the whole I don't do serious thing.*

I, of course, don't say any of that. Not now and maybe not ever.

I wake up with Knox's arms still wrapped tightly around me. We fell asleep naked and him still hard, and it looks like that's how we're waking up too. For someone who claims he doesn't cuddle, Knox Holland is a superb cuddler.

I snuggle back into him without opening my eyes. We've only slept over together a couple of other times and it usually ended with him needing to get home quickly the next morning.

"Morning, princess."

I mumble my reply with a yawn.

His laughter tickles my ear. "You'd think you were the one who drank too much last night."

"I was the one making sure you ended up back in your room in one piece."

"That is not how I remember you spending the evening." His lips press to my neck just below my ear, and he whispers his next words. "Unless I dreamt you on your knees with that fucking mouth around my cock."

My insides turn to liquid. "You didn't dream that."

"Not last night, but I have many, many times."

I turn around in his arms. His crooked smile surrounded by dark scruff and mussed morning hair make him more handsome somehow.

"I'm so happy for you."

"Thanks." His brows pinch together. "Yeah, I keep forgetting. What a wild day."

"When do you think you'll leave for New Mexico?"

His hold on me loosens and he lays his head back on the pillow. "I need to check with my brothers, but I'll probably drive out Thursday morning. Flynn has a game on Wednesday so if I can stay for that, I will."

Three more days. My chest squeezes.

"Wow. That is soon. I bet you have a lot to do before then."

He sits up. "Not really. Plenty of time to take you to breakfast."

While Knox gets up and starts getting dressed, I find myself unable to move. Like if I just stay here in this bed then everything will be absolutely fine. Who needs food or the rest of the world?

"How often will you be able to come back?" I ask, still rooted in the same spot with his scent lingering on the sheets around me. He never did answer me when I tried to get an idea of what his schedule would look like.

"Weekends when I can before the season starts. During the season it just depends. With Flynn graduating in May and going to college, there'll be less of a rush to get back."

I swallow down all my pride and summon every last ounce of courage as I gather the sheet up around me and sit with my back against the headboard. "What about us?"

I don't know why I chose to call us an us for the first time now. We aren't an us. Not really. Maybe because that's how I've been thinking of me and Knox for weeks now. Us. Together. Really together.

He pulls his black shirt down slowly, meeting my gaze. The look he gives me makes my stomach tighten in dread.

I can't take it back, though, so I decide to lay my heart out on the line. "I know we're supposed to be just hanging out, but I like you a lot. We're having so much fun and I don't want that to end."

"I like you too."

"But?" I ask because I can see it coming on his face.

"We can still hang out when I'm in town, but I don't want to promise things when we might not see each other for weeks or months at a time." A flash of vulnerability pulls the corners of his mouth down. "You're going to be busy with competition season too."

I will be, but I still want this and believe it's possible. Only it's not, because he doesn't want that.

His smile pulls back into the easy, playful one I've grown so accustomed to. He walks over to the bed and takes my hands, pulling me up and into his arms. "Trust me. I know what it's like to have people you care about pop in and out of your life. Always waiting around, always hoping for things that don't happen, always disappointed. I don't want that for you, and I could never let myself do that to another person."

I smash my lips together to keep them from quivering.

"New Mexico isn't that far. Maybe you can visit one weekend," he says as casually as if he were telling an old friend he hoped he'd see them around town sometime.

"Yeah. Maybe." Surprisingly my voice comes out much steadier than the beating of my heart as it cracks.

Knox brushes a kiss over my lips and smiles. "Come on, let me feed you and then we can drive back to Valley. We have a few days before I leave, and I know just how I want to spend them."

# CHAPTER THIRTY-SEVEN
## Knox

The next few days go by quickly. I chat with Burt, the team owner of Neon Punch, and dig him immediately. He raced when he was younger before deciding he wanted to be a lawyer. He did that for fifteen years and then, in his words, decided he was tired of sitting behind a desk.

His team is new, but they already have a lot of backing from heavy-hitting sponsors, one of which they poached from Thorne. I'm excited.

But there's this underlying emotion that's been nagging me all week. My brothers were stoked for me and they all reassured me that it was fine, that this is what I had been working for. I've been gone before, so it shouldn't feel any different. Maybe it's because Flynn's almost done with school and his days and weeks are filled with school activities that tout it being the final or last. It's funny, really, since I didn't care about those things during my own senior year.

And then there's Avery. I can't get her out of my head. We've hung out as much as we can, but there aren't that many hours between her school and practice, and me hanging out with my brothers and getting ready to go.

Things are weird between us. She hasn't said anything else about wanting to keep hanging out, but I can feel her disappointment. I'm bummed that we won't be able to see each other as often, too, but I couldn't bring myself to promise that things will be the same.

I saw what it was like for my mom and for our family when my dad came and went when it was convenient for his schedule. I won't do that to someone, least of all Avery.

Tonight is my last night in Valley. Avery had a late practice, but she's going to meet me after Flynn's basketball game. It could be a big game for him. Scouts from two of his top universities are in attendance. He's still not sure if he wants to play basketball in college, in addition to baseball, but having options is great.

While the team warms up, I think through my schedule for the rest of the week. The initial meeting should only take a few days, so I can probably get back mid next week. I'm lost in my thoughts, wondering when I can squeeze in time to see her, when Archer and Brogan take their usual seats in the row in front of me and to the left. Brogan hands over a bag of plain M&Ms.

"Thanks." I kick one foot out onto the bleacher in front of me.

Hendrick drops down into the seat beside me, Jane on his other side.

"The gang's all here," I say, leaning forward to wave at my brother's fiancée. "Hey, Hollywood."

"Hey, Knox." Her smile is tight.

"I gotta talk to you about something," Hendrick mutters, tipping his chin toward me and speaking quietly.

"What's up?" I'm distracted by the buzzer and the players jogging over to their

respective benches.

"Dad's here."

"What?" I ask loudly, snapping my attention to him. There's no way I heard him right.

He tilts his head toward the door, and I turn to see our dad walking in.

*What the actual fuck?*

I start to stand to tell him to leave, but Hendrick places an arm out to keep me in my seat.

"Wait," he says. "Look at Flynn."

Clenching my jaw, I do as he says. We're not the only ones that spotted our prick of a father. Flynn's noticed Dad's here too, and he's got a tentative smile on his face. My blood is boiling.

Dad scans the gym like he's taking it all in for the first time in years, which I guess he is. About ten years too late. He must feel the fury of our stares because his gaze lands on us and his steps slow.

"Hi, boys." He tips his head in greeting.

None of us say a thing and he continues on, taking a seat in the first row just past half court.

The players on the opposing team are being announced, but I barely hear anything. I can't believe he showed up here.

"I gotta say something." I stand and all three of my brothers sitting with me move in front of me.

"I don't think that's a good idea," Hendrick says.

Brogan shakes his head in agreement.

Archer looks torn. Like maybe he wants to be the one to go over and deck our old man, but he doesn't want to make a scene.

I have zero issues doing either of those things. All I want is him gone.

"Let's just wait until halftime," Hendrick suggests. "And if he does anything before then, I'll go over there with you and help you toss him out."

I glance back at Flynn. The hopeful smile on his face is broader now and it breaks my heart. I can count the times I had that exact same smile on my face when Dad would show up. Only to have it snatched off the next time he let me down.

The game starts and I do my best to focus only on my baby brother, but when Dad stands up and cheers after Flynn makes a three-point shot off the wing, I lose it. Like he has any fucking right to stand here and act like he's some dad of the year, proud and present.

I'm aware of Brogan calling after me and the looks I get when I face off with Dad, but I'm driven by a singular force to remove him from my life, and my brother's too. He doesn't get to just show up and act like everything is hunky-dory.

"I don't want any trouble, Knox," he says when he sees me.

"Then you shouldn't have shown up here."

"Flynn looks happy to see me. He should have his dad here."

"Yeah, he should," I agree. "If he had one that wasn't a piece of shit."

A woman clears her throat in the row above Dad.

"What are you doing?" Flynn asks, catching me off guard. He jogs by the sideline slowly, watching me and Dad. The expression on his face is a mixture of embarrassment and anger. My stomach drops. That look isn't aimed at Dad, but at me.

"Everything's fine. We're just talking. Get back out there and show the other team what you're made of, huh?" Dad assures him, and after a moment of hesitation, Flynn runs off to catch up to the action on the court.

Hendrick's voice booms behind me. "Knox, let's go. He isn't worth it."

Dad's jaw tightens as he stares past me to my oldest brother.

When I don't move, Hendrick lays a hand on my shoulder. I know it's meant to be reassuring but my skin crawls. The only touch I want to feel is my fist against Dad's jaw.

I spin, clenching my hands at my side.

The rest of the first half I'm anxious and counting down the seconds until I can step outside. Archer suggested we go, but there was no way I was letting him run me off or cause me to do exactly the thing he's known for. The only one that would have hurt is Flynn.

"What do we do?" I ask, looking to Hendrick because I can't think rationally. And I can't stop seeing that look on Flynn's face. Is he upset because we were making a scene or does he actually want Dad here?

"I don't know. We can't force him to leave," he says.

"Unfortunately," Archer adds.

Dad ambles over to us before we've decided. "Good to see you, boys."

The man is ballsy, I'll give him that. Hendrick is the only one that acknowledges him, grunting something that might have been "why are you here?" He steps partially in front of Jane like he wants to shield her from the shitty human parading around as our father.

No one else speaks. I'm clenching my jaw so hard I wouldn't be surprised if I've cracked a molar.

He doesn't take the hint and fuck off. "Flynn's good. Probably the best kid on the team. Is he planning to go to college?"

I'm not sure what part pisses me off more. The fact he's just now realizing how talented Flynn is or that he thinks he has some right to ask about his future plans when he hasn't been present in years. He should already know all of this and so much more. He should have been the one staying on Flynn about his grades and helping him research colleges and filling out financial aid applications.

Hendrick was lucky enough to get a full-ride football scholarship. Archer and Brogan stayed in Valley for college at least in part because it was cheaper. I'm sure they didn't feel like they could leave me alone with Flynn either.

But I want my baby brother to go wherever the hell he wants. He deserves that because he's not had it easy growing up like he has and he's still somehow the best parts of all of us.

"Why are you here?" I ask through gritted teeth.

"I guess the same reason you all are."

"No." I shake my head adamantly. "We're here to support Flynn. You're here to what, make a point that you can still pop in whenever you want and jerk us around?"

A flicker of shame passes over his face so quickly I can't be sure I saw it. He should be ashamed. What kind of man leaves his kids without so much as sending a card on their birthdays? God, I was so devastated when he'd make a promise to be there and then inevitably break that promise. I cannot stand by while he does that to Flynn.

He's good and deserving. I want so much more for him.

"I just want to watch my son play. That's it," he says, but all I hear is, 'I didn't show up for you or Hendrick or Archer, but here I am. I found my way to one fucking game in seventeen years. Aren't I great?'

"*If that's it, then after the game you'll leave again, and we won't see you back here?*" Archer signs the question without speaking the words like he usually does.

I could almost laugh. Dad never learned to sign for Archer, and I doubt he took it up as a hobby since the last time we saw him. Where would he possibly have found the time, what with all his work and being a giant asshole loser?

Dad's damage worked on us all in different ways. Hendrick tried to escape it all by leaving and making something of himself, which he did before deciding that wasn't what he wanted. I guess I dealt with it by letting my hate guide me to be different than him in every way I could. But Archer's never run from it or rebelled in any visible way. I think he blames at least part of Dad's disappearing act on his accident, the one that caused his hearing loss. I remember it well enough to know that it wasn't like Dad was around that much before anyway, but he's not wrong that Dad was gone for longer stretches of time after that. So, for Arch, I think being himself has always felt like the ultimate fuck-you.

"He won't be back after tonight," I answer for him, then shoot a pointed glare at Dad. "Right?"

His face goes red and he opens his mouth like he might speak, but then thinks better of it. The Valley High team jogs back out onto the floor. Flynn watches us as he grabs a basketball and dribbles it while walking toward the basket where his teammates have started shooting around.

Without a word, Dad leaves. I know it's too much to hope that he's fleeing the entire building, but we take a breath anyway.

Brogan's eyes are comically wide as he lets out a giant sigh. "Well, that was awkward. You guys cool?"

Arch shrugs. "I'm fine."

Hendrick doesn't look that calm, but he nods and wraps an arm around Jane.

"I'm gonna take a walk," I say.

"Do not engage," Hendrick demands.

"I'm not." Though I want to. I walk off toward the locker rooms. There's a back door near them that opens out into the parking lot, and more importantly is in the opposite direction from where Dad went.

I pull out my phone without realizing my intention. Tapping on Avery's contact, I start to send a text: **Guess who showed up at the game?** 😵 😵 but then delete it. She's got her own shit and I'm sure she's tired of hearing my daddy sob story.

ME

How's the training going?
Miss watching me do
handstands yet?

I pace the gravel lot while I wait for her answer. My heart leaps at the sound of the incoming message. It's a selfie of her on the beam.

AVERY

**If what you meant to ask is if I miss watching you shirtless then the answer is yes.**

A short laugh escapes into the night and against all the shitty odds, I smile.

When I get back to the gym, the second half of the game has just started. I pause and stand near the wall watching the action in front of me. Flynn makes a steal and takes off at warp speed with the ball toward the other end. The other players sprint to catch up, but he gets to the basket first, jumping high and laying it in.

What happens next seems like slow motion. One of the players on the other team makes a last-ditch effort to stop him. He jumps, but Flynn is already coming down and they collide midair. My brother's legs go out from under him and he comes down on his right arm.

I'm moving forward before he's made impact. Flynn lets out a guttural scream and the gym goes eerily quiet.

# CHAPTER THIRTY-EIGHT
*Knox*

Brogan extends a cup of shitty cafeteria coffee in my direction.

"No thanks." I shake my head and continue walking the length of the waiting room, not meeting anyone's gaze.

The seats are filled with Flynn's teammates and the parents that drove them. His coach is here, too. Then there's all of us. Hendrick and Jane sit not talking, Archer and Brogan are keeping the vending machine busy, and Dad is sitting as far away from me as he can. Wise choice.

I don't remember much from the moments after Flynn got hurt. It felt like a bad dream as they helped him off the court. One look at his elbow and we all knew it was broken. I drove him to the hospital, and they took him back immediately. The only update we've had is that it needed immediate surgery. Surgery. I swallow the lump in my throat.

A quiet murmur sounds across the waiting room while we all

do our best to will the time away. I'm counting the tiles on the floor, stepping on each one as I go. Thirteen, fourteen, fifteen.

The sliding doors open from outside with that electronic humming noise, followed by the honk of horns and the steady plink of rain hitting the asphalt. She stops in the doorway. Avery's worried gaze scans the room until she finds me and then she rushes toward me. I can't move, but when her arms wrap around me, I melt into her embrace.

Sliding her fingers through mine, she guides me down into a chair and takes the one next to it.

"Have you heard anything?" she asks.

"Not yet."

"I'm so sorry." She squeezes my hand. "Flynn is tough. He's going to be fine."

Fine, but will he be able to play again? None of us have mentioned it, but I know the others are thinking the same thing. He broke his right elbow. His pitching arm. I don't know what that means for him now or in the future, but it feels like everything good in my life is slipping through my fingers like quicksand and I can't do shit to stop it.

Flynn's coach stands and gets himself a cup of the crappy waiting room coffee and then wanders over to Dad. The doctor did the same thing, assuming he's the person responsible for Flynn. What a fucking joke.

"I feel so helpless," I tell her. My leg bounces with frantic energy that needs to be dispelled. "I wish it were me in there."

"I know," she says.

I finally look at her. Really look at her. Black joggers thrown over a pink leotard, sneakers, hair thrown up in a messy ponytail.

"You didn't need to quit practice early to come here."

"I didn't," she says quickly, then offers a sheepish smile. "Okay, I did. But there will be plenty of time to obsess over my routine tomorrow."

We sit there holding hands in the dimly lit room on cheap plastic chairs with the smell of burnt coffee in the air. I have the errant thought that she's the only thing keeping me together right now.

The doctor comes back out and the family gathers around to hear the news. Dad joins us, but so does Avery and she squeezes my hand tight.

He explains in complicated medical terms what was broken and how he fixed it. Under normal circumstances I'd be taking in every word and asking for clarification to better comprehend exactly what's happened, but I'm consumed with the need to get to Flynn and see with my own eyes that he's okay.

"Can we see him?" I finally ask when the doctor stops talking.

"Yes, but keep it brief. He's groggy and needs to rest. His pain is under control right now, but he's going to experience a lot of discomfort over the next twenty-four hours. I want to keep him at least for tonight. If things look good in the morning, you can take him home then."

"I'll let everyone else know," Brogan says, pointing to Flynn's teammates and coach, who watch us anxiously.

The rest of us head back with a nurse to the recovery room. Well, almost everyone. Dad disappears somewhere along the way. Probably afraid he's going to get stuck with the hospital bill.

Flynn is high from the meds. He smiles and cracks a joke about not being able to sign autographs for a few months.

We each take turns hugging him and offering bullshit words of comfort. He can barely keep his eyes open by the time it gets to me.

My throat burns as I say, "I'm going to run home and get you some clean clothes. Anything else you want?"

His eyes close and he shakes his head.

In the parking lot, Avery walks next to me hugging her arms across her middle. "Do you want me to come with you?"

I want to say yes, but I know there isn't anything she can do, and it's not like I'm going to be any fun. Flynn needs me and that's all I can focus on.

"No, that's okay. I'm just going to grab his stuff and come back for the night. I'm sorry to bail on our plans."

"No, of course. You should be with him." We stop at her Bronco.

"Is he going to be able to pitch again?" I ask her. She's the only person I trust for the answer. She's been through this. Not this exactly, but she had a traumatic injury and came back from it. If she says Flynn can too, then I'll believe her.

"I don't know," she says and some of that hope disappears into a puddle at my feet. She takes my hand and then links our pinky fingers. "But if he's as stubborn as his big brother, then I think there's a good chance."

My lungs expand to take in a deep breath, but my chest still feels tight.

"Hey," she says, swinging our joined hands. "I don't have anywhere to be the rest of the night. I could pick us up some food and meet you back here, keep you company."

My lips curve up on one side. She has no idea how nice that sounds but sitting around the hospital while I take care of my baby brother isn't exactly the night we had planned. "It's okay. I'm probably not the greatest company right now and I know you have classes tomorrow."

There's a beat of hesitation before she replies, "If you change your mind or need anything, I won't be far."

I nod and she turns to open the door of her vehicle.

"Avery." My voice is low, but she stops and flicks her gaze over her shoulder to me. "Thanks for being here."

# CHAPTER THIRTY-NINE
*Avery*

Knox texts on Thursday, thanking me again for being there last night and letting me know that Flynn was home. He didn't ask me to come over or mention his upcoming departure. I offered to bring food or help play nurse, but he just told me they had it covered. That was it.

I know he's dealing with a lot, but I want to be there for him. I want him to let me in, so I can take some of the weight off his shoulders.

Showing up unannounced doesn't feel right either though, so I sent one more text offering whatever he needed if he changed his mind.

I can't make him let me in or need me. And I can't make him miss me the same way I miss him. He isn't even gone yet, and I feel like I've lost him.

Sure, we've hung out this week, but he's been distant since the moment I opened my big mouth and told him I wanted more than hookups when we happened to be in the same town.

I have my answer even if he didn't say it explicitly. Suggesting we might occasionally be able to see each other after spending nearly every day together would be torture. It's already torture. I fell hard for him. Rough-edged and prickly Knox Holland has my heart, even if he's tried to pass it back to me daily.

I've missed the idea of people before. Ex-boyfriends and crushes, great aunts that passed that I never really knew. But the way my chest aches thinking about never seeing Knox again is something I am entirely unfamiliar with.

In movies there's always a scene where the heroine is brokenhearted or down on her luck. She eats tubs of ice cream and barricades herself in her room while wearing the same pair of sweats day after day.

I am an expert on throwing a pity party, but with everything that has happened to Flynn and Knox, I don't see how I can feel all that sorry for myself. I'm healthy. I have parents that love me, and I can still do the thing I love most, even after an injury that should have stopped me.

So, I don't cry or eat massive amounts of sugar, or reread every text Knox and I have ever sent and replay every moment we spent together. Okay, I am guilty of the last two, but that's as far as I let it go. Then, I throw all my energy into training.

Or I'm trying to. I'm lying on the beam, staring up at the ceiling. It's always been my favorite place, but today it isn't soothing me like usual.

I shake my head to clear it and push myself into a stand. I have a brand-new dismount to work on and another meet in two weeks. If

I had been looking for the perfect distraction, Coach Weaver gave it to me.

"Looking a little sleepy this morning, Ollie," Tristan says as he struts past me.

My skin prickles with irritation and I swear I catch a grin on his face as I go into the first move of the routine.

The ache will still be there later, but for now I'm ready to get to work.

# CHAPTER FORTY
## Knox

"Flynn." I knock on his bedroom door as I call his name.

"He hasn't come out since we got home from class an hour ago," Brogan says from the couch where he and Archer appear to be giving the video games a rest and are actually doing homework.

"He hasn't come out all day," I say, dropping onto a chair in the living room. I know because I've been trying to coax him out since breakfast.

"On the bright side, not a lot of trouble he can get into in there," Brogan says.

My phone buzzes in my pocket and I pull it out and press ignore on the incoming call. Archer is watching me as I turn the screen upside down and set it on my leg.

"When are you leaving for New Mexico?" he asks.

"I'm not sure."

He and Brogan share a look, but it's interrupted by Hendrick coming in through the garage.

He sees the three of us and then immediately glances toward Flynn's room. "How is he?"

"Same," we say in unison.

Hendrick turns his attention to me. "I thought the truck would be loaded. What time are you leaving?"

I shrug. "I told them I needed more time."

I'd called the day after Flynn's injury to let my new team know I couldn't be there until Friday. That was five days ago.

I really did intend to leave, but while Flynn's elbow will eventually recover, his spirits are low. He still doesn't have any answers on the future, and while the rest of his team is continuing their season—one even signed a letter of intent to play basketball at one of Flynn's top schools—my brother is brooding in his room.

Burt's called twice today to check in, but I don't know what to tell him yet so I'm ignoring him until I do. Nothing else matters.

"We've got it handled here," Hendrick says, hands on his hips. "I've got the bar covered. I can stay home with Flynn and take him to his appointments."

"I'm not leaving. It'll be fine. I can continue practicing here and meet the team in a month or two."

Though I haven't been to the track in almost a week, it's true that I could get back in my routine here.

"Knox." It's Archer's voice that speaks up. "You have to go. Hen's right. We've got things covered here."

I shake my head, but I'm not sure what to say to make them understand. "I appreciate it, but it makes sense that it's me. It's always made sense for it to be me."

Archer's brow furrows. "Why does it make sense for it to be you?"

"Hendrick has the bar and Jane, you two have football and classes. Flynn and racing are all I have." The truth of those words scrapes up my throat. A quick vision of Avery flashes in my mind, but I'm not sure I have her anymore. We've barely spoken since Flynn's accident. That's my fault and I know it, but the weight of my responsibility has reminded me why I've never gotten this involved before.

"And you'll still have both of those, but you are risking a lot by staying here," Arch says, and the others chime in to agree.

"I don't care."

Usually Arch backs down pretty easily, but not this time. "I know you'd do anything for Flynn. You've proven that more times than I can count. We all should have helped out more before and we didn't, but we can now. You just have to let us."

"I don't care about any of that," I say truthfully. "I don't resent it or you guys. But I can't just flake on him now. Not when he really needs me."

"You're not flaking on him." Hendrick's face drops and a large pit forms in my stomach. "You think leaving him makes you like Dad."

My ears ring with those fears being spoken aloud. It sounds dumb. Maybe it is. But Flynn should have someone who always shows up for him, even if it isn't his dad.

"You dropped out of school, got a job, paid the bills, learned how to cook and how to do the fucking laundry. You took Flynn to and from school, bought him clothes, and so many other things I probably don't even know about. *You* made sure he had everything he needs…" My oldest brother's voice trails off.

"So?"

"You aren't him. You could never be him."

Not today, but how many times does it take to flake on someone before they stop looking for you?

I open my mouth to protest, but Flynn's voice cuts through the room. "He's right."

I stand and face him. His reddish-brown hair is a mess on his head, and I don't think he's changed clothes in several days. The sling on his right arm holds it close to his body. Over the last year he's started to fill out and he's this odd combination of man and boy. I'm relieved in some ways that he's going to graduate and become an adult, but in other ways I'm sad and more anxious about him making all his own decisions and not needing me anymore.

"You've done so much for me and I will always be grateful, but hanging around here isn't going to fix my elbow. I've held you back for so long. Please don't let me be the reason you lose another team."

"Your elbow will be fine," I tell him because I can see that flicker of uncertainty in his eyes. "And I want to be here for you. It's not a burden. *You're* not a burden."

He shuffles his feet and won't quite meet my gaze, so I step forward and duck my head so he can't avoid me. "Do you hear me? You are not a fucking burden."

"But you would have left Valley years ago if it weren't for me." There's a hint of a teenage whine in his voice.

"Maybe I would have, but you're my family. I'd do anything for you."

"Then do this for me," Flynn says, voice small. "I can't stand the thought of you missing this opportunity. You were born to do this. No one deserves it more."

I hear him. I hear all of them, but I'm still uneasy about leaving.

"It's what we all want," Archer says. He walks over to our youngest brother and places an arm around his neck gingerly, avoiding jostling his hurt arm. "We'll send hourly updates on Flynn if that's what you want."

Brogan rubs his hands together. "I love it when the group chat is popping off. New group name: Baby Holland Updates."

Hendrick laughs and shakes his head. The tension in the room dissipates with the sound.

They're all looking at me expectantly. An anxious and excited energy works its way under my skin.

"You're sure?" I ask them. "I can put off going another week, maybe two, or I can see about bringing my training to Valley full-time." Other guys have done it. I could hire the help I need with my training and check in virtually with my team. Assuming they'll sign off on it. It means not getting as much face time with my coaches and teammates, but I could manage.

"Positive," Hendrick says.

Archer and Brogan nod. I look back to Flynn.

"Positive," he echoes.

"If something comes up or you change your mind. If you need anything—"

"We will text you," Archer cuts me off.

"Holland Brothers Emergency Hotline." Brogan throws out another group text name idea with a smile.

"We've got you. Go and kick some ass." Hendrick closes the distance between us and hugs me.

Brogan joins in a second later. "Holland Brothers Hugs & Kisses."

I hear Archer snort a laugh as he comes on my other side.

"If you kiss me, I'm going to kick you in the balls," Hendrick mutters to him.

And then Flynn quietly wraps his good arm around my back.

I get to New Mexico Tuesday afternoon. I spent the entirety of the five-hour drive wondering if I'm making the right choice and was half-tempted to turn around. The only thing stopping me was Flynn's voice in my head telling me I was born to do this. I hope he's right.

There's lots of time to make up for and my new team doesn't miss a beat. Days blur together with practices and making adjustments to my bike. Burt has put together a great group. We mesh and see eye-to-eye on so many things. It gives me a lot of hope for the season.

At night when I finally have a chance to sit still for a moment, I call Flynn and check in on everything in Valley.

"Sitting on the bench is so frustrating," he says late Friday night. My eyes burn with exhaustion. "I just want to be out there. We lost by two points. Two!"

The season is coming to an end and he's not going to be back in time to help his team. I know how tough that is. "Baseball will be starting soon though."

"Yeah." He bobs his head. "How's it going there?"

"Good," I answer quickly, then add, "Tiring."

"It's week one. Better suck it up." My baby brother grins at me.

I laugh quietly and run a hand through my matted hair. "Yeah. No doubt. I need a shower and sleep."

"What time is it there?"

"Same time that it is in Valley."

His brows lift. "It's early."

"Not when you've been awake since five."

"I'll let you go, old man. I'm going to meet up with some friends to celebrate Charlene. She got accepted into Stanford."

"Is Hendrick driving you?"

"No, they're swinging by to pick me up." He's already moving around his room like he's getting ready.

"Have fun. Be careful. I'll call tomorrow."

As soon as we hang up, I scroll through my missed texts. The group chat, currently titled **Brogan STOP changing the group name**, has several new messages.

> ARCHER
>
> **Major Flynn update**
> **he showered!**

> BROGAN
>
> **I think I caught a whiff of cologne too.**

> HENDRICK
>
> **A whiff? I can smell it all the way out in**
> **the garage.**

I smile as I type out a reply.

ME

Tell 'em to F off, little bro.

FLYNN

🔥 You're all just mad because you're old.

BROGAN

Oh snap. No he didn't call me old.

I have other texts. Colter and Oak, even Brooklyn. They're in Texas this weekend and it feels weird not to be with them. I doubt I'm going to have a chance to keep up with practicing freestyle with my current schedule.

After I've sent a few replies, my eye is drawn to Avery's contact. She was there for me when I needed her, and it meant more than I could ever say. I'm not great at accepting help, but just knowing she was willing made my load lighter.

I've thought about texting her more times than I can count.

I left without saying goodbye and that has weighed on me. It just felt too final.

I wish things were different and that it was possible to be in two places at once. Of course, I want to keep seeing her, but she deserves more than scraps of my time and energy. She thinks that she'd be good with it, but I know how much it hurts to be the person left behind. She might be able to live with it for a while, but eventually she'd be let down.

And in the meantime, I'd hate myself for not protecting her from that. But maybe we can still hang out when I'm in Valley. I plan to go back most weekends until the season starts. If everything works out, we can see each other then. It'll be just like before.

At the thought, a little spark of anticipation spreads through me.

I'll be home next weekend. I'll check in with my brothers and then I'll text her and see if she's free.

I lie back on my bed, feeling instantly calmer with a plan. I just have to survive without seeing her for seven more days.

# CHAPTER FORTY-ONE

*Avery*

O n Friday, Quinn talks me into getting out of the dorm and to the track to hang out with Colter and his friends. They had their final big event last weekend and are going to break for a few weeks, then do some smaller events and Supercross shows.

A few of the riders are doing tricks, others are sitting on their bikes talking in groups. Colter is sitting with me and Quinn on the tailgate of his truck. Oak has traded his dirt bike for a skateboard and is riding it in front of us while he and Colter brainstorm group tricks.

"Colter said Knox really likes his new team," Quinn says, bumping my elbow with hers.

"That's good." My stomach twists at the mention of him, but I keep my emotions carefully tucked away. Not that I'm fooling anyone, least of all Quinn.

"He also said—" she starts, but I reach over and squeeze her arm when the object of our conversation steps into view.

My heart stops. God, I've missed him.

He's in his uniform of jeans and a black T-shirt under his leather jacket. How many days has it been since I've seen him? I don't know, but it feels like a million.

"Knox!" Colter jumps down to greet him, and other riders gather around.

He looks up from the group and meets my eyes while holding a conversation. The butterflies in my stomach swoop low.

"Did you know he was back?" Quinn asks.

"No. We haven't talked," I reply, forcing my gaze away from him. It stings that he's back and didn't even text to let me know. Almost as much as it stung that he didn't let me know when he left Valley.

"Aren't you going to say hello?" Quinn asks with a big smile on her face. "He keeps looking over here."

Before I can answer, he cuffs one of the guys on the shoulder and starts in my direction.

"Oh, I think that's my cue to get lost," my best friend mutters before she hops down from the tailgate. She runs by Knox as she's fleeing, waggling her fingers at him and chirping, "Hello," as she goes.

I slide off the truck as he comes to a stop in front of me. "Hi."

"Hey, princess." There's a friendly taunt to his voice that pulls on my heartstrings.

We step toward each other. I stop just short of hugging him, but then he wraps his arms around me. Leather and soap and a hint of cologne.

"What are you doing here?" I ask, a little breathless and nervous as I move away and cross my arms over my stomach.

"Colter said the guys were hanging out tonight and that you were here."

I glance toward Quinn. She's watching me and Knox with a hesitant smile. Her boyfriend is now on my shit list. He couldn't give a girl a heads-up?

"I meant in Valley. I thought you were in New Mexico."

"I was." He nods. "I'm just home for the weekend. Flynn has his last home game tomorrow night. He's obviously not playing, but I still didn't want to miss seeing him take the court for the last time."

"I'm sure it means a lot to him that you came. How's his elbow?"

"Better. His doctors say he's making great progress. He might be able to pitch some later in the season."

"I'm really glad to hear that."

"Thank you for the PT recommendation. Flynn said you made a call for him."

"Oh, that was nothing. John did some of my therapy on my knee."

"He really appreciated it, and so do I."

"You're welcome." A beat of uncomfortable silence passes between us and the noise around us infiltrates our bubble. I motion toward the track, where one of the riders is doing a trick I watched Knox practice not that long ago. "Missing all this yet?"

"I actually do miss it," he says. "And you."

My lungs struggle to pull in air. His words are a relief and yet still make me ache. I push past the discomfort and smile. This is Knox. However things were left between us, I don't ever want us to not be able to be friends. Or at least friendly. "Yeah, I miss you too, but I hear you're really liking the new team."

"I am, yeah." He nods again.

We're joined by Brooklyn and another rider who was out on the track when Knox walked up. They say hello and immediately pepper him with questions. Pretty soon nearly everyone has crowded around him.

Quinn falls in beside me and takes my hand, squeezing it lightly. She whispers, "You good?"

"Yeah," I reply.

For the next couple of hours, Knox is constantly flanked by someone wanting to talk to him. I hang with Quinn until around eleven when most everyone has stopped riding and instead, they're sitting around and cracking open beers.

"I think I'm going to go," I tell her.

"No. Already?" she asks as she hugs me.

"Yeah. I need to be up early." I give her my best nonchalant smile that she absolutely interprets as, yes, I am running away from Knox because I'm in love with him.

"Text me when you get back so I know you made it."

"I will." I wave at Colter. No one else really notices my departure. They're all friendly, but I'm still very much Colter's girlfriend's friend to most of them. Knox is talking with Brooklyn and has his back to me. I debate whether or not I should say goodbye, but ultimately decide it's better than slinking away. I really do want us to be able to be around each other and talk without it being weird. Today isn't that day, but maybe eventually.

"Hey," I say when I step into his line of vision.

Brooklyn offers me a polite smile, then ducks away with an excuse of needing to grab another drink.

"Hey." Knox's smile is bigger than it was earlier. It's almost hopeful as he angles his body toward me.

"I'm getting ready to head out, but I wanted to say bye."

His smile dims. "You're leaving?"

"Yeah. It was nice to see you though. I'm really glad things are going well. I'll see you around." I step away quickly. I can feel the tears building and I do not want to cry here.

"Wait." He hurries to step in front of me. "Where are you heading?"

"Home."

"Do you maybe want some company?" His mouth falls into a crooked smile. "I barely got to talk to you. I thought about you nonstop since I've been gone."

My heart skips and races. "I have an early morning. We have a competition Sunday so practice in the morning to run through routines."

"Right. Is it in Valley?"

"Yeah. It's our home opener." It's on the tip of my tongue to invite him, but I know he has to go back to New Mexico.

"What about tomorrow afternoon? Are you free after practice?"

It would be so easy to say yes and to let us fall back into the way things were, but then he's going to leave, and it'll break my heart all over again.

"I don't think it's a good idea," I tell him, glancing down. "I missed you too and, of course, I want to hang out, but then what?"

"I don't know," he admits. "I don't have it all figured out, but I know that I want to see you when I can. I'll be back most weekends. Things don't have to change."

His hand reaches out and he hooks his pinky finger with mine.

"That's the thing, though. I don't want to just keep hanging out when our schedules align. I mean, I do want that, but it's not all I want. I want *more*. I want you all the time, even when we're not together."

"You think you do, but then what happens if you get bored with having a boyfriend that's only around every other weekend? It's a lot of pressure on both of us. What we have is good. Why mess with it?"

I suck in a deep breath and stare into his beautiful hazel eyes. "Because I'm in love with you, Knox."

The panic on his face is immediate. Is he really that surprised?

"I—" he starts and then stops. His jaw tightens and his throat works with a swallow.

"You don't have to say anything. I know you don't feel the same or want a relationship. One of the things I admire most about you is how honest you've always been with me. But if *I'm* being honest, I can't keep hooking up with you, pretending like it's what I want. I know I said that I didn't want a relationship, and I meant it at the time. But somewhere along the line I fell hard for you anyway."

"Avery." His voice cracks on my name.

"It's okay," I say, letting him off the hook. Knowing he doesn't feel the same is one thing but hearing it would break my heart. "I have to go."

I take a step and then pause to look at him. His brow is furrowed, and he looks…lost.

"It really was good to see you. Good luck in New Mexico."

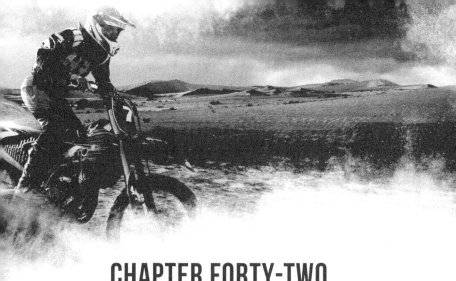

# CHAPTER FORTY-TWO
## Knox

The Valley High School gym is packed tonight. Hendrick and I share a look as we walk in and head to our usual seats. They're taken, but Archer and Brogan wave from a section over.

"Did you know?" Hendrick asks me.

I shake my head. It's Parents' Night, which explains why there are nearly double the number of people. All the players' parents made extra effort to be here and show their support.

The whole premise of the night annoys me, but I realize I'm probably just bitter that Flynn doesn't have parents to show up for him like his teammates do.

He didn't mention anything about tonight, but every year it's the same. There's always shirts or signs or some designation that all the parents have to stand out among the crowd. This year it appears it's buttons. Big, circular ones with the player's team photo on them. Good god.

"Awww. You're gonna look so ridiculous with one of those pinned to your chest in eighteen years for a little Hollywood. Promise you'll send pics?"

Hendrick shoots me an annoyed look, but there's a spark of excitement that he can't quite conceal.

We take our seats without saying anything. Flynn is under the basket rebounding balls one-handed while his team warms up. He has a tentative smile on his face as he glances over. I try to read into it. Is he feeling left out by the whole thing? Missing Mom more than usual? It probably feels like an added gut punch that it's his senior year. Or maybe he's thankful he won't have to endure another one of these.

*"Any sign of Dad?"* Archer signs to me and Hendrick.

"No." Hendrick's jaw flexes. Dad hasn't shown up again since the hospital. He stayed while Flynn was in surgery, but then didn't even bother to go back and see him when he was out. I wish I were surprised.

*"What a piece of shit,"* Brogan says quietly, signing it for Arch.

We're all in agreement there.

"If he was going to show up any night, the least he could do is show up on Parents' Night and make himself useful," Hendrick says. "I used to fucking hate this night."

"Same," Archer and Brogan say at the same time.

"He doesn't deserve to be recognized as a parent," I say.

"It's not about that," Archer says. "It's about Flynn. He just wants to be a normal kid with a normal family on nights like this. That's what we all wanted."

My stomach clenches. I never thought about it like that. I glance back at Flynn. Fuck. "I'm gonna get some air."

I leave without another word. I pull out my phone when I get to the cafeteria. The smell of burnt popcorn makes me queasy. Or maybe it's staring down at my dad's contact on my phone. I unblock his number and then hit call without letting myself think too hard about it.

He answers on the second ring. I walk toward a quieter corner, but there's background noise on his end too.

"It's Parents' Night," I say, skipping all other greetings.

"O-kay."

I grind down on my molars before continuing. "Can you make it to the game or not?"

"I'm already here," he says, and this time his voice sounds closer and I realize I'm not only hearing it through the phone. I spin around and face him. He drops his phone from his ear slower than I do. If he wants me to act happy or surprised he's here, then he's not getting it from me.

"Flynn called last night to let me know about the game," he says.

So many questions sit on the tip of my tongue, but I'll be damned if I ask them or give him another opportunity to feed me bullshit answers.

The buzzer sounds and I turn to walk back into the gym. Dad follows. When we get to my brothers, I pause and so does he. I wave my hand indicating he should sit with us. His brows lift slightly, but he sits without comment.

*"What the fuck?"* Archer signs and mouths as our father takes a seat with all of us for the first time in…too long.

"This doesn't change anything between us," I say to Dad, motioning between me and him. "Flynn is good. The best parts of all of us. I don't understand why he wants you here, but know that when you break his heart, it will be a relief. I'll finally be able to forget you exist."

I take my seat without another word. Hendrick nods like he's agreeing with everything I did or said. Jane's shown up since I left and gives me a thumbs-up. Her approval makes me smile.

My heart hammers in my chest, but I don't have long to calm down before Flynn walks over. He has his red Valley High warmups on, ready to sit on the bench. And in his hand are two buttons with his team photo.

We all greet him like the seconds before weren't tense and uncomfortable.

"They, uh, gave me these." He holds them up with a bashful smile. He stretches one out toward Dad. I hate every second of it, even if I understand that it's more about partaking in the ritual than proclaiming him parent of the year. Then Flynn hands the other one to me. His face is flushed. My throat is thick with emotion as I take it. I hold it up in thanks and he backs away, then spins around to head back to the bench.

My fingers fumble as I slide the pin through my shirt and attach the button. When I glance up, Hendrick is grinning wide. "Who looks ridiculous now?"

I scratch the side of my nose with my middle finger and put all my attention forward as they announce the starters for the game.

After the game, we all hang around to wait for Flynn. Dad does too, but he keeps his distance. Our baby brother comes out quickly since he didn't play. He goes to Dad first. I can't hear what they say, but

Flynn looks happy.

"He'll be okay," Brogan says, as if reading my mind.

"Dad is one hundred percent going to let him down."

"And when he does, Flynn will be okay. You three survived it and so will he. Besides, he has us. We more than make up for one deadbeat dad." He elbows me with a cocky grin.

I hope he's right.

When Flynn saunters over to us, Dad leaves. None of us say anything about him or the fact Flynn asked him to come.

"You want to grab dinner?" I ask him.

"Yeah. That'd be cool."

We go to The Hideout because Hendrick wants to swing by the bar after and it's the closest restaurant nearby. Once we settle in, Archer and Brogan see some friends sitting on the bar side and leave us to go say hello to them.

Flynn is on his phone, ignoring us.

"Have you seen Avery while you've been home?" Hendrick asks. Jane suddenly sits straighter, obviously eager to know as well.

"Yeah. I ran into her last night."

"And?" Jane prompts.

"She's doing good. She has a meet tomorrow."

"Are you going?"

"No," I say slowly. "I wasn't invited and I don't really think she'd be too excited to see me."

"Why not?" Flynn looks up from his phone, brows furrowed.

Archer returns without Brogan.

I shoot him a very clear *save me* expression, but he ignores it and asks, "What?"

*"He's about to tell us how he screwed things up with Avery,"*

Hendrick says and signs.

It's loud in here and even though Archer can read lips, it's a struggle sometimes for him to follow along with a group conversation.

*"She wanted more or nothing at all."*

"More?" Hendrick asks with one brow lifted.

*"She wanted more than casual,"* I admit and then clear my throat. *"But I'm leaving again tomorrow and only going to be back on the occasional weekend until after the season is over."*

"So you just turned her down?" Jane asks. Disbelief makes her big, green eyes go wide and her jaw drop.

Damn, it's hot in here. I take a drink of my water.

*"It's the best thing right now. I can't be there for her when I'm not going to be around."* She should have someone that can spend time with her, take her out to dinner, and watch her compete. And someone that will be there for her to hear about every detail of every boring day, too, because those are the moments that matter. A lot of life happens in the days that don't get marked on a calendar.

It's quiet for several long seconds and then Archer nods.

"Yeah. Long distance is hard," he says. "I know several buddies that have tried it and almost no one has made it more than a semester."

Hendrick takes his time choosing his words, but also nods his agreement. *"You haven't been seeing her that long, so maybe keeping it casual is best. Distance and time can give you space to work out how you feel about her."*

*"Sure,"* I say, but I don't really need either of those things. I know how I feel about her. But somehow that just makes it all the more important that I do the right thing by her.

I thought my chest was going to crack open as she stood there telling me she loved me.

"What do you think, Hollywood?" I ask.

Jane shrugs slowly. "I really like Avery, but if you're not sure about her than I think you made the right decision."

Not exactly what I was hoping for, but at least she didn't tell me I'm an idiot.

*"I liked her too,"* Flynn says. *"And I liked how you were with her. But I guess I've never seen you with a girl before so maybe that's just your face when you're getting laid regularly."*

I level him with a look that makes him blush and go quiet. "I hope you don't talk to girls at school like that."

His shy smile widens.

Brogan plops down into his empty seat. "What'd I miss?"

*"Knox turned down Avery. They're over."* The way Archer signs the words as he says them makes it feel especially brutal. I don't like the way that sentence looks or sounds.

Brogan turns to me. His usual friendly and playful expression is gone. "You moron."

Archer nudges him, still signing as he speaks. *"He's trying to do the right thing and save them both the headache of long-distance bullshit."*

Brogan's *you're a moron* stare doesn't let up.

"What exactly did she say?" Jane asks. "Maybe it's not as bad as you made it sound."

*"That she was in love with me and wanted to be mine all the time, not just when our schedules conveniently aligned to hook up."* I guzzle more water, but it doesn't do anything to cool the inferno raging inside of me.

*"She said she was in love with you?"* Hendrick asks.

*"Yeah."*

*"That's pretty big."*

*"Huge,"* Brogan says. *"You know this guy didn't make it easy for her to get close enough to fall for him."*

Ouch, but probably true.

"But it doesn't matter if he doesn't feel the same way," Jane says.

*"He does."* Brogan waves a hand at me, still looking irritated. *"Look at him. He's got that same miserable look on his face as Henny had when he was pretending not to be into Jane."*

Jane snuggles closer to my oldest brother and lays her head on his shoulder.

*"I do feel pretty fucking miserable,"* I admit. *"More so since we started this conversation."*

I glance around at all of them, and my idiocy is all I see staring back. Brogan arches a brow like he's daring me to disagree with him.

"Of course I fucking love her," I say a little louder than intended. Saying the words out loud has a new kind of panic washing over me. I think I have for a while, but I didn't realize that's what this gnawing, awful feeling I've had since I left was until she said the words to me.

Brogan waves his hand again with a "duh" expression.

Does it really matter though? I'm still me.

*"So what if I love her? That doesn't change the situation. I saw what it was like for Mom when Dad popped in and out. I never want to make someone feel like that."* I won't make his mistakes. I swore it years ago and I still stand by that.

*"Dad was a prick to her even when he was around,"* Hendrick says. *"It had nothing to do with his location."*

*"Long-distance might suck, but are you really going to just walk*

*away when the person you love is telling you they feel the same?"* Archer asks, cocking a disbelieving brow.

I don't have to answer for them to know that isn't what I want. But still…*"What if I end up hurting her or what if I screw it up?"*

"You will absolutely screw it up," Jane says, laughing softly. "Everyone does, and you have even less experience than most. It's what you do after you screw up that makes you who you are."

"Fuck," I mutter again. *"I need to go see her."*

Archer places a hand on my shoulder to keep me from standing. "You can't go now. She has a meet tomorrow and she's probably already sleeping."

*"I'm leaving tomorrow,"* I say.

*"Not until after her meet, you're not."* Brogan grins and clinks his glass against mine. *"Now let's figure out what the hell you're going to say to make up for being such a clueless idiot."*

# CHAPTER FORTY-THREE
*Knox*

"This was a bad idea," I say as Brogan and I walk into the gym. My stomach is in knots and my palms are sweaty.

He places both hands on my shoulders from behind like he's stopping me from turning around and leaving. The thought has crossed my mind. What the hell am I doing here? She's getting ready to compete. The last thing she needs is a distraction. Which is exactly what I feel like. The chump that showed up uninvited. She might not even want to see me.

"Just stick to the plan, Casanova," he says. "It's a great plan."

"You're only saying that because you came up with it."

He beams proudly.

I wanted to go talk to her last night, not show up at her meet unannounced like some sort of creeper. I can't believe I let him talk me into going along with this.

I shrug out of his hold and take a seat. The gym has bleachers on one side. It's a small crowd, but the events are far enough away that I feel safe from her spotting me right away.

I scan the room until I find Avery. She's standing in the farthest corner of the gym, warming up next to the vault. My pulse races.

What if she's changed her mind? I hurt her. I could see it on her face. Avery is fierce. She's strong. She might have already decided I'm not the kind of guy she wants to put her energy into.

"You didn't need to tag along," I say as I bounce my leg.

"No way I was going to miss this," Brogan says. "You pouring out your heart to a girl? These are going to be once-in-a-lifetime memories that I can taunt you with until the end of time."

I glare at him, but he's not paying me any attention. His gaze is intently locked on the floor. "Plus, gymnasts are hot."

The first event is bars. Avery isn't among the six members of the Valley team competing. She stands on the sidelines cheering for the first couple of routines, then takes off her warmup jacket and moves to the sideline. She jumps in place, then does high knees, and jogs the sideline, stopping each time one of her teammates finishes on bar so she can congratulate them.

When the rotation is over and Valley moves to vault, her expression changes. I can see the concentration on her face and nearly feel her nerves.

"Knox!" someone calls my name.

I glance down to see Hope smiling and waving to me. She says something to the woman behind her and then they start up the bleachers toward us.

"Hope." I smile easily at the teenager in front of me. "Hey. Good to see you."

"You too."

The woman comes to stand close to her. She has Hope's same hair color and straight nose.

"This is my mom," she says and then to her, "This is Avery's boyfriend, Knox."

Brogan chuckles quietly and mutters under his breath, "He wishes."

"Nice to meet you." I tip my head to the mom. Hope takes a seat next to me and her mom next to her.

Hope leans over to me. "It's easier than explaining to her what you actually are. Which is what currently?" There's steel in her voice that lets me know she stands firmly with Avery.

Brogan leans over. "I like you, kid. I'm Knox's brother, Brogan."

Hope lifts a hand in a wave to him and then blushes. Looks like I might be her second favorite Holland now.

"This is her first time competing on vault since last season," Hope says as she stares out toward where Avery is still warming up.

"Nice," Brogan says, clapping with the crowd. "She's got this."

I don't tear my gaze away from Avery when the first of her team members begin their vault rotation. The first girl must nail it because everyone around us cheers loudly.

A woman that I assume is her coach talks to her while they wait for the judges. I'm sweating more than I did before my own races.

Avery is third in the vault rotation. The closer it gets to her turn, the more confident she looks. I feel like I'm gonna throw up. When she takes her position at the end of the track, she lets her head fall side to side, gaze locked straight ahead. She folds her toes underneath her foot and stretches each one. When she's ready, she raises her arms and smiles at the judges. Her shoulders lift and fall with a big breath and then she takes off, sprinting forward. She raises her arms, does a round-off into a back handspring before pushing off the vault with her hands and twisting in the air over it. Or at least that's what it looks like. It all happens so fast it's hard to pick out the individual skills.

I let out a sigh of relief as Avery sticks it, but it's short-lived because almost immediately I can tell something is off. Her smile is strained and the way she holds herself as she raises her hands for the judges is just...wrong.

I open my mouth to ask Hope as Avery crumbles to the mat.

"What happened?" It looked perfect, but something must have gone wrong.

"I don't know. Maybe her knee."

My heart pounds in my chest and my stomach twists. No, no, no. She's worked too hard to have this kind of setback. The gym goes quiet until Tristan and another guy help her off the floor. Concerned applause follows her as they take her out of the main area through a door on the other side of the gym.

"I'm gonna..." I start to say to Brogan.

"Go," he says.

It doesn't occur to me that she might not be excited to see me, especially now, until I'm hovering in the doorway.

Avery is lying back on a makeshift exam table while a guy in a blue polo shirt and khakis looks over her knee. My lungs finally let in a little air at the sight of her. I can't see her face. She has both hands up over her eyes.

My heart is in my throat when she lets her head fall to the side and looks right at me. She blinks away the tears in her eyes. "Knox?"

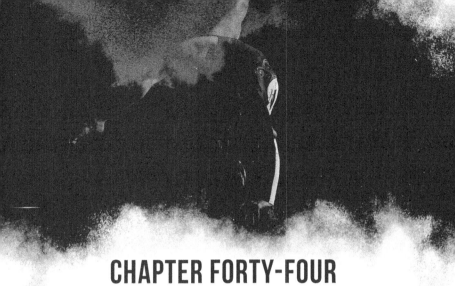

# CHAPTER FORTY-FOUR
*Avery*

H e lingers in the doorway while Coach Weaver and one of our trainers check my ankle.

"I'm fine," I tell them as I sit up. "I think I just rolled it."

It scared me more than it hurt. As soon as I came down on it wrong, I panicked. Too aware of how every injury could take months or years off my training, maybe even end it.

My nerves are shot, and I can't stop my hands from trembling, but I don't think I injured it. It hurts, but it doesn't feel broken. Thank goodness.

Adrenaline is still surging through me as I try to relax and let them look me over. I hold out my hand toward Knox and he rushes forward like he'd been waiting for any signal from me to move closer.

"Hi," I say quietly as his fingers wrap around mine.

"Hey, princess." His deep voice and that familiar nickname

soothe something inside of me. "You scared the crap out of me."

"What are you doing here?" I ask him.

Before he can answer, the trainer jumps in. As I thought, it's not broken, but he and Coach Weaver think it would be best if I sit out the rest of the meet.

"No." I shake my head and move to stand.

Everyone moves toward me at once like they think I'm going to fall over. I ease myself down on my left ankle to test it out. It's tender and there is some pain, but I can put weight on it.

"Beam is our last rotation. I'll be fine by then."

Coach Weaver's brows pull together in the middle, and she studies me closely. Whatever she finds must convince her I'm telling the truth because she nods. "After it's wrapped, test how it feels with some light warm-ups, and we'll decide then."

I smile, knowing she's going to let me. I won't push it if I think I could make it worse, but I need to go back out there for reasons I can't explain.

Knox holds my hand, squeezing my fingers tightly while his thumb brushes over my knuckles the entire time the trainer works on me.

When I'm ready, Knox helps me to my feet, and we walk back out to the floor. A few of my teammates send questioning looks, but I hang back with Knox a few seconds longer.

"I thought you'd be back in New Mexico," I say.

"Me too." He faces me, meeting my gaze head-on. "I had to see you before I left."

My heart wants to shatter into pieces at his feet. He's here to say goodbye. We never did actually say it before he left the last time. I know it's going to hurt to watch him walk away, but at least I told him how I felt. I don't have any regrets. I'd do it all again even knowing the outcome.

"Thanks for being here." I swallow the lump in my throat. "I better test out this tape job."

"Yeah, right. Of course." He clears his throat. It seems like something is bothering him, but maybe this is just the weirdness that's going to be present between us now.

"Are you staying until the end?"

"Yeah. I'll be here. I was hoping we could talk."

My pulse picks up speed. "About what?"

"I, uh…after would be better. I think."

"Tell me now." I can't wait another hour to hear what he has to say. I'll drive myself crazy.

"It's no big deal. Go focus on kicking ass." He tries to smile but it isn't at all convincing.

"Knox?"

His lips fall into a thin, straight line and his jaw tightens. If he's worried about hurting me worse than he has, I don't think that's possible.

"Avery." Coach Weaver calls my name. We're about to move to our third rotation and I really need to rejoin my team.

"Just tell me, Knox. It's okay. Whatever it is. I'll be fine."

"I love you," he blurts out, then squeezes his eyes shut. "Fuck. Wait. No. That's not right."

Everything around me seems to move slowly as my brain processes his words and the adorably frustrated look on his face. "So, you don't love me?"

"No, I do. It's…Dammit. I'm fucking this up. I had a whole speech."

My heart pounds in my chest and I fight a smile.

"I'm sorry for being a coward. I should have told you how I felt sooner, but I didn't think it mattered. Maybe it doesn't now. I wouldn't blame you if it's all too little too late, but I couldn't leave without telling you. I love you, Avery. You are the most impressive person I've ever met. You're beautiful and smart, and so talented. You work harder than anyone I know, chasing your dreams, and yet you still always have time to help everyone else with theirs too. There's nothing you wouldn't do for the people you care about. Quinn, Colter, Hope, Flynn, me…" One corner of his mouth lifts. "It's been a long time since I've let anyone in, but you didn't give me any choice. You pushed and pried your way in just by being you, and I was a goner. Maybe I didn't do a great job of showing you that I was already all yours, but I was. I still am. I want you to be mine. Not just when we're in the same zip code, but all the time."

He stares at me, waiting for a response. Adrenaline courses through me, and my heart feels like it's going to beat its way out of my chest.

The announcer gives the lineup for the next event, and I know I need to go. There are so many things I want to say, but all I can do is hug him quickly like I've thought about doing all week. My eyes sting with tears and I let them spill over as I smile at him and take a backward step toward my team. "I have to go. I'll find you as soon as it's over."

A flicker of worry and doubt creases his forehead, and he nods. I track him as I take my place on the floor, and he sits in the bleachers with Brogan and Hope. She waves at me, clearly excited to see I'm not out for the rest of the meet. She gives me a questioning thumbs-up as if to verify, and I return the gesture, making her smile grow bigger.

I cheer my teammates on during floor with a renewed spirit. I try not to glance up at Knox too often, but every time I do, he's watching me. And as much as I try to push all distractions away, I keep hearing his words all over again. He loves me. Knox Holland loves me. I think I already knew that he did, but I never thought I'd hear him say it.

By the time we get to beam, I am an anxious, excited ball of energy. I feel like I've been waiting to do this routine for years. I'm the anchor today, so I have to stand by and watch everyone else go ahead of me.

The other team is on vault, and they finish before us, so when I salute the judges, all eyes are on me.

I close my own eyes briefly and let out a breath, then I place my hands over the beam and pull myself up. As I do each skill, I have brief flashes of all the times Knox and I worked out together. What a pain in the ass he was, how much he pushed me, the way he was with Hope, and the ridiculously hot image of him shirtless and sweaty, muscles pumped from an hour of working hard.

I can't pinpoint the exact moment I fell in love with him. It happened in all those moments, little bits at a time.

When I do the triple wolf turn, I can hear Hope screaming louder than anyone else. I go into my acro series next, side aerial layout stepout. I feel like I'm floating above myself watching. My chest lifts proudly and I smile bigger than I ever have. I never want to take this feeling for granted again. Up on the beam is my favorite place to be and I know that every opportunity is a gift.

I land my leaps cleanly, no wobbles on my turns, and my dance movements are graceful. Hours of practice and it all came together.

The only thing that's left is my dismount. I test my ankle as I lift my left foot and point. Only a small ache is left, thankfully. I want to do this, but not at the expense of the rest of the season.

I have practiced the new dismount for a couple of weeks now, landing it more often than not. But it's always different in front of a crowd. I swallow the tiniest bit of doubt trying to throw me off and focus. Knox's voice plays in my head. *You've got this, princess.*

Once I start the acro series toward the end of the beam, everything goes quiet. The doubt in my head and the crowd too. I don't know if they really fall silent or if I just stop registering everything else, but when I explode off the end and go into the full twisting double tuck, I swear there's an audible collective intake of breath in the gym.

My feet land on the mat, my chest a little lower than some of my practices, but I quickly stand, snapping my feet together, and throw my hands over my head.

The silence lingers a second longer and then noise explodes around me. My Valley U teammates scream my name, and the crowd cheers and claps loudly. I jog off toward Coach Weaver. She has a relieved expression on her face as I throw my arms around her.

"Thank you for believing in me," I say as I squeeze her so tightly she struggles to respond.

"Good job, Avery."

As soon as we part, I'm surrounded by my teammates. We hug and high-five, and when the judges come back with a perfect ten score, we scream in delight.

Tristan approaches me with a look that's somewhere between smug and proud. "Nice work, Ollie."

"What was that?" I ask, holding a hand up to my ear.

He rolls his eyes. "Way to not back down. You're back."

"I was never gone." I bump my fist against his and then take off into the crowd toward Knox. He hasn't moved yet, so I race up the bleachers to him.

Hope attacks me first, hugging me while she bounces around. "A perfect ten?! I can't believe it. You are so cool."

"Thanks. I'm glad you made it." I glance over at Knox. I don't think I've ever seen his smile so big.

"Congratulations. That was…I'm speechless."

"A rare thing for sure." Brogan steps closer. "You were dynamite."

"I had a little inspiration," I say to him, and cut my gaze back to Knox.

"I'm glad you found it inspiring because I was freaking out. What kind of idiot tells a girl he loves her for the first time before she competes in front of a big crowd?" His expression goes sheepish.

"My idiot." I wrap my arms around his neck. "I love you too."

I'm about to kiss him when I hear Brogan say, "Wait? You already told her? What happened to the plan? He had a whole speech prepared for after you won."

Knox's lips twitch with a smirk.

I arch a brow at him. "I can't wait to hear it."

"Later," he says and then crashes his mouth down onto mine.

# CHAPTER FORTY-FIVE
*Avery*

"Is that Knox?" Hope nods toward my phone when she walks over to the beam where I'm sitting, taking a break and catching up with my boyfriend.

*Boyfriend.* Knox is my *boyfriend*. Weird. I haven't tried out the word yet, but I like it.

It's been two weeks since he told me he loved me and then had to leave for New Mexico. Two weeks of daily phone calls, hundreds of texts, and missing him like crazy.

I hold out the phone for Hope to see Knox.

"Hi!" She gives him a huge smile and waves. "When are you coming back? Avery is all mopey without you."

"I am not," I say a little too defensively. Fine. I was at first. It's weird not having him around all the time. There are so many things that happen every day that I want to share with him and at first, I felt weird about spamming him with messages about mundane topics I was sure he could care less about. But when I told Knox that, he scoffed. "I want to know it all, princess," he said.

And so our epic text conversations began. Does he need to know what I ate for lunch today or vice versa? No, but somehow sharing little bits of our days makes the distance feel smaller.

"I'm hoping I can come home this weekend or next," he tells her. "How was your meet last weekend?"

She takes my phone and gives him the rundown, leaving no details out. I smile as I listen to them. I'm pretty sure she misses him almost as much as I do.

When there's a pause in the conversation, I motion for my phone back.

"Wait," she says to me and then to Knox, "I need your advice on something."

"Shoot."

I lean over to see him on the screen. He called from the gym where he trains and he's sitting on the floor, still shirtless and sweaty.

"This boy I like told me he had a crush on someone but couldn't tell me who. My friend Janet says that means it's me, but I'm not sure. I went through our class roster guessing and he said no to everyone."

"O-kay," Knox says the word slowly. "What do you need my advice on?"

"Does he like me?" she asks, a hint of exasperation in her tone. "And how do I get him to tell me?"

Knox's brows lift and he opens his mouth like he wants to say something, but no words come out. He rubs the back of his neck. He's so out of his depth right now it's hilarious.

I jump in to save him. "When you went through everyone in

your class, did you ask him if he liked you?"

Her face pales. "No way. I'd die of embarrassment if he laughed or something."

Fair. First crushes are tricky and so are first rejections.

"You go to Valley Middle School, right?" Knox asks.

"Yeah. Why?" Hope's mouth purses as she studies him.

"If he laughs, I'll have to pay him a visit the next time I'm in town."

I press my lips together to fight a laugh. Do I think he's kidding? Absolutely not.

"Knooooox." She groans.

"Okay." He gets a contemplative look and then nods. "Yeah, I think your friend Janet is probably right and that he's trying to tell you he likes you without actually saying it. He's being evasive for the same reason you haven't told him how you feel. You can either wait him out or ask him."

Her smile falls, but she nods.

"If you ask him, then at least you'll know. You don't want to waste time on some boy who doesn't realize how awesome you are."

"Yeah," she says solemnly.

"If he doesn't like you, he's an idiot," Knox tells her. "You're the coolest kid I know."

Her full smile returns. "You're right. I'm amazing. Thanks, Knox!"

With that, Hope hands me the phone back and takes off to warm up.

Laughing, I bring the phone back out in front of myself so I'm in the frame. "I think you just made her day."

My boyfriend lets out a breath that puffs out his cheeks. "Growing up with brothers did not prepare me for girl talk."

"You did good."

His shoulders slump and he shakes his head. "I really hope I don't have to make an emergency trip back to tell off a middle schooler."

"If anything, it better be an emergency trip so I can kiss the crap out of you."

"Not kissing you definitely feels like an emergency," he says with a smirk.

On Friday after class, I get back to the dorm and have a note in my mailbox that I have a package being held at the front desk.

The girl working lights up when she sees me. Standing, she grabs the big vase of pink roses on a desk behind her and holds them out to me.

"Somebody is awfully smitten with you. This is the third time this week," she says.

It's actually the fourth, but someone else was working on Tuesday afternoon.

"Thank you." I take them from her and bring the flowers closer to sniff them.

"This came for you too."

I shift the heavy vase to accept the bubble mailer. "Thank you."

I call Knox as soon as I get to my room and can set everything down. I've run out of space on my desk, so I've had to start placing the flower arrangements on the floor. It's like a very pretty obstacle course in here. It turns out, Knox doesn't know how to do anything without doing it all out.

He was so worried about being a good boyfriend and not being there for me while we're apart, but he's the most present person even from another state. I know these gifts are his way of making sure I know he's thinking about me.

Some days are harder than others, but most of the time I just feel incredibly lucky that we both get to do the thing we love.

"Hey," he answers, sounding out of breath.

"Thank you for the flowers."

"You're welcome."

"I also have a suspicious looking package in my hand," I say as I stare down at the bubble mailer from a New Mexico address.

"Did you open it?"

"Not yet. I just walked in." Tearing it open feels like Christmas morning. The only other person I ever get mail from is my mom. I also have this weird vision of Knox standing in line at the post office like a regular human. Who would have thought?

Reaching inside, I pull out a folded hot pink T-shirt. When I hold it up in front of me, I smile at the Neon Punch name and logo in black on the front. On the back it has his number, 18, and Holland. My insides go squishy, and I hug it to my chest.

"I love it. Thank you." I'm already peeling off my shirt to put this one on instead. It smells faintly like him.

"You're welcome."

And then it hits me, "Oh my gosh, their color is pink?"

"*Neon* pink."

I burst into laughter.

He makes a noise that's a mixture of a scoff and a groan. *"And black."*

I'm laughing so much it's hard to talk. "You're going to have to wear pink? This is too good."

His own quiet chuckles join in a second later. "At least now it'll make me think of you."

# CHAPTER FORTY-SIX
## *Knox*

I'm in my truck driving when Avery calls.

"Hey, princess," I say when I answer.

"Hey." Her cheery voice replies, and it's like a hit of dopamine directly into my veins. "How was your day?"

"Good. How was yours?"

"Pretty good. Practice was tough. I'm working on another vault combination and it's similar to one I did last year, and my brain keeps trying to do that instead. It's frustrating."

"You'll get it," I assure her.

She hums a sound that's not exactly agreement. "What about you? How's everything there? I miss you. Oh, I got some fun news today!"

"Miss you too." I take the first Valley exit off the freeway. "I met with the new trainer today. He's agreed to let me put together some of my own off-track training."

"Handstands galore?" she asks, mocking me.

"You know it. Shirtless handstands."

"Oh no. Shirt on. I don't want anyone ogling you when I'm not around to throw down."

I laugh at the image of her fighting anyone. Not that she'd ever need to. I'm all hers.

"Are you back at your dorm for the night?" I ask her. "And what's this fun news?"

"Actually, I just stopped by to see Flynn." She must move the phone toward my baby brother because a second later he mutters a quick, "Hey, man."

I freeze, wondering if he's going to give me away. He knows I'm coming back this weekend, but Avery doesn't. I wanted to surprise her, but I wasn't expecting her to be at my house.

"Okay, so I got a call today from one of my USA teammates and she's putting together a summer tour of some of the top gymnasts in the country, and she invited me to join."

"Princess, that's awesome."

"I know! She's only asking ten total gymnasts and I'm one of them. Can you believe it?"

"Of course, I can. Congratulations."

"Thank you. I wish you were here to celebrate. Quinn is taking me out. Oh, and Colter says hi. I think he misses you. He keeps watching videos of your freestyle routines and talking about how much progress you made in such a short time."

I shut the engine off and grab my bag from the back seat. "He might not need to miss me for long."

"Are you coming back soon?" she asks, and I don't miss the

hopeful lilt in her tone.

I throw open the door, my steps faster. I'm eager to see her. The weeks are long. We're managing on phone calls and lots of texts, but every time I leave Valley, I'm counting down until I can get back.

"Yep. Real soon."

"When?" she asks, and I can hear her voice from the kitchen.

I toss my bag on the floor and she whips around, jaw dropping as she takes me in. She lets out an ear-piercing squeal and runs toward me and jumps. I catch her and hold her up so I can kiss her.

Damn. I missed her, and the way she's kissing me, I'm pretty sure the feeling is mutual.

Flynn clears his throat, and I chuckle as I break away from my girl. Avery flushes as I set her on the ground, but I don't let her get far. I circle her waist with an arm and walk toward my brother.

I let her go only to hug him. I've missed him too. "I swear you grew another two inches this week."

His lips curve and he puffs out his chest. "I'm taller than Hendrick now. He hates it."

"Yeah, I bet he does." I ruffle his hair. "Arch said you went to dinner with Dad last night. Everything good?"

I hate asking, but I know Flynn won't talk to me about Dad after everything I've said about the man. And I want to know, for no other reason than I'll never stop looking out for my baby brother.

He pauses like he isn't sure how to respond. "Yeah. He took me out to celebrate."

His elbow isn't completely healed, but he's making progress every week, and he accepted a scholarship to his top choice college in Houston, playing for his dream coach, Luka Champe. It doesn't cover the full cost of tuition and room and board, but the way he lit up with excitement when he got the offer, I knew I'd do whatever it took to make it work. I'd do anything to see him achieve his dreams. It's going to be tough when he goes, but I couldn't be prouder.

"Good. I'm glad."

He chuckles. "You are?"

I consider my words carefully. "You should have lots of people who want to celebrate your wins."

Do I think Dad will stick around and start acting like the father Flynn deserves? No. But I'm not even sure Flynn expects that at this point. And at the end of the day, I guess all I can do is be there for him. I'll just keep showing up in all the ways I wish someone had for me.

Flynn grabs his phone off the counter. "They're expecting you at the bar. Can you give me a ride to the school on your way? There's a school dance tonight."

"Wait. They knew you were coming?" Avery asks, looking from me to Flynn and back.

"I wanted to surprise you. Quinn told me you had big news. There was no way I was going to miss your celebration."

She lunges at me, hugging me again. I glance over her shoulder to Flynn, really seeing him. He's wearing a button-down shirt and his jeans aren't at all wrinkled. "Wait, did you say you wanted to go to a dance?"

After we drop off Flynn and swing by Avery's dorm so she can change, we head to The Tipsy Rose. Archer and Brogan greet me from behind the bar. Arch doesn't bartend, but he likes to hang back there sometimes when Brogan is working.

"Good to see you, bro," Arch says.

Brogan sets a shot glass in front of me with pink liquid.

"What is it?" I ask.

"I'm calling it Neon Punch." He winks.

I toss it back, grimacing at the sugary sweet taste that has a bit of a kick to it. Accurate name. I sit down and pull Avery onto my lap. I can't stop touching her.

Colter and Quinn show up not much later. Avery stands to hug her friend, and Colter walks toward me. He holds his hands out as he looks me over and then steps forward to hug me and slap me on the back.

"How is the new team?" he asks when he pulls back.

"Good. Really good. I think it's going to be a hell of a season."

"I'm so stoked for you," he says. "Miss you around here though. Everyone at the track does. Even Brooklyn has been less sunshiny, if you can believe it."

I bark a laugh. "Yeah, I can believe it. And I miss you guys too."

I have. Of all the teams I've been a part of, that one was effortless, like family. "You think you might still have room for me during the off-season months?"

He dips his head, eyes widening. "You want to come back?"

I nod. "I've been thinking about it. I already kick your ass in one sport. I should probably see this one through so I can show you up in freestyle too."

He laughs loud and long. "Dream on, Holland."

Avery and I are the first to leave the bar. As glad as I am to see everyone, I need some time alone with my girl.

Outside of the bar, we walk hand in hand toward my motorcycle. I hand her the helmet without a word, and she slides it on over her blonde head.

"Where to now?" she asks as I help her onto the bike.

"Anywhere you want, princess."

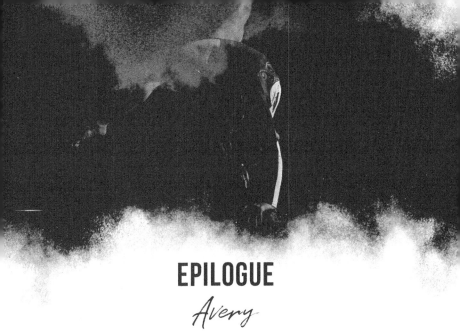

# EPILOGUE
## *Avery*

"**H**ere he comes." I grab hold of Flynn's arm as Knox rounds the last corner of the track and speeds toward the finish line. His pink jersey will never not make me smile.

I scream for him, like I've done every time he's passed us. I doubt he can even hear me over the noise, but it's the only outlet for all my pent-up anxiety. There's still five minutes left, but with every lap, my nerves grow.

His face is mostly covered from his goggles and helmet, but when he makes the jump in front of us, whipping his bike with flair, I swear he's grinning. He loves being out there and I love watching him.

His bike, including the number eighteen plate attached to the front, is covered in mud. It rained after the first race of the day, making a mess of the dirt track. But the sun is out now, not a cloud in sight, and Knox is tearing it up out there, leaving everyone else quite literally in the dust.

He's had a great season so far. He's leading in points and race wins. He's been unstoppable. All while continuing to cheer me on as I finished my second year and captured my first NCAA all-around title, making sure Flynn graduated and has everything ready for college this fall, spending time with Archer and Brogan, and helping Hendrick with wedding stuff.

I am in awe of him and his big heart.

He's here and then he's gone. Just like that, zooming out of view.

I remove my fingers from Flynn's bicep with an apologetic smile. "Sorry."

For a second his smirk is so much like his brother's that I feel like I'm staring at a younger Knox, but then I get one of his sweet Flynn smiles. "He's got this. No one can catch him unless he messes up."

He won't mess up. He's been perfect out there today.

The whole family came, and I know he won't let the opportunity to win pass him by. He wants to share this with all of them. So very Knox.

Flynn and I came with Knox, so we've been here a few days getting the full race weekend experience. Archer and Brogan arrived last night and are currently tent-hopping to meet cute girls. Hendrick and Jane got back from their honeymoon in Fiji just yesterday and drove up this morning to join us. They have a glow about them. Even Colter and Quinn came, but they're out in the crowd somewhere with some riding friends of Colter's.

I love that Knox has so many people here supporting him. They all showed up the same way he has always showed up for them.

Riders continue to pass us by. I half-heartedly cheer for Knox's new teammate, Ronnie. He's young, only a year older than Flynn, and has this whole blond, blue-eyed charm going for him that's made him a big hit with the female fans. Knox says he's a good kid. I think he enjoys having someone so close to his brother's age as a reminder when he's traveling. I've only met him once and he seemed nice, but I still want Knox to beat him.

A crash in front of us draws an "ooooh" from the crowd.

"Who was that?" Flynn asks.

Hendrick chuckles from his spot on Flynn's other side. "Link."

I watch as a guy picks up his dirt bike and jumps back on it. He tries to restart it a few times before getting off, pushing it over, and kicking the crap out of it.

Our tent howls with laughter. Petty? Probably.

The time ticks down slowly, but every lap Knox increases his lead. It doesn't feel like anyone else is even trying to catch him anymore, but the crowd is on their feet to cheer him along.

On the last lap, I bounce on my toes. Flynn glances at me out of the corner of his eye and grins at me but says nothing. He's playing it cool, but I know he's excited too.

When his pink jersey comes into sight, I don't care how ridiculous I look, I jump and clutch onto Flynn. He humors me and joins in, and we scream our heads off as the black and white flag waves Knox across the finish line.

All of us head down to the Neon Punch trailer to meet him. Knox is off his bike and removing his goggles and helmet when we get there. I throw myself into his arms, probably with more gusto than I should, considering how tired he has to be.

"You won!" I yell as I squeeze him.

"Was there any doubt?" His breathing is ragged, but he still wraps his strong body around me and hugs me tight against him.

"Never." I pull back and look up at him. "I love you. I'm so proud of you. You freaking did it!"

"I had to win, otherwise my brothers would keep giving me shit about how I'm not pulling my weight in this relationship because you've won more trophies than me."

My head tips back as a laugh breaks free. "I didn't realize we were keeping track."

"*We* aren't. Unless it's about something a whole lot more important than trophies."

"Like… who owns the most pink clothing now?"

He shakes his head, eyes dancing with amusement. "I love you too, princess."

"But I love you more," I counter, just to see his handsome, dirt-covered face pull into a smile.

"Not possible."

# ACKNOWLEDGMENTS

Thank you to my team: Devyn, Jamie, JR, and Tori. I couldn't (and wouldn't want to) do this without you guys.

Amy and Catherine, I love you two so much. Thank you for continuing to motivate and inspire me.

My editors, Jamie, Margo, Becky, and Sarah—my books are so much better because of you.

Erica, your kind words and knowledge on all things motocross were so helpful. I hope I did the sport justice! Shout-out to Monsoon Mike!

Aurora, thanks for double checking all my gymnastics content.

Sarah Jane, you are so talented. I gasp every time you send me a new illustration. You're a gem. Thank you for bringing Knox and Avery to life!

Lori, I know I can always count on you for the most stunning covers. Thanks for taking my random half-baked ideas and turning them into something beautiful.

To my publicist and agent Nina, you're the best. I'm so grateful for you. The entire team at Valentine PR, you are rock stars!

Katie, I absolutely adore you. Your feedback makes me a better writer and human. None of my books would be the same without your insights.

Sahara, thank you for always cheering me on and for your amazing video content! I love our hockey conversations. Someday, we're going to a game together!

To The Love-Shak, love you all!

And to everyone who picked up this book and gave Knox and Avery a chance, thank you so much! I love this job with my whole heart and am endlessly grateful to everyone who's played a part in allowing me to continue doing this.

# ALSO BY REBECCA JENSHAK

**Wildcat Hockey Series**
Wildcat
Wild About You
Wild Ever After
In Your Wildest Dreams

**Campus Wallflowers Series**
Tutoring the Player
Hating the Player
Scoring the Player
Tempting the Player

**Campus Nights Series**
Secret Puck
Bad Crush
Broken Hearts
Wild Love

**Smart Jocks Series**
The Assist
The Fadeaway
The Tip-Off
The Fake
The Pass

**Standalone Novels**
Sweet Spot
Electric Blue Love

# ABOUT THE AUTHOR

Rebecca Jenshak is a USA Today bestselling author of new adult and sports romance. She lives in Arizona with her family. When she isn't writing, you can find her attending local sporting events, hanging out with family and friends, or with her nose buried in a book.

Sign up for her newsletter for book sales and release news.

Made in United States
North Haven, CT
26 April 2024

51807831R00275